Praise for *The Blame*

'This thriller is a read-in-one-gulp triumph'
Claire Frost, *Fabulous*

'This absorbing mystery also takes a look at police conduct'
Heat

'I love a police procedural, and this debut ticked a lot of boxes.
The tension kept me swiftly turning the pages'
Nina Pottell, *Prima*

'Fun as well as thoughtful, this will be gobbled up
by fans of Cara Hunter and the like'
Jake Kerridge, *Daily Telegraph*

D1375960

THE
BLAME

CHARLOTTE
LANGLEY

NO EXIT PRESS

First published in the UK in 2023 by No Exit Press,
an imprint of Bedford Square Publishers Ltd,
London, UK

noexit.co.uk
@noexitpress

A CIP catalogue record for this book is available from the British Library.

This is a work of fiction. Names, characters, places, and incidents either
are the product of the author's imagination or are used fictitiously,
and any resemblance to actual persons, living or dead, businesses,
companies, events or locales is entirely coincidental.

ISBN
978-1-915798-10-7 (Hardback)
978-1-915798-12-1 (eBook)
978-1-915798-11-4 (Paperback)

2 4 6 8 10 9 7 5 3 1

Typeset in 10.4pt Garamond MT Pro
by Avocet Typeset, Bideford, Devon, EX39 2BP
Printed and bound in Great Britain by
CPI Group (UK) Ltd, Croydon CR0 4YY

PROLOGUE

'THERE SHE IS!'

Erin watched through the glass doors, her stomach sinking, as newspaper reporters and TV crews swarmed the entrance of Wakestead police station. She'd dealt with the press more times than she could count, but never a mob like this. This was rage; the real thing. As soon as the automatic doors slid open, and she stepped out into the cold September air, the reporters' questions descended on her in a relentless tirade:

'Do you blame yourself, DI Crane?'

'Is there anything you'd like to say to Sophie Madson's parents?'

Camera flashes pierced her vision. Overwhelmed, and half-blinded, she followed two officers into the crowd, already imagining the pictures in tomorrow's paper, of her, fleeing from the station with her head bowed – *see, here it is, the proof: she's out of her depth…*

The two officers in front cleared an escape route through the throngs of people. At last, one of them reached her car and wrenched the door open. Erin clambered inside. Even once the door was shut, the reporters surged forwards, crashing into the side of the vehicle like a wave against the face of a cliff.

OK, you're out. Now just get home.

The crowd spilled onto the road behind her as she drove away. Only when watching the crowd grow smaller and smaller in the wing mirror did Erin realise how fast her heart was beating. She waited for the relief to sink in. But even after driving down a quiet, open road, past the familiar corner shops and cafés that signposted her route home, that relief never came. Instead, the noise and the flashes and the shouting faces, twisted with contempt, stayed fixed in her mind.

She ran a hand through her hair, tugging at the roots. She'd thought she'd known what she was doing. She'd thought she'd done the right thing.

1

Two weeks earlier

ERIN LOOKED AT THE TIME on her phone. Nearly 6 p.m. Five hours since Sophie Madson was reported missing. Together with DS Lewis Jennings, Erin had been put in charge of a vehicle checkpoint near the outskirts of Wakestead, where it was their job to take the names of every driver that came this way to search the woods for the missing girl. In other words, a job for constables. The biggest case Wakestead had seen in years, and instead of going door-to-door with the other detectives, interviewing possible leads, or planning the investigation from the office, here they were, shining torches in car boots like glorified border security.

Just when she thought she'd finally been accepted. Just when she thought she could put it all behind her.

Lewis was making short work of the sandwiches they'd picked up from the corner shop. 'It's getting dark. What do you think the chances are we're going to find her before night comes?' he said through mouthfuls.

'Low,' said Erin, studying the woods at the bottom of the hill. Lewis's chirpy demeanour had been annoying her all afternoon. 'He's probably dumped the body by now.'

She took the can of full-fat Coke he was holding out to her, snapped it open and chugged the lukewarm fizzy liquid. Lewis had fallen into an uneasy silence.

'Isn't that a bit pessimistic?'

She arched an eyebrow at him. 'Did that phone call sound good to you?'

Missing persons were categorised into one of three risk levels – low, medium or high. Sophie Madson was high risk. All because of a single ten-second phone call to the emergency services, which she had made just after 1 p.m. that day.

The Major Crime Unit was already all over the case by the time they summoned in every detective and PC in Wakestead to listen to the recording, received by the emergency services not an hour earlier. There'd been a map of the town projected onto the whiteboard in the main office. Next to it was a photograph pulled from Sophie's Instagram, showing the sixteen-year-old on holiday, with sunburn on her cheeks and a coppery tint in her dark hair. Under the buzzing florescent lights, the police force had listened to the sound of the dial tone ringing out four times. 'Which service do you require?' the operator had asked. But another sound had almost drowned them out. Rustling. Loud and distorted. As though the call was being made from inside a wind tunnel. Then they had heard a young woman's voice. 'I'm Sophie Madson,' she had yelled, 'I'm—' But her screaming had quickly become muffled. Erin had felt her blood go cold. After a few moments, the recording had cut out.

'Maybe it was just a struggle,' suggested Lewis.

Erin lit a cigarette and leant against the car. 'Maybe,' she said, before taking a drag and slowly releasing the smoke. 'But say you kidnapped a girl and she started screaming her head off down the phone to the police.' She looked at him. 'What would you do?'

'Well, make a run for it, obviously.'

'Sure, but not before finishing her off first. Knowing every officer in a twenty-mile radius would be out looking for you.' She noticed how defeated she sounded and added, 'Sorry. We should hold out hope. I'm just grumpy because we're stuck here doing vehicle checks.'

His brows knitted together. 'Yeah, why is that, by the way? Shafting me, I get. But you've been here for years.'

Erin felt her ears burn red. She shrugged and took another quick drag of her cigarette. Lewis had only recently made DS – he hadn't been here long enough to know where she stood in the pecking order, or that there even was one. She didn't fancy being the one to break it to him.

She forced herself to focus on the positive. Thanks to that 999 phone call, the police had been able to trace her location to a field beside the local woodlands, which were now swarming with uniforms and local people who'd come out to help. All day their cars had arrived in a steady stream. Just when she thought everyone in Wakestead must be out by now, another car would pull up with a tired-looking family bundled inside, teenagers in wellies, mums and dads in puffer jackets, usually with the sound of the radio bleating out through the rolled-down window: 'police are requesting anyone with information to come forward'.

The next car to roll up to the checkpoint made her stomach turn. A flash silver Mercedes she'd recognise anywhere. The window rolled down and DSU Walker stuck his head out, manoeuvring carefully so his coif didn't scrape the car frame. Walker had gone grey years ago but that hadn't stopped him from gelling up his hair like a teenager.

'Oh dear,' he said. 'You two look… chilly.'

'Piss off,' said Erin.

'Anything to report?'

'Nothing. Just delivery men and search parties.'

'Hmm. Shame –' he checked his oversized watch '– anyway, as much as I'd love to stay and chat, we've had a lead. Someone rang in to say they saw Sophie Madson with a man near her school, Wakestead Academy.'

Erin's heart leapt. 'What? Really?'

'We're redirecting the investigation. I'm heading up there now. We need to clear these woods – get constables over there now.'

'We can go,' said Erin.

'Oh no, I wouldn't want to distract you from –' he looked around pointedly at the empty country road '– all the great work you're doing here.'

Erin gritted her teeth. 'Walker—'

'Should be quite a nice evening for you two, just sitting around watching the cars go by.'

'Your knees gonna be alright? It gets quite hilly up there.'

Walker ignored her. 'Honestly, you look freezing though. Remember you can always snuggle up for warmth.'

Lewis's ears were red as they watched the Mercedes glide past.

'He's a laugh,' he said weakly.

Erin stamped out her cigarette on the gravel. This was Walker all over. He probably fancied himself making an appearance on the national news, one hand sweeping through his hair as he assured a pretty reporter that everything was under control.

'For Christ's sake. When this is over, I'm complaining to Peters.'

Lewis fidgeted against the side of the car. 'I don't want to seem like we're kicking up a fuss though.'

'We're being messed about. You think it's an accident we've been pushed to the sidelines?'

He still looked uncomfortable. She straightened up.

'Listen. Now you're a DS I can tell you this. Most detectives here are solid. They work hard and, if you need help, they'll give it to you. But there's a couple of people who'll try and palm stuff off on you because you're new, OK? Say someone rings in late one night with a case that looks like it'll drag on for months. Some dickheads will pretend they didn't hear it and leave it for someone else in the morning because they can't be bothered. Or, in Walker's case, because they enjoy watching other people shovel the shit. But that doesn't mean you have to, alright?'

She'd been trying to reassure him. But, if anything, Lewis looked even more nervous than before.

'I'm not trying to scare you. It's nothing personal; they do it to everyone. I'm just saying it so you know you can push back.'

Lewis did a lot of nodding. 'That's useful to know. Thanks.' He stared straight ahead, processing this, like he'd just been told Santa wasn't real.

Green turned to grey as night approached. About twenty minutes after Walker passed through, a wall of officers in high-vis jackets emerged from the trees, an army of neon advancing onto the field. There was no barking from the sniffer dogs, no chatter among the police. Just a deep, searching silence.

The civilian searchers were giving up the ghost. More and more of them who'd passed through the checkpoint earlier now returned, looking exhausted.

It was getting cold. Lewis started rocking back and forth on the balls of his feet for warmth, hands tucked into his armpits. Most people would be searching til the early hours. That was fine with Erin. She functioned well on little sleep. After enough all-nighters and 3 a.m. calls to miserable domestic cases, she'd learnt how to jumpstart her body like an engine, running on nothing but adrenaline, cigarettes and shitty filter coffee from police HQ's tragically under-stocked kitchen.

She looked at her phone. The time glowed at her in the darkness, making her tired eyes hurt: 10:23 a.m. Over nine hours now since Sophie made that phone call. You really didn't want that number to hit twelve. The first twelve hours were the best for gathering evidence. Miss something now and the case could drag on for years and years.

And the cases that did, those were a detective's worst nightmare. Like Annie Dodds' case. Reopening that investigation last year – seven years after Annie's death – Erin had been painfully aware of the stretch of time that had passed just from the contents of the evidence bags. A Mars bar wrapper pressed flat, its wrinkles ironed out. A bus ticket with the colour almost faded away. A pot of cherry-flavoured lip balm, now discontinued, still indented with the fingerprint of its owner. Like all that was left of Annie's life was a museum of odds and ends.

And the reason her case had taken so long to solve? The murder weapon. In the post-mortem, the pathologist had said the precision of the bruising on Annie's neck suggested she'd been strangled with a long, thin strip of fabric pulled tight. It matched the description of the long piece of ribbon her mum had used to tie Annie's hair up that morning, but at the crime scene it was nowhere to be found.

Erin would never forget when she'd showed a photo of that ribbon to Alan Vogel – their main suspect after the case was reopened – sitting there in the interrogation room. He'd had a dusting of dandruff over the shoulders of his dark-grey jumper and an eyebrow hair almost an inch long that curled down over one eye. He'd given the photograph a single contemptuous look.

'Never seen it in my life,' he'd said.

She hadn't been there when they'd found it. But despite that, she could picture the scene with total clarity. She still remembered Alan Vogel's house; how it had smelt of dog food and how one of the windows was blocked by the tendrils of an overgrown rose bush. There had been so much dust in the air you could see it hovering in the shafts of light like a small galaxy. She could imagine the forensics in their white plastic coverings, wiping down banisters and swabbing surfaces. Two of them entering Alan Vogel's bedroom. A gloved hand reaching into his bedside drawer and pulling out the slither of silky fabric.

'No one can hide forever,' Tom, her partner, had said afterwards.

In the darkness next to her, Lewis jumped.

'Christ. What?' she said.

'Do you see that?'

He was pointing towards the woods. By now, it was cleared of searchers. But deep in the trees, a silver light was fluttering – someone's torch beam, dancing across the forest floor. For a moment it stuttered out. Then it reappeared again, moving through the woods in strange looping arcs.

'Why are they moving so weirdly? Wait. Are they—'

Erin finished his sentence for him:

'Carrying something.'

The whites of Lewis's eyes glowed pale blue.

'Oh shit. Oh shit shit shit.'

When was he going to grow up? Ignoring him, she stepped away from the car, eyes fixed on the flickering beam of light.

'Call it in just in case. Maybe don't go all out and get an armed response unit. But flag this to HQ.'

'What, you're going by yourself? Come on—'

'Someone needs to stay at the checkpoint. And I'm the DI here.' She started walking down the hill. 'Anything happens, call me,' she said over her shoulder.

'OK. Likewise.'

She waded through the thick grass towards the wood. Only now, approaching it, could she feel the threatening atmosphere radiating off that seemingly endless row of dark trees, like a veil into another world. The darkness closed overhead as she stepped inside. A twig snapped beneath her foot. She paused, worried the torchbearer could have heard. But the beam continued to shrink into the wood. She set off after them.

Soon she was close enough that she could hear the undergrowth crunching beneath their feet. They were wading forwards, heavy-footed. She and Lewis had been right: this person was carrying something.

Erin tripped over a fallen branch and quickly righted herself. She could barely see anything. But she definitely couldn't afford to turn her torch on.

She shivered. It was cold now. That cold deep in your bones that couldn't be solved by just adding another layer.

Then something happened. Up ahead, the torchlight went out.

She froze.

Her eyes had adjusted to that silver light in the distance – without it, everything went pitch black. She waited, heart pounding.

Should she keep going?

Then she heard someone crashing through the undergrowth. To the right of her. She turned around sharply and caught sight of the torch beam slicing through the woods, flashing across the tree trunks. She couldn't see the person holding it. She just watched the light swing away into the distance. They were moving faster now, much faster. As if they'd suddenly become lighter.

Did that mean…?

Erin's pulse rocketed. Pulling the torch out of her pocket, she turned it on and fired the beam in all directions. Silver trees reared up around her. Then something else appeared, about ten metres ahead, that made her hand holding the torch freeze.

A bright shape on the forest floor. Trainers; white ones. A leg bundled on top of another.

Oh no.

Holding her breath, Erin crept forward.

They'd folded her over at the base of a tree, beneath a thicket of brambles. Half her face was in the dirt. On the side that was visible, there was blood furred around her nostril, turned black in the harsh glare of the torch light. She had a bruise around her eye socket. Part of Erin almost expected her to start groaning and trying to lift herself up. But touching her cold neck she found no pulse; she was gone. Someone's baby, never coming home. A family facing a lifetime of anguish. Erin looked up at the dark-blue sky and had to take a few moments just to breathe deeply.

Within five minutes of her putting the call in – requesting cordons at every access point; he was on foot; they might still catch him – the place was swarming with Forensics. Other torches bobbed through the trees, a fire-lit procession of officers marching in the darkness.

Among them was Walker, who came striding over.

'You think it was them who dumped the body, Crane?'

'Sounded like it to me.'

'Did you see them?'

'No.'

'So no description you can give us? Height? Clothing?'

Erin's chest tightened as she realised the killer had been right there, and she'd seen nothing that could help them identify him. She shook her head.

14

Walker left a very deliberate, excruciating pause before saying, 'Right. I'll take it from here, Crane.'

'I was first on scene.'

'Exactly. First witness. Go sit down; have a cup of tea.'

Erin opened her mouth to retort but Walker was already turning away from her, barking orders at SOCOs: 'Come on, people. Let's get fingerprints, snagged clothing fibres, shoeprints.'

Sophie's body had vanished behind the white tent set up by forensics. Thoughts of the girl's peaceful, almost-sleeping face shuddered through her. She'd missed him. He'd been right there, just metres away, and she'd missed him.

One of the detectives skidded across the forest floor towards her. She felt a wave of relief when she recognised Tom Radley, her partner.

'Are you alright?' he said.

'I should have just – you know, run after him. I didn't—'

'It's not your fault,' he assured her. But he was stone-faced. 'I don't get it. We've been searching these woods all day, and now he dumps her body here? What happened? Why weren't there more officers out?'

'It was this lead at the school. Most officers left to search the grounds. Do you know what the intelligence was there? Why did we trust it so much?'

He shrugged. 'I know as much as you do.'

'So we don't know if it was legit?'

She watched the forensics traipse in and out of the white tent. The school tip-off – could that have been the killer? Were they trying to divert them, so they could dump the body without getting caught?

After they left the scene, Erin took a lift in Tom's car. The forest stretched out to their right, invisible.

'He took a risk moving during the manhunt,' Tom was saying. 'He went out of his way to put the body here. He wanted us to find her.'

Erin was grateful for the darkness. It hid her. She made sounds of agreement so Tom would know she was listening, but really her mind was elsewhere.

You can't afford to make mistakes like this, a voice in her head told her. Not after what happened.

When she got home, she hauled her exhausted body up the stairs, pulled the curtains closed and crawled into bed, waiting for sleep to come at any moment. Instead she lay awake for another hour, with a whirring brain and a horrible tightness in her chest that wouldn't go away.

2

IT WASN'T YET 8:30 A.M. WHEN Erin and Tom entered the main office the next day, and already constables were heads down, clacking away at their keyboards with caffeine-fuelled intensity, while the senior detectives marched in and out of meeting rooms, hurling questions at their bowed heads: where's that neighbour's statement; how long til the fingerprints come through; any update yet on the transport system's CCTV footage? When a case this big came in, it was like your first day all over again. Only once in their careers might any of them get the chance to investigate a murder that was dominating the front page of every national newspaper, and Erin could practically feel the excitement crackling in the air that morning.

The chief superintendent, Peters, never came looking for you himself. He'd always send the last person he'd spoken to on a mission to find you. He was still having his morning latte, bought from the deli round the corner, when she and Tom were summoned in.

One of that day's papers dominated the available space that Peters' monstrous house plant had left on the table. He pointed at the two-page spread, as though showing them a plot of land he was vaguely interested in buying, and took a sip of his coffee. 'The back of your head's in this one, Radley.'

When Erin had first heard Peters speak, she'd thought she'd gone deaf. He had such a low, quiet voice he was practically murmuring to himself. She'd soon worked out it was deliberate. He wanted to have you leaning in, focusing all your attention on him to try and catch what he was saying.

He wasn't about to turn the newspaper the right way up for them so she tried to make sense of the photo from her upside-down perspective. There were splashes of white and bright yellow – the forensic investigators in their plastic coverings. She was looking at the site where they'd found the body. In the background, a man in a dark coat was facing the other way; Tom, potentially. She must have been there next to him, but she was out of sight.

Peters looked at them. 'I'm giving this to you two.'

Even though she'd seen it coming, Erin felt the ice-cold rush of adrenaline. It was just the feeling of being picked. Childish and immediate like having your name called out while stood up against the wall in PE. Even six years in, it hadn't gotten old yet.

'You did well,' he said. 'Both of you. Things have been said.'

That was the useful thing about having Tom as a partner; there was never any shortage of people singing his praises.

'I don't need to tell you how much is riding on this one,' Peters continued. 'We were all there. Almost the entire force. And the bastard dumped the body right in front of us. I'd be surprised if we're not a complete pissing laughing stock, wouldn't you?'

Erin was glad he wasn't looking at her, so he couldn't see her wincing. But Tom nodded, sincere and understanding, just what Peters wanted.

The super's eyes roved back to the page in front of him again. 'So all the more reason to throw everything at this one. You've got free rein on resources. Anyone specific you want me to assign on this with you?'

Tom looked into the plant, and then back at Peters. 'Lewis Jennings,' he said.

Peters' owlish eyebrow lifted slightly. 'Jennings who only just made DS?'

'He's ready for a case like this.'

For a moment Peters looked like he might say no. Then he nodded. 'Alright. Use as many people as you need. Find who did this.'

*

When police had searched the Madson family's house the day before, nothing was missing apart from Sophie's keys, phone, wallet and a yellow handbag. This wasn't a runaway case: Sophie had planned on coming back that day.

The handbag wasn't found on the body, and nor was her phone. That was a pain – they could find out who she'd texted from her phone company, but without the mobile the actual messages were lost.

A conversation with the digital forensics team revealed she'd been captured on the transport system's CCTV, getting the 133 bus into town at 11:12 a.m. The staccato images showed a girl in a white top sat on the lower floor of the bus who got up and left when the bus stopped at the high street. That put her in the centre of town just under two hours before she called 999 from the field.

A team of forensics had combed that field from top to bottom. They'd found nothing. So far, the only crime scene they had was in the woods. According to the CSI, the blood patterns at the base of the tree confirmed Sophie hadn't died there; she'd been moved and repositioned. When Erin had asked the CSI what that said about the killer, he'd replied: 'Considering the risk they took to hide the body there, and the publicity of the place, an exhibitionist. Someone who wanted her to be found.'

Something else supported the theory that this killer enjoyed the limelight: they'd picked a fairly high-profile victim. 'Sophie appears in a Google search more than your average sixteen-year-old,' said Tom, on the drive to the Madsons' house. 'Looks like the gymnastics was more than just a hobby. Bronze in last year's regional championships. She's pictured in a lot of blogs that follow these things. I think they're mostly run by people's mums.'

He held out his phone. Erin, who was driving, glanced away from the road to register the photos of Sophie in a spangly uniform, body bending into bizarre, zero-gravity movements. Without knowing it was Sophie in them, she wouldn't have recognised her. She had her hair scraped off her face in a tight ponytail and her expression was one of morbid concentration.

'So it wouldn't have been hard for someone to find her,' she said grimly.

'Exactly.'

'One of the researchers – Joel—'

'The one who downs Lucozade like he's not sitting around on his arse all day?'

'Him. He said most of the girls in that team were all double-barrelled names and grammar schools. Sophie was the only one at that level who came from a lower-income family.'

'You think that had anything to do with it?'

Erin shrugged. 'Maybe she felt isolated there. Or it could have made her seem more vulnerable to someone who was targeting gymnasts.'

She stopped at a red light and Tom ran a hand over his mouth, thinking. Watching him, a glow of warmth spread through Erin. Times like this, when it was just the two of them, embarking on another case, reminded her how lucky she was to have Tom as a partner. Out of training, she could have been lumped with any one of the officers who'd joined at the same time. Instead, by sheer luck, she'd landed the high-flying homicide detective several years' her senior, adored by every probationer. She'd never forget the case that had brought them together. Close her eyes and she was there: only a few months into the job, with no homicide experience, speed-reading the incident report as she followed Tom into the interview room where the suspect was waiting for them. For three gruelling hours they were in there. At a few points Erin thought they should pack it in. But they kept going, her and Tom, rallying back and forth, sticking with the strategy they'd planned outside, then – when that didn't work – relying on their own intuition, and on each little signal from the other.

That was the first time Erin appreciated the importance of the partner-to-partner relationship. It was like a marriage, really. You learnt how to read the other. Sense their discomfort. Anticipate their next move. Except, unlike a marriage, it was built on grim foundations, not candlelit dinners and cinema trips, but traumas. Shared experiences of the stuff no one should have to see.

Wakestead was still littered with reminders of last night's search, missing posters of Sophie trodden into the pavement, disintegrating into blue sludge after the early morning shower. The sight was made all the more disorientating by the swarm of TV crews. Everywhere they looked there seemed to be at least one white van parked up with tired-looking cameramen crowded around outside, drinking from Thermoses.

About six of these vans were parked right outside the Madsons' house. As soon as Tom and Erin left the car, the reporters who'd arrived in them surged forwards in a wave of noise and lights that flooded the road in front of this otherwise dreary row of suburban houses.

Inside, the house had a horrible nether zone feeling. They'd shut the curtains to get some privacy from the cameras but turned none of the lights on, casting the room in a thin, dusty light.

Sophie's parents were called Richard and Andrea. They were sat on the sofa together, holding hands tightly, when Erin and Tom entered the living room. Erin got the impression they'd been sat here all day and all night, braced against the endless stream of forensic investigators who trampled back and forth through the house, arms piled up with Sophie's belongings.

'We know you've already given a statement to the family liaison officer who was here with you yesterday,' said Tom. 'That will really help us try and narrow down where she was going and who she was meeting. But there's still a few things we need to ask you.'

Richard nodded. 'Go ahead.'

'The first thing it would be good to hear is what Sophie was like as a person,' said Erin.

He looked at the wall. 'Just… a wonderful kid. Loved the outdoors. Loved gymnastics. Stubborn as anything, but you never met a kid more determined, more hard-working…' All through this, Andrea stayed silent. Her dark fringe hid her eyes as she looked at the carpet.

'You said in your statement that you're not aware of any boyfriend in the picture,' said Tom.

Andrea cleared her throat. A brittle sound. 'Nothing like that.'

As soon as she said it though, she looked sceptically at Richard, who was still staring at the wall. When he looked back at them, his eyes were hard.

'The truth is, we have been feeling like something's been going on,' he said. 'We put it down to her growing up. You know, our friends say their daughters are going through the same thing.'

'And what was that?'

'We used to joke that she lived with one foot in the virtual world. You know, on her phone all the time.'

'I think that's definitely normal at that age.'

'I know. But she's been distant the whole of the past year. Locking herself in her room. Getting grumpy at dinner. Plastering herself in make-up and going off to meet friends all the time.' He paused, looking stony. 'And then obviously the stuff with the gym just made it worse.'

'What's that?'

'Sophie was kicked off the team about six weeks ago,' said Andrea.

'What for?'

'They said she was slacking off. Ridiculous.'

Andrea added, 'We didn't think it was fair. But her coach wouldn't take her back.'

'How often was she there?' asked Tom.

'Gymnastics practice was generally four or five times a week. Two hours each time.'

Christ. Poor bugger, Erin thought to herself.

'What's your opinion of her coach, Fraser Jones?'

There was silence, and then Richard gave a huff of bitter laughter through his nose. 'That's a hard question to answer right now, isn't it?'

They gave it a few moments before he continued, 'We've never had a problem with him before. He was really committed to Sophie. She was like his star pupil. When she was seven, he said she might even make Olympic level, if she stuck it out.' His knuckles clenched on the sofa's arm. 'But the whole drama with him kicking her off the team… he wouldn't even speak to me, would he, Andrea? I turned up to ask for a proper explanation and he just mumbled through it. Could barely keep eye contact with me.'

Erin glanced at Tom; he had that look he got when he could see the start of the trail in front of him.

It was misting with rain when they dashed back to the car and the cameras flashed at them through the windows as they drove away. Erin shivered, relieved to be out of there. The intensity of the last twenty-four hours had worn her down. Sophie's blue body in the darkness shot through her mind.

Tom swept the damp hair off his forehead. 'Slacking off,' he said. 'I wonder if that's really true.'

'Sounds like something happened between her and this coach, doesn't it?'

'If they're right about how seriously Sophie took gymnastics,' said Tom, 'then it would have been quite easy for an older man to take advantage of that.'

'The thing is,' she said, 'if she'd been meeting her coach the day she went missing, wouldn't she have told her parents?'

'Not if she was in some kind of relationship with him.'

The rain blurred the suburban houses outside. 'Any chance Richard's trying to take the attention off himself?' she asked. She found it hard to imagine either Andrea or Richard had been involved, but you could never rule out the parents.

'We know he didn't move the body,' said Tom. 'He and Andrea were with the family liaison officers in the evening and then they were out with the other searchers all night. So if it was them, they'd have had to get help.'

'Which would be weird in a domestic killing,' Erin concluded. '"Hey, do you mind helping me move my daughter's dead body?"'

'Exactly. Right now, Fraser's the one we need to speak to.'

3

Erin's shoes squeaked on the linoleum flooring of the gymnasium, which was so vast it felt almost like entering a cathedral. To Sophie, the significance of this place was probably borderline religious. Right here was where she focused all her time and energy. Where her hopes and dreams would either come toppling down or spring miraculously to life. For the first time, Erin felt like she could envisage Sophie padding over the training mats, lifting up her gym kit and swinging it over her shoulder before heading to the showers. She saw her clamber up onto the balance beam and stand with her arms elegantly outstretched; perfect poise, perfect command over her body.

A lot of detectives would tell you to put up a wall between yourself and the victim, not just for the case but for your own sanity. Erin disagreed. If nothing else, you owed it to them to remember they were once flesh and blood, not just a headshot on an incident report.

A line of teenage girls were queued up in front of the balance beam, waiting their turn. This was a far cry from the gym classes Erin remembered. No messing about; no sick notes and fake period pains. Each girl studied the performance of the one before them with complete focus, stretching out a leg or rolling their shoulders in silence.

There was still silence when Tom and Erin spoke to them. They explained that they needed to know if anyone had seen Sophie on the fifth and whether, in the days leading up to her death, she'd acted strangely. The gymnasts stared back at them with a kind of morbid fascination.

The coach – Fraser – watched from the benches. His eyes looked red.

'You started training with her when she was seven, is that right? You must have known her pretty well.'

Like the rest of the centre, Fraser's office carried the strong smell of chlorine from the indoor pool. Although his gymnastics days were over, he took care of himself. Erin noted the clearly defined muscle in his forearms.

'You're always hoping you're going to get someone who really has the passion for the sport,' he said. 'A lot of parents, they enrol their children just because they're looking for an extracurricular activity. It's rare to find someone who genuinely cares. Sophie... she cared alright. She had the perfectionism you need to have. The desire to finesse everything til you get it right. She could have gone professional, if things had been different.'

'When did you hear she was missing?'

'When it made the news. Must have been 3 p.m.? I was at home.'

'Do you have anyone who can verify that?'

'Not as such. I live by myself.'

'And what time did you start searching for her?' asked Tom.

'Not long after.'

'And where was this?'

'In the woods.'

'I'm assuming you drove there? Can you show me where you parked?'

Tom got out a map on his phone. Fraser squinted at it and pointed to a section of the screen. 'It must have been around there. It was one of these car parks they have for walkers. You should be able to see it on a map of the footpaths.'

His car should have been stopped by one of the officers. They'd check later if his name was written down.

'What about between 8 and 11 p.m.? Where were you searching?'

He pointed at another section of the map. Erin could see just enough to know that it was a long distance from where Sophie's body had been found.

Looking back up at him, Erin said, 'It surprises me, to hear that she had so much potential, but you kicked her off the squad at the end of July?'

'That was really hard to do. She cared so much about gymnastics. But the truth is her performance had been worsening. She was making more and more mistakes. I wanted to keep her on, but I had to be honest with myself.'

'Do you know if anything caused it? Her losing focus like that?'

'I don't know exactly. Maybe there was some boyfriend in the picture who was distracting her. But I can't say for sure.'

Erin couldn't help noticing that, as he said this, his right knee started juddering silently up and down, like he suddenly couldn't wait to get up and start moving.

They held the next interview in an empty squash court opposite the main sports hall. Alisha Iqbal, fresh off the balance beam, sat on the bench in front of them – zipped up in a bright-orange sports jacket with the sweat still curling her dark hair. She gripped the edge of the bench like it was the lip of a pool and she was about to plunge herself down.

'Sophie told her parents she was going to yours on the day she went missing. But she never mentioned any plan like that to you?'

'No.'

'Did she speak at all about what she planned on doing that day?'

Alisha shook her head.

'Any theories?'

'Maybe seeing a guy.'

'Which guy?'

'It was a bit hard to keep track with her. For a while there was this guy two years above us. Then there was Theo in our year.'

'Any of these serious?'

'Just fun.'

Sounded like she could have gotten on someone's bad side, in that case.

'Did she do that a lot? Use you as an excuse.'

'I don't know. She never told me she did.'

Teenagers could be like this – put a detective in front of them and suddenly they were twelve years old again.

Erin tried to soften her tone. 'Really? I would've thought she'd tell you she was using you as an alibi. In case her parents checked in.'

Alisha's hands clenched and unclenched on the edge of the bench. 'Yeah, I guess that would've made sense. But she wasn't really speaking to me…'

'You had a falling out?'

She nodded, looking relieved Erin had said it for her.

'What happened?'

'Gymnastics was everything to her. Getting kicked out, she got really, really upset. I think she thought maybe I should leave too, you know, in solidarity, because it was unfair. We had a big argument about it.'

'Was it unfair?'

Alisha looked at the squash net behind Erin. Then her gaze darted back, apprehensive.

'I don't want to get someone in trouble if they didn't do it,' she said.

'If they didn't do anything, we'll find that out.'

'She said Mr Jones kicked her out because he fancied her.' The words tumbled out of her – as if by saying them quickly she couldn't be held responsible for them.

'Did he?'

'I didn't think so. She was his favourite student, definitely. But he's not like that. I didn't think he would ever – with a student—'

'So what did she tell you had happened?'

27

'That he'd kicked her out because he was angry he couldn't have her.'

'But you think it was something else?'

Alisha fidgeted.

'She had been getting distracted. She'd slipped up a few times. To be honest, I thought it was unfair, him letting her go, but I thought he just expected better from her. I thought he might take her back on.'

Alisha's chest lifted up and down as she breathed out heavily.

'I didn't say that to her. But she could tell that was what I thought. We never really spoke about it after that. Which is why…'

'What?'

Her eyes – filled with distress – flashed up to meet Erin's.

'Which is why I don't want it to be him. Because if it is him, then I didn't believe her.'

Alisha's words stayed with Erin as she made her way back to the car with Tom. Before she'd joined the force, she would have assumed that murder made people paranoid of everyone around them. Surely you viewed anyone as a potential suspect. Your dad could have done it; your teacher, your friend, your husband. But people didn't usually think that way. People were surprisingly unwilling to let go of their preconceptions of others: 'Oh no, he couldn't have raped her – he's a really nice guy'; 'He's not violent. It doesn't make sense'. Alisha didn't owe this coach anything; why was she so certain he couldn't have done it? But Erin knew why, because she'd seen the same pattern in others so many times before. It was easier, even for the friends and relatives, to face a hopeless scenario with very few suspects, if any, than it was to admit that there'd been something so profoundly wrong with another person, and you'd missed it.

Walker was waiting for them in the corridor outside the main office when they got back to HQ. He made it look like he was minding his own business, leaning against the wall with one hand in his pocket, scrolling through his phone. But Erin knew that this was premeditated. As they approached, he put his phone away and looked at them, smiling demurely.

'Afternoon, you two. I want to know what lines of inquiry you plan on making.'

'We'll explain in the briefing tomorrow.'

'Bad idea, hiding your ideas right up until curtain call. Back in my day, you ran every little detail past your gaffer. So come on, what have you got?'

Tom and Erin exchanged a look.

'Sophie told Alisha Iqbal that Fraser was interested in her,' Tom said.

Walker's eyes lit up. 'Does he have an alibi?'

'A flimsy one,' said Erin. 'He was alone at home most of the day. Then he joined the search. We're going to check if his car was searched before he parked up.'

'And after that? Are you bringing him in?'

'Not yet. We need more.'

Walker smiled incredulously. 'Really? What are you waiting for? You think he's just going to swing by, knock on the door, and say, "yeah, you're right, I did it"?'

Erin resisted the urge to roll her eyes.

'Just a little warning,' he continued, 'it's important you tackle this as quickly as possible. Before patience runs out. Because spending months trying to be dead certain about the suspect, only to have it blow up in your face, that's just the worst thing in the world. So no cut corners. No hiding.'

His smiling eyes settled very deliberately on Erin. She tried to keep her face impassive even though her heart rate had just leapt.

'Anyway. Everyone's very excited to see what you turn up,' he said. His coiffed head bobbed back into the main office.

Slowly, she and Tom looked at each other. She was relieved to see her own exasperation mirrored in his expression.

29

'Notice how he managed to sneak in a reference to the good old days?'

Erin scoffed. 'Back in my day…'

'Back in my day they made you swim through a river of shit in the physicals. Shawshank-style.'

'Back in my day you had to arrest your own mother just to prove you were hard enough.'

'My mother's been in prison for twenty-four years now and I don't regret a thing…' Tom opened the door to the main office and held it there for her. 'He won't get off our backs with this one, will he?' he said. 'No hiding? What was that supposed to mean?'

Erin felt a twinge of panic shoot through her. She managed not to show it; instead she shrugged. 'You know what he's like. He's just micromanaging.'

For a moment Erin thought he was going to say something, but then he shook his head to himself. 'Ridiculous.'

A wave of nausea crept over her as they re-entered the office. Walker felt like a walking contagion zone. Alone, she could handle him. It was the creeping influence he could exert on other people – on Peters, on Tom – that scared her.

If she'd known Walker would suspect something, she might never have done what she did.

4

IN ERIN'S SIX YEARS AS a detective, so far no feeling had compared to the unbridled relief that had washed over her the moment a judge had stood up in Oxford Crown Court and sentenced Alan Vogel to life in prison for the murder of Annie Dodds.

As the judge's words had echoed around the courtroom, eliciting a harsh, animal cry from Annie's mother on the bench behind her, Erin had felt every knot of tension that had built up during the investigation, in her shoulders and neck and around her spine, slowly start to unwind. She'd left that court high as a kite, knowing that as soon as she got home, she'd have the best sleep she'd had in months.

Right up to the end, Erin had been terrified Vogel might get away with it. Now it was certain he'd be locked up for what he'd done, every tiny pleasure had been amplified. The cigarette she'd had by the side of the car afterwards had been heavenly. On the way to the station, she and Tom had stopped off to get fish and chips, which they'd eaten in his car with the doors open. She couldn't remember what they'd talked about but she remembered Tom's easy grin in the sunlight, and how he had his takeaway box elegantly outstretched in one hand while the other wiped traces of salt from his best suit trousers. If only the sentencing had been later in the day, they could have gone for a pint straight after.

And the whole time, the words of Annie's mum had kept ringing in her ears: 'You have no idea what you've done for me. This is the first time I've felt peace since she died.'

Hearing that had made her glow with pride. But the feeling hadn't lasted for long.

Because then they'd returned to the station, and once the round of applause to welcome them back had died down and the team had returned to their seats, one person had remained standing.

Walker, head bowed, hands clasped behind his back, had slowly woven his way round to where Erin had stood at her desk, filing the court documents.

Immediately she'd looked around for Tom, but he was off accepting praise from Peters. She was alone.

She'd made a point of not looking at Walker as he'd come close. But out of the corner of her eye, she'd seen him staring out of the window. He could have been in deep concentration, except there'd been a mean smirk on his face.

'What luck, eh?' His voice had been low. 'Years pass by without any progress. Then you get the case. And the forensics just so happen to find that ribbon right there. In your only suspect's bedside table.'

Fear had shivered up her skin like an electric current. But she'd shrugged, still gathering up the papers into Vogel's file. 'Makes sense to me. Vogel wasn't exactly a criminal mastermind.'

The high she'd experienced moments before had already become a distant memory. Instead she'd felt cold.

Walker still hadn't moved. 'Lucky.'

He'd turned around then and left, but she'd hardly noticed.

Because she hadn't been in the office anymore. Instead, she'd been back there, in Vogel's house, the dust circling around her and the floorboards creaking beneath her feet. Climbing up to the bedroom. It hadn't taken her long to find a virtually identical ribbon online. She had contaminated it with one of Annie's hairs taken from one of the evidence bags. And now the ribbon, laced with the murdered girl's DNA, was coiled up inside Vogel's beside drawer where it would remain, untouched, until Erin called in the search.

*

Just to get to her front door, Erin had to squeeze past an old wardrobe and step over several bin bags packed full of baby clothes when she got home after the first day leading the Madson case with Tom. The family who lived next door to her were moving, so they'd turned their house inside out on the pavement. It was late and the glow from the security alarm inside cast her hallway in a bright green light through the frosted glass as she turned her key in the lock, like she was about to step into an evil lab.

At times like this she wondered if she should have moved to London like most of her school friends had, instead of staying here in her hometown. But she always tried to shut out thoughts like that. She'd stayed for the job, not the place. A sleepy, post-1950s housing estate in Wakestead was the trade-off.

She dropped her bag next to the door and kicked off her boots, wondering what she was going to have for dinner. Fancying something comforting, she made toast and scrambled eggs and took the plate through to the sitting room, where she ate while streaming the evening news on the TV.

A reporter was stood in Wakestead's old town centre in the dreary, lightless morning. 'Yesterday, this town in Oxfordshire became the scene of a huge manhunt, as dozens of officers were taken off ongoing cases to search for the missing girl.' Overhead shots showed bodies weaving through the wood like trails of ants. The elderly couple who ran the post office were interviewed against the backdrop of postcodes and envelopes and Haribo sweets. Erin frowned as she chewed. This news report made Wakestead sound idyllic. Maybe that was how it seemed to a London news reporter who'd been helicoptered in for the day. In reality, Wakestead's relatively high crime rate had tarnished its reputation, making it one of the least desirable towns in the area.

A photo of Sophie at age five or six, clutching a rubber ring round her middle at the poolside, came up on screen. As more and more photos appeared, Erin felt her appetite drain away.

The reporter said, 'Sophie's death is bound to restart the debate about the safety of young girls in Wakestead, where Annie Dodds was found dead eight years ago—'

A school photo of Annie. One she'd seen a million times before. Round cheeks and uneven teeth. And long dark hair tied up in a ribbon.

Erin had to put the plate to one side and put her face in her hands and breathe deeply through her nose.

5

THE TEAM CROWDED IN FOR the morning briefing. While the more senior detectives stood arms-folded at the back of the room, the new DCs sat up front, watching Erin and Tom take the floor with hungry eyes. She always enjoyed this bit; the rare chance to actually perform in front of the team, and to do it with Tom.

'Sophie was last seen getting the one-three-three bus into town at 11:12 a.m. Wearing these clothes.' She clicked through the photos on the screen. 'Let's get these images circulated on social media – find out if anyone saw her after this footage was captured.'

Tom said, 'We haven't found her bag or her smartphone, but she left her laptop at home. Tech is going through her social media now. That will tell us if she was actually speaking to anyone in the lead-up to the murder. But, at the moment, our focus is on Fraser Jones. Sophie's gymnastics coach.'

A photo of Fraser appeared on screen. 'We have it from another gymnast, Alisha Iqbal, that he may have propositioned Sophie sometime in July. He claims he drove to the woods at just after 3 p.m. to join the search party and parked in this area. Have we been able to confirm this yet?'

One of the probationers who'd been stopping cars that day sat bolt upright, like this piece of information could make or break the case. 'We've got him driving past the checkpoint on Kings Road at 3:30 p.m., on his way to join the search. Nothing suspicious in his car.'

'And there's no record of him coming back the same route?'

The probationer shook his head.

'That still leaves about seven hours between him arriving in the woods and the body turning up,' said Tom. 'Maybe he had the body somewhere else. When DI Crane found Sophie, it was about 10:40 p.m. So we need to know: where was Fraser between 8 and 11 p.m.? Did anyone see him go back to his car at any point? Let's go through those drivers' names and narrow down a list of people who might have seen Fraser, then approach them for interview.'

Heads ducking down. Scribbling in notepads and clacking keyboards.

When they wrapped up, chair legs scraping against the floor, Erin became aware of a fizzing in the air around her, like static electricity. She knew what was happening to her. She'd felt this way plenty of times before. Like you'd been knocked off balance, like something in the world had tilted and your whole perspective was shifted; walking around in a winter chill in the middle of summer. She'd slept badly the night before, overheating beneath her sheets, her head whirring. But it wasn't anxiety. It was the same feeling of alertness before a job interview, the same jitteriness kids get in their beds at Christmas. It was your head saying to you what are you doing sleeping, get out there and do something, you can't miss it.

After the briefing, they met Shergill, head of the digital forensics unit, in one of the station's less glamorous rooms – a space the size of a broom cupboard, with wires everywhere and no light except for the blurred glow of the computer screens. Tom, Erin, and Lewis Jennings had to stand shoulder-to-shoulder just to squeeze in.

Shergill reached over to turn on the speakers. 'I hope none of you plan on sleeping well tonight,' he said.

When she'd first heard the 999 call, the screams had shocked her so much that thinking rationally had been impossible. But here, listening to the chaos a second time, she found herself honing in on details she hadn't noticed before. Like a blind person feeling through the dark, the sounds started to form solid shapes in her mind.

'Jesus,' said Lewis quietly when it was finished.

'What do we think?' said Tom.

Lewis was frowning. 'It sounds like she's far away,' he said. 'Not just because she's muffled. It sounds like she's not near the receiver.'

He was right. Even if her face was covered, the screams should have been horribly close and breaking up the noise.

'The phone's out of reach,' she said. 'It must be, otherwise the attacker would stop the call sooner. Maybe she got the chance to dial the number and then the attacker knocked it away and covered her mouth. That sound at the end, that's them grabbing the phone and ending the call. Shergill, did you find anything else in there?'

Shergill, it seemed, was already getting used to listening to this disturbing time capsule of Sophie's last moments – he put on the headphones and nonchalantly hit play again. 'We've tried to isolate certain frequencies, and we've turned up the compression.' When Tom, Lewis and Erin just stood there in a clueless silence, he added, 'That helps to bring down loud sounds and bring up quiet ones.'

They waited while he listened to the clip, scrolling sideways through the audio software.

'So there's another voice in here.'

He said it so casually, like it was nothing. Erin's head snapped up. She stepped forward and placed her hand on the back of Shergill's seat.

'It sounds like just a short phrase.' He pulled down his headphones, reached round and toggled the speakers. 'Have a listen yourselves.'

The screaming had died down to a morbid background noise, like a shrieking bird. Over the top, there was now a sound that had been completely indistinct before. Shergill was right. Someone was speaking.

'No way,' said Lewis.

Shergill edged up the volume. 'It must be quite close if we can pick this up,' he said.

'Play it again,' said Erin.

He replayed the clip. It was almost certainly a man's voice. But no matter how desperately Erin tried to decipher any of the words, it was too washy. And it came in only briefly, a short bark, like an order.

'Maybe he's telling her to keep quiet,' said Lewis darkly.

'Can you get that any more precise?' she asked.

'I'll see what I can do,' he said. 'We might not be able to get actual words. But I can possibly get the tone of the voice coming through more. You never know, maybe you could match it against someone.'

'What else have we got from her electronics?'

'Her internet history is fairly tame. Just Netflix and clothes websites and gymnastics.'

'And what about messages? Any conversations with blokes?'

Shergill raised his eyebrows. 'Where do you want to start?'

Erin was grateful that Shergill had already narrowed the conversations down to a couple of options. Reading through a bunch of teenagers' chats would make anyone question their career choices.

Pretty quickly, Erin saw why Alisha had said she found it hard to keep up with Sophie's love life. Sophie had conversations going with five boys. Most she'd initiated herself. They largely showed a girl confident with her sexuality, testing her power over the invariably starstruck males in her life.

The last conversation they looked through was the most interesting by far. When the name came up on the screen, Tom raised his eyebrows at her.

'Fraser didn't mention this,' he said.

The first text had been sent on the twelfth of June.

Got a couple of friends down from Henley; out for a few pints. Setting a bad example, aren't ?I! Hope you're having a nice evening

Sophie had responded:

Haha well you dont have a competition coming up you can get away with it. I'm having salad for dinner...

A minute later, Fraser had sent:

That's what I like to hear!

Sophie had replied with a few laughing emojis. Fraser had sent a smiling one back.

Brief, awkward exchanges like that had continued throughout the month. The last one had been sent on the twenty-third of July. As mundane as the contents were, Fraser's texts were keen as anything. By comparison, Sophie's were so reserved it was hard to imagine what she thought about all this. Probably, she was just texting back out of politeness, or perhaps curiosity.

'There's nothing actually here,' said Tom. 'If he'd asked her out, we'd have him. He's not as dumb as he looks.'

'But dumb enough not to mention this to us,' she said. 'Because now it looks like he's hiding.'

Fraser hadn't touched the breakfast tea they'd made for him. Instead he sat there with his hands politely folded in his lap, as though afraid to leave a mark on anything in the interview room.

'You said you knew Sophie well as an athlete. Did you try to get to know her outside of that?'

Fraser sat very still. He knew where this was going. She could see it in his eyes.

'We texted, now and then.'

'You didn't think it was important to mention that?'

'I'm her coach. It's not inappropriate.'

'Seems inappropriate to me. Tom, you were quite sporty growing up, right? Tennis? Did your coach text you?'

'Can't say he did.'

'You feel confident her parents would be alright with it? If we showed them those texts?'

Fraser shifted uncomfortably in his seat. 'Well, if they did have a problem with it, that's – that's ridiculous.'

But his face had gone pink. He knew as well as they did that the tone of those texts wasn't innocent, and he was embarrassed they'd read them.

'It just seems strange to me,' she said, 'that you started texting her just weeks before you dropped her from the team.'

'It's exactly what I told you before. Her performance was slipping. I thought speaking outside of the gym might improve the communication between us.'

'Alright,' said Erin, 'so maybe you were just looking out for her. To be fair to you, Fraser, there isn't anything here that worried us as such. Although there was just one thing I wanted to check with you.'

She searched through her folder and pulled out a printout of the conversation.

'A message you sent back on the twenty-third of July. Quite late at night this one. Almost 10 p.m. "Hope you're doing OK. See you next week."'

Erin let that linger in the air for a second.

'Why did you need to check if she was doing OK?' asked Tom, all concerned.

'She was on bad form that day. Distracted. She could hardly keep her balance on the beam.'

'Was that really all it was?' she said. '"Hope you're doing OK." Something must have happened for you to say that.'

'Well. You know, I was worried about her. In case something was up. I was just trying to show I was there for her.'

'Right,' said Erin. 'It didn't seem to work though, unfortunately. She didn't reply to that one. In fact, it's the last message you ever sent her. That "hope you're doing OK"… that wasn't because you'd made a move, was it, Fraser?' said Tom.

His eyes went wide. 'What? No. Never.'

'That's what her friend told us.'

'What? Who? I never did anything like that.'

'Not even something she could have interpreted in that way?' said Tom. 'Maybe you said something and she got the wrong idea?'

Fraser blinked rapidly, looking away from them. 'I'm trying to think… No. Honestly, I don't know why she'd have said that. Who was this friend? How do you know she's telling the truth?'

He pressed his lips together. Then he leant forward, putting his arms on the table. 'Look,' he said, 'I know you're trying to suggest there was something I'd done that upset her. And that I therefore had something to do with this. But I'm telling you, for that whole last month, she was distracted. And I think it must have been something going on in her personal life. A bloke, I'd say. You know, I think she must have met someone and I think he must have been the one to… you know.'

It was convincing. The way he worked through it; the emotions that passed over his face. There was just one problem: Erin didn't believe him.

The interview with Fraser left her feeling wired all day. She could still see his simpering blue eyes when they went for an after-work pint at the Bull and Butcher, the force's watering-hole-of-choice. Along with Lewis, they found a table for three in the corner, away from the senior detectives crowding up the bar.

Lewis pulled up a stool and ripped open a packet of cheese and onion crisps. After Erin had finished relaying the interview back to him, he paused for a moment. 'Fraser saying "I think she must have met someone"… weird thing for her forty-year-old coach to say, don't you think? None of his business if she's seeing someone.'

'Agreed, it was weird. He might be trying to take the heat off himself,' said Erin.

She waited for Tom to chip in but he was busy checking his emails on his phone. You either had Tom's attention or you didn't. When he was concentrating on something else, Erin had learnt to wait until he was back in the room before she spoke.

Something did finally catch his attention, and it wasn't either of them. It was the young woman bringing their drinks over. As she lifted their pints off the tray and placed them on their table, she gave a naturally coy smile that left a dimple in her cheek, eyelashes curving downwards. Her skin was miraculously clear. Erin caught a glimpse of her own reflection in the large pub window – wiry body, faded old jacket, tired face – and thought she looked like a scarecrow by comparison.

Tom said thanks, then kept staring at her as she walked back to the bar, hips swaying.

Lewis noticed. 'She's quite fit.'

'Can we not?' said Erin.

Tom shook his head playfully like he was coming out of a trance, pocketed his phone and edged forward in his seat and Erin knew then that they had him back. 'So,' he said after a sip, putting his pint back down, 'Sophie was meeting someone that day. That much is clear. But there's no arrangement like that in her texts with anyone. My bet is that she'd bumped into Fraser at an earlier point, and he suggested they meet up to talk about her re-joining the gym. As angry as she was with him, she'd have leapt at the chance to come back.'

'And he picked her up and took her to the edge of the wood?'

'Until we have the post-mortem results, it's difficult to say whether it was premeditated. Perhaps he planned to do it; perhaps she refused another advance by him and he lost it. But it's likely to be one of those.'

'Sounds about right,' said Lewis, stuffing his whole hand into the packet. He nodded in her direction. 'What do you think, Erin?'

'The problem is,' she said, 'that it sounds like Sophie and Alisha didn't speak much after the Fraser thing first came up. Or at least, they didn't talk more about him. That means we've got this stretch of time of about six weeks between her leaving the club and her murder. Why the long wait? What happened then?'

A man came in from the rain, and the lead he was holding started undulating frantically as his dog, hidden behind the tables, shook itself dry. At the opposite end of the room, barking erupted; another dog going mad because it was no longer alone.

'Where are we at with the others she was texting?' asked Tom.

Lewis dusted crisp fragments off his trousers. 'I asked the teams how the interviews were going. So far, they've all had solid alibis. There is one I thought we should talk to ourselves though. This kid called Theo McPherson.'

'One of the boys she was stringing along?' said Erin. 'Why him specifically?'

'Based on their texts, it seemed like she was actually friends with this one. You never know, he might be able to help us fill in that six-week gap.'

Tom nodded. 'Great, we can talk to him tomorrow.'

'Brilliant,' said Lewis, necking back some of his pint triumphantly.

She knew it was unfair, but Lewis was annoying her. This was the first time he'd been welcomed into a detective's inner circle before, and he was loving it; chomping his way through his crisps, almost knocking over their pints with his swooping arm gestures, dominating the conversation. He wasn't thinking about Fraser or Sophie. He was just thinking how nice it was they were all getting along. After they'd finished their drinks, they started getting ready to make a move, but not before Lewis insisted they both come round to his for dinner on Saturday, which only made Erin more pissed off at him. They were on a murder case, and the only thing on Lewis's mind was when they could next get smashed together.

Just as she was about to push through the door, she realised she only had Lewis behind her. 'Where's Tom?'

She glanced inside and immediately found the answer to her question. He was propped up against the bar, one knee dropped casually as he spoke to the woman who had served them, whose white teeth flashed as she laughed at something he'd said.

'For God's sake,' said Erin.

Lewis was gawping at him. 'That is bold.'

Other detectives had noticed too; a couple of red-faced, pint-sloshing seniors were laughing and cheering him on from the unlit fireplace while Tom pretended not to notice.

Gritting her teeth, Erin shouldered the door open and stepped out into the rain, pulling up her hood. With enough women around, men would sanitise their conversations. But not when you were the only one. Throughout her time as a detective, she'd had to get used to colleagues leering at hot mums on drive-alongs or flirting with ticket-inspectors in the car park. But only ever from the likes of Walker. Never Tom. By the time he emerged, slipping his phone into his pocket – presumably with a new number added – Erin was seething. She watched Tom exchange a conspiratorial smirk with Lewis through the drizzle. 'Are we done?' she snapped, and they headed back to the car with her leading the way.

6

'WOULD YOU SAY YOU WERE good friends with Sophie?'

Theo McPherson – one of the boys she had been texting – shrunk back into the sofa in his family's living room, as though hoping he might get suctioned between the cushions and be able to escape this interview.

'Pretty good friends, yeah,' he said. Eyes darting nervously between them, he added, 'but, you know, lots of people were.'

Theo wasn't the killer. A receipt from the Co-op – which his parents had been desperate to shove in their faces as Erin and Tom had stepped foot inside the house – placed Theo on a shopping trip with his family at around the time of Sophie's 999 call. But even knowing the detectives had his alibi didn't stop Theo from staring at them with panicked eyes, like they were seconds away from escorting him off to prison.

'You messaged quite regularly, didn't you?' said Erin.

His wide eyes went even wider.

'You – you read those?' he said.

'Not in detail, don't worry –' no need to tell him the truth there or he might off himself in front of them '– but you'll understand that we need to speak with anyone Sophie was in regular contact with before she died. Seems she went a bit quiet on you in the last few weeks?'

He squeezed his arm nervously. 'Yeah, she did seem off, to be honest.'

'How so?'

'Well, just that. She was quiet. She was really upset about gymnastics. About her coach kicking her out.'

'Did she say why he kicked her out?' asked Tom.

Theo said, 'Yeah. He fancied her.'

Said with disdain and full confidence that it was true. Christ, Sophie really did have them wrapped around her little finger, thought Erin.

She was about to ask him another question when Erin saw the spark of memory in his eyes. He looked out of the window onto the garden.

'Actually, she did say something weird about that,' he said.

Tom and Erin waited expectantly.

'It was a few weeks ago.'

'It could still be useful,' said Tom.

'We were in the park after school. She was telling me how angry she was that he'd kicked her off the team. Gymnastics was the only thing she cared about. And it was gone, just like. So I said maybe she should tell someone. Like her parents or some staff at the gym. And she said she couldn't do that because it wouldn't make a difference. But then she got this weird look on her face and she said, quietly but with confidence, "I've already worked it out anyway. I know what I'm going to do. And then he'll regret the fact he ever did it."'

7

THEY DIDN'T NEED TO BE there for the post-mortem itself, just the pathologist's report, but Erin had skipped breakfast anyway that morning. Even without a dead body in sight, the smell of chemicals and rubber that lingered in the examination room always made her stomach churn.

Working in a morgue for half of her life had deprived Cecilie of sunlight and blinded her to changing fashion trends. She had very pale skin, a helmet of tightly curled hair that resembled an 80s wig, and a pair of thick-rimmed glasses. Stood on the other side of the metal table, she pushed these glasses up her nose before shuffling the photographs like a deck of cards.

'Shall we start?'

After watching so many news reports, Erin had gotten used to seeing footage of Sophie alive. That made it much worse now, looking at the photos of her bruised, slackened face. Thoughts of her lying dead beneath the tree came in long dark waves. She hoped Cecilie couldn't see her jaw clenching up.

'The first blow was to the side of the face,' said Cecilie. 'The shape of the bruising around the eye socket suggests this was likely to have been made by a fist. However, the bruising this caused was minor, suggesting the attacker didn't use much force at this point.'

She pushed forward a photo showing the upper part of Sophie's face.

'Then we have this more serious blow. This one is interesting,' she added casually, as though showing off her butterfly collection.

47

'This blow caused more extensive bruising and also burst the blood vessels in the nose. So it could have been that they used more force to hit her and, possibly, that gravity was on the attacker's side at this point. Suggesting they were on top of her.'

Erin stole a look at Tom. He always managed to stay composed during post-mortems, but Erin was relieved to see that even he looked drained of colour.

'Neither of these blows were serious enough to cause bleeding in the brain. Ultimately, the cause of death was asphyxiation. You can see this from the petechial haemorrhaging in the eyes and on the surface of the lungs. You can also see distinct bruising on the neck. Notably the patterns suggest the person used their hands. Not a cord or anything like that – that would leave a much more precise line.'

'Anything you can tell us about the struggle?'

'She has very good muscle tone, as you would expect for a gymnast. The person who restrained her was physically strong. There were no skin cells or fibres under her nails, which would usually indicate a struggle.

'The other thing to note was the blood pattern. As I said, the blow to the nose was delivered before death. But it continued bleeding afterwards. The blood flowed down and left this pattern on the side of her face. This would be consistent with her body lying on its side. Perhaps on a floor, or in a car, if that was the mode of transport to the site.'

'Any signs of sexual assault?'

She shook her head. 'No vaginal abrasions, no external fibres, no other DNA present.'

'So as far as you're concerned, there was no sexual element to her murder?'

Cecilie scanned her photos. 'No. No sexual element.' She pushed forward the toxicology report. 'I have one more finding for you. Traces of a benzodiazepine in Sophie's blood.'

Erin looked at Tom. There was an intense look in his eyes now. 'Which one?'

'Alprazolam. Often marketed as Xanax. A short-acting tranquiliser, as you probably know. Can cause drowsiness and memory problems. It's not uncommon to fall asleep under its influence. Given the low concentration in Sophie's blood, she took this some time before her murder. Maybe a week before her death.'

'Any evidence she was a long-term user?'

'If they're a long-term user, the drug shows up in their hair. No trace was found in Sophie's. Single use or very occasional use is most likely.'

'Single use. Except she wasn't using it, was she? Someone's drugged her,' said Erin.

They turned through the sterile corridors of the morgue, having left Cecilie to pack up her photos and get to work on another body.

'There's a chance it was recreational,' Tom said. 'But I agree. Most likely she was spiked. Which means she might have been assaulted as well.'

'It doesn't really tie in with what Theo told us. Based on what he said, she thought she was in control of the situation. I know what I'm going to do. She had a plan to get Fraser back. Then a few weeks after that someone drugs her and, a week after that, she's dead.'

'Maybe whatever plan it was backfired. Maybe she decides to get incriminating evidence against him. And ends up getting too close.'

The sound of the door opening out onto the gravel scraped against her nerves. The post-mortem always made it real for Erin. The clinical breakdown of the violence one person could inflict on another.

'Whoever it is, they didn't keep it very clean,' she said as they headed to the car. 'He hit her a few times. Eventually strangled her.'

'It's someone who hasn't done it before.'

49

'And possibly someone who didn't mean to kill her either.'

She thought of Fraser's puppy-dog eyes and the messy, fumbling way Sophie had died. She could visualise it now, for the first time – him lashing out, underestimating his own strength and not realising what he'd done until it was too late, then blubbering like a baby.

They stopped for diesel on the way back. Queuing up to buy their coffees in the service station, she noticed a baby in a pushchair, gurgling happily at the other shoppers. One woman gave him a big smile and waved hello with both hands, bracelets jangling – the instinctive reaction of someone who'd had babies before and missed them. Catching Erin's eye, the woman smiled sheepishly. Erin looked away and stepped up to the coffee machine. Haven't visited Mum in a while, she thought. She'd been putting off stopping by for weeks but she made the decision then to pay a visit that evening.

She took the coffees back to the car. While Tom was paying for the fuel, she looked at the dark hedges across the road, at the strips of a plastic bag snagged and fluttering there. Out of nowhere she heard the laugh her mum did when she was drunk, shrieking and too loud. She saw him sat on the green sofa, thick hand on the armrest, wearing a shirt the colour of corn. His belly hanging over his belt. She could smell his sour breath.

The door opened and Erin's head snapped around. She tried to compose herself but it was too late; Tom had noticed and he frowned at her from the open car door, eyes darting between each of hers.

'Are you OK?' he said.

She straightened up, hands on the steering wheel, and made a point of checking her reflection in the wing mirror. 'Fine. Just that post-mortem. Getting to me.'

It didn't usually get to her and he knew that. But he got in the car, nodding sagely, and said as they pulled out, 'Yeah. I know how you feel.'

She went round that evening. Her mum hadn't changed the way she dressed since she was forty, and it made her look older, with her thigh-hugging jeans and her long, thin hair and too-bright lipstick. Watching her narrow hips as she stirred pasta over the cooker, Erin wondered if she was eating enough.

It was feeling more autumnal by the day, but their respective nicotine addictions drove them to pull up a couple of plastic chairs in the garden despite the encroaching cold and smoke while the sun set. She looked at her mum cuddled up in a pink woolly jumper, watching the spilled yellow on the underbellies of the clouds, totally still apart from the wind stirring her dry blonde hair and one hand lifting a cigarette to her lips.

'Work OK?'

'Walker's being an especially huge knob.'

'Is he?'

'He hates seeing someone else catch a big fish. If he can, he'll find a way to slip us up.'

'He won't find a way. The case is in good hands with you two.'

Conversations with her mum usually went like this. She'd never admit it, but she didn't have the stomach to hear what Erin actually did in her day-to-day. When she first started on the force, and, brimming with excitement, gushed about the domestic violence case she was working on – without thinking to edit out the grisly details – she had seen in her mum's eyes the realisation that her daughter's life would now revolve around the worst things people could do to each other. There were more texts and calls than usual in the weeks after. Now Erin made an effort to sanitise every case she mentioned.

But the Madson case was different. It was everywhere; an unavoidable topic of conversation in any workplace or down the supermarket. So when Erin talked her through the text messages and the toxicology report, her mum listened attentively. Once she was finished, she shook her head.

'I know I shouldn't say this,' she said, 'but you can't help thinking the parents should have done something.'

'What? Wrap her up in clingfilm?'

'You know what I mean. Teenage girl bouncing off the walls like that… You feel like they should have taken more responsibility for her. The mum especially.' She tapped the ash off the end of her cigarette onto the paving stones underneath them.

'She was pretty secretive, by the sounds of things. I'm not sure they knew what she was up to.'

'It's not even that. You need to teach girls to stand up for themselves. That's what I taught you.'

Erin downed the last of her drink. The wine tasted sour at the back of her mouth.

Rather than sleep over at her mum's, Erin walked back home under the streetlights, watching the insects circle frantically in the yellow beams. She hadn't stayed overnight at her mum's in years. Despite being the house she'd grown up in, it felt unfamiliar. It had done ever since he'd turned up.

It had started with a new toothbrush in the bathroom. Then had come the fragments of beard hair in the sink. The lager cans in the fridge. She remembered running into her mum's room and coming to an abrupt stop because there'd been a man with no shirt sat on the bed, putting his socks on. One day, the presence of a stranger in the house had arrived and, even long after he'd left, that presence never did.

He was good for her – Erin remembered her mum saying that. She'd been thirteen at the time and had thought it was a weird thing to say. She couldn't work out at first if he was her boyfriend or some kind of live-in therapist. But she'd got used to him being there. And, for the most part, they'd given each other a wide berth and lived together without any issues.

Then had come the day she'd never forget. She'd been kicking the football against the garden shed, rattling the door in its frame. He had leant against the wall of the house, watching her. He'd annoyed her that morning. Erin had watched TV all morning in the living room. She'd wanted to keep watching it but he'd come in saying she must have homework to do and switched it off. Erin had known he just wanted to watch the rugby, but her mum had sided with him and now Erin was venting her frustrations by battering the door of the shed. She'd wished he'd go away.

'That wasn't a nice thing you said in there.'

The ball had bounced back. Back and forth, back and forth.

'What wasn't?' she'd said.

'"Shut up." She's your mum. You shouldn't speak to her that way.'

I was here first, Erin had wanted to say. But she'd kicked the ball again and it had hit the door and bounced past her. Turning around, she'd seen he had the ball trapped underneath his shoe.

'Give it back.'

'Are you sorry for what you said?'

'No.'

He'd smiled, which had made Erin feel confused and then he'd hit her.

It had hurt so much that she'd stumbled backwards. The wall of the house had reared up in front of her. He'd grabbed her by the front of her top and she had been so shocked that she'd hung totally limp as he'd pushed her backwards into the shed.

His weight had pinned her down. The hard concrete floor had pressed into her shoulder blades. He hadn't looked at her and she'd stared at the bucket in the corner of the shed and the row of paints on the shelf and tried to become nothing, hear nothing, feel nothing. When he'd finished he'd let his whole body weigh down even more, crushing the breath out of her.

You always knew to stand up for yourself. But whatever value her mum thought she'd instilled had left her in that moment. She hadn't reacted. She'd been scared that if she did, he might do it again. So she'd lain there in silence as he'd crouched on his knees and pulled his pants up over the nest of pubic hair. Some loose change had rolled out of his pocket. When he'd asked her to pick it up, she'd obeyed without thinking. Later, the memory of watching her hand extend and drop the pound coins into his had felt like an act of complicity.

Once he'd gone, she'd walked into the house, filled a plastic tumbler with orange squash and tap water and drank it in the middle of the kitchen while looking out of the window.

8

ERIN WOKE UP JUST BEFORE 6 a.m. and took her time showering and getting dressed. There was nothing like sunlight and the sensation of warm water to clean out whatever junk had filled up your brain the night before. But her morning routine didn't have the effect it usually did. She hated the way she looked and redid her hair three times and made herself another coffee even though she knew it'd give her the shakes. She was silently grateful for Tom's physical presence and his reflections on Fraser as she drove him into work for their fourth full day on the case.

Why was this happening? These were things she thought she'd dealt with years ago. She'd decided she was going to lock them away in the back of her mind and throw away the key. And it had worked. She could think about it and feel almost numb. It was what it was.

Now that wasn't true. Now she saw that it had all been seeping in slowly, like the horrible drip-drip of a stain on the ceiling, and she'd let it grow out of control.

Tom's voice saying 'Erin' snapped right through her like a gunshot. There was a car coming out in front of them, moments away from collision. She slammed her foot on the brakes so hard their bodies jolted forwards, the seat belt constricting around her waist.

The other car escaped down a residential road. Tom's angry voice filled the car. 'Fuck. It was his right of way.'

'I know. I know.'

He dropped his head forward, breathed out deeply, trying to calm himself down. When he looked at her again, there was that same searching expression in his face.

'Seriously, what's wrong?'

'Honestly, I'm fine. I just wasn't thinking. I'm fine.'

'Do you want me to drive?'

'No. I've got it. Just relax, alright.'

She put the car into gear but her mouth was dry and her heart was still beating frantically. She needed to get a grip. This case had set her off-kilter. Pushed her off balance.

'DCI Radley. DI Crane. There's something we need to tell you. It's about Sophie Madson.'

Erin had seen the two constables around but she'd never known their names until now. PC Drummond stood with his feet wide apart, presumably to compensate for the fact he only came up to their shoulders. The other officer, Saunders, was much taller, with a wiry build, narrow face and a scrappy moustache.

Whatever this was, Drummond was excited about it. Once they were in a meeting room, he removed his cap with an air of solemnity and started tapping an agitated rhythm into it with his fingers.

'The victim,' he said, 'we've seen her before. With a bloke.'

Erin saw Tom raise his eyebrows.

'This was back in July,' he continued. 'Must have been 8 or 9 p.m. We'd been carrying out speed checks all day. We'd just stopped off at the Welcome Break to grab some food. We were coming back to our car when he heard a bloke's voice, distressed, saying something like "no, don't do that" and a door slamming shut.'

'We passed the car and there was a girl and a bloke up front,' said Saunders, the tall one. 'The bloke was much older. Maybe forty? He was talking really intensely to her. And it just didn't look right. We thought maybe he could have been her dad but even if he was, it didn't look like a normal argument. He was going off on one, like he was trying to persuade her of something, and she was all hunched up against the inside of the door.'

Drummond said, 'We thought, you never know. So we went knocking on their window. They looked like we'd just caught them trying to steal the car. In the end, nothing came of it. You know how it is, they said it was just an argument, she's there looking terrified of us and insisting everything's fine. It was definitely her, Sophie Madson. We're certain of it. She was a gymnast, and the bloke, he was her coach.'

9

It was cold in the interview room today. The wind was whistling in through the draughty windows. Fraser kept his scarf and hoodie on. It pissed Erin off, seeing him all wrapped up in front of them while she felt jittery and almost light-headed with the cold.

She said, 'Seems like there's something else you've failed to mention to us, Fraser.'

He blinked rapidly under her glare.

'One evening in July, two officers bumped into you and Sophie. In the Welcome Break. They said you were having a little tit-for-tat. What was the argument about?'

'Like I said, her performance was slacking. I just brought it up with her and she took it badly. That was all.'

'Very badly, by the sounds of things. The officers said she was curled up like a little mouse.'

He winced at that. 'It wasn't a big argument. Those officers overreacted by coming over.'

'We asked them when this was. It was obviously a small incident. Nothing to write home about. But they made a note of your number plate, as well as the time and date. And guess what day it was, Fraser? The twenty-third of July. Just an hour before you sent Sophie that text... "Hope you're doing OK."'

'Well, there you go. That's why I sent that message.'

'That's not what you told us before. Before, you said –' flicking back through her notepad, reading out loud '– she was on bad form that day. No mention of an argument. No mention of police coming up to you. You'd think you'd remember something like that.'

'It wasn't a big deal. That's why I didn't remember it.'

'Did you often have arguments then? If it wasn't a big deal?'

'No, no, not at all,' he said quickly.

Something had happened. Something he didn't want them to know.

Erin made a point of breathing out deeply. She sat back in her seat, arms folded. 'This isn't really making much sense to me right now, Fraser. I've got a bunch of texts between you two in the weeks leading up to her being suspended. I've got what sounds like quite a bad argument between you and Sophie that seems to have slipped your mind.'

'And then there's this whole thing about her performance slacking,' added Tom.

Fraser's eyes darted between each of them. 'It was.'

'It's a difficult one, that,' said Tom. 'Because only you can say for sure whether it really was. Her parents can't give an opinion either way, and neither can the other staff. No one else knows what her performance was like. No one, that is, apart from your other gymnasts.'

'We spoke to Alisha Iqbal,' said Erin. 'And she agreed Sophie had been making mistakes. But she also told us how incredibly talented she was. How dedicated. It didn't sound to me like she deserved to get dropped, that's for sure.'

Fraser didn't have anything to say to that. Just sat there, his face gradually colouring.

'Are you absolutely sure that argument was about her performance, Fraser?' said Tom. 'Because if it wasn't, then now's your chance to say.'

As he said it, Tom shuffled his weight and subtly flexed his shoulders. Erin knew that unconscious mannerism off by heart. That was a signal. He was gearing up.

Fraser had his hands clasped in front of him on the table, one thumb pressing down on the other. They were getting close now. They needed to push in.

Tom said, 'You see, this is how it works, Fraser. Something like this happens. A girl dies. Someone who spent their evenings watching her prance about in skimpy outfits doing the splits… you know, they start to look a little suspicious. Silly me. What's the world coming to?'

Every interview was a performance. You could choose who you'd play. And Tom always played the same character. A version of himself without inhibitions, prepared to demean the suspect until he had them backed into a corner. For the people on the other side of the table, it must have felt like torture. But Erin always got a small kick out of it.

The temperature in the room had shot up. She saw Fraser swallow. 'That says more about the way you think that it does about me,' he said.

'Does it? Maybe you could enlighten me then.'

With his eyes still locked on Fraser, Tom lowered his arm into the satchel under the table and pulled out a brown paper file. He placed it on the table in front of him and carefully unwound the clasp. When Fraser saw what was inside, his face darkened.

'I saw these on the website. And I could use your help, because I'm a little unclear where the line is,' Tom said. 'Would you say this is normal?'

He pushed the first photo forward. It showed Sophie poised on the gym mat, elongating her chest, her arms stretched high above her. Fraser stood behind her, one hand looped around her waist, the other grasping her inner thigh, his body supporting hers. The longer you stared, the more obscene it looked. Fraser's fingers dug possessively into Sophie's bare thigh, pliable as dough.

'I asked you a question,' he said.

Fraser's forehead was shiny with perspiration, reflecting the glare of the overhead light. He hadn't yet looked up from the photo.

'Alright, let's try another one.' Tom pulled out a second photo. This time, one of the girls was flat on her back. Fraser crouched in front of her, holding her foot and bending her leg up to her torso.

'Do the girls' parents see these photos, just out of interest?'

'They might have done. They're taken for the website.'

'Really? Wow.' Tom raised his eyebrows. 'I don't have kids myself, you see. But I can't imagine feeling very comfortable if I saw a photo like that of a man with my daughter.'

'Come on, Radley,' said Erin. 'Behave.'

'Crane's right. I'm being unfair. I'm sure we could find photos like this of every gymnastics coach in the country.' He leant forward. 'But still. It's interesting. Because if we found photos like this showing anyone else with Sophie, it would be incriminating. Very incriminating. But you. It's different for you. You had a special pass, I guess you could say. Special access.'

The photos were still splayed over the desk. They'd shifted the dynamic of the room so the ceiling felt lower and Fraser looked smaller. His hands had left the table, and now his arms were folded tightly across his chest.

'You can't just put these photos in my face. And treat it like it's something wrong. I've never... never done anything to my students. None of them.'

He was angry now. She could tell by the slight tremor in his voice as he spoke.

This was how they were going to get him. By turning up the heat until he couldn't help but interrupt: 'no, it wasn't like that; you've got it wrong.' Like how you kill a crab; slowly bringing the water up to boiling point so it doesn't even notice it's dying.

'You're right, it's not evidence. It's just us trying to work out what this story is, if you like.' Erin put her hand flat on the table. 'We just want to know your side, Fraser. These photos, we didn't request them from someone. They're up online. Anyone can see them. And people will reach their own conclusions about what they mean. So now's your chance to tell us what really happened. Why did you have an argument with Sophie? Was it because you'd made a sexual advance on her?'

'No.'

'Did you suspend her so you could keep seeing her, without worrying you might lose your job?'

'No.'

'Or was it because she wanted your sexual advances to stop?'

'No.'

'It was the second, wasn't it? You did it to punish her. Maybe she'd never wanted it to start in the first place.'

'Listen to me.'

And that was what did it. The sudden bark in his voice. Erin felt a stab of vicious anger. Before she knew it, she was leaning across the table. The words rushed out of her.

'No, you listen to me, Fraser. For years, you had close contact with that girl. She saw you more than her own family. And her parents, they were only too happy to go along with it. They had absolute faith in you. I bet you started when she was young, didn't you?' As he stared at her fixedly, the skin under his left eye twitched. 'I bet you did. I bet you started touching her during one-on-one training, and she was too young to understand or even say anything. I bet you told her it was normal between coaches and students. I bet you told her she needed to do it, if she wanted to make it as a gymnast. I bet you told her she could never tell anyone. How old was she when you got confident enough to try penetration? Fourteen? Twelve? Nine?'

'You're sick in the head.'

Erin could feel the adrenaline spiking through her.

'But then she grew up, didn't she? She got older, and then she knew what you'd done. And she didn't want to be your little star performer anymore. You started sending the texts because you knew you were losing her. You knew you couldn't get away with what you had before. And you couldn't stand it. You gave her an ultimatum: if you won't have me, then you're out. And when she wouldn't have you, you suspended her. But you still couldn't stand it. The idea that she was out there, outside your sphere of influence, living her life, where you could never touch her again. So you met up with her, promising to let her back on the team. Then you drugged her.'

'What?'

'You drugged her and did everything you wanted to do to her. But she knew, didn't she? She knew what you'd done. And she arranged to meet up again. Confronted you about it. And you knew then there was only one way out of this. And if you couldn't have her then no one could.'

'That isn't what happened.'

'Then what happened, Fraser? What did you do to Sophie?'

There was the deafening silence that follows when words have been spoken that could never be unspoken.

'Are you done?' he asked.

His face was blank but Erin could see how shaken he really was. He wasn't in there with the room with them anymore. He was somewhere they couldn't follow.

He told the floor, 'I think I'd like to go for a walk.'

'This interview isn't over,' said Erin, her voice scratchy.

His neck turned; he looked at her with the eyes of someone who'd aged years in the space of ten minutes. 'It is over. I say it is.'

As he slowly got up from his seat, Erin's mind was blank. Fraser was right; if he wasn't under arrest, then he was free to go whenever it suited him. She could only watch, powerless, as he got up, pushed his chair carefully under the table, and then left her field of vision. She heard the squeaking of his trainers echoing around the interview room, followed by the sound of the door closing.

That was when the tiredness hit her.

'You led well,' said Tom, after a long silence.

'You don't have to say that,' she said.

'No, you did,' he said. 'He just wasn't budging.'

She ran her fingers through her hair, across her temple. 'It still doesn't all add up though. The suspension, for instance. Would he let her go like that? If he wanted her?'

'It's like you said: he thought that would get her out of his head. But it didn't. So he got rid of her for good.'

'Maybe. Maybe.' Her head felt hot. 'But then there's the Xanax. Why use it? And why then?'

Tom had his body turned towards her now. 'Look, we haven't got the motive figured out. But we're closing the walls around him. That's good. That's what we need.'

She wanted nothing more than to lean over and rest her head on his shoulder. She felt scared of herself. The anger had reared up before she could stop it. Everything from the last few days bubbling to the surface. She thought about the dull throb in her head. Too much coffee and not enough sleep. She had to be more careful than this.

Then the door opened.

Walker grinned at them. Someone was forking up a lot in dental fees; his teeth never used to be this American-white.

'What are you doing here?' she asked, wincing internally at how clipped and irritated she sounded.

'Nice to see you too, Crane. It's come to my attention that you might be needing some help with this.' Only the tone in his voice suggested anything but. It was scalding, patronising. Teacher coming to check in on the naughty kids.

'What made you think that?' asked Tom.

Walker's eyes glittered. He stuck his thumb out towards the two-way mirror. 'I was watching that,' he said. 'Part of it, anyway. I don't have all day to watch you two natter away. And what I wanted to ask you is: what are you expecting?'

Tom's eyes narrowed.

'Sticking those pictures in his face. I mean, come on. What's he gonna say? Yes, I do love feeling up those gymnasts, now that you mention it?' He stepped forward, big hands gesticulating. 'Don't just pit yourself against him from the start. Find something you can use to get through to him.'

'I disagree,' said Erin. 'He's a soft touch. The more pressure we apply, the sooner he'll give in.'

Walker smiled at her. 'Actually, I have a question specifically for you, Crane.'

Erin really hated the long pauses Walker left between speaking. Like she was five years old.

'What's the most important thing about a case? What's the end goal?'

She wasn't going to dignify this by sitting there gazing up at him. So she got up and started clearing up the polystyrene cups of cold coffee off the table. 'Bringing justice to the victim and their family.' She said it flatly, because it was obvious. Two plus two equals four.

It was what he'd expected her to say. He pointed a finger at her. 'Wrong.'

She exchanged a glance with Tom, who looked as annoyed as she felt.

'The most important thing is what you carry around with you every single day. The badge. Maintaining trust in that. That's the only thing that matters. The truth is, we all get the urge to step out of line. To teach a lesson to the jumped-up teenager who's off his face and screaming at you. To start threatening the suspect in front of you because you both know it's them who did it. I've known men like that. Men who are all about locking the doors and rolling up their sleeves. They're just looking for any reason to give a suspect a good slap around. You never can. As soon as you give into that urge, you've already lost.'

What did he seriously expect her to do after these philosophical ramblings? Break into applause; you're so right, mate, well done, you've cracked it.

Tom was better than her at not letting what Walker said get to him. He sat with his legs apart, angled towards Walker but not fully facing him. His voice was calm. 'We put some pressure on him, Walker. We didn't break his knees.'

'My point is,' said Walker, 'that you're here trying to provoke a reaction from him. When you need to be following the evidence. In the event that Fraser gets an interview with a paper, and tells his side, what do you think he might say, after an experience like that? My bet is he'll say we berated him. Humiliated him. Roughed him up.' He smiled. 'All I'm asking is that you think about the bigger picture here.'

Tom waited for her while she crammed the coffee cups into the recycling bin down the corridor. Then she went to the toilet. As she washed her hands under the freezing sputter of water, she thought how dull her skin looked in the white light. She needed to eat better. Sleep better. She splashed cold water on her face then went out into the corridor.

That's when she saw them. Something about the way they were stood sent alarm through her body. Tom had his back to her and Walker was leaning in conspiratorially. It looked like he'd caught him off guard. She might have been able to convince herself it was nothing, if not for the leer Walker shot her over his shoulder and the look on Tom's face when he turned around and noticed her.

They broke apart. Walker disappeared down the corridor. Tom walked briskly in her direction, facing the floor. As he passed her, she asked, 'What was that about?'

His eyes flashed to hers, but only very briefly. 'Don't worry about it.'

But it was impossible to believe him after the way he'd just looked at her in the corridor. Like she was suddenly a stranger.

10

'THEY FOUND THE HANDBAG.'

It was Lewis's voice. Erin looked up to see him rushing across the office to where she and Tom were sat writing their reports.

'It was in one of the bins in the town centre.'

Erin frowned. 'The town centre? Why would the killer dump it there?'

'So here's the thing. The strap's broken. Which could be nothing, right? Maybe it was on its last legs, it broke while she was out, and she decided to chuck it. Or—'

Erin finished his sentence for him: 'Or it broke during a scuffle with the killer.'

'That's what I'm thinking.'

So the killer could have pursued her out of town, or driven her to the field from here.

'Did they find anything else?'

'Nothing. No phone. I'm guessing the killer took whatever was inside.'

Erin's heart was racing. 'And if we're right, then that means—'

'I know. Fingerprints.'

Hallelujah. Erin turned to her right. 'Did you hear that, Tom?'

Tom didn't respond at first. After an excruciating pause, he nodded at his computer screen.

It was the day after their interview with Fraser, and Tom had been like this all morning – working in silence, barely acknowledging her, with his shoulders hunched forwards, a posture that warned everyone *don't come near me, not today.*

Lewis, suddenly noticing the tension between them, bit his lip awkwardly. He scratched behind his ear and mumbled something about chocolate digestives before sloping off towards the kitchen, leaving Tom and Erin alone.

She kept trying to tell herself it was the case. But he never usually got like this. Especially not with her.

Please. Please don't be what I think this is.

She noticed how hot and clammy her skin was underneath her clothes. Christ, she needed to get out of here. A cigarette break. As she was heading down the stairwell – she smoked in the downstairs car park, not out the front; imagine the photographs the journos would get – she thought she heard the sound of the door banging open and shut behind her.

Was someone—?

Following her—?

No. Ridiculous. It was just someone heading to their car or coming out for a fag. Get a grip, she thought.

She welcomed the emptiness of the car park, the smell of diesel, even the wind blowing her hair into her face. She'd just lit up, shielding the flame against the cold breeze, when she heard the fire door swing open. She whirled around to find Tom moving so quickly and deliberately towards her that for one swooping moment she thought he was going to kiss her. But the look in his eyes was pure venom. It shocked her so much she backed away instinctively, shoulder bashing into one of the car park's concrete pillars.

Tom stood squarely in front of her. 'I want to ask you something,' he said, 'and I want you to give me an honest answer.'

The conviction in his face terrified her.

'The ribbon. The one they found. Was it the real thing? Was it Annie's?'

'I didn't—'

'I just need to hear you say it.'

There was nothing between them but smoke and the smell of his cologne. Erin found herself struggling for breath.

She choked out, 'I'm sorry. I'm so sorry.'

She hated how childlike she sounded – pathetic and pleading.

'But it had traces of her DNA. Her hair,' he said desperately.

'I-I took it. From the evidence room.'

He stood there, taking in her answer. 'You're joking. You're fucking joking.'

'Vogel did it, Tom. We got the right person. We did the right thing.'

He stepped back, shaking his head. Seeing him physically move away from her, like she was contaminated, made her chest ache and she edged closer, feeling her heart rate accelerate in panic when he didn't respond, just turned his head to stare across the car park, jaw clamped shut and eyes wild with fury. No, not this; not with Tom.

'Was it – was it Walker?' She had to know. 'Did he say something?'

'He suspects,' he said. 'Do you realise that? Do you understand what he would do if he worked out he was right?'

'You know why he's telling you this,' she said. 'Because of the Madson case. He can't stand the fact we got it. He's trying to drive you away—'

'Did it ever occur to you that you weren't just putting your career on the line? But mine as well?'

'Tom, please—'

But he was already turning around, shouldering through the fire escape door, which banged shut behind him. Erin listened to his footsteps disappear up the stairwell.

Her fingers flinched. The cigarette was still hanging limply between them, forgotten, and the hot embers had crept up and burned her.

She lit another to try and calm herself down before heading back upstairs. Immediately she regretted it. One was enough; the second made her mouth feel claggy and her throat scratchy and she was hyper-aware she must be reeking of smoke as she stepped back into the main office.

Tom wasn't at their desk. Walking back to her seat, she let her gaze roam around the room in search of him. Had he gone somewhere without her? There weren't any interviews or meetings on now that she was aware—

Then she saw him. In the glass office at the other end of the room. A slice of fear slid up her spine.

He was talking to Peters.

About fifteen minutes later, the thing she was utterly terrified would happen happened. An anxious-looking probationer crept up to her desk and said:

'DI Crane? The super wants to speak to you.'

Erin had to stand up very slowly and carefully so they wouldn't see her legs shaking. The glass walls of Peters' office seemed to shimmer under the hot overhead lights. As she approached, she looked at the bulk of Peters sat there, studying some documents on his desk, his face impossible to read.

Tom wouldn't. He wouldn't report her, just like that. Would he?

Her mind raced as she tried to work out whether he might, and, if he had, what would happen now. Unbelievable though it seemed, she'd never allowed herself to dwell on the consequences what the punishment was for a miscarriage of justice like this – it was too painful to think about. Dismissal, obviously. And she'd be barred, unable to work in the force ever again. Would there be a prison sentence too? If so, how many years? Her insides churned. Why the fuck had she done this? Why had she ever thought it would be worth it? By the time she reached Peters' office and obediently sat down opposite him, she felt like she could unzip down the middle and come undone at any moment.

Peters sat incredibly still, resting his forearms on his desk. Slowly, he looked up from the reports in front of him to fix her with a pale, unblinking stare.

'We don't hide here. We don't bury our heads in the sand.'

Erin noticed she'd stopped breathing.

Peters continued, 'If an officer has something to say that could affect a case – anything, even if it makes them look bad – they come forward. The case always comes first.'

This was it. Erin could feel her body swaying in the chair. Get ready to hear it. You're suspended, we're letting you go, we're referring this to the IOPC—

'I don't know why you can't tell Walker himself. But I will. He shouldn't be sticking his oar in.'

She blinked. For a second she thought she'd misheard him.

'Guv?'

'You're leading this, not him. It doesn't help, having detectives bickering over every detail of an investigation.'

She realised her mouth was hanging open. She quickly shut it.

'I'll tell him to back off. But you need to learn to deal with this stuff yourself, Crane. You're not ten years old. If you need to report something to me, just report it. Radley shouldn't have to speak up on your behalf.'

He raised an eyebrow at something behind her. She let herself turn around and saw Tom working alone with his head down. Apart from the light blush in his cheeks, his face gave nothing away.

After work, they walked down the high street towards the river and found a bench to sit on. Next to her, Tom leant forward with his hands clasped together between his knees, staring into the dark water. For a long time, there was no sound apart from the chatter of water birds and the occasional flapping of wings as a group of geese broke away from the bank.

She said what she'd been waiting to say all afternoon: 'Thank you. For not telling Peters.'

Still not looking at her.

In a quiet voice, he said, 'Obviously I wouldn't have told Peters, would I?'

She felt a rush of affection.

Tom straightened up a little and glanced at her hand. 'Give me one of those.'

'Really?'

He nodded.

She held the lighter for him. A triangle of yellow appeared on his cheekbone as he bent towards the flame. There was a flutter of wings nearby. He breathed out smoke, staring into the twilight blue as two pigeons took flight above them.

He said, 'I'm in this now, alright? I didn't ask to be. But as far I'm concerned, this is our problem. We're going to control it together. And to do that, we need to start being honest with each other, alright?'

She nodded.

He leant back so they were shoulder-to-shoulder. 'So, what does Walker have on you?'

'Nothing. He just suspects the ribbon was planted.'

'You didn't actually touch it?'

'No. I wore gloves.'

He nodded. 'There's no evidence that you can think of that proves you planted it?'

'None.'

'And what would he need to do to get some?'

'Find the original ribbon. That's the only thing. But Forensics have been all over Vogel's place and never found it. Besides, it's just a ribbon. And it was eight years ago now.'

She was surprised at how confident she sounded. Sometimes she lay awake at night, wondering if there was anything she'd missed; any trail she'd forgotten about that Walker could follow.

When she'd hidden that ribbon in Vogel's room, Tom had been downstairs, mid-interview. Deep down she'd always known that if this ever went to Professional Standards, he'd be implicated too. They might even conclude he'd helped her. A wave of nausea passed over her at the thought.

'There's something else I want you to be honest with me about,' he said.

His voice was gentler now,

'I want to know why you did it,' he said.

Erin shifted uncomfortably under his gaze.

'Seven years without an outcome. I was worried he'd get away with—'

'That's not the reason. You risked your whole career on this. Why?'

Between his long, thin fingers, the end of his cigarette burned amber in the gloom.

She searched for the right word. 'He was… I don't know. Familiar.'

'What? He reminded you of someone?'

She nodded.

'Who? Someone from another case?'

She followed a vapour trail in the sky.

'Have you heard of the Three Crowns?'

He shook his head.

'One of my first jobs was a raid at that pub. They were trading without a licence. Just someone's living room with a beer tap installed. I knew about it and snitched on them. And it was kind of a family betrayal because, when I was growing up, my mum was there all the time. Since it stayed open later than everywhere else.

'When I was about thirteen, she'd stumble in sometimes at 2 a.m. and come and wake me up by making too much noise. She'd pretend it was an accident but really it was so she could stand there in the doorway chattering away while she sobered up. Mostly that was all it was. Sometimes it was worse than that. One night I heard her fall coming up the stairs and I had to help her brush her teeth and get her into bed.

'At the Three Crowns, she met this guy. She was a lot better-looking than him; everyone must have thought he was punching. But for some reason Mum seemed to think he was going to turn her life around. I was fine with him. He seemed to calm her down, at least.

'Then one day something happened.'

*

When she finished telling him, she took a long drag on her cigarette, filling her lungs with smoke. Saying it out loud hadn't been cathartic. Instead, it had left her feeling unsteady. Like she'd given away a part of herself she'd never get back.

She could sense Tom watching her. After a long pause, he asked quietly, 'Did your mum suspect—'

She shook her head.

'So what happened?'

She stared at the purple waves lapping against the riverbank. What had happened? Nothing. A man had attacked her in her own home, and four days later, when he'd next come round – taking off his coat in the hallway, handing her mum a bottle of Lambrini from the corner shop – he'd smiled at her and said, 'Hey, kiddo'. He'd gotten drunk with her mum in their living room, as usual, forcing Erin to lie awake in bed listening to the high-pitched, alienating sounds of him laughing and watching TV downstairs. He'd carried on as normal, and she had too, sitting down for dinner with him, answering his mundane questions about school and homework, pretending to laugh at his shit jokes. Desperate to convince herself that what he'd done had meant nothing to her. Because she could see it had meant nothing to him, and in a horrifying way, that had given her hope – hope that one day maybe she could be in the same room as him without feeling like her whole body was on fire.

But none of this she could tell Tom. She barely understood it herself. So how could she expect him to?

She said, 'Eventually, he walked out on her. That was when the stories started to come out. One night, a woman told her that a man using a different name had wormed his way into her life too. It had seemed to be going really well at first, and then she'd caught him taking photos of her little girl. Mum did one of her 2 a.m. visits to my bedroom after she heard that. Only this time she's crying. And she's crouched next to my bed in the dark and asking me "did he do anything?", but her face is saying "don't say yes". So I didn't.'

There was a long silence. Then Tom said, 'You didn't tell her?'

She shook her head.

'So you didn't press charges?'

Another headshake.

'What about your friends? People at school? What did they say?'

'I didn't tell them.' Should she say it? It felt like she had to; this was beyond her control now. 'I've never told anyone, actually.'

And now her heart was pounding – she could feel her hot, rapid pulse skidding through her. She made herself look at Tom in the darkness. She saw him realise she meant she'd only told him in her whole life.

Shit. This was too much; what was she doing? She suddenly felt as though she had their entire relationship in her hands, as fragile as glass.

She added, 'I'm not saying it so you feel sorry for me. I'm also not trying to excuse what I did to get Vogel charged.'

His face was very still. 'I know that. It's just... do you ever think about reporting it now?'

'Like I said. He used different names. I don't even know what he's called. Besides, nothing puts you off reporting a rape like investigating them. Think about how many times people get let off. Would you do it?'

He stared across the river. 'I understand you not wanting to tell people something like that. You don't want to be defined by it, because you're not. I just don't know if I could stand it. Him just out there. Walking around.' As he said it, he looked down the path, like a figure was about to emerge and come down the path towards them.

Hearing that, Erin felt her shoulder blades stiffen. 'When we started on Annie's case, and we had that interview with Vogel. And he was right in front of us. Just the lack of remorse on his face, the lack of engagement with the horror of what this girl had been through. It made me realise that's what I was to this guy. This thing that I'd spent the rest of my life wishing hadn't happened, to him, was an inevitability. Some collateral damage he shouldn't be held responsible for. And I couldn't stand it.'

They'd known each other for years but neither of them had ever shared anything like this before. She realised she was terrified of what he'd think. Terrified he'd judge her for what had happened, or – and somehow this idea hurt most of all – that he'd secretly think how he'd never be willing to share as much with her.

'Jesus, Erin. He doesn't deserve to live.'

Erin never wanted to forget the way he said it. Gently and frankly, like stating a fact. This was the kind of thing she'd deprived herself of by never speaking about it. She felt a glow of warmth in her chest that was almost overwhelming. She swallowed it back.

She'd made the atmosphere between them spiky with tension. She needed to say something. Change the subject. She was grateful when Tom said teasingly, 'I always thought you were just born hard as nails.' He smiled a little.

She softened. 'I know right?' she said. 'Now you see why I never told anyone. It'd blow my whole cover.'

There was another moment of silence. The atmosphere felt tense again. She still wasn't sure whether she'd done the right thing by telling him. Tom stared across the river, contemplative. She badly wanted to know what he was thinking. Then he checked his watch and started getting up.

'We're going to freeze to death if we stay here much longer.'

'Yeah,' she said, getting up and dusting off her coat. She looked around. 'Do you want to go for a pint?'

For some reason she didn't want to be alone tonight. She wanted to keep talking. Usually her home was a comfortable retreat but right now the prospect of going there made her feel cold inside.

But Tom was already preparing her for a rejection; he pulled his phone out of his pocket and checked it, biting the inside of his mouth. 'It's a bit late. I'd better be heading back.'

'Sure,' she said. She looked down the road they'd come from, at the grey houses with their dolly lace curtains, unlit rooms and overflowing bins outside. Maybe he had another drink arranged with someone else. She remembered that girl in the pub with the dimple in her cheek. Maybe he wanted to slip away so he could text her freely. She imagined the girl doing the same thing; reaching for her phone behind the bar, making her excuses to the other staff, getting changed in the pub toilet and escaping into the night in her heels. Erin crushed her cigarette butt into the bench. 'Alright. Let's head.'

Opening the front door, her hallway felt as lonely as she'd imagined. Somehow the conversation amplified the silence and made her more aware of the empty space around her. She decided to take a shower. As she was pulling off her trousers in the narrow space beside the shower unit, she felt hot embarrassment come over her. Because there'd been a moment there, in the dark blue, cradled by the sound of running water, where an impulse had crept up on her, unexpected, and the thought of it now made her scared of herself.

But beneath that, there was this tantalising voice: things don't have to go the way you always thought they would. You made your own rules. You don't have to play by them.

Several things hit her at once. The smell of his cologne. Tom coming out of the fire escape towards her. The imagined pressure of another body. A feeling of horrible, clawing need.

Erin breathed out and turned on the shower and stood there under the freezing stream of water until her scalp went numb.

11

IT WAS SATURDAY NIGHT – the night of Lewis's dinner. After a gruelling week, all Erin wanted was to order a pizza and go to bed early. But no, here she was chopping veg for a side salad in Lewis's kitchen while he wrestled with his own oven like he'd never even used it before – which, given the number of microwave meal sleeves in the recycling, was possibly true.

Clearly Lewis still saw Erin and Tom as seniors to impress. So he'd chosen an elaborate meal that chained him to the oven. While they tried to make themselves useful around the kitchen, Lewis dipped in and out of conversation, not really listening, occasionally throwing them an anxious grin from where he was crouched on the tiled floor in his oven gloves, exuding the frantic energy of someone trying to disable a bomb while entertaining their in-laws. And it was taking forever; Erin had started to worry that the sad bowl of crisps laid out might be it for the evening when he heaved a steaming fish pie onto the table.

Watching Lewis gulp down half his glass in one go, Tom frowned, smirking. 'How hard are you going tonight?'

Lewis made a face as he swallowed his last sip. 'I hate wine. I'm thinking if I have bigger sips maybe I won't notice.'

Erin snorted. 'Why'd you buy it then?'

'It's what you do, isn't it? Dinner and wine.'

'You're definitely outshining me on your first case,' she said. 'I think I bought Adlington a coffee once and got his order wrong.'

'Novice error, that,' said Tom. 'You need to shower your seniors in gifts.'

'Is that what you did?' said Lewis.

'It's what I would do,' he corrected, 'starting over again.'

Lewis cocked his head to one side. 'You never talk about what it was like for you starting out.'

There was a moment where a reproachful look came over Tom's face as he looked at Lewis. Then he smiled. 'When you're as old as me, neither will you.'

There was a wall with Tom. Some things were off-limits.

Lewis disentangled himself from his seat to go to the kitchen. He returned, carrying another bottle of wine, and they moved over to the sofa.

Tom said, 'I've always thought it was strange, him moving the body like that. But I'm starting to get a sense of why he did it. Maybe seeing all these families out and about, he realised someone might find her and get scarred for life.'

She nodded. 'I could imagine Fraser thinking like that. Or thinking he didn't want the Madsons finding her. He'd known the family for years.'

Lewis kept absentmindedly combing one hand through his hair so it stood up cartoonishly, like he'd been electrocuted. 'Personally, I struggle to imagine him doing it. Just the little I've seen of him... he's quite wet, isn't he?'

'An innocent person wouldn't lie as much as Fraser has,' said Erin.

Tom nodded. 'If he was innocent, he'd have just come out and admitted they texted. And he'd have admitted they'd had that argument. Not sat there bricking it. He's hiding something.'

He directed most of this to Lewis. While he did, Erin studied his face. It was funny. She looked at him all the time, but did she ever really properly look at him? Tom was extremely good-looking; a straight, Roman nose, high cheekbones, dark eyes. No wonder he had the gall to just stride up to women in pubs and ask for their number.

Tom noticed her stare and returned it, expecting her to say something. Erin felt a shot of panic and looked away, her face burning hot.

By the time they called it a night, all of Erin's initial cynicism about this evening had melted away. She felt an unexpected rush of affection for Lewis when he squeezed both hers and Tom's shoulders in the doorway as they said their goodbyes.

They barrelled out into the cold air. Checking the time, she realised it was almost midnight, which seemed absurd to her, borderline offensive. They decided to keep going. There was only one pub still serving. It was a twenty-minute walk away. Yet somehow the walk felt totally effortless, like they were gliding over the streets, kept warm by the booze that had set a fire inside them.

They picked a tall, rickety table barely big enough for the two of them and leant their elbows across. Gulping down pints. The drink shining in his eyes. Everything was funnier. The coaster kept sticking to the bottom of her glass and clattering onto the table. The door to the pub kept opening and closing, sending unpredictable and intermittent gusts of cold wind against her back. It happened about four times before Tom started insisting they swap around but Erin stood her ground and he came around to playfully shoulder her out of the way while she booted his shin, and her hand was on his arm and the grin on his face was making her heart go high up in her chest.

It felt like not even ten minutes had passed before the barman rang the bell for last orders. Then it felt like only five minutes since they'd got their final round, and suddenly they were being shunted out into the rain with their pints sloshing around in plastic cups, a group of bald-headed men hooting at each other.

The next thing she knew they were surfing the bus as it splashed around corners. Tom turned his head to read the destinations. She looked at the space between his neck and ear. Aware of the space his body filled. She thought about what she was going to do, how she was going to do it. You had to savour this moment. The moment before you knew. The moment before the jump, when you were filled with anticipation and want. The increasing surge of confidence, addictive, like a drug.

She tapped his shoe with the toe of hers. 'That better not be the case you're thinking about.'

Tom had started looking out the window. His face had gone serious. A small smile crept over his lips, but he didn't move. 'No.' Then he looked at her, right at her this time, and she knew and he knew. The wall was down and the knowing was there. His eyes were kind. 'I'm thinking that you should get off at your stop,' he said. 'And I should get off at mine.'

Erin felt it all at once. The sting of the rejection, followed by the hope that maybe there was regret in his voice, that he was only saying that so she'd change his mind. A couple of hours ago she might have played it cool; 'what are you talking about?' Now it was too late; she'd had too many drinks for that. All her emotions rose to the surface.

'Why?' she said.

'You know why,' he said. 'We're partners. It's not...'

She knew then, just from the gentle tone of his voice, that he meant it. Partners. In this context, clinical. Twisting her hand around the pole, she shifted her body so she was looking out the window, watching the town bend around them and the car lights create streaks on the window.

'Alright,' she said. 'I think mine's the next one.'

It wasn't and they both knew it. She knew it might look petty but she didn't care. She wanted him to feel the blunt force of her anger. His face barely moved, but his eyelids wavered and he said, 'Erin—'

The bus juddered to a halt. There was the hiss and squeak of the doors automatically pulling open and she tore through them, walking fast through the rain, hitting her in the face, fists balled in her jacket pockets, wanting to get round the corner as soon as possible, aware that his eyes would be on her back the whole time as the bus pulled away.

She was on her third cigarette by the time she got home. She'd needed something to do with her hands. She sat on the cold steps outside as the rain turned to drizzle, finishing up her last one as the rain turned to drizzle. In a puddle on the pavement, she saw a square of light appear – the light from someone's bedroom – and then, after ten minutes, turn out. She wondered if Tom was home yet. She imagined him taking off his clothes and getting ready to go to sleep. She finished her cigarette and stayed there for a few minutes out in the damp, watching a thin grey fox sniff around a bin across the road.

12

Bright white sunlight prodded her awake. She forced her heavy eyelids open, drawing in the biggest intake of breath that she could. It hurt to swallow. Her mind was blank.

Then she saw her leather shoes on the floor, one lying on its side. Her rain-soaked socks stuffed on top of the radiator.

Weird. She didn't usually take her shoes off in—

And then it all came tumbling over her.

The pub door opening and closing. The freezing drizzle on her face on the walk home. Tom's sympathy smile.

Oh no. Oh fuck no.

She sank back into the mattress like her whole body had turned to stone.

After about fifteen minutes lying there with her hands over her face, she forced herself up into a seating position. If she stayed in bed, she'd never leave. So she got up, even though she'd only had five hours' sleep, and stood under the scalding hot shower.

Chores. She'd distract herself with chores. She took the bins out in the ashen morning and scrubbed grease and toast crumbs off an unwashed plate. Then she washed the floor, and hoovered the carpet in the hallway and up the stairs. When she felt exhaustion creeping back in, she made herself an instant coffee and retreated into her bedroom, where she planned on staying for the rest of the day, or possibly for all eternity.

Stupid, selfish, needy. She had a sudden memory of Tom pulling her in the direction of the bus stop while she giggled like a teenager, tugging playfully on his arm. The image made her want to die of embarrassment. He'd been trying to make her go home. She should've slowed down, should've realised.

They'd have to work together tomorrow. She'd have to sit next to him and carry on as normal, knowing she'd acted like a teenager with a crush.

She heard his voice in her head. 'You know why. We're partners.' People always gave you the nicest reason, didn't they? This was what he really meant: he didn't find her attractive. Sometimes Erin thought she had a hard face; thin nose and narrow eyes and a strong jawline. She didn't look soft and open like some women did.

And why would he want her anyway, after what he'd just found out about her? She'd been an idiot to think he'd just forgiven her for the Vogel case. Of course he'd reached the conclusion that she was damaged goods, someone to steer clear of.

She'd have to forget about it. Pretend it had never happened. They were adults. A few days and things would be back to normal.

But deep down, she wished she'd been more careful. She pictured Tom in the golden glow of Lewis's living room light, his hand on her seat. She'd felt valued, safe, happy in an innocent, childlike way. For a moment there, it was like a door had opened, giving her a teasing glimpse into another life. And she'd recklessly slammed the door shut.

The next morning was a new start. She'd gone to bed at the embarrassingly early hour of 8 p.m. and woken up with no trace of yesterday's hangover. She was washing her face in the mirror when her phone rang.

An unfamiliar voice. She couldn't catch their name. Then she made sense of what they'd said. It was the forensic investigator.

'The forensic report from the handbag's come through,' the voice said. 'We have a match on the fingerprints. They're Fraser's.'

Erin watched Fraser's balding head disappear into the police car. There was a dull thump as Lewis closed the door shut behind him.

The officers would drive Fraser to HQ, where he'd wait for them in one of the custody suites. They didn't want to interview him just yet. Not until they'd turned his place inside out.

She walked through the house with Lewis close behind, weaving past SOCOs who were wiping down bannisters, rummaging through cupboards, sifting through Fraser's bins, until she reached the glass doors leading out onto the back garden. There, Tom was striding down Fraser's garden path, supervising the forensics during their sweep of the garden.

It was worse than she'd imagined. On the drive here, he'd been deathly quiet and, when they'd arrived, he'd been the first to get out, like a moody teenager impatient to escape their parents.

Tom turned around unexpectedly and started walking back to the house. He was too far away to tell, but for a moment she thought he might have been looking at her. She felt a confused rush to the senses.

Behind her, the grass crunched under someone's footsteps. Lewis appeared, holding out a flask of tea. Erin took it, unscrewed the cap, and sipped.

'Everything alright?' he asked cautiously.

'Fine. Why wouldn't it be?' Erin realised with a pang of embarrassment that he might have noticed her watching Tom.

'I don't know. You're both just… quiet. What time did you guys get back on Saturday?'

She gave the flask back to him. 'Not that late. Like twenty minutes after we left you.'

The look in Lewis's eyes was anxious. Did he know? Already? Then she realised it was something else. Lewis had been puppyish and excited about their burgeoning friendships. Now their little trio was already falling apart, and Lewis was the only one who didn't know why.

Tom came over, hands in his pockets. 'Nothing yet.'

Lewis drummed his fingers nervously on the flask of tea. 'You guys want to come round mine this Friday as well? The other night was fun. Be nice to do it again.'

Neither of them said anything. Erin listened to the gentle sound of birdsong, determined not to be the one to speak first. Tom was staring into the flower beds like they'd delivered him an unforgivable insult.

'I don't think that's a priority right now,' he said curtly.

'Obviously, yeah,' said Lewis quickly. 'No worries.'

After a horrible pause, Tom said, 'The woods aren't far from here. I'm going to walk around for a bit. See how easy it would have been for Fraser to get from the woods to his house.'

Any excuse to get away. This was really starting to annoy her now. 'I'll join,' she said. 'I'd like to know as well.' If he wasn't going to be an adult about this, then she would. Whether he liked it or not, they still had to work together.

The gravel crunched beneath her feet as she stepped through the back gate onto the pathway that ran alongside the house. 'Which way?' she said.

Maybe by refusing to give him the cold shoulder she'd made him feel guilty, because he looked sheepish now. His tone was softer when he replied, 'I think it's down here.' They followed the path and started walking into the woods.

Yesterday evening, once the almost overwhelming sense of self-loathing had started to subside, she'd had an epiphany. She'd realised Tom was right. 'Partners' wasn't just a convenient excuse. It was a recognition of the professional consequences that – stupidly – she hadn't even considered until now.

Getting involved with a partner might not get you fired. But it could still ruin your career. At best, the two of you would be moved onto different cases; at worst, you'd be bumped all the way back down to night shifts and high-vises and the kind of cases no one wanted. Everyone around you would know why you were really there, and no one would ever be able to look past it. To the seniors, you'd always be a punchline – someone who'd tried to screw their way to the top of the career ladder.

And who'd have been the one deciding their fates, if their involvement was ever reported? The head of Professional Standards.

Walker. Erin pictured him grinning at her across the table in the interview room, her entire career in his hands. She couldn't believe she'd almost let it happen. Almost risked it all. Everything she'd spent the past six years working for. Just for Tom's attention. He'd made the right call.

It was just them in the woods this morning. No dog walkers, no joggers, no families out for a stroll. No one was going near this place after Sophie's body was found here.

'Look, I'm sorry about the other night,' she said.

Tom was walking in front of her. He jerked his head to the side a little, listening.

'I was pretty far gone. I shouldn't have drank on an empty stomach.'

Immediately she worried it was the wrong thing to say. How would she feel if a man made an advance on her and then blamed it on alcohol? She waited anxiously for Tom to reply as they skirted some tree roots. She relaxed when she heard him exhale deeply.

'It's fine. Don't worry about it.' He added, 'I'm sorry. I didn't handle that well.'

Then he stopped and she stopped and he turned his body half towards her. His hands gesticulated, like he was trying to find the words. 'I didn't make myself—'

He stopped, looking away again, and kept walking. Whatever he was going to say, he'd decided against it. She was glad. She wasn't prepared to listen to Tom explain exactly why he didn't find her attractive.

They were approaching the top of a steep hill. From their vantage point, they could see a shallow bridge emerging briefly from the trees. Crumbling bricks strangled with ivy, it looked disused, like a remnant of some ancient civilization.

'That's the same railway that passes near me,' she said. 'I can hear the trains from my place.'

She looked sideways at Tom. Something had made him thoughtful. She could tell from the set of his jaw and the way he looked off to the right. Then he bowed his head and continued down the slope. They wound their way down in a comfortable silence. She listened to the sounds of their footsteps crunching through the bed of leaves. They turned off towards the bridge, a dark arch at the bottom of the hill.

When she thought back to this moment later, she realised that she already knew what was about to happen. Something in the air had changed. As he approached the underpass, he looked back over his shoulder at the space above her head, scanning the path they'd just come down, as if to check whether they were being followed. Before he turned around, his eyes briefly met hers before flitting away again. It was accidental, she could tell. There was no message in his eyes. He was just looking.

And then Erin felt it, like a flare that started deep in her stomach and arced right through her body. As she followed him under the bridge, where pale light cross-hatched the bricks in the wall, roots climbing down from the curved ceiling, she watched the back of his neck, studying his hairline and the slope of his shoulders.

He turned around. The same way he had done coming out of the fire escape. He moved closer until she could only see a slither of light shrinking and then he was reaching out to touch her face and his head was turning and he was kissing her. A needle of pleasure slid down the top of her spine, pinching her shoulders in. When had she last been kissed… when had it last felt like this; had it ever felt like this? As compulsive as eating or drinking.

She wasn't sure whether she stepped back or he pushed her. But the next thing she felt was the brick wall pressing into her back. His hands pushed past her coat, circling around her waist. Checking if this was OK before slipping them under her top. Just the sensation of his bare hands made the breath leave her. Erin realised she was going to do anything he wanted, but only if he moved first, so she waited for a signal. She saw it when his eyes met hers, searching. His hands went to unbutton her jeans. Erin started undoing his belt. She was so nervous her boot skidded in the earth as she felt his hands slip into her pants. He moved decisively around her body, like he'd always known this would happen and what he would do. He put one hand underneath her thigh and lifted her leg, bending it up slightly so it hurt a little, squeezing her body between him and the wall, and then he was inside her. They panted into each other's mouths.

It was over before she knew it. Before she'd had the chance to get over the amazement at what was happening. She shakily lowered her leg, taking her hands away from the wall. She looked down – at his belt still hanging loose, at her jeans scuffed green from the moss on the bricks. She didn't want to speak first. She wasn't going to say anything until she knew how he felt.

Then he looked at her and let out a breath of silent laughter through his nose. His eyes searched hers and he kissed her again, more lightly now. It felt different this time. There wasn't the same unrestrained hunger behind it. He was doing it to reassure her, because he knew it was what she wanted. Not because he necessarily did. Already Erin felt the high fizzing out. Anxiety crept in.

The sound of a phone ringing – Tom's – broke through the silence. He almost bent double retrieving it from his pocket. As soon as brought it up to his ear, he straightened up, looking down the alleyway.

'Lewis,' he said, 'has anything come up?'

Erin watched him take the call, speechless. She wouldn't be able to speak to anyone right now, let alone someone from work. Was that it? Had he used up his desire just like that? Was it gone?

The call ended. He pocketed his phone.

'They've found something.'

His eyes were bright with excitement. By comparison, she couldn't really give a shit right now. Then he looked her up and down. They both realised at once that she was still standing there, a complete mess. He quickly reached into his coat pocket, pulling out a pack of tissues.

'Here,' he said.

'Thanks.'

She felt self-conscious cleaning up in front of him but Tom didn't seem to mind. In fact, to her relief it seemed to bring him back to the real world and remind him what they'd just done; the longer he looked at her face the more she saw desire returning to his eyes. By the time they left the bridge, the atmosphere between them had softened, and as they climbed down the slope, his hand touched the back of her arm gently, steadying her as their route down became rocky, making her heart double in size on their way back to the car, back to normality, back to Lewis.

Surely he'd work it out, Erin thought, as they climbed into the car. Surely Lewis would take one look at their faces and immediately know what had happened. But he greeted them both in total nonchalance and said:

'It's a burner phone,' he said. 'He had it in a drawer in his desk.'

But her head was spinning so much she struggled to even register what Lewis had said. She was aware of not much else except Tom's outer thigh brushing hers through the fabric of their trousers and the closeness of the space in the backseat and the way his head moved around, ducking to look out the window.

13

T<small>OM PUSHED THE PHOTOGRAPH ACROSS</small> the table.

'Can we stop playing games now?' he said.

The photograph showed the yellow handbag with the strap torn. Fraser eyed it like it was a snake poised to lash out and strike him.

'Sophie was last seen wearing this when she got on the bus to head into town. We found it in a bin in the town centre, with your fingerprints on it. So stop lying, Fraser. You saw her that day.'

Erin watched Fraser swallow.

'Why's it broken?' she asked.

He said nothing.

'Did you have another one of your arguments?'

Silence.

'Did you hit her?'

'No.'

'Did you pull her into your car?'

'No. That's not what happened.'

'This phone –' Tom pointed to another photograph '– there's only one number on it. A few texts were exchanged between the months of August and September. Arranging meet-ups. Three in total. I'm willing to bet the phone's Sophie's. And the person texting her. That's who killed her. Is this why you tried to grab the bag off her? So you could get this back?'

Fraser's cheeks hung heavy and pink, pulling his face down.

'The phone's with Forensics right now. What are we going to find,

Fraser? Are we going to find yours and Sophie's fingerprints all over this?'

Fraser pointed shakily at them. 'You've got it totally wrong.'

Erin lifted her hands and said, 'We're just doing our job. If we've got it wrong, Fraser, then please help us understand.'

'It wasn't me texting her. It was someone else. The person who actually killed her. I swear.'

'Oh yeah? So all your arguments and texts, they're irrelevant, are they? Nothing was going on?'

Fraser wiped a hand over his face, now damp with sweat. 'OK. OK. The way you're spinning this… like I'm a monster…'

Fraser started studying the wall to his right. Erin got the feeling he'd reached a decision. They sat in silence, waiting for him to formulate the words.

'I think people can be a good fit,' he said, 'even a perfect fit. But meet at the wrong place. At the wrong time.'

And be born at the wrong time? Erin almost said, but she bit the inside of her mouth.

'I had this idea that I would wait until she was older and had left the club. I had a plan of how I was going to do it.'

There was a misty look in his eyes. He was entering that place people did, where they just started talking and didn't stop. Because they'd never told anyone this in their lives and once someone was willing to listen, they couldn't help themselves.

'I'd get in touch and suggest we meet for a coffee to catch up. She'd be at university and I'd listen to her talk about her studies, the new club she'd joined, anything she wanted to talk about. We'd get on better, once I was no longer her coach. And I'd tell her I'd be there for her for anything, anytime. And we'd keep meeting up like that.

'I never would have pressured her to do anything she didn't want to do. I just would have been there for her. And then, when she was ready, I'd make it obvious that I'd be there for her in another way as well, if she wanted it.'

The expectant tone in his voice made Erin's skin crawl.

But Tom nodded, all understanding. 'You were willing to wait.'

'Exactly. That made it easier to keep my mind off it, I guess. I made my rules and I stuck to them. And it wasn't too bad, at first. But she was a woman now, you know. She'd always been so graceful on the mat but this stiff, awkward kid off it. And now…' He shook his head. 'I mean, if you'd seen her. She'd glide into the room and put down her gym bag and her ponytail would swing behind her head. She just sucked the air out of rooms.'

'She was stunning. Anyone could see that,' said Tom.

Erin knew he was saying it just to empathise with Fraser. But that didn't stop her from feeling an anger so immediate and vicious that it shocked her.

'I started breaking my own rules without even realising it. I was out having a few drinks with some friends one night. And I don't usually drink so it went to my head. I messaged her on Facebook. The message you saw. Saying what I was up to and asking what she was doing. And obviously you know the rest. But she responded. Quickly as well, in about ten minutes. And I couldn't help myself. I knew I shouldn't but I kept messaging her. Not regularly; I didn't want to worry her. But just getting to know each other outside the gym, you know.

'Then the atmosphere in the gym. It changed, you know. There were little looks. Little smiles. I started dropping her off and picking her up more. At competitions I'd sometimes buy her a tea at the hotel bar or something like that. I was careful that all of it could have been platonic. But obviously it wasn't.'

His mouth tensed.

'I'm not an idiot. I knew I was playing with fire. I love my job and I knew from the way it made me feel it wasn't right. I had every intention of sticking to my plan.'

But he hadn't, and they all knew it. He needed a push now.

'That must have been difficult,' said Tom.

For a brief moment, Fraser's eyes flickered defensively towards Erin. 'It wasn't leering. I don't get physical pleasure out of touching students, I don't. It's just with her there was… an appreciation, I suppose.

'One day, on the mat, when it was just us two training, I was helping her get into position. And she just looked so beautiful. There was an atmosphere. Or I thought there was. I thought there was some mutual understanding going on between us. But obviously I got that wrong.

'I kissed her when I was taking her home and we'd stopped off at the services to get a coffee. I hadn't been planning to. It just happened. She looked disgusted with me. Immediately I said I was sorry. She got upset. Said she'd walk home from there. She couldn't, it was too far, so I was insisting I drop her off. That's what your officers saw when they came round to talk to us.

'I apologised again, at our next training session. She said it was fine, nothing. That's what she said: "nothing". And it broke my heart hearing her say that. Because it was nothing to her. She just wanted to keep training. There were no feelings she had to push down. Nothing like that. You're going to think I'm a fool, but I'd never realised until then that it was genuinely just about the gym to her. I'd never stood a chance.

'It was torturing me. I still had feelings for her but I had to see her every day and it was just making it worse. So I knew I had to do something. Once and for all. That's why I did it. That's why I suspended her from the squad.

'She was livid. I still remember what she said. "You're only doing this because you can't get what you want."' He shook his head. 'I should have handled it better. More carefully.'

'Wasn't she right?' said Erin. 'Weren't you punishing her for your own mistake?'

'It was the best thing. For both of us.'

The selfishness of it made Erin's hand clench underneath the table.

'So when did you next see her after that?'

'I didn't see her for a long time. And then…'

He looked at his hands.

'What?'

'And then I got a phone call.' He was grimacing. 'Out of nowhere. From this bloke.'

'When?'

'The day before she went missing.'

'And what did he say?'

His face darkened.

'He said, "do you get off on being a pervert?" I said, "Who the fuck is this?" He didn't say. Just said, "I know what you've been up to. Creeping on little girls. Punishing them for rejecting you." And then he told me, "if you don't get Sophie Madson back on the team, there'll be consequences. You'll deal with me." And he hung up.'

Erin stared at him, heart pounding, waiting for him to continue.

'So I went to her house first thing the next day. I was going to knock on the door. Then I saw her head out by herself. I admit it, I followed her into town. Eventually I caught up with her, just ahead of the bridge. I demanded to know who'd spoken to me, who she'd told. She was saying, "leave me alone". Refusing to tell me. I-I got angry. I grabbed her bag. That's how it snapped. It burst and all its contents tipped over the pavement. Sophie dived for all these papers that had spilled out, I don't know what they were. And I saw the burner phone. And I don't know, I was so angry, I thought, that's it, and I grabbed it. She was already leaving – she'd gathered up her things and she was gone, leaving the broken bag behind. I-I took the bag and dumped it in the bin. But I kept the phone. I thought it might be evidence or something. Maybe it would show me who'd threatened me. It was only after then I heard she'd gone missing. I swear.'

'What time was this?'

'It must have been about twenty to twelve.'

They were silent for a moment, and then Tom said, 'You never thought to mention any of this?'

'Why would I admit to any of this? If I'd done it?'

As Erin sat there, watching Fraser's gaze flit desperately between hers and Tom's, she realised she believed him.

'The thing is,' said Tom, 'if Sophie had just managed to escape one creep, why would she run straight into the arms of another?'

They'd let Fraser go. Now Erin and Tom were filing their reports in the office, which was nearly empty. It was late. The sky outside was pitch black and there was barely anyone left in the office now. But Erin felt wide awake.

'"I'm going to show him." That's what she told Theo,' she said. 'This is what she meant. Maybe she tried to get someone to help her with that. To scare Fraser.'

'Start sleeping with someone new and then rile them up?'

'Exactly. We know she played games with men; I wouldn't be surprised.'

Tom looked unconvinced. 'Would you really go that far though?' he said. 'I mean, it's just a gymnastics club. Could she not have just gone to another one? Or found a new hobby?'

'It was more than that though, wasn't it? He took away the only thing she'd ever been good at. All because he couldn't keep it in his pants. She wanted payback.'

They considered this in silence for a moment, then Tom said, 'If it's true, though, and there was another guy in the picture helping her get revenge, why would he kill her? What would be the motive?'

'If you wanted a guy who'd help you scare someone, you'd look for someone unhinged, wouldn't you? Maybe this guy really was. Maybe things got out of control.'

'Well, he's smart, whoever he is,' said Tom. 'Using a burner phone. He knew not to leave any phone records.'

Lewis came skating towards them.

'I was watching in the observation room,' he gasped out. 'I would've come out sooner but I wanted to check I'd heard correctly, so I replayed the recording.'

'Heard what correctly?'

His eyes darted between each of them. 'You guys noticed, right?'

'Noticed what?'

'The bridge. He says he saw Sophie at the bridge. So she got off the bus in the town centre, but then she kept walking towards the outskirts. Which explains why we haven't picked her up on any CCTV. Because from the bridge to the field where she called the police, it's just country roads. And it's a long walk as well. So someone probably picked her up and drove her.'

Erin had felt a glimmer of hope for a moment while Lewis was speaking; now it dwindled. 'Great. So we've found out she was even more out of sight than we thought.'

'Not necessarily. I had an idea about that.' Lewis dragged a finger over the phone screen, following the river. 'The walk she was doing. I've done it loads of times on my way to that pub, the Old Cross. You know the one?'

'Yeah. Pretty rough place. There was a mugging there recently.'

'Exactly. And around the same time Sophie was in the area, the Old Cross held a police press conference about that mugging. Tom, I think you were there.'

Tom stared at him blankly. 'I think we'd have all noticed if Sophie Madson had met someone inside, if that's what you're suggesting.'

'I know, I'm not saying she went in. It's just there were local reporters outside it, right? You never know, someone might have caught something on camera.'

Erin nodded. 'Good idea. Let's put a call out on social media. I wouldn't just limit it to cameramen either. Anyone who was in the area at around midday.'

'OK. I'll do that now. Then I'm out; I'm spent.' Lewis yawned. 'You staying much later?'

She glanced at Tom. Something passed unspoken between them.

'Yeah, probably another hour or so,' said Tom.

Lewis stared at them both in disbelief and shook his head. 'You two are tanks,' he said, closing his laptop and gathering up his things. 'How am I supposed to compete?'

They'd wait for five minutes after Lewis was gone before leaving, just in case he came back. It would have been typical of Lewis to leave behind his bag or his scarf.

'Admit it. You didn't know who I was at first.'

'Yeah, I did.'

She scoffed. 'No, you didn't.'

'OK, I didn't know your name. But I noticed you.'

They were lying in her bed, with the sheets fresh and cool over their bodies. Outside they could hear the gentle roar of a car driving past and the sound of TV chatter emanating from someone's open window.

'Yeah, right. When?'

His eyes searched the ceiling. 'Must have been your first week. When you were shadowing Adlington. You were listening to something he was saying. White shirt, hair up.' He shrugged. 'You just looked really good.'

They'd worked together for so long that she'd assumed he viewed her asexually, like a family member. Imagining him thinking about her in that way gave her a shot of pleasure.

'You never did anything about it,' she said.

'Yeah, because I want to keep my job, thanks. I don't go near girls at work. I just chat to girls on the job instead.'

She snorted. 'I know you do.'

He looked at her out of the corner of his eye. 'I'm quite subtle in front of you.'

'No, you're not.'

He turned over onto his front and smiled at her. A wave of giddiness hit her and she did her best to hide it. All evening she'd been shocked at the strength of the emotions that kept arcing through her. He'd come round to hers; it was only the second time they'd had sex. Get a grip, she told herself.

Then his expression turned serious.

'We're going to have to be careful,' he said.

She'd been enjoying not thinking about work. The familiar twinge of anxiety returned to her. 'Like you said, we'll just leave and come in separately.'

His gaze slid up to the ceiling. He lay flat again. 'It's not just people at work we need to worry about. It's reporters.'

'Isn't that pretty paranoid?'

'No,' he said. 'A case like this, I'm surprised we haven't had more people knocking on our doors.'

It hadn't occurred to her before. Now, she had a nightmarish image of both of their faces all over the news.

'Alright, nothing public then,' she said. 'We'll just be careful when we're outside.'

But he was working through it in his mind. She could see the wheels turning in his head. 'What if someone followed me here one evening? How would anyone explain that?'

'It wouldn't be so hard,' she said. 'Just claim your place had a gas leak or something and you needed a place to crash.'

'Yeah, but you don't even want the question out there. Think how suspicious it would look if one of us even released a statement explaining something like that.'

This conversation was making her nervous. The truth was, she was scared he was edging towards the conclusion that this wasn't safe at all.

'We'll just be careful,' she said.

He slid his palm over hers and gently wound their fingers together. The touch felt not quite real yet. Playing at intimacy.

'Any sightings from the Old Cross?' she asked Lewis, dropping her satchel beside her desk and turning her computer on.

It was early in the morning. Lewis stretched his arms out above his head. 'Oh, loads,' he said. 'Someone who was looking shifty at a petrol station about thirty miles away from the murder scene.

Someone who reported seeing a girl out with a man at around the time Sophie went missing, except she was eight years old, not sixteen. Really helpful stuff.'

'Brilliant,' said Erin.

'The best one, though, was this bloke who refused to tell me his story over the phone. Which means you have to go see him in person.'

'For fuck's sake,' she said. 'What is wrong with these people? Are they literally conspiring with the killer to waste my time?'

'Name's Mark Gale. He sounded pretty old and senile as well, so enjoy that,' he sniggered.

'And it has to be me?'

'Actually, it was weird,' he said thoughtfully. 'He asked who would come over – as in, he asked for our names. And he picked you.'

This was possibly that most inefficient part of the job, and Erin resented it. Ninety-nine per cent of potential sightings were completely useless. Erin remembered one woman who'd rung up just to say she had a really good feeling that the murderer would be caught.

Abruptly, Lewis asked, 'Any plans this evening?'

'Huh?'

'You look nice, is all.'

'Oh. Thanks.'

Self-conscious, she tucked a strand of hair behind her ear. Here was what she usually wore to work: white shirt and black or grey trousers, paired with either her faded old bomber jacket or long grey coat. That was it. Anything figure-hugging or colourful or vaguely feminine was strictly off-limits. Not since she was a probationer had she actually dressed up for work. It was pathetic how much exhilaration she'd felt that morning, smudging eyeliner around her eyes and slipping on one of her best tops, a silk grey one she hadn't worn since a friend's birthday, back before she had made DI and work had decimated her social life.

She was starting to wish she hadn't bothered. Ever since she'd arrived at her desk, she'd been waiting for Tom to notice her. She was within his line of sight from where he stood speaking to Shergill. But he still hadn't so much as glanced in her direction. Embarrassment prickled over her skin. The reason she didn't usually dress like this because she wanted to be taken seriously by her co-workers – and here she was drawing attention to herself, and not getting attention from the one person who—

Then Tom's eyes drifted over to her, looking her up and down. Her heart beat faster as she watched him slip away from Shergill and approach Lewis's desk, gesturing with his thumb towards the door.

'I need to run something by you quickly,' he said.

She followed him out of the main office. As soon as the door was shut behind her, Tom did a quick scan of the corridor. Then he came close and pushed her through the fire escape. The stairwell was empty. He leant in as close as he could without touching her.

His eyebrows furrowed helplessly. 'You know it's not going to work if you do this. You need to come in wearing a potato sack. With a bag over your head.'

'I think I could make that work.'

He shook his head. 'You're enjoying it, as well. That's the worst part.' He kissed her, the first time he'd done that at work, and Erin drank in the moment, the fact that she'd made him break one of his unspoken rules.

He pulled back a little, but his body now pressed against her. 'I'm going to ask the gym staff if they saw Sophie getting into the car Fraser mentioned. Are you coming?'

'Can't. I've got a witness to meet. Every sign it's going to be pointless.'

'Well, enjoy that. I hope it's not a bloke. You'll knock him out wearing something like that.' He ducked, running a hand through his hair, something she'd seen him do around other women but never her. 'Are you doing anything this weekend?'

'I thought you were worried about reporters hunting us down.'

'Obviously I didn't mean we should stop. I thought maybe we could get out of Wakestead. Take a break. Stay at a hotel. Arrive at different times.'

Even though they'd spent entire weeks working together in close proximity, this suggestion felt totally different; brand new. Erin was pathetically happy he didn't consider that too much or too soon. And she liked the way he'd said 'obviously...' in that incredulous tone.

'Yeah. That sounds nice.'

'Alright. I'll take a look at places.'

He beamed at her, eyes searching her face. She smiled back, knowing what the expression meant. *Look at us now. This is new.* As he turned and walked down the stairs, she could tell he knew she was watching him because he touched his hair once again before disappearing through the door.

She felt a brittle, precious happiness. Brittle because she already knew what was going to happen. He was going to cruise in and out of this like it was nothing, just another exploit, and she was going to fall hard. But even knowing that, as she visualised him standing there grinning at her with the sunlight slanting in through the windows, she realised she didn't care. She wanted to remember that forever, even if he didn't.

On the drive to the caller's house, she turned on the radio. Usually she preferred to drive in silence but not today – today she wanted music. While the radio played, she watched a stream of schoolchildren walk in single file down the road, led by a couple of teaching assistants who swung one of the children between them, their face lit up with glee. How long had it been since she felt like this? Like she was carrying around a secret garden of happiness inside her wherever she went? She loved this song she'd never heard before and the smoothness of the car seat through the thin fabric of her trousers and the people she passed and the way her hair looked in the wing mirror. When she got out of the car, she imagined Tom watching her and she walked with poise all the way up to the front door, thinking of what it would feel like heading into that hotel this weekend.

Mark Gale wasn't as old as Lewis had made out – he must have been in his late fifties. He delivered kegs of draught beer from a local supplier to the Old Cross. His van had been parked outside the pub during the press conference.

They sat at his kitchen table while he searched through his laptop.

'I'd never looked at the footage before,' he said. 'The dashcam's just there in case you have a collision. But when I heard your guys on the radio, I thought, do you know what, let's take a look. Good thing I did as well.'

Remembering her skin-tight top, Erin awkwardly zipped up her jacket.

'Where is it?' Mark muttered. 'There's an icon I need to press, somewhere…'

He hunched forward, squinting at the screen in bewilderment. Oh man. This might take a while. Erin let her mind wander to Tom again. Happiness fizzed over her scalp and behind her ears.

She zoned back into the room when she realised Mark was adjusting his glasses and straightening up in his seat. The laptop was working. But before he turned the screen towards her, something made him hesitate. He looked at her and she was jolted by the look of sincere apology in his face.

'I would've said over the phone. But I didn't. Just in case. I'm sorry if I should have done. I really am.'

Immediately she felt spooked. But she tried to hide it, nodding and leaning forward to see the screen as he turned the laptop around.

It took her a few moments to fully grasp what she was looking at. She saw a white-painted wall and a hanging basket; the corner of the Old Cross. Then her heart stopped. It felt like a block of ice had formed right below her ribcage, and was slowly melting over her insides.

Parked directly in front of Mark's van was a black Audi. Erin recognised the number plate immediately. At what the footage told her was 12:14 p.m., a teenage girl came around on the passenger's side. It was – unmistakably – Sophie Madson. All high cheekbones and dark hair. She didn't get in the car. Instead she hovered there for a moment, talking to someone off camera. Then the driver joined on the other side. The sight of his black coat collar and the deliberate way he opened the car door killed something deep inside Erin. Because there, getting into the car with Sophie Madson and driving her away just one hour before she made her final phone call to the world, was Tom.

14

FIFTEEN MINUTES SEEMED TO LAST forever. Erin wished she'd stayed at her desk and preoccupied herself up until the very last moment. All she could do now was pace in the corridor beside the vending machine, waiting.

Finally Peters shuffled around the corner. Somehow he managed to look almost bored as he toed the carpet, hands in his pockets, as though this press conference held no significance to him. Erin wondered what was really going on in his head.

The media liaison officer emerged from the press conference to usher them over. Erin let Peters go first and followed after him. When they got to the doors, he would step back and she would come to his shoulder. It looked better if they went in together.

Two lighting stands were turned towards the empty desk, drenching it in bright white light. Erin pulled out her chair and squeezed in beside Peters. A wall of journalists loomed over them. It felt unbearably hot under the lights.

Peters started them off. He spoke calmly and clearly. Only it was difficult to hear most of what he said. Because as soon as he used Tom's name, the crowd began to murmur, conferring with each other, and the room became filled with the rapid clicking of dozens of cameras.

Then it was her turn. She cleared her throat and looked down at the statement in front of her. The words made no sense; they might as well have been splashed onto the page at random. She felt suddenly and viscerally that she wasn't in the room. The last twenty-four hours came crashing down on her.

THE BLAME

*

After she'd left the delivery driver's house, she'd walked back to her car, only she didn't remember doing that. All she remembered was that spaced-out feeling of a fever coming on as she'd sat alone in the car, overwhelmed by the sickly smell of leather in the car, looking at the blue veins under the skin of her hands gripping the steering wheel. She realised in retrospect that she must have been in shock. Slowly, a tingling feeling had started to come into her fingers and the numbness had been replaced by total, heart-clutching fear. She'd wanted to ring Lewis. She'd wanted to tell someone what she'd just seen. But she'd known she wouldn't be able to bring herself to do it. There'd been only one person she could speak to right now.

She'd texted:

Meet me in the car park in 15 minutes.

She'd hit send. Her hands had been trembling.

There were a few seconds when he hadn't noticed yet. When he emerged from his car and walked over to her with an easy grin on his face. Then, as he got closer, he really looked at her. The smile fell, to be replaced by an expression of complete terror. She felt the realisation right there, like a punch in the stomach, so that what she said came out before she had time to gather her thoughts or even pause for breath:

'You'd have told me. You'd have told me you'd seen her. If it wasn't you. I know you would have.'

She was certain. She held a hand over her mouth. Her vision was blurring but she saw the shape of Tom jolt as he dropped his satchel and came towards her, fast.

'Erin. Erin.'

She backed away. She felt the car's exterior press against her back. 'You know what I've just seen. If you lie to me right now, you're dead, you're dead to me.'

He stopped. His eyes were wild.

'I-I should have told you,' he managed.

It seemed to her like the worst thing to say in the world. She felt like a gaping hole had opened in her stomach, a vast black nothingness.

She said quietly, 'Were you having sex with her? Was that why you did it?'

And Tom's face fell open and the blackness swallowed her whole. Because she didn't know what that look meant. She didn't know if it was the horror of a false accusation or the horror of getting found out. She didn't know anymore.

'Erin, no. Erin, I swear. I'd never met her before. Not before that day. Never, I swear.'

It had only just occurred to her in the last few moments that he might have touched her. She thought of Sophie's yellow, slackened face in the post-mortem photos. She thought she was going to be sick.

'God. Oh god.'

He crossed the space between them and grabbed her shoulders. The feeling of his hands on her suddenly disgusted her.

'Look at me, Erin. Look at me. This is not what you think it is.'

She smacked her palms against his chest, pushing him away. 'You can tell that to Peters. You can tell it to everyone.'

He swayed from one side to the other. He brought his hands up in front of him, all slow and steady. 'You don't have to do that. We can deal with this, just us two.'

'I'm turning you in. I'm turning you in.'

His eyes pleaded with her. 'Erin, just think for a minute—'

'Get upstairs. We're doing this right now.'

Peters had his hands clasped together and his knuckles against his forehead. His eyes lingered on the carpet. The air around them was dusty and the light coming through the blinds was grey.

After a while he said, 'Does Jennings know?'

'Not yet.'

He nodded, processing this. 'Bring him in now.'

The constable at the door left the room, reappearing moments later with Lewis, who filed in like a school child and sat silently beside Erin while Peters studied the desk.

'I need to ask you something,' said Peters. 'At any point during your investigation, has DCI Radley mentioned having any connection whatsoever to Sophie Madson?'

'No way,' said Lewis.

It made Erin's body stiffen, hearing how horribly upbeat his voice was. Peters stared right through him. Somehow, Lewis hadn't picked up on the hostility that was coming off him in waves. Like a child that hadn't noticed the cat's tail gently flicking.

'You've never uncovered any evidence of a connection like that?'

Lewis shook his head, eyebrows furrowing.

'I see,' said Peters, looking away. 'I hope that's true. For both your sakes.'

That was when the penny dropped for Lewis. All at once, he'd noticed the atmosphere in the room.

'What's happened?' he asked quietly.

'A delivery driver has dashcam footage of Sophie Madson getting into Tom Radley's car on the day of her murder,' said Peters.

'What?' said Lewis, half-laughing, unable to keep the disbelief out of his voice.

Peters leant back in his seat, straightening his shoulders. 'As of today, Radley is suspended from the force. He'll be put under investigation. We'll keep it internal, if we can. But it's up to the IOPC to decide that.'

This was it. It felt like the chair had disappeared beneath her.

'This can't be right,' said Lewis. 'This can't – it's got to be something else.'

Peters' blue eyes fixed on him. 'I need you two to understand this very clearly –' his eyes switched to Erin '– we are now investigating the possibility that Tom may have murdered Sophie Madson.' The tone of his voice was flat, cold. 'In twenty-two years, I have never been in this position. If the case were further along, or if you two were implicated in any way, I would immediately disband this squad.'

Lewis was sat bolt upright by now, as though an electric current had gone right through him.

'For now, you two are in the clear. This case is important and I don't want to do anything to disrupt your progress. However, I know it will be hard for you to disconnect yourselves from this. You need to forget everything you thought you knew about him.'

She couldn't even feel relief. The warning behind Peters' words was obvious. 'For now, you two are in the clear.' For now.

His chair creaked as he leant back, looking tired. 'Alright. Out with you both. You'll hear more about this later today.'

They rose from their seats and half-stumbled out the room. As soon as the door was shut behind them, Lewis looked right at her, his eyes wide and questioning.

'What the fuck?' he said. 'What the fuck?'

In another situation, Erin would have put her hand on his shoulder and told him everything was going to be fine. She would have suggested they get into a room right now and work through this together. But she just stared at him. She couldn't find the words.

15

SHE HADN'T WANTED TO COME. She hated the publicity of it; the idea of them all leering through the glass at him like some exhibit in a zoo. It was Lewis who'd convinced her to. Everyone was going to hear what he had to say for himself; did she really want to be the only one who hadn't?

Walker was already there, which Erin could've predicted. He acknowledged them with a knowing look. He'd found himself a comfortable spot close to the glass and he looked smugly settled in, like he'd secured the best seat in the pub before a football game.

Seeing Tom through the double-sided mirror was more of a punch in the gut than she'd expected. The first thing she noticed was that he was sat on the other side of the table, with his back to the wall. Where the suspect always sat. The other thing that surprised her was how devastated she felt looking at his face. She'd expected – hoped – to feel repulsed by him. Instead, he looked ethereally beautiful – his eyes half-lidded, darkened by the day's ordeal.

Over the next ten minutes, more and more detectives filed in. Among those who'd been closer to Tom, there was a sombre, respectful silence. Others spoke in gossipy stage whispers Erin tried her best to tune out.

For the longest time, there was no movement in the room. Then the door opened. Peters stepped inside and slowly closed the door behind him. The entire team was dead silent as he made his way over, pulled the other chair out with a painfully loud screech and shuffled his weight into the seat. Tom hadn't moved. But perhaps his eyes were slightly wider now. There was a horrible silence.

'Was it busy that day?' asked Peters.

The question sounded uncomfortably sincere, as though he was genuinely concerned about Tom's workload. Peters waited patiently for an answer. Tom stared at him, his face unreadable.

'Did you forget?' Peters continued. 'Did it slip your mind? Did you not notice that the girl whose body we found in the woods was the same one you saw, just before she was killed?'

Tom said, 'I should have reported it immediately.'

'No shit you should have. Now, describe to me what happened in between her getting in your car and her screaming down the phone to the emergency services.'

Tom was shaking his head. 'I only had her in my car for twenty minutes. She wanted to speak to me about something. Then I dropped her off near her house. It was twenty minutes later. I swear.'

'So let's hear it then. What did she want to speak to you about?'

The observation room felt airless.

'She wanted to know,' he said, 'if she could trust me to help her arrest someone who was abusing her.'

She had no idea whether to believe it or not. His voice sounded different: soft, slow and defeated.

Peters was totally still. 'Did she at any point describe that person?'

'No, she wasn't comfortable naming them. It was impossible to tell who she was talking about.'

'You understand that, if what you're saying is true, you've not only failed to disclose a connection to the victim but also withheld information related to a potential suspect?'

Tom said nothing. He nodded stiffly.

'You hid this. And in doing so, you've stabbed every member of this team in the back.'

She saw that hit Tom hard. A muscle in his neck shifted.

'I would do anything to keep investigating this—'

111

'Don't,' said Peter sharply. 'Don't even try. This affects everyone, you understand that? Everyone on this team is sullied by this. Me. DI Crane.' She thought she noticed Tom's head pull back a little, but she couldn't know for sure. 'Everyone. And every single case they've worked on. Cases could be reopened. Criminals let back on the street. Officers sacked. You care about your team?'

'You know I do.'

'What I'm trying to make you understand is that this isn't just about you. The sooner I know what happened that day,' he said, 'the smaller the fallout zone.'

He stood up, putting one hand inside the pocket of his suit jacket. Before leaving, he turned to the side and looked down at Tom.

'I am still your gaffer. That means I will drop everything to help you out of a tight spot. If you are innocent. We're going to work this out together. Whatever the outcome is.'

Tom bit his lip and gave a brief, sincere nod. Once Peters was gone, he turned his head and looked towards the glass. Erin's throat tightened. For a moment, it felt like he was looking straight at her.

The muttering gradually resumed, this time with a darker, more accusatory tone. 'Did you see his face when Peters came in?' someone whispered. Then the door to the observation room opened, revealing Peters.

'Crane. Jennings. I want you two in the other interview room in ten minutes. First I'm going to have a word with Walker and Adlington.'

His eyes moved between them. Erin didn't nod but Lewis did, and that was enough. Peters abruptly turned around and left. As if on cue, Walker moved like a shark through the room and brushed up close against Erin. She pretended he wasn't there, keeping her eyes fixed on Tom.

'Must have been a big shock for you, Crane,' he said quietly.

'No kidding,' she muttered.

'I should hope so,' he said. 'Because if Peters finds out you did anything to protect him in all this, you are in deep water.'

Before she could answer, he turned away, leaving her there looking through the one-way glass, watching Tom.

She took an automatic swig of coffee while it was still hot and burned her tongue. It tasted like iron. Sitting here in one of the meeting rooms with Lewis reminded her of lingering in a hospital waiting room, physically exhausted but too wired and distracted to comprehend sleep.

The door opened and Adlington shuffled inside, suit jacket open and hands weighted in his trouser pockets. Behind him, Walker sloped inside and leant against the inside wall.

'What happens now?' asked Lewis.

'We've been speaking with the IOPC. In all likelihood they'll want what's called a managed investigation. Where we take control but they monitor our progress.'

'Who'll be on it from our team?' asked Erin.

'The Professional Standards Department will handle this. So Walker.'

Erin's teeth clenched. She'd suspected as much. She glanced at Walker and said nothing.

'Is there anything we can do?' said Lewis.

'No. This has to be independent of you both. The two teams will share information, of course. But that's it.'

Hearing this, Erin felt any last vestige of hope drain out of her. This was official now: Tom was out. And by the time the investigation was over, he might also be charged for Sophie's murder.

Adlington was mumbling a few closing remarks. Walker opened the door, signalling that they were done. No. This wasn't over yet.

'I want to speak with him.'

Adlington turned around, studying her. Out of the corner of her eye, she could see Lewis watching her too.

'Just once,' she said. 'Before the investigation begins.'

Adlington paused for a moment, then nodded. 'Alright.'

'Not alone,' Walker cut in. He pointed through the wall. 'In there. In front of the cameras.'

'What's she going to say that you need to hear?' said Lewis.

Erin felt a little twinge of warmth for him. It was probably the first time he'd stood up to Walker, or any senior for that matter. But they all knew Walker was going to win this one. 'I think, given the circumstances, Jennings,' he said, eyes narrowing, 'you might agree that now isn't the time for covert little chit-chats.'

Lewis glared at him, thinking of a rebuke. But Erin caught his eye and shot him a look. She looked at Walker and nodded. 'In front of the cameras,' she agreed.

In the women's bathroom, Erin splashed water on her face. Thin watery light filtered in through the windows. She looked like trash. Pale skin, dry lips and dark circles under her eyes. But for the first time in a while, she felt absolutely no urge to fix her hair or put make-up on before seeing him. It was a statement. Look what you've done.

'Five minutes,' said Adlington, when she returned. He opened the door for her and she stepped past him into the interview room.

Tom looked smaller somehow. His shoulders were slumped forward so that his suit jacket fell off him. Just this morning they'd been kissing in that stairwell. She couldn't believe it.

As soon as the door opened, he looked up at her. The relief in his eyes was excruciating. She felt like she'd lost all feeling in her body as she took the seat opposite him.

'Erin,' he said, pleading. She heard him exhale, then he said clearly, but with a tremor going through his voice: 'I shouldn't have to say it.'

Erin bowed her head and looked at the floor. The room was subterranean. The only light came in through a few slotted windows at the top of the walls. It was raining outside and silver shapes stretched across the floor, rippling with the movement of the rain on the glass.

'I do need you to say it,' she said finally. 'I need you to say it.'

Out of the corner of her eye, she saw Tom move forward and lean across the table. 'Look at me.'

She did.

'It wasn't me.'

She swallowed, feeling a painful lump in her throat.

'Sophie turned up out of nowhere. Asking to speak to me at the press conference. She asked me to help her. I dropped her off. And then a few hours later—' His eyes were filled with anguish. 'Please believe me.'

She looked away. She felt so overwhelmed that her thoughts seemed to be sliding away from her. Instead of listening to him defend himself, now all she wanted was to stay here for as long as possible, locked away from the rest of the team; to not have to think about anything at all, but to just feel his presence there across the table, and pretend none of this was happening.

'Erin,' he said shakily, 'I'm sorry but can you – can you say something?'

'Sorry,' she said quietly. 'Thinking.'

He went quiet again, waiting obediently. The one-way glass shimmered out of the corner of her eye, dark and obtrusive like a row of surveillance cameras.

She had to pull herself out of this. When she did, it was with the effort of someone hauling themselves out of deep sleep. Even speaking physically drained her.

'Alright,' she said. 'Say what you're going to say.'

She could see how desperately he wanted to talk, how he wanted to race through every single reason in his defence, and she hated it. Even the simple act of defending himself seemed duplicitous to her. He could sense that and so he made his case slowly, cautiously.

'She wanted to speak to an officer. I can tell you what she said. Exactly what she said. She was scared for her life. But she was afraid to draw attention to herself. So she wanted to find a way to speak to me privately.'

'That's why she went to the press conference. Not to the station.'

'Exactly,' said Tom.

'Why you?' she said. 'Why did she specifically want to speak to you?'

'I don't know,' said Tom in a desperate voice. 'Maybe she just happened to hear about that press conference. I don't know. But that's all it could have been. I had no idea who she even was before the case.'

She shook her head. 'There's an hour between that dashcam footage and that phone call. It's not enough time. It doesn't make sense.'

'You know me, Erin,' he said.

And that broke through to her. All of her rage rose to the surface and bubbled over. 'I thought so too,' she said. 'I really did.'

He flinched. 'You think I – you think I had something to do with her death? You really think that?'

'You're the last person who saw Sophie. And you said nothing. And you want me to believe you just dropped her off and someone immediately killed her? Right then? Really?'

'Someone must have followed her. They must have seen she was telling on them.'

'Who?'

His eyes darkened. Then he reached across the table and opened his hand.

'Let me see that file,' he said. 'I want to show you something.'

For a moment she hesitated, but then she decided there would be no harm; there was nothing in there he didn't know already. She slid it across the table. He picked up her pen and quickly noted something on the page.

'The guy who threatened Fraser,' he said. 'That's still the most concrete thing we have. We need to find out who he is.'

He pushed the paper back towards her across the table. Erin

noticed that his expression had changed. There was a calculating look on his face, as if he was testing her.

She looked down at the paper. Right where Fraser described the phone call, Tom had written a note in the margin: Walker.

Adrenaline shot through her. Tom's face was unreadable except for the flicker of anxious expectation in his eyes. Would the others be able to see the note through the glass? She moved her elbow to hide it from view.

She wanted more than anything to scribble back, 'How?' But in that moment the door to the interview room swung open.

'That's five minutes, Erin,' said Adlington.

The door to the observation room was open. Inside, Walker watched Tom through the glass with his arms folded. He turned his head when she walked in. 'Wasn't that sweet,' he said, and winked at her. There was a nasty smile on his face like a grimace.

16

When Adlington had told her about the press conference, she'd been incredulous. 'We can't name him in the press,' she'd said. 'Not now. He has a right to anonymity.'

But he'd shaken his head. 'It's too high-profile, Erin. I'm afraid, in this circumstance, the public's right to know who he is comes first.'

For the first time, she felt something resembling fear on Tom's behalf. There was no turning back from this.

'You'll go. With Peters.'

'I'm here to do my job. Not the PR.'

'Your job is PR. Now more than ever. I know Tom was more—'

Erin shot him a look.

'Well, I know he took care of that side of things. You're not meant to dazzle them with your performance. You just need to seem solid. State the facts. Make them trust you.'

He looked at her. 'But there's something else you need to do first.'

Andrea and Richard were waiting for her in the interview room. The hope in their face was unbearable. Their daughter had been murdered; the worst had already happened. They must have thought any development would be good news.

'I'm going to have to ask you to prepare yourselves for this. It will come as a shock.'

Their eyes followed her all the way to the table. Sitting down, she felt aware of how united they looked, shoulder-to-shoulder, them against the world once again.

'This morning, we obtained footage from a delivery driver's dashcam. It shows Sophie outside the Old Cross pub at 12:14 p.m. leaving a police press conference in DCI Tom Radley's car.'

At first, they blinked at her in confusion. Then the lower part of Andrea's face sank. Richard twitched horribly; his neck jerked and his arm came up, pointing at the door.

'Him?' As if Tom was standing right there behind her. 'His – his car?'

'DCI Radley has been suspended with immediate effect. An investigation will be carried out to determine if he had anything to do with Sophie's murder.'

'Police – police press conference, I don't understand.' The words were spilling out of him. 'Why was she at – why was he – why didn't you know?'

'Who do you people have working for you?' said Andrea, in a voice thick with grief. 'Don't you vet them?'

'DCI Radley has no criminal record. He has been a committed detective for nine years. He insists he had nothing to do with her death and there is a chance he is telling the truth. But that's what we need to work out now.'

She was surprised at the certainty in her voice. Richard had gone rigid like a statue, his eyes fixed on Erin's.

'Where is he?' he said.

She looked from his clenched fists on the table to his face. 'I can't let you speak to him.'

'You two sat there in our house,' he said, voice trembling, 'and you asked me about my daughter. To describe her. My wonderful daughter. And the whole time, he'd seen her. He'd been with her, right before she died. That piece of shit.'

'I understand how you feel. Everyone on the force has been completely shocked by this. But there is a process for this situation. We've alerted the IOPC and we'll be following their instructions—'

The words came out of her lifelessly. She abruptly stopped speaking when Richard swore and stood up and left the room, the door banging shut behind him.

Andrea stayed where she was. She was rocking slightly. Erin couldn't tell if she'd even noticed her husband leave.

'Do you know how long it takes to die from strangling, DI Crane?'

The walls closed in around them. Caught in Andrea's fierce gaze, suddenly Erin was a little girl. She shook her head weakly.

'I do. It takes eight to ten seconds. Once you've applied enough pressure. But it could take longer. Minutes perhaps. Why do I know that? Not because anyone told me. Because I researched it. I know, I know. Why would I do that? Why would I torture myself? Richard doesn't do that. He can't. But I have to. Because I investigate this as much as you do, every day, every night. More than you do, I bet. Because I have to know, DI Crane. I have to know even though every new piece of information tortures me. I have to know even though the truth will kill me.'

Her eyes were bright with manic rage. The tendons in her neck stood out.

'That's how I know that if you gave a single shit about her, you'd never have missed this. You can claim to be as innocent as you like. Either you noticed something you're not telling us. Or you missed it. The only thing more shameful in this world than a man who hurts girls is a woman who sees it happening and lets it happen.'

The lights splintered across her vision like white-hot suns. She made it through her section without paying any attention to what she was saying. It occurred to her that she was speaking down at the page, when she should have been directing her words all around the room. But she couldn't face looking up and registering the dozens of reporters with their eyes trained on her.

'We are now appealing for witnesses who know of any connection between Sophie Madson and DCI Tom Radley – or who may have seen them together before her death – to come forward,' said Erin.

Then came the questions. She remembered what Adlington had said: 'Almost every answer will be no. Just keep the no's varied.'

'Are there any other leads?'

'I can't reveal that at this time.'

'Was there any prior connection between DCI Radley and Sophie?'

'Not that we're aware of at this current moment.'

The next reporter, an immaculate woman with a glowing complexion and a spotless camel-coloured coat, stood up. 'Could you tell us about your relationship with DCI Tom Radley?'

It felt like a trick question. Like she was about to pull a mask off any second now and reveal Walker's grinning face beneath. Erin felt the heat crawl up her neck.

'It was a close professional relationship. He was my partner.'

'For three years, is that right?'

'Yes.'

'Is your relationship with him going to make this difficult? How can the public trust that you'll investigate impartially?'

Erin exchanged a glance with Peters. 'The way we are managing this, I will be distanced from the investigation into DCI Radley,' she said.

Peters shuffled closer to the microphone. 'DI Crane is one of our most accomplished investigators. I have no doubt that she is the best person to carry this case forward.'

That was probably the nicest thing he'd ever said about her. Shame it was probably bollocks.

Her legs were shaking when they made it back into the corridor, escaping the reporters and their cameras. Peters immediately sloped off with his hands in his pockets. Adlington was waiting for her with a bottle of water.

'Thanks,' she said. She gulped down a mouthful. 'Did it look alright?'

He shrugged diplomatically. 'It went as well as it could have done, all things considered.'

The circular patterns in the carpet were making her feel sick. Out of the corner of her eye, she saw Adlington rub at the bridge of his nose underneath his spectacles.

'There was something I couldn't get out of my head,' he said, 'from the moment this case started.'

She waited for him to continue.

'We made the decision – Peters, Walker and I – not to send too many officers into the woods. We thought we'd have a better chance of catching her alive if we focused on roads. Access points in and out of town. But the woods were where we found her.

'There could be any explanation,' he said. 'Maybe that was where she died. Maybe the tree held some emotional significance for the killer. But I couldn't help wondering… what if they put her there because they knew that was where we weren't looking? What if, when Peters and Walker and I were giving the orders, the killer was listening in over a police radio, planning their next move?'

Everyone had warned her about going outside. Even so, she'd underestimated just how many of them would be waiting for her. She pushed through the reporters thrusting smartphones and microphones in her face. Finally, with the help of two officers, she managed to squeeze her way into her car, relishing the sudden quiet that came as soon as the door was shut. But even once she'd sped away from the crowd and turned onto the next road, she couldn't shirk the feeling that their cameras were still capturing her every move.

She needed a drink. Did she have anything in? She thought about picking up wine from the corner shop on the way home. But then she imagined how it would look if a reporter photographed her coming up the porch, bottle in hand. No, she had to have something in. What? Once home, when rummaging through her kitchen cupboards, she discovered half a bottle of vodka left over from a birthday party years ago. She poured herself a double shot, added a few ice cubes from the freezer and took it through to the living room. Then she sat down on the sofa and opened up her laptop.

It was years since she'd had vodka straight. The icy, chemical taste hit her right in the back of the throat and her nose burned with the smell. She waited until the alcohol had spread a fiery warmth across her chest, and only then did she feel brave enough to type his name into the search engine.

The story was everywhere. She clicked on one of the first that came up in Google – a BBC news report. As the clip started playing, she took a sip from the vodka, listening to the gentle clink of ice and biting down on the glass.

The woods were dark. A reporter strode towards the camera, gesticulating to the wilderness around him. 'Sophie Madson's body was found here two weeks ago on the fifth of September. Ever since, police have been searching tirelessly to find the person responsible for her death. Now, they're investigating the possibility that someone on their very own force may have been involved in her murder.'

Cut to Peters reading his statement at the press conference earlier. With a shock she recognised herself next to him, looking exactly as uncomfortable as she'd felt.

Cut to Tom. It was a photo she'd always liked of him. On a balcony somewhere, she'd never known where exactly, but on holiday with friends, half-turned towards the camera with a relaxed smile, wearing a white shirt. Just looking at that photo, the feelings of the last few days came rushing back to her; all the possibility and electric nerves. Except now the emotions were tinged with an edge of something else, like the iron taste of blood.

The reporter's voice faded back in: '… top homicide detective, but Tom Radley has now been suspended from the police force. Why he failed to mention his encounter with Sophie Madson is the number one question on everyone's mind.' As he was speaking, the image changed. Now, Tom was coming out of the station with Walker stalking beside him, stepping out into the mob of journalists Erin had just battled through. His expression was inscrutable. The camera zoomed in as they shepherded him to the police car.

Something Tom had said hit her then, out of the blue.

'I understand you not wanting to tell people something like that. You don't want to be defined by it, because you're not.'

The words, comforting before, now made her guts go cold.

17

Tom

Nine years ago

THE LIGHTS IN THE MORGUE were so bright that the body stretched in front of them seemed to emit a yellowish, alien glow. Tom glanced sideways at Kapil. Thankfully, his partner looked as nervous as Tom felt. Back straight, jaw clenched, fists balled at his sides – like he half-expected to have to make the incisions himself.

Officers didn't need to be present for the post-mortem. The real reason they were here wasn't lost on either of them. This was a test. A rite of passage. Something new detectives had to endure to prove they were man enough.

Tom bit the inside of his mouth as the pathologist reached for the table next to him and picked up a large pair of surgical scissors.

'Are we ready?'

He had expected the motions to be smooth cuts. He'd thought the blades would glide through the skin like paper. Instead, the pathologist went to work like a butcher. After all, why take it slow? This was just one of many bodies they had to deal with today. He made rough chopping actions straight through the torso, then started tearing the skin open with his gloved hands where it wouldn't give way. The air was thick with the smell of blood.

Tom's mouth and throat went dry. He clenched his teeth as tight as he could. Not now. Not in front of Kapil. It would be over soon. An hour, they'd said. An hour and it would stop. Then he could go outside, where he could look at the white walls of the corridor instead of the body being ripped open in front of him.

The pathologist started sawing, causing the corpse's internal organs to slosh and slap like waves in the pool of his abdomen. Tom tried breathing in very slowly through his nose, keeping his mouth firmly shut. Maybe he could do this. If he just kept breathing steadily. If he tried to think about something else—

Then the pathologist turned and grabbed what looked like a pair of garden shears, and snapped through the man's sternum. The ribcage sprung open like an animal trap released.

Tom was out of the room before he knew it. The corridor rushed past him. He barely made it to the toilet before he vomited.

He wished he could say that joining the police had been a calling. Or that he'd signed up because he felt inspired to give back to his community. But that wasn't true – not for him, or anyone who had joined the force. TV was the only reason anyone became a detective. As a child, Tom had been captivated by the high-functioning characters on screen – those men who knifed through crowds to get to the places no one else wanted to be, who would stare down death when everyone flinched away. He wanted that. He wanted to be the one who had the answers. And when the time came, he wanted to be the one to look a killer in the eye and know that he'd been the one to put them away.

This was not what a twelve-year-old starstruck Tom had pictured. Before he'd even reached the ranks of detective, he'd had to spend two years in uniform, patrolling sleepy streets and waking up at 2 a.m. in order to respond to noise complaints and convince drunken sixteen year olds to vacate the park and go home. Shovelling down meals before bed so he could catch enough shut-eye before the whole painful charade started all over again. It wasn't just physically taxing – it was emotionally gruelling.

He couldn't believe he'd thrown up at his first port-mortem. He was so mortified that he lay awake in bed half the night, torturing himself with thoughts of what Kapil must have said to the other officers once he went home. His restlessness wasn't helped by the fact the walls of his flat were paper thin, forcing him to eavesdrop on what a great time the Polish couple were having next door. There was only so much noise cancellation a pillow over the face could provide.

The next day, he was so tired he was hardly worth an hour of work. He stared bleary-eyed at his computer screen, scrolling mindlessly through a witness statement without reading it. He didn't notice the officers leering over a computer screen, laughing conspiratorially. Then one of them shot him a grin.

'You're quick, Radley. You must have smashed the bleep test.'

Tom looked at their screen. Immediately he felt the blood rush up his neck. They were watching a clip of CCTV footage, stuck on repeat. Every time it circled back to the start, a couple of the officers collapsed with laughter. It was him, crashing out of the examination room and pelting down the corridor towards the toilets.

Tom found Kapil emerging from one of the early morning briefings. He'd thought Kapil might leap at the sight of him stood outside waiting for him. Instead, he barely acknowledged he was there. Still flicking through his notes from the meeting, and without looking up, he said, 'How're you, Tom?'

'There's a video being sent round. It's—'

Kapil looked up from his notes.

'Oh. Yeah. That one.'

The corner of his mouth twitched upwards subtly. That wasn't...? Was that a smirk?

'Do you know anything about that?'

'Er.' It was a smirk. Trying to conceal it by pressing his lips together, Kapil looked guiltily up and down the corridor. Tom wanted to punch him. 'I don't know who would've got a hold of that. Maybe someone from IT—'

'Did you tell them about it?'

Kapil's pale eyes locked onto his. 'Yeah,' he said awkwardly.

'Surely, taking that footage from the morgue isn't allowed? And sending it around like that—'

He trailed off when Kapil let out an impatient sigh.

'I'm not being funny, Radley, but do you really want to make a fuss about this? If you complain, everyone's gonna know – Walker, Peters. It won't look good, trust me. It looks better if you just take it on the chin.'

Tom had no idea what to say.

'If you like, I'll ask people to stop sharing the clip with each other,' he said.

If you like. Obviously I'd like that.

Tom nodded; his jaw and neck were so tense it was all he could manage.

'I'm sorry. I didn't know you weren't in on it.'

He wanted to say, Sure. *Sure you fucking didn't. Because I'd really want people to know I puked my guts out, wouldn't I?* But instead he said, 'Fine. That's fine,' and walked back to his desk on unsteady legs.

An elbow jabbed into him, sloshing his pint over the floor.

'Sorry, Bradley,' said the detective, before immediately launching back into conversation with Adlington.

The Bull and Butcher was heaving. There were so many bodies crammed into the wood-panelled front room that the windows had steamed up. It was strange seeing the detectives he respected and feared pink-faced and shiny-eyed, shouting at each other over the tinny pop music.

His confrontation with Kapil – if you could even call it a confrontation – had demoralised him for the rest of the day. So when the office began their mass exodus to the pub, all he'd wanted was to make his excuses and leave. But that wasn't an option. It was still early days for him. You had to put the hours in.

'Radley,' said a voice.

He turned around to find Shergill, the head of digital forensics, standing there. Small police forces like theirs didn't have the resources for tech, so there were only three people on Shergill's team. But he was well-respected in the force, and that was why Tom felt his guts liquidise when Shergill said, wincing apologetically: 'About that video.'

Tom wanted the ground to swallow him up. So the seniors knew about it.

He was shaking his head. 'It's an absolute disgrace. I'll be having words with anyone I see watching or sharing it.'

Tom nodded, not knowing what to say. Then Shergill asked, 'Do you know where it came from, by any chance?'

Out of the corner of his eye, Tom could see Kapil leaning against the windowsill, sucking up to Adlington and Peters.

'I'm not sure,' he said.

For a second Shergill looked like he might say something, then he nodded. 'Alright,' he said.

Tom watched Shergill duck underneath a low-hanging beam, returning to where his team was huddled in the corner.

Maybe he should have said something. But Kapil's words echoed in his head. *Do you really want to make a fuss about this?* He hated it, but Kapil was right. It looked better if he just ignored it.

Only then did he realise he was completely on his own in the middle of the pub. Face burning with embarrassment, he made straight for the group nearest him. Someone had dropped their drink an hour ago and now the floor was so sticky that Tom had to peel the soles of his shoes off the floor as he squeezed in next to Walker.

Walker had his phone out and was showing something to the rest of the group. A woman's selfie. It took Tom several moments to register who it was. When he did, he thought his eyes were about to pop out of his head.

'Isn't that the witness?'

They'd interviewed her last week about the man whose body had been examined this morning. Now here she was, squinting sultrily at the camera with her cleavage on show.

'You just got that off her socials,' said one detective.

'Oh really?' Walker swiped through his phone, revealing the selfie situated inside a text conversation. Some made noises of outrage; others, approval.

Why were they reacting like this? Communication with witnesses and victims outside of work was highly inappropriate. You could get done for it.

Walker obviously registered his shocked silence because, as he put his phone in his pocket, he smiled knowingly at Tom.

'If you ever doubt your career choices, there's one thing you should remember,' he said. 'Women love the badge.'

18

WALKER STARED UP AT THE projection on the wall. He hit pause on his laptop and the footage froze.

'That's my favourite bit,' he said. 'Where you turn your head. So we get a nice, good look at your face. Just in case there was any doubt that it's Tom Radley there, climbing into Tom Radley's car after a press conference Tom Radley attended.'

Tom said nothing. He hadn't spoken since the interview had started. He'd just sat there looking at the table, unbearably still.

Erin was alone in the observation room, watching through the glass. This was the first interview in Walker's investigation, and he was enjoying himself.

'I'm interested,' said Walker, shifting his weight onto one arm. 'Did you notice her? In the crowd?' When Tom didn't say anything, he continued, 'She must have stood out. Pretty girl all on her lonesome.'

Tom shook his head. 'No. I didn't see her.'

'So you only noticed when she approached you?'

'Yes.'

'And she said...?'

'She said she had information that she could only give me if we were alone.'

'Had she ever approached you like that before?'

'I have never had any interaction with Sophie Madson before the fifth of September.'

Walker smiled. 'You see, that I don't buy, Radley,' he said. 'She'd planned this. She didn't turn up at the station and ask to speak to a detective. She went to a press conference where you – specifically you – were present. Not to mention, she's quite young, right? Sixteen? To have the nerve to do that at that age. You need assurance, don't you? You need to know they're going to listen to you. So how do you explain that?'

There was a long pause. Then Tom said, 'I can't explain why she chose me. I wish I could. But clearly she decided I could help her.'

Chose me. The way he said it made her stomach sink.

Walker smirked secretively. He said, 'Or she liked the look of you, Radley.'

The comment left an ugly silence in the room. Erin's nails dug through her shirt and into her upper arms.

When Tom said nothing, Walker leant across the table.

'Did you enjoy that little ego boost? Teenage girl following you down the road, clutching her school books, twirling her hair around her finger?'

He was shaking his head. 'Nothing like that happened.'

'No?' said Walker. 'She didn't proposition you? You didn't make a move on her?'

'No.'

Walker leant back in his chair.

'Alright. So she gets in your car. You have this conversation you've mentioned. She says she's scared for her life. That she wants protection. But she can't tell you who she needs protection from until she knows she can trust you. Right?'

'I've already told you.'

'And how long does this conversation last?'

'About twenty minutes.'

'And then what? She says "thanks for the chat, officer, just drop me off at the corner here"? What note did it end on?'

'I dropped her off near her house. Not at the house. She didn't want her parents to see me. I was going to meet her in that same place again the next day. After she'd decided whether or not she could trust me.'

'And then what?'

'Then I drove to a victim's house to give them an update about the press conference. A couple of hours later, Adlington called. Telling me to come back to the station.'

Walker narrowed his eyes. 'You didn't think to mention, once you got back and saw Sophie's photo on the board, that you'd met her just that morning?'

'I knew what it would look like.'

Walker let that hang in the air. He shook his head.

'Hours searching for that girl. And you never said a word. You're either a killer or a coward, is what I'm hearing, Radley. Anyway, so the search has started. Thinking about it, I don't remember seeing you around much. Remind me: after we were briefed in the office, where were you?'

'Taking statements at people's houses.'

'Go on then. Which house at what time?'

'First I went to interview Alisha Iqbal, one of Sophie's friends. That was at about 4 p.m. I was there for about forty minutes. Then I visited one of the other gymnasts, Kaitlin Brown. Then I visited two of her teachers' homes. Each visit took forty minutes at most. Then I joined the search in the woods.'

'What time was that?'

'Late. Around 9 p.m.'

'We'll see if your interviewees can confirm that for us.'

Erin studied Tom closely. Maybe she was just imagining it, but she thought she saw a shadow of fear pass over his face.

'It's interesting,' said Walker, smiling, 'because most officers would have had someone to vouch for them during the search. But you... you did the whole thing alone. Funny that, isn't it?'

Lewis must have slept badly too. Once Walker's interview was finished, she found him with one elbow on the table, knuckles pressed into his cheek, staring at his computer with unfocused eyes.

A handful of officers were eyeing them over the computer monitors. She ignored them. Keeping her voice down, she said, 'Alright. Let's talk, just you and me.'

Slowly, Lewis pulled himself out of his seat. Leading him into an empty meeting, which he processed in a daze, running his hands through his hair, she thought how much she hated this; skulking around like they had something to hide. Already, battle lines were being drawn in the office. And she and Lewis were alone in their own trench.

'OK,' she said, 'the burner phone.'

Lewis looked like he'd forgotten there was one.

'Have we made any progress there?'

Lewis blinked, shaking himself awake. 'Right. Yeah. As you know, we only found one number there. She exchanged a few messages with this person over the past few weeks that suggest they met up at least three times. "Things like running ten minutes late." But once Sophie mentioned a location. She asked if they were meeting by the bridge again.'

'Have we checked CCTV footage in that area for that day?'

'They're checking it now.'

'And this number. Is it one we've seen before?'

'It's the same number that Fraser received a call from.'

'What about the one that rang in to give us the school lead?'

'No. That was different.'

So either they used another phone for that, or got someone else to make the call. Or it was unrelated, but Erin didn't buy that.

'Was there any mention of the plan to meet at the Old Cross?'

Lewis blinked at her.

'Well, was there?' she snapped.

'No.' He looked as though she'd slapped him. 'You don't think Tom…? You don't think he did it?'

She really didn't want to have this conversation with him.

'Didn't you hear what Peters said? We need to forget everything we thought we knew about Tom. Right now, he's just a suspect. Nothing else.'

Lewis frowned. 'Nothing else? What if it was the other way around? What if it was one of us in there? Imagine if he gave up on us. Just like that.'

She forced herself to say, 'Look, we need to keep an open mind going forward.'

A cold silence fell between them. She hated the way Lewis was staring into space, misty-eyed, like an abandoned lamb.

Seeing that he'd mentally checked out of their conversation, she said, 'So that CCTV footage near the bridge. That's our next point of focus.'

Still Lewis said nothing.

'Can I leave that with you?' she said.

Lewis gave a small nod.

'Good,' she said.

He didn't reply before he left her alone in the empty room.

She wasn't angry at Lewis for his loyalty to Tom. She was angry at him for being so oblivious.

Could he really not see that she didn't believe what she was saying any more than he did?

It was raining when she got home. Street lights shone through the window, so the unlit hallway trembled with underwater shadows. When she went to the toilet, she saw the silky grey top and black trousers she'd worn yesterday crumpled in a heap on the floor where she'd undressed before her scalding hot shower. She picked them up and put them in the laundry basket. She couldn't imagine ever wearing them again.

She wanted something methodical to do. Something mindless. She felt relieved when she saw the pots and pans she'd left out after the meal she'd made two nights ago. She cleaned them and put them away, then added washing-up liquid to the shopping list. After that she stood in the silent kitchen, wondering what to do next. She decided she'd eat so she opened the cupboard and ate a biscuit, then two, then three. She wanted a drink. Another glass of that vodka.

She got out the bottle and a glass, then looked at what she was doing and put them away again.

What she wanted more than anything was to lie down. But it was 8 p.m. and she knew that, if she did, the same thing that happened yesterday would happen: she'd lie there staring at the ceiling while a lead weight pushed down on her chest, crushing her until she thought she might sink through the mattress and down beneath the foundations of the house.

19

WALKER SMILED AT HER. 'THAT'S it?' he said.
Erin must have had dozens of interviews in this room. But
being on the other side – in the suspect's chair – transformed the
space completely, making the walls seemed much closer and the
lights brighter and hotter. Her shirt stuck to her armpits.

Clearing her throat, she said, 'That's everything I can think of
about Tom's conduct on this case. There was nothing out of the
ordinary, as far as I'm concerned.'

Walker still hadn't stopped smiling. 'Are you sure you're not
forgetting one detail?'

Her heart raced.

'You and Radley drive each other around a lot, don't you?'

Cautiously, she said, 'Yes.'

'Drive out to interviews. Give each other lifts to and from work.
That kind of thing.'

'Yes.'

'In the days following Sophie Madson's death,' he said, eyes
narrowing, 'whose car were you in?'

Her blood went cold as she recalled receiving the text.

You wouldn't mind giving me a lift tomorrow, would you?

She hadn't questioned it. Not even when he'd asked again the next
day. It was just the kind of thing they did for each other.

'Mine.'

'Yeah. That's what I thought.' Walker smirked. He didn't need to say it out loud.

Why wouldn't Tom have wanted to use his car in the days following the murder? One explanation rose up in Erin's mind, and made her mouth dry out.

Because he was cleaning out the inside.

Walker held the door open for her on the way out of the interview room. Then, to her surprise, he started walking beside her down the corridor, hands behind his back. She felt her shoulder blades stiffen. What was he up to?

Walker said, 'I know we haven't always seen eye to eye, Crane. But I just wanted you to know that I'm here for you.'

The air conditioning in the corridor chilled the sweat on her skin; she felt shivery and clammy all at once.

'Thanks. But I'm good. I know what I'm doing.'

'And you have Jennings, I suppose. A big fan of Radley's, isn't he, Jennings? I can imagine that might make things... difficult.'

She said nothing.

Walker held the next door open for her again.

'This case,' he said, 'it's a lot. It's a lot for someone with only a few years in the game. Trust me, Crane, you need all the help you can get.'

'I thought the plan was for us to tackle this from different sides. I investigate Sophie's murder. You handle the IOPC investigation. So what exactly are you asking for?

His shoulder brushed up against hers as they walked. 'Any further developments, I want to know as soon as they happen. The longer there's a question mark around Radley's innocence, the deeper the shit we're in, Crane. We need to get this sorted quickly.'

He left her to go back to her desk alone. Once there, she pulled the interview transcript out of Fraser's file. Immediately she was confronted with the words Tom had written there. Walker's name in neat, deliberate capitals.

Did he mean Sophie had explicitly named Walker? Surely if she had, and Tom was in the clear, he'd have mentioned so before.

No, Tom was just trying to take the spotlight off himself. There was no evidence Walker had anything to do with this.

But then again... Walker hounding her for updates on day two of the IOPC's investigation. Walker confronting them about Fraser. Walker taunting Tom in the interview room. What if it was more than a grudge? What if the reason he'd been so delighted by Tom's arrest was because it made everyone look elsewhere? Away from him?

She could feel herself swaying on the spot a little. Last night she'd barely slept. Instead, she'd laid awake in the darkness with a pounding heart until, at 5 a.m., she'd given up and started getting ready for the day. The fatigue left her fuzzy-headed and there was an ache behind her eyes and nose as she stood at her desk, painfully aware that every officer around would be sneaking glances at her while they worked in an uneasy silence.

She needed a moment alone. A cigarette. She pulled her coat on and headed downstairs. Although it was only drizzling, the wind blew the rain into her face with such force that, even while using her hand as a shield, it took about five go's before she could light a cigarette. But on some level, she wanted the cold, how it zapped through her fingertips and woke up the brain, the relief it brought, like pressing her overheated head against freezing glass.

She knew it was irrational. But she couldn't shake the feeling that seeing Tom in person again might make things better.

Watching Walker interview him, there was no way of knowing if he was telling the truth or not. If they could get a moment alone together, she'd know just from looking in his eyes and hearing his voice; she was certain.

But how to get him alone? Right now he was escorted in and out of the station by several officers. And once he was in, he was with Walker, who'd definitely make it impossible for them to share a quiet word together. Turning up at his house was out of the question.

Reporters had set up a barricade outside, just like they had done at the Madsons'. Surely they didn't camp out there all night though, waiting to pounce if he so much as moved a curtain? She could turn up at some ungodly hour and speak to him then. No one would ever know. She imagined sitting with him on the sofa while morning light crept in through the blinds, his tired eyes, his vulnerability, and felt a strange, dragging-down sensation—

The sound of the door opening made her jump. Adlington shielded his face from the spitting rain with a raised arm. She fumbled in her jacket pocket for the straights and held the packet out to him. Adlington pulled a face and waved it away.

'Just fancied a bit of fresh air?' she said, arching an eyebrow at Adlington's flyaway hair and flapping lapels.

Adlington glared into the rain. 'Something like that.'

This was Adlington all over. He had an awkward way of broaching serious topics one-on-one. She could only imagine what he was like with his teenage daughters. *Lovely weather we're having. Honey, I do like your miniskirt and crop top; the only thing is…*

He cleared his throat.

'Don't try to contact him,' he said.

That was the other thing about Adlington. He was good at thinking one step ahead.

Even though she could have seen it coming, it still hurt. She scanned the car park, feeling the tension in her jaw and neck and hoping Adlington couldn't see it. She nodded.

'I mean it. No contact until this is cleared up.'

She scoffed and kicked at the gravel.

'You know, don't you, how close Peters was to taking you and Jennings off the case,' he said. 'One of the reasons he didn't was to reassure the public. Another was to keep some stability in the team. And another is because… he became convinced that you could distance yourself from Tom.'

Became convinced. In other words, Adlington had had to vouch for her.

'So I'm telling you. If you give him any reason to suspect you can't, then you could lose this.'

'Tapped my phone, have they? Hired someone to tail me?' She looked theatrically over her shoulder.

'Imagine what even one text from you would look like. If he was charged and this went to court.'

'I get it,' she said, not wanting to hear anymore. 'I get it.'

'I'm not trying to rile you up. I'm just trying to stop this from getting any worse.' He tucked his hands under his armpits for warmth. 'That's another thing I came out to tell you. The Criminal Cases Review Commission have been in touch. They want to look into the Vogel case.'

The ground lurched beneath her feet.

'They need new evidence to do that. What's happened?' she said.

'Radley happened. Alan Vogel's always claimed he had no idea how that ribbon turned up in his house, hasn't he? Well, he's arguing that if Radley obstructed justice once, he could have done it before. Planted the ribbon to frame him. The CCRC's going to look for evidence to see if they can get his conviction overturned.'

She noticed her breathing had become faster and shallower. 'That's bullshit.'

'I know. It's ridiculous they're giving it the time of day. Do they plan on re-investigating every case Tom ever solved?' He shook his head. 'Anyway, they'll want to speak to you.'

She nodded, concentrating on the cars as they travelled past. Through the blur of rain, they seemed to crawl by in slow motion.

'We'd better go back in,' said Adlington. 'It starts in ten.'

In a windowless room, surrounded by the hum of computers, breathing in the same recycled air for two hours, the Major Crime Unit went over Tom's case with the IOPC's investigators.

There was no digital link between Tom and Sophie. They hadn't so much as Googled the other's name. From the perspective of the digital forensics team, these two looked like strangers in every way – apart from the footage proving that one had sat in the other's car just an hour before her death.

There were no blood stains in his house or car either, although they'd taken some items away for further analysis. As they discussed the likelihood of finding Sophie's DNA on his sheets, she thought about what Adlington had said and was secretly breathlessly thankful she'd never slept round Tom's – otherwise it would be her DNA they'd find there. Maybe that had been a precaution. Maybe the real reason he'd never invited her around was because he knew one day they might be combing through those sheets in search of evidence.

The thought distracted her so much so she almost missed the next thing that was said. She only registered its importance because Walker's hand flexed on the table like a living thing. Michael, one of the officers who'd manned the checkpoints that day, had stood up. He shuffled his feet nervously.

'There's something you should all be aware of,' he said.

The microphones picked up on every sound in the interview room. Watching through the double-sided mirror, Erin could hear Walker's lapels rustling as he leant across the table towards Tom.

'We've been over your previous statement. I have to say I was a little disappointed in you, Radley. Because I'd have thought you'd know how we work and get your accounts straight.'

Tom's head was angled down, his face half in shadow. When he said nothing, Walker continued, 'You say your conversations with Sophie's teachers took forty minutes, is that right?'

'Roughly.'

'And then you wrapped up and joined the search at around 9 p.m., is what you're saying.'

'As far I can remember.'

'We've spoken with those teachers. Mrs Connolly and Mr Haslett. Both said you couldn't have been there for longer than fifteen minutes.'

'I might have misremembered.'

Walker arched an eyebrow. 'See, here's why this is awkward for you, Tom. If you really did speed through those interviews, then it sounds like you weren't as busy in the search as you claimed. Do you mind telling us where the time went? Maybe you had a little nap in the car? Stopped off for a bite to eat?'

'Like I said, I was in interviews all afternoon. Either I'm misremembering or one of them is.'

'There is one thing you seem to have got right. And that's the time you joined the search – 9 p.m. We've got you on record, coming past the checkpoint.'

A photo appeared on the screen on the wall. It was Michael's notes from the day she went missing. Tom's name was scribbled down among the others.

Walker looked at the mirror. 'Michael? Would you mind joining us for a second?'

Behind her, Erin heard the scrape of chair legs as Michael got up and left the observation room. When he appeared on the other side of the glass, his head was bowed.

Walker got up, pacing back and forth in front of the table. 'See, the question everybody has been asking,' he said, 'is how did they do it? How did the killer move the body, with police crawling all over the place? So we've got Michael in here today to help us try and work that out. You checked the cars that were passing through. Is that right?'

'Yes.' Michael was squirming under Walker's gaze. He looked like he'd rather be anywhere in the world but in this room with them.

'How many cars did you check?'

Michael fidgeted. 'Hard to say off the top of my head. Thirty?'

But that wasn't the answer Walker cared about. 'Any police pass through in that time?' he said.

'Yes,' said Michael. 'Most of the team passed in their cars.'

'And you checked all the cars, is that right?' he said. He didn't even look at Michael as he spoke; he just stared at Tom, who stared back, apprehensive.

Michael swallowed. 'No.'

'No?' Walker's voice was all false surprise. 'Whose car didn't you check?'

Michael bit his lip. His face went pale. 'Police cars,' he said.

Even though she'd known what was coming, Erin felt the walls around her come tumbling down. Tom looked away from Walker and stared into space; the same look he made when he was thinking hard.

'You didn't check police cars,' said Walker, 'because why would you check the people who were on your team?'

'Exactly,' said Michael.

Walker watched Tom's face with a pink glow of excitement in his cheeks, and a barely suppressed smile at the corner of his lips. 'So Radley's car. You just let him pass?'

Michael was looking at the floor again. 'That's right.'

'You didn't check the back seat? The boot? Nothing?'

'No. I saw the front seats. That was it.'

Tom's face had drained of colour.

Walker nodded in satisfaction. 'Thanks, Michael. That will be everything.'

Michael scurried out. He hadn't looked at Tom once.

Walker said, 'It's strange, Radley. Because we know Sophie was in your car. But the forensics have been all over it. And you honestly couldn't tell. There's no fibres from her clothes. No stray hairs. Nothing.'

Tom said nothing.

'You know what Crane told us?'

Surprise entered Tom's face when he heard her name. Erin felt sick.

'Crane told us she gave you lifts in her car all week after Sophie Madson's death. Why is that, Radley? Why did you suddenly need to be chauffeured everywhere?'

'You know why.'

'But I need you to say it.'

Tom's voice came out quiet and muffled through the mics: 'Because I was cleaning the inside.'

144

Erin felt the hairs on the back of her neck stand up.

A devastating silence followed, which Tom was quick to fill: 'But not because I killed her. Because I had a murder victim's DNA on my front seat.'

'That's still obstruction of justice, Radley. You won't just be dismissed, you'll be barred for life. Assuming you were innocent and just trying to remove any connection you had to her. And not cleaning Sophie's blood out from the boot of your car.'

Tom said nothing.

'What prompted it? Did she threaten to leave you? Was she shagging some other bloke on the side? Or was she going to tell someone? I keep asking myself: what would Tom Radley hate more?'

Tom glowered at him across the table.

'Not the first one. Not being left. Because it wasn't love, was it, Radley? You were just enjoying feeling like a big man. So then there's the question of two-timing. It sounds like she had a lot of offers. Obviously, no one likes being cheated on but I bet you'd especially hate it, with an ego like yours. But I still don't buy it. Men who kill out of jealousy, they're sentimental. A lot more sentimental than you.

'So that leaves just one option. She threatened to tell someone. Maybe she'd fallen for you and she was going to rat you out if you didn't give her more. You knew it had always been just a shag, nothing serious, so you knew immediately it wasn't worth losing your whole career over. So you did the only thing you could to shut her up. Well, I hope it feels worth it now, Radley.'

'I'm telling you,' said Tom, 'she came to me for help because she was scared for her life. And within an hour of her leaving me, someone had killed her.'

There was a horrible, twitching sneer at the corner of Walker's lips. 'Keep lying to me,' he said through his teeth, so quietly Erin almost didn't hear it. 'I want you to lie to me right up until the moment this all comes crashing down on your head.'

20

SHE WOKE UP THE NEXT morning trying to catch the end of something. It took her a few moments to adjust to the fact that she was in her room and not still in the dream with him.

Eventually she pulled herself out of bed and into the shower. She put toast on and made an instant coffee. The whole time, her head was elsewhere.

She'd never had a dream like that before, where you could actually feel the person; hear them, smell them. He'd stood barely an inch away from her, the side of his body pressing up against hers. In the dream, he'd just been cleared. He wasn't the killer. But it hadn't been a good dream. There was hostility that hadn't been there before. He'd been distant and difficult to understand. When they kissed, his face felt hard against hers.

She slammed the car door shut behind her and pushed the dream right down to the bottom of her thoughts.

Right there, she made her decision.

She needed to see him. One way or another, she'd find a way how.

The sound of reporters and photographers shouting had come to signal Tom's arrival at the station. If you went to the window, which Erin usually didn't, you'd see two uniforms shouldering their way through the crowd with Tom in tow, walking quickly to escape the encroaching mob.

Erin went to the window this morning. Almost immediately she could tell that something had changed. She didn't know what.

146

Maybe there were more reporters than usual. Maybe the shouting was angrier this time, more accusatory than it had been in the initial days. But whatever it was, it meant that there was a threatening hum in the air as Tom stepped out into the cold, glinting sunshine.

Even from their vantage point on the first floor, none of the force had seen his attackers coming. The crowd was so tightly packed in that the men didn't create any kind of channel as they wove their way towards Tom. So no one even knew they were there until he fell to the ground. The shouting intensified and the crowd moved to swallow him up.

Later, after the officers managed to clear the throngs of people, you could see no evidence anyone had been there at all, except for the vehicle Tom had been escorted over in. It was still parked in front of the station. Scrawled in yellow graffiti down one side were the words *police protect killers*.

'Where's Radley?'

Walker's voice travelled over the heads of the officers gathered around the window. Erin froze, listening.

'He's just been attacked, Walker. Saunders is going to check him out and take a statement if he's up to it.'

Walker snorted. 'Come on, Adlington. He's just trying to get out of this interview.'

'Don't be ridiculous, Walker. I'm not having you interview a suspect while they're bleeding all over the table.'

As the crowd gradually dissipated, Erin stayed where she was, watching the officers sponge the graffiti off the car.

They'd taken Tom to one of the smaller interview rooms on the bottom floor. Through a small window in the door, she watched Saunders photograph his injuries, collecting evidence of the assault. Erin stepped out of view of the window, took a deep breath, and knocked twice. After a few moments, Saunders appeared. Seeing Erin, his eyes widened.

'DI Crane,' he said, shutting the door behind himself quickly. 'Can I help you with something?'

She glanced up and down the corridor, doing one more check for any officers who may have followed her down here. Lowering her voice, she said, 'I just want one conversation with him, Saunders.'

Saunders' scrappy moustache twitched. 'It's not allowed.'

'I need to hear it from him. Without anyone listening.'

'I'm not supposed to let anyone near him,' he said.

His tone was robotic but there was panic in his face. She could tell that saying no to a senior detective was going against every impulse in his body.

'He was my partner,' she said. 'For years. One conversation. Just one.'

Saunders stared at her unblinkingly. She could see him weighing up the options in his head. 'OK. But no one can know about this, alright?'

He stepped to the side before opening the door, as if to physically distance himself from the act of helping her. Erin had spoken to this person almost every day for the past few years of her life, but suddenly the idea of approaching Tom terrified her. She trembled as she entered the room.

Tom looked up. Barely a second passed before he rose from the table. Erin had to concentrate very hard to stop herself from flinching at the sight of him. His lower lip was split, and the skin under his right eye was mottled pink and swollen, giving him a permanent watery-eyed glare.

'Why are you here?'

'I needed to speak to you,' she said.

His jaw clenched. He said nothing.

Confused, she edged towards him. She considered reaching out and touching his shoulder.

'Are you – are you hurt?' she asked.

He flexed the fingers on one hand. 'Just say what you're going to say.'

She didn't come any closer. This wasn't what she'd expected. She remembered how he had looked in the interview room, leaning towards her, eyes filled with pain, as if desperate to close the distance between them and touch her. This Tom stood in front of her now felt like a stranger.

'Explain it to me. What came out in the interview yesterday.'

He flashed a hateful glance at her. 'What do you mean?'

'The timings. The car. The cleaning. All of it.'

'I don't know what to tell you. My head was in pieces. I decided not to tell anyone I'd seen Sophie. And then I covered it up.'

'Why?'

'Because I knew what would happen. This.'

She hated the resentful, self-pitying way he said it.

'Why did you write Walker's name down?'

'Use your head,' he said. 'It's obvious.'

'Not to me it's not.'

'She needed the police. But she went out of her way to get a detective alone instead of calling or going into the station. Why is that?'

He was speaking quietly, and his voice was croaky with exhaustion. She shook her head.

'Because she couldn't risk just any detective getting the job. In case it was the person she was scared of.'

Erin's heart quickened.

'Then there's what Fraser told us,' he said. 'How he was threatened. It's not what the average person would do, is it? But it's what a copper might do. Someone self-righteous. Who's used to putting pressure on others like that.'

'You never mentioned any of this before.'

He looked away. 'It didn't occur to me until I was arrested.'

'Why?'

'I'm not so paranoid that I'd immediately suspect a member of my own team.'

'Why are you being like this? I'm just trying to work this out—'

A calm hate filled his face as he looked at her.

'You did this.'

The cold accusation in his voice was so unexpected she lost her breath.

'I did this?'

He put his hands over his face and wiped them down. Erin could see he was sweating. 'You've ruined my life. You have.' He looked at her, and now the cuts on his face made him look violent and wrong, a torn-up painting. 'My career is gone. Even my friends – everyone I've ever known, even people in the street, they all think I could have done it.'

She'd never seen him like this before.

He stared at her with desperation. 'Why did you tell Peters? None of this had to happen.'

'You wouldn't have done that,' she said, 'if it was footage of me with Sophie, you wouldn't have—'

'Wouldn't I? You framed Vogel. And I didn't tell a soul.'

The look in his eyes was devastating. Her heart dropped.

'That's – that's different.'

'You're right. It is. I knew for certain you'd framed him and I chose not to tell anyone. You had no guarantee I'd done this and you told the world.'

She heard herself say, in a small voice, 'I was trying to do the right thing.'

But he was somewhere else now. Rage flared in his eyes as shook his head. 'What if I go to prison over this? What if? And even if I don't... you know what this amount of publicity does to a person. Everything they're saying about me – that's there forever. No matter what I do, even if I get out, there will always be people who believe that I did it. This is never going to end for me. Never. Do you understand?'

He looked away from her and took a step back. She felt a rush of guilt and a strong desire to hold him. Suddenly she wanted to take back everything she'd said.

After a few moments, he took a deep breath out. 'I know you came here for more. But I can't give you more. I don't have the answer, Erin. I don't have some alibi I can magic up out of nowhere.'

His voice was softer now. She considered moving closer.

Then he said, 'They'll be wondering where you are,' and sat back down.

It took all of her strength to leave him and his bruised face and walk out alone.

21

She trudged up the stairs. She'd only just reached the front desk when a woman she didn't recognise leapt forward, thrusting out a hand for her to shake.

'DI Crane? I'm Pauline Chadwick. From the Criminal Cases Review Commission.'

She had blonde, flattened hair and wore a navy suit. She looked untouched by the wind and the drizzle outside, like she'd sealed herself in an airtight packet before leaving her house that day.

'We're investigating Alan Vogel's sentencing. Could I have a word?'

Erin had a dull, thumping headache that was making it hard to think. Pauline looked fresh and alert; had probably spent the last hour going over her notes.

'Now might not be the best time.'

'It won't take long.'

She watched Pauline turn each page of Vogel's file with excruciating care. They were sat in one of the meeting rooms. Beneath the table, Erin could feel her hands trembling where they knotted together in her lap and hoped Pauline couldn't see.

'Mr Vogel has always insisted that he had no prior knowledge of the ribbon that was found in his property during your investigation. He believes it was planted there by someone else.'

'That was his defence in court. And the jury rejected it.'

'Quite. But that was before one of the detectives on the case was investigated for a possible obstruction of justice.' Pauline sat totally still while one hand methodically turned pages in the file. 'When you found the ribbon, that wasn't the first time police had been inside Mr Vogel's property, was it?'

'No. DCI Radley and I had interviewed him there a few days previously.'

'How long would you say you spent at the property?'

'No longer than twenty minutes, as I remember.'

'Which room were you in?'

'Mr Vogel's living room.'

'You weren't there the whole time though, were you?'

'Maybe we used the bathroom. I can't remember.'

'So he could have searched the house? He could have gone, for instance, into the bedroom?'

'There's nothing to suggest DCI Radley planted that evidence and the court decided as much. Just because he's being investigated now doesn't change that fact.'

Pauline cocked her head to one side. 'Doesn't change it? I'm a little surprised to hear you say that. DCI Radley saw Sophie Madson right before her death. And he kept quiet about it. If you can't trust him to be honest about that, how on earth can you trust anything he says?'

Erin thought of the bruises on Tom's face. The crowd pulling him down. It was because of her. And so was this.

Her mouth had gone dry. Before she could think of a response, Pauline leant in and said, 'That case was cold for years. Then it's reopened and in no time at all Mr Vogel is charged with Annie's murder. You know what that looks like to me?'

'What does it look like?'

Pauline's blue eyes flashed.

'Like the police had a vendetta. A personal vendetta against Alan Vogel.'

*

Pauline marched down the corridor in her heels, navy coat buttoned up, umbrella at the ready, as immaculate as she had been when she'd arrived. Erin watched her go, then headed back into the office. She was so shaken by their conversation that she almost yelped when someone tapped her on the shoulder. She turned around to find Lewis there.

'Are you alright to talk?'

A few desks away, she saw Walker, deep in conversation with Adlington, subtly tilt his head in their direction.

She nodded at Lewis.

As soon as the door was closed, Lewis said, 'It's not good news. There's no CCTV cameras near that bridge.'

Tom would know where the cameras were, she thought.

Judging by Lewis's expression, he thought he'd failed her by delivering this news. He scratched the back of his head and stared at the floor.

'If you want someone else on this with you,' he said, 'I understand.'

She said nothing.

'You could have Adlington. Someone more experienced.'

'Lewis, listen to me,' she said. 'You know this case. You were the one who remembered there was a press conference at the Old Cross. Not me. You. This is as much yours as it is mine, alright?'

Lewis's ears turned pink.

'I'm sorry about before,' she said.

But Lewis was already shaking his head. 'You were right. We need to be impartial. It could have been him. Especially seeing as there's no other suspect right now.'

He was still staring at the floor, jaw clenched. She sensed something else was up.

'Was that all?'

He looked at her, wincing.

'Something's come up. It's grim, Erin.'

They entered the IT room, picking their way over the cables, spread across the floor like tree roots. Shergill's expression was serious.

'We found it on a folder in the phone. Password-protected but we managed to get through.' His eyes focused on Erin. 'Has he already told you? You know what to expect?'

Erin nodded.

Shergill wheeled his chair back around and clicked on a file in the folder. Even though she'd known what was coming, Erin still felt her ribcage tighten, squeezing the breath out of her lungs, when the photograph appeared on screen. It showed the blurred form of Sophie sleeping on a white bed, her head to the side, lips parted, peaceful, gone to the world. She was naked.

'Was this sent to her?'

'No. It was taken on the phone.'

'When?'

'The day before she went missing.'

Erin's heart was pounding. Maybe Tom was right. Maybe she was scared for her life. Because this, this was blackmail. This was: do what I say, or everyone sees this. Do what I say, or you're fucked.

Then she remembered something.

'There weren't any others, were they?'

Shergill frowned. 'No. Why?'

'Other photographs. Fraser, her coach, he mentioned that she had a load of papers with her. They haven't been found. They could have been printouts, is what I'm thinking.'

'Sorry, Erin. We've been all over her files, her internet history. There's nothing else.'

Erin dug her nails into her palm. 'This is maddening,' she said. 'He's right there. Right behind that camera. But still we have nothing on him.'

Lewis said, 'Could we listen to that clip again? With his voice?'

Shergill put his headphones on. 'I don't know what you're expecting to get out of it. But worth a shot, I guess.'

They listened through once again to the sounds of Sophie screaming. Presumably anyone working on the tech side got

155

desensitised to this sort of thing. But Erin felt terrified. What if she recognised Tom's voice there, underneath her screams?

Then she realised.

'The other voice,' she said. 'It's coming from a TV or a radio.'

Shergill raised his eyebrows at the screen. 'Yeah, might be,' he said.

'Any way of working out what programme that is?'

'I mean…' He grimaced, gesturing helplessly at the screen. 'It's just some bloke's muffled voice. Very monotone. No theme music or anything like that. I don't see how you can.'

She glanced at Lewis to see if she was on the right track. But he looked back at her like he was still waiting for her to get it.

Shergill replayed the clip several more times. Each time he did, he focused more and more on one particularly muffled section just as the voice came in. It boomed out of the speakers again and again, an ugly plosive sound. Erin didn't think she could listen to it many more times without going insane, but Shergill continued, unphased, zooming in and pinching and pulling the clip on screen.

'There's this bit of distortion here and here that I can't really place,' he said. 'You can barely make it out because of all the other noise. But it's kind of distinct and it happens twice.' He paused, and then said conclusively: 'Weird.'

That was when Lewis leapt away from the wall. 'Alright, that's great. Thanks so much for taking a look at that. Shame it didn't tell us more.'

Shergill hesitated. For a moment he seemed to sense that something was up. Then he said, 'OK. If you're sure. Shall I send you what I've got?'

Lewis's foot tapped the floor in a nervous, repetitive motion. 'Yeah, send us what you've got. Brilliant.'

He was rushing to get them away. Whatever he'd worked out, he didn't want to say it in front of Shergill.

Further down the corridor was a meeting room. Erin could see through the half-open blinds that it was empty. Lewis led them in. He wandered into the centre of the room and hugged himself.

She closed the door behind them. 'Talk to me.'

He had his back to her. Slowly, he turned his body in her direction. When their eyes eventually met, his face was pale.

'It's a police radio,' he said.

Erin felt like the floor had just given way beneath her feet.

'He can't tell,' he said quietly. 'He doesn't have to listen to them all the time. But I knew as soon as he said about the white noise. It's the sound of the other person cutting in and cutting out.'

And suddenly it seemed totally clear. That abrupt burst of white noise. The monotone voice. It had sounded like someone reading an announcement, but it wasn't. It was someone putting out a call to other officers, giving an order. Erin had to grab the chair in front of her to stop herself from swaying.

'Christ,' she said. 'It is a copper. Sophie was in a police car.'

Lewis stared at the floor with his hand over his mouth. 'When we tell Peters, that's going to be it for Tom.'

'We're not telling him, Lewis.'

His eyes widened. 'What if he works it out? Shergill? If someone finds out we knew and didn't say anything, we'll be gone. No questions asked.'

Erin was shaking her head. 'We can't afford to. Right now, I know it's not you. And I know it's not me. That's literally it. Anyone else here is a potential suspect. Did you recognise the voice?'

Lewis shook his head.

'Me neither. Maybe it wouldn't help anyway. Except to cross someone off the list.'

She hadn't planned on showing Lewis just yet. But now was the right time.

'When I was speaking to Tom in the interview room,' she said, 'he wrote this on the transcript. I'm sorry I didn't show you before.'

She unzipped her bag, pulled out the file and pushed it across the table towards him. When Lewis had finished studying it, he looked up at her with wide eyes.

'No way.'

'At first I thought Tom might just be trying to take the heat off himself,' she said, 'but Walker keeps sniffing around this case. He has been from the very start. Right before the first briefing, he asked me and Tom who our main suspect was. Like he needed to know right away. And then he told us to get a move on and interview him.'

'You think he was looking for someone to frame?'

'Maybe.'

Lewis stared at her for a few moments, then sat down at the table, running a hand through his hair. She could see the conflict already forming in his eyes; between the hope he felt at the prospect that Tom might still be innocent, and his newfound disbelief.

Lewis grimaced. 'I don't know, Erin,' he said. 'Walker, he's – he's a prick, but he's a solid detective, you know?'

'He's been here for donkeys' years. No guarantee that he's clean. Besides, Walker likes a power trip. If he could find a way to flash the badge or use his rank over you, he would. Maybe he did that with Sophie.'

They both went quiet. She could see Lewis fighting with himself, swaying from one side to the next.

There was a buzz in Erin's mind that kept building, making her feel dizzy. 'We're going to investigate the people in this building now. Work out where everyone was on the day of Sophie's disappearance. Not just Tom. We won't be able to palm it off on any of the researchers. We're going to have to do this ourselves.'

They were silent as the gravity of what they were about to do slowly dawned on them. She looked through the gaps in the blinds, at the officers at their monitors, a few of them leaning back in their seats to laugh and chatter amongst themselves. People she'd spoken to every day for years. Any one of them could have done it.

They were silent for a few moments. Then Lewis said, 'It's weird. Whoever it was, how did they meet Sophie? She didn't have contact with anyone from the force.'

That was when it hit her.

'Yes, she did.'

22

'Sophie's name's not in the system, so I take it you didn't log it?' she asked.

Drummond shook his head. He and Saunders looked a lot more sheepish than they had done less than a fortnight ago, when they'd first reported seeing Fraser and Sophie in the car park. Now Saunders' scrappy moustache was turned downwards in a mopey triangle. Erin probably wasn't his favourite detective after she'd asked to speak to Tom. You owe me, the expression in his eyes seemed to say.

'Is there any other way someone could have found out about the argument you saw? Did you call someone about it? Did you talk to anyone in the office?'

'I don't think so,' he said.

Erin didn't buy that. They'd said something and they knew it.

'We have no evidence of a previous connection between DCI Radley and Sophie Madson. Right now, we're in the dark. Anything you know could make a difference.'

They exchanged a nervous glance.

'Well, we did mention it once,' said Saunders. 'Just in passing in the office.'

'I really don't see how it could be relevant though,' Drummond added.

'What made you bring it up?'

They looked at her guiltily. It took Erin a few seconds to get it, and when she did she had to resist rolling her eyes.

'It was dark and she had lots of make-up on,' said Drummond apologetically. 'I didn't know she was sixteen. I thought she was about twenty.'

'So you mentioned to the guys that you'd seen this good-looking girl out?'

'No, no, it wasn't like that. You know Walker?'

The hair on her arms prickled. She nodded.

'He was – well…' He gave her a guilty look. 'It's a bit awkward. It's just lads, you know.'

'I've been here long enough. Trust me, I've heard it all.'

'Well, he was showing everyone in the office photos of this woman he'd just interviewed,' he said, 'and he went round everyone, asking them who they'd come across on jobs, getting these girls' profiles up. And you know, telling them whether they had good taste or not.'

She could imagine this clear as day. She'd seen Walker do it before. Making a big performance out of the fact he hadn't lost his virility or whatever, as if anyone would go for a crumbling relic like him.

'It's not like I was really into it,' Drummond added. 'It's more that he's senior. You want to be on his good side.'

'So you brought up Sophie?'

'I couldn't remember her full name. Just Sophie. Thank God. Can you imagine? He'd have got her profile up and we'd have seen she was still in school. I'd have looked like a complete creep.'

'But you said you'd seen this pretty gymnast arguing with her coach? You described her?'

He nodded.

'I don't think that would have been enough – if it is DCI Radley…'

'Can you remember who was there when this happened?'

'Everyone, it felt like. Lots of uniforms. I think yourself and Adlington were on the other table and Radley on another. I'd say he was within earshot.'

She went in search of Walker first thing the next day. The base of her spine stiffened as she walked through the office. The space felt unfamiliar to her now. She snuck glances at the officers working at their desks, no longer trusting a single one of them.

She found him in the kitchen. With the kettle boiling, Walker closed the door behind her, sealing them in together, alone.

'Got an update for me, Crane?'

'On the twenty-third of July, PC Drummond saw Fraser and Sophie arguing in a car park, on the way back from training. He talked about it in the office. It's possible that's how Tom found out about Sophie.'

Walker's eyebrow ticked up. 'Interesting,' he said.

'You were there, apparently,' she said. 'He mentioned a gymnast called Sophie. Does that ring any bells?'

She studied him carefully for a reaction.

Walker squinted. 'Can't say I remember that,' he said. 'Thank you, Crane. Coming round to the idea, are you?'

'It's too early to say. It's just a connection I thought you should be aware of.'

He opened the cupboard and took out two cups.

'Whatever bogieman you're imagining did this, you need to get him out of your head.' Then he turned around and rested his hands on the counter behind him, puffing out his chest. Big man about to deliver a speech. 'Let me tell you something, Crane,' he said. 'The other month, I was working on a case. The body was the stuff of nightmares. They'd smashed his face in. Right around the cheekbone. His eyeball was crushed into jelly. You know what I did that evening?' He paused, as though Erin was about to guess. 'I ate liver and bacon for dinner. I took my son to the pub to see his friends. I watched *Strictly* with my wife. Then I picked up my drunk son. Then I went to bed and slept like a baby.'

Erin stared at him. She wasn't sure she'd ever heard anything more sociopathic come out of Walker's mouth.

He kept going. 'The people who get it right in this job – they know when to stop themselves. They know that when you go home, you need to be home. Have your tea, put your feet up. Disconnect yourself from everything that happens in here. Not just for yourself or even your family. But for the job. When you're watching a witness cry her eyes out, you can't be the one going into the toilets straight after the interview to burst into tears over how shit life is. You put a wall up. Because that's the best thing you can do for them.' He looked at her. 'The people who get it wrong are the ones who put too much of themselves into it. Kill themselves overworking every case. Because every little kid they come across who's dead or hurt or abandoned is them twenty years ago.'

'Fifty for some.'

That got a glower, but he kept going. 'All I'm saying is, if you want to solve a case, you need to be prepared to disconnect from it. Otherwise you overlook things. You miss clues. When I have a suspect in front of me, I don't sit there thinking, "what do I know about men like this? Does he have it in him?" I just look at the evidence. And the evidence says I have a man who drove the victim off in his car and then got the timings muddled for the rest of his day. Sugar?'

'No thanks.'

'You like yours incredibly bitter. I should've guessed.' His head disappeared into the cupboard again. 'You keeping up with the news, Crane?'

Her nose wrinkled. 'I don't need everyone and their aunty giving me their opinion on this case.'

'Have you seen some of the things they're saying about him though?' Closing the cupboard door, he raised his eyebrows at her. He made a whistling sound as he placed the sugar tin beside his coffee.

She didn't like where this was going. Suddenly her blood felt like it was pumping around her body a little hotter. 'Well, they would, wouldn't they?'

'I don't mean the commentators discussing whether or not he did it.' His back was to her, spooning sugar into his mug. 'I mean the stories that have come out.'

'What are you talking about?'

Walker turned around in mock-surprise. 'He didn't tell you either?'

Her face had gone red, she knew it.

'Well. That does surprise me.'

This was Walker all over. He was playing games. The problem was, it was working. Erin kept thinking how she really hadn't needed to hear that. Her stomach had turned over and she didn't fancy that coffee anymore.

Walker handed over her cup, smiling demurely.

'It's not just gossip in the press. There's something I think will surprise you.'

Walker must have had the email drawn up and ready to go, because it arrived in Erin's inbox as soon as she was back at her desk.

There were five articles in total. Reading the first one, she had to resist the urge to scoff out loud. This was exactly why she'd been avoiding the press coverage. Everyone who'd ever crossed paths with Tom suddenly seemed to think they understood him better than anyone else. It was pathetic. She closed the email and tried to concentrate on her work.

But then, she thought, for several newspapers to cover the same story, there must have been something in this. Surely she had to read the rest as well. So after she got home, putting her bag down next to the door and taking off her jacket, she gave in. She opened her phone and read the other articles while sat on the edge of the bath. And that was when her heart started to race.

They all said the same thing.

Locker room culture. Predatory behaviour. Sexual harassment.

She should've stopped reading. It had become compulsive and she hadn't noticed the buzz of panic that was building inside her as she sat there in the unlit bathroom. Then the next thing she knew she was halfway through an article describing stories from an anonymous source in the police. About how, on patrol, when there were no female officers around, he'd point out every attractive girl walking down the street. How he'd flirt inappropriately with witnesses. How he'd once bet with someone that he could have the girl behind the bar and slept with her that night. And it was pathetic and it didn't matter and it shouldn't have hurt but then there was a quote from someone claiming to be a former colleague in the force that made her close the phone and stare through the window vents, at a cobweb that was gently fluttering there. 'No question, it's a game to him,' they had said. 'He has to prove to himself he can have anyone.'

23

THE CEILING FAN ROTATED SLOWLY and silently above their heads. There was no one else in the café apart from a sullen teenage waiter who placed their drinks on the greasy plastic table like he resented them for ordering.

Erin studied Sandra Wilson as she tipped one, two, three sugars into her coffee. She must have been about fifty, and she was small – mousy-faced, with wrists so thin she had to keep rolling up the sleeves of her knitted cardigan as she stirred the sugars in. She couldn't have looked less imposing if she'd tried. And yet Erin was utterly terrified of her.

Sandra had rung in yesterday, not long after the stories broke. A sexual health worker, she'd read the articles on the way to the local community centre that morning.

'You work with vulnerable women, is that right?' said Erin.

'Survivors of domestic abuse. Rape victims. Sex workers. You know, the ones you lot ignore.'

For a moment Erin thought she'd misheard her.

'What does that mean?'

Thoughtful, Sandra took a sip of coffee and swallowed.

'Exactly what I implied. We pick up the pieces after you're done.' She smiled unpleasantly.

A muscle in Erin's temple twitched painfully. 'Excuse me?'

'When I read that stuff in the paper about a locker room culture in the police, I can't say I was surprised. I don't think many people were. For years now I've been trying to raise this issue with the local

166

council. I've never got anywhere. Seems like now, with this Tom Radley investigation, people are finally waking up.'

'Waking up to what?'

'I want to tell you about someone. A woman named Maia Andrei. She worked as a sex worker. We were there to make sure she and the other girls were safe. We gave them condoms, pregnancy tests, health checks. And we gave them something no one else was giving them: we gave them the space to talk.

'Nine years ago now, Maia was raped by one of her customers. He'd given her something. I don't remember what – something to put her to sleep.'

Erin felt the hairs on the back of her neck stand up. Xanax.

'Seems he liked it that way, her not being awake. He left as soon as he was done with her, just passed out in the bedroom. For all he knew, she could have been dead. The other girls found her, lips gone blue, not breathing, and phoned for an ambulance.

'The doctors called the police. Maia never would have done herself. But it didn't matter. Because the police didn't catch him. What they did do, though, was charge Maia for assisting in the running of the brothel. She got three years in prison.'

Erin thought she'd heard her wrong.

'What? But she wasn't part of a brothel?'

'Didn't matter. If you live with someone who's also in sex work, the police can do you for running a brothel. Surely you know that?'

Erin didn't know that.

Three years. The words sank through her.

Erin had never heard of this case before. But then again, why would she?

'Having the job you do, I'm sure you know all about the criminalisation of sex workers. Most are scared to call the police in case they get done for drug abuse or for having an unstable immigration status. But I knew as soon as I heard about it that there was something more to this. Not once has Maia given a description of her attacker, even to the other girls she worked with. As though she was scared to reveal him.'

'What are you saying?'

'I'm saying I think there's a reason Maia got charged. I think the police wanted to shut her up.'

'You mean it was an officer who did it?'

She hesitated.

'I wanted to ask you, Erin… can I call you Erin?' she said. 'What do you think of the team you work with?'

Erin stared at her.

'I shouldn't expect you to answer that. They're your co-workers, after all.'

'I'm a safe pair of ears.'

'It's come to my attention,' Sandra said, 'that some of the vulnerable women who deal with the police in this town come out worse than they went in.'

The walls behind Sandra seemed to shiver like a mirage.

'Maia's not the only one. There was another girl, Megan Sadler. A sixth-former. Two years ago, she was sexually assaulted coming home from a night out. The way the police dealt with her was totally inappropriate. They demeaned her. Embarrassed her. And when she complained, nothing happened. The police ignored it.

'The amount of women I've encountered whose lives were made worse – not better – after they came into contact with the criminal justice system. Migrants who were deported after they reported their abusive partners. Women who came to us after they were raped and the police wouldn't help them.'

Erin's chest hurt.

'What you're talking about,' she said, 'that's not my experience.'

'You're on the inside. Have you had your eyes closed?'

Erin said nothing.

'I don't need to tell you that Wakestead has a crime problem. In my opinion, we threw more police at the problem when we should have created more community support. And as far I'm concerned, more police on the streets, more police in people's lives, is bad news. Especially for girls like Maia Andrei and Megan Sadler. Neither cases were taken seriously. Nor was Annie Dodds. Why else did it take so long to solve?'

Erin's breathing had become shallow.

'Maia's case,' she said. 'Who were the detectives on it?'

'That's the thing.' Sandra's eyes glinted. 'The detective on Maia's case. It was Tom Radley.'

Erin drove straight from the café to the station, where she opened the Police Records Management System on her computer and looked up Maia Andrei's case. There it was, in black and white. The incident report and, alongside it, a record of Maia's arrest. In her headshot she looked hollow-eyed, scared. Ein forced herself to look up Megan Sadler as well. Again, Sandra was right. There was no record of a complaint there. Just Megan's original interview.

Every time an officer looked up a case, the system recorded the search. She checked the records to see who else had accessed these files. The answer was no one, not since the early days of each case being opened. But the detective who'd uploaded Maia's – Erin noted, her mouth going dry – was Tom.

She showed the files to Lewis, waiting in silence while he scrutinised one after the other with a hand lost in his hair. He bit his lip.

'This is the kind of thing Walker's been hoping for,' he said, and Erin felt her body go cold.

24

THE RECEPTIONIST KNOCKED GENTLY ON the door before opening it.

'Someone here to see you, Maia. A detective.'

Watery light streamed through the thin curtains into the small, unlit bedsit, where a woman was curled up on a brown sofa watching TV. Seeing Erin stood there, she lifted herself upright.

If she hadn't just heard the receptionist refer to her by name, Erin would never have recognised her as the girl from the photo in the police file. Maia Andrei had aged two decades in the space of one. Sat down at the table and chairs beside the threadbare curtains, Erin looked at the long lines on either side of her mouth, dragging her face down in a mask of permanent gloom. Ex-convicts often shared the same look. Even after they got out, things were never the same again.

Sandra had told Erin that after Maia was released, she'd worked alone for six months, feeling that she couldn't risk working with other girls and getting arrested a second time. But that meant losing the safety she'd had working in a cooperative. Alone, she took more risks, went out alone at night, had no one to protect her if the man proved dangerous. She drank to get through it. It got bad and eventually she ended up here, at a housing association on the fringes of Wakestead that Erin had never known existed, providing accommodation to women in need.

Maia was squeezing her thin, pink-knuckled hands together on the table between them. The way she stared at Erin, shoulders pinched in, made Erin think of an animal watching a predator from the safety of its warren.

'Sandra reached out to me,' she said. 'Do you remember her?'

Maia said nothing.

'She told me about what happened. Are you OK to talk about it?'

Maia looked down at her hands, picking at the skin around her nails.

'I'm not here to make things harder for you, Maia. Anything you have to say about how the police treated you, I'll listen.'

Still nothing. The picking became more aggressive.

'I know what happened. They raided your house for menus of services, bills with your name on them, and used them to incriminate you. They made your life worse, when they should have helped you. If you tell me what happened, Maia, we can try and get the officers who charged you held to account.'

Maia didn't even react. Erin glanced up at the staff volunteer, but they were watching Maia calmly, giving no indication that this behaviour was out of the ordinary.

Erin said: 'Maia, we're worried he may have hurt somebody else.'

This time, that sent a shiver of emotion across Maia's face. The watery light had turned her complexion grey.

Still, she said nothing.

'If you're not comfortable speaking,' she said, 'you could write it down. A name.'

Maia's eyes drifted to the piece of paper Erin had placed on the table. For the first time Erin thought she noticed a glimmer of life in her eyes. As though she was imagining the world of secrets she could spill onto this blank canvas.

With careful deliberation, Maia picked up the sheet of paper, held it out in front of Erin's face, and tore it in half.

25

Lewis covered his mouth anxiously as she described the interview to him.

Annoyed, she said, 'Can you not do that? Someone will notice.' A few rows away, a group of probationers were working with their heads down. At any moment one of them could look up and see them. Who was to say word wouldn't then reach Walker that Erin and Lewis were hiding away in the far corner of the office, talking in low voices?

'Sorry, sorry.' He brought his hand down. 'It's just... you know, you're a woman. If she won't speak to you, who's she going to speak to?'

'Sandra never got anywhere with her either.'

'There must be other people who could tell us. Other officers on the case.'

'Yeah, they're really gonna admit to something like this.'

'Surely someone on the force would have seen what was happening and thought it was messed up. Surely.'

Erin's mouth felt dry. 'It's the same guy, isn't it? Xanax. Contact with the force. Maybe this has been going on for a while.'

They both sat in silence as it sank in. If the cases were connected, this wasn't a boyfriend who'd lost his temper. This was a serial abuser.

Erin stared at the probationers working at their computers. Did others here know? Had they always suspected? Had they deliberately covered it up because they knew who was responsible, and chosen to protect him?

'So who else can we speak to?' asked Lewis.

'Kapil Manek's one,' she said. 'He was the other detective on the case. He left right afterwards, which is strange. Maybe he suspected something. Let's look at his notes in the file again and then check in with him.'

Lewis glanced nervously at her. 'Actually… I've got some bad news,' he said.

Erin waited.

'The file on Maia's case. I went to look it up again. And I saw someone else had as well. Walker.'

Her insides went cold. 'Fuck,' she said. 'He must have looked at one of our computers. The complete creep.'

She glanced over her shoulder. Walker was at the other end of the room, deep in conversation with one of the DCs. Were they discussing Maia's case? Then she saw the DC clock her. The two of them must have been waiting for her to get back, because Walker immediately turned around and started heading their way.

'What do we say?' asked Lewis.

Erin said nothing. Her feet were rooted to the floor.

Walker had printed out Maia's case file. He held it outstretched in one hand as he arrived at their desk, grinning ear-to-ear. 'I'm a little concerned you didn't immediately report this to me, Crane, I must admit.'

'Only just found out about it myself, Walker.'

He started flicking idly through the file. 'So, would you like to tell me what you make of this? Because, from where I'm standing, it's unclear what connection this has to the Madson case.'

She swallowed. 'A sexual health worker who knew the girl involved flagged it with us.'

'And why's that?'

'She was concerned about the way the police treated her.'

Walker stared at her, unblinking.

'The way Radley treated her, you mean?'

'He wasn't the only officer on this case.'

'Except no one else is a suspect in Sophie Madson's murder, are they, Crane? You spoke to this Maia? What did she say?'

'Nothing.'

'She said it was nothing or she wasn't willing to say?'

Erin's heart drummed in her ears. 'The second.'

'That's interesting. That's very interesting. Well, thank you for telling me, Crane. Even if you did take your time.'

From his tone of voice, it sounded like he was about to leave. But he remained standing over her desk, hands in his trouser pockets.

'I've got an interview with Radley in ten. How about you take this one with me?'

'What?'

Suddenly he'd become very interested in the floor. He traced it with the toe of his shoe, his raised eyebrows the only indication that he was still in conversation with her. 'I think your input could prove very useful for this next part.'

She looked at Lewis, but he was watching Walker with the same silent panic she felt.

'I'm out of this, Walker,' she said. 'That's the whole point.'

'So you are,' he said. 'But one interview won't hurt.'

'I don't have anything,' she said. 'I haven't prepared a—'

'You'll catch up,' he said, and sloped off down the corridor, hands still in his pockets.

26

WALKER WENT IN FIRST, THEN Erin followed.

It disturbed her that even now her body reacted so immediately and viscerally to him. Just being in the same room as Tom made her heat climb up her neck. She glanced at the camera in the top left-hand corner of the room. The footage was always washed-out and grainy, wasn't it? Hopefully it wouldn't show the flush that had just entered her cheeks, or the unsteady wobble in her legs as she pulled out the chair beside Walker and sat down at the interview table.

Tom gave her no sign he'd experienced the same thing. He stared at Walker as though she wasn't there. She wasn't sure if that made this better or worse. But she ate up the chance to look at him unobserved. He'd lost weight. His cheekbones were sharper and more clearly defined than before, carving distinct shadows into his face. Did she look thin too? She hadn't been eating much lately; she couldn't remember when she'd last cooked a proper meal for herself. Compulsively, she checked her reflection in the double-sided mirror and was startled to see her unfamiliar, hard slice of body beside Walker's bulk.

Next to her, Walker's arm jerked up. He was pointing to his own face. 'That's healed up well, hasn't it?'

He was referring to Tom's split lip, now vanished. Tom said nothing.

'We both know there's a lot more where that came from, Radley. People are angry. I'm getting it too, you know. Harassment in the street. We all are. Especially bad for you, isn't it, Crane? Being a woman.'

Erin couldn't think where this was going.

'You should see the stuff they send her, Radley. Death threats. Men saying the disgusting things they'll do to her if they find out where she lives.'

That wasn't true. Erin hadn't received anything like that – thankfully – and she definitely hadn't said as much to Walker. For the first time, Tom looked at her with alarm in his eyes. *Really? Is that happening?* She looked away, her cheeks blazing with heat.

This felt wrong. She never wanted this – to be complicit with the questioning, the goading.

'And you know why, right, Radley? Because as long as you're out, walking around, innocent until proven guilty, people think we're protecting you. The sooner you tell us what really happened, the sooner the rest of us can start sleeping soundly in our beds. So I'm going to ask you again. That window of time, during the Madson search, where you're unaccounted for… what were you doing?'

'I already told you.'

'I'm disappointed, Radley. I really am. For a second I thought maybe you cared enough about your team to do the right thing. I guess maybe you never actually gave a shit about anyone in this place, did you?'

Tom stared at him.

It was pathetic, but Erin wanted nothing more than for him to fight back. Defend himself. Tell them both publicly, on camera, how much he cared.

He said nothing.

'Bit of a pattern that,' said Walker, 'looking out for number one. Not caring about the consequences for those in need.'

Tom frowned.

'Crane, why don't you tell Radley what you've found?'

Tom looked at her, puzzled, sending the blood rushing to her face.

Decisively, Walker lay his palm flat on the table. 'I'll leave you to it. You need anything, I'll be right there on the other side of the glass.'

The sound of the door closing behind Walker seemed to echo endlessly inside the small room. Tom watched her in silence.

She knew what Walker was doing. All that bullshit about death threats. The accusations that Tom didn't actually care about his team. They were meant for her as much as Tom. He was trying to rile her up, push her buttons, turn her against Tom.

And it had worked.

'Maia Andrei,' she said. 'Does that name mean anything to you?'

There was a flash of recognition in Tom's eyes.

'She was my first case,' he said.

Her heart was beating so hard it hurt. Was she really going to do this? She tried to think how she'd normally approach this with a suspect but her mind was slow and fuzzy.

Walker had left her with Maia's file. Her hands trembled slightly as she unwound the clasp and slid the incident report onto the table.

'Then you'll already know what's in here. Xanax. Neck bruises. After Sophie Madson's post-mortem, the similarities with Maia Andrei's case didn't occur to you?'

Tom's eyebrow twitched. 'Maia was a sex worker. The case was almost a decade ago. No, it didn't occur to me.'

'But you admit they're similar?'

Tom stared at the incident report. 'I would have to really look at the evidence again. But yes, I can see there are similarities.'

'One of those being you, of course. You were a detective on both.'

Tom said nothing.

'So do you want to tell me what happened? Why didn't you catch this?'

'Maia wouldn't tell us anything about him. She was afraid.'

'Afraid of what?'

'You know what it's like dealing with vulnerable people like that. She just wanted to get out of there.'

'So you thought you'd just charge her instead?'

Tom looked at her coldly. She hated the careful pause he left before he said, 'That isn't how it happened.'

'Really? So what happened?'

'I don't know who charged her. The case fell to the wayside. I wanted to keep investigating but the seniors weren't interested. And next thing I knew, Maia had been arrested.'

'And you just sat back and let that happen?'

There was something almost helpless in the way he shrugged.

'I was young and new. I regret it. I really do.'

'Why have you never mentioned any of this to me before?'

'It was a long time ago. And I was ashamed of it. I didn't want you to know.'

'Kapil Manek. Your partner before me, and I've never even heard of him. Why?'

She knew the emotion was rising in her voice. She knew Walker would pick up on it. So would the IOPC investigators when they listened back to the recording. But she was too angry to care anymore now who heard.

Tom opened his mouth to speak, but she kept going.

'We spoke to a sexual health worker who knew Maia at the time. She claims that Maia became – and I quote – "scared of the police" following the investigation. Your investigation.'

Tom's eyebrows furrowed. But he said nothing.

'It doesn't look good. Here you are implicated in one murder case. And a girl from a previous case of yours appears to have come out traumatised. What did she have to be scared of, Tom?'

'I only ever treated Maia as a victim.'

He said it with such conviction that Erin was almost knocked off her stride. To her surprise, he kept going.

'However,' he said, 'I can't say the same for everyone else on the team.'

She almost missed it, but just for a second Tom's head tilted towards the double-sided mirror. She knew what he was trying to say. Walker.

Except this time, she didn't believe him. This time she saw it for what it was. A cheap trick.

At that point, there was the sound of knuckles rapping on the mirror. She knew what that meant. Time's up.

She sat in the stairwell, nursing a filter coffee between her hands. Walker leant over her, shoulder against the wall, polished shoe on the step in front of her, edging into her personal space.

'That was good in there,' he said. 'There were a couple of points where I thought you'd make him cry.'

The hot coffee churned in her stomach.

She didn't want to ask. But she didn't think she could bear not to. 'What do you make of it?'

After everything, Walker seemed to glow with satisfaction.

'Maybe you've never seen him this way, Crane. Perhaps you didn't want to. But Radley's a man who thinks he can have everything he wants without paying for any of it. Always has been.'

She stared down at her filter coffee. It looked grey.

'If you'd been here for as long as I have, you'd see that. He never deserved the respect this place gave him. He never worked as hard as me – or you for that matter. He just took and took and took.'

She remembered confronting Tom in the interview room downstairs after his attack. The anger in his eyes. Everything he'd said. It had felt so genuine at the time.

Walker leant towards her, resting his arm on his knee. 'I can see what he's doing to you, Crane. Do you think I missed that little point he made? "I can't speak for everyone on the team"? He's trying to convince you it's one of us. He's trying to turn you against your own team. Isolate you. Don't let him win.'

There was a strange paternal warmth in his voice. Erin stared at her shoes.

'We've been waiting for you, Crane,' he said. 'Waiting for you to see it as well. This will go a lot faster if we're all on the same page.'

Her chest was bursting. If Walker wasn't right in front of her, she might have cried. Because everything he was saying, deep down, she agreed with. A few days ago, she couldn't have imagined feeling that way. But fighting for Tom's innocence, when every piece of evidence that emerged continually pointed to his guilt, had exhausted her. She couldn't do it anymore.

She cleared her throat, hating the brittle sound that came out. Then she said, 'Let's put him away.'

27

SHE DIDN'T WANT TO SPEAK to anyone on her way out. She timed it so she'd leave after the young officers had shot out the door but before the seniors had called it a night. She was scared that if she tried to hold a conversation right now, the other person would see right through her and know she was going to fall apart.

Driving home, she watched the yellow headlights drift past her in the darkness. She'd always told herself that Tom had been a miraculous force in her life. Someone she'd never seen coming but who'd appeared to her at exactly the right time. Now, as she imagined him sat next to her in the car, the profile of his face against the blue window, she began to wonder if it really had been so outside her own control. Secretly, maybe she had wanted some stable force to arrange her life around. Someone to rely on. Perhaps she'd wanted it so much she'd stopped asking if he was someone to rely on at all.

That was the thing about looking for things in people. You'd always find what you were looking for, one way or another. How much had she excused, or overlooked? How much of him was real and how much of him had she made up in her head?

A long figure in a tan coat opened the door, bringing a shock of cold air into the pub. Kapil Manek crossed the room and sat opposite her in the booth, pressed up against a thin window clouded with condensation. They felt so close to the road that every time a car crashed through a puddle outside, Erin expected to be hit by the freezing spray.

181

He'd left the Wakestead force years before Erin joined. She'd have probably never crossed paths with him if it weren't for his name on that file, marking his connection to the Maia Andrei case and, therefore, to Tom.

At first, she'd wondered if it could have been him. But he hadn't been in the area for Sophie Madson's murder, or the Megan Sadler case. It seemed unlikely. Especially now that he was in front of her. Kapil looked more like an accountant than a copper and he was thin and skittish. Erin wondered if he'd always been like this. Getting dropped from the force the way he had, as early as he had, would knock anyone's confidence.

'Walk me through the case,' she said. 'What happened with Maia?'

'From the start, it felt unlikely we were ever going to find this guy. In a place like that, no one knows who these men are passing in and out, no one keeps any kind of record. But then we spoke to her in the hospital and I knew for certain it was a dead-end. She didn't want to speak to us at all. She just wanted to forget about it. We spoke to her housemates and checked the CCTV down the street. Nothing came up. It seemed to go off everyone's radar. Then one day Maia was getting charged for assisting in the running of a brothel. And the next thing I knew I was fired.'

He smirked bitterly. He was still sore about it.

'Sounds like you think there was a connection? Between the girls getting charged and you being let go?'

'Management told me as much. They said I wasn't pulling my weight – said I'd missed the obvious signs that Maia Andrei was running a brothel. It didn't look like that to me. Besides, I was sent in to solve a rape case. Not punish people for working in the sex trade.'

Erin frowned. 'That seems extremely harsh. As a reason for letting someone go.'

Kapil said nothing, but he looked pleased she felt that way.

'So who was behind it? The girls getting charged?'

'I don't know. Really couldn't say.'

She paused; then said, 'During the case... did DCI Radley behave strangely at all?'

Kapil frowned. 'No.'

'He didn't speak to Maia alone at any point, did he?'

'No. He was brand new, no way was he getting trusted to do interviews alone.'

He had quite startling eyes, Kapil, such a pale shade of brown they looked almost golden. Apart from that his face was long and narrow. Erin looked at his tan coat and golden eyes and tried to imagine being attracted to him.

He put his hands up. 'Look, if this is about the Madson case, you should know Tom was never inappropriate with Maia. Or anyone for that matter. He's clean. All this Sophie Madson stuff – I don't believe for a second he did it.'

'You don't?'

He shook his head. 'Not a guy like that. No way. He was straight-down-the-line. I can't believe what I'm hearing – all this stuff about him. Like he's some killer. It's a witch hunt.'

Erin finished her drink and didn't stop Kapil when he went to get them two more. As they spoke – about work now, not the case – the wine, as well as the black coffee she'd had on the way here, rattled through her bones and made the lights skid over the veneered table.

Kapil became more and more stoic. She could tell it was because he was nervous. The conversation felt forced. When he asked her where she lived – in a way he probably thought was subtle – and she told him her house was near here, he frowned and nodded like she'd told him she was recently bereaved. By the time they left together, not touching, still continuing their jarring, overly formal conversation, she'd already accepted what was going to happen. It didn't feel like a decision so much as an inevitability, the tide rolling in, invisible in the darkness.

The way he moved was nothing like Tom's silky, fluid approach. Kapil immediately came too close. Erin thought there was something pathetic to his hurried frisk of her body, like someone scrambling to pick up your loose change off the floor before you realised you'd dropped it. Her hand kept going to her drink, like a reflex. He hadn't touched the one she'd poured for him. She wished he would. She wished she'd convinced him to buy her two, three more rounds.

His body was like a metal frame; narrow and angled, with bones close to the surface. When he grabbed her hips and pulled her on top of him, he felt simultaneously too hard and at the same time completely immaterial, like he was made of air. She looked for the gold in his eyes. But the darkness of the room had dilated his pupils and dulled them to unreflective black.

28

MEGAN SADLER KNEADED HER UPPER arm self-consciously, squeezing the face of the tiger that was tattooed there.

'I don't remember much about the attack. I remember leaving the club by myself. My friends had asked if they wanted me to come with them but I said I'd be fine. I was outside, heading for the taxi queue. Then everything went black.'

She and Lewis had driven to Bristol, where Megan was studying her undergraduate degree. She sat cross-legged on the bed of her student flat, a bohemian rug stretched on the wall behind her, towers of tattered books in one corner, and a tray of incense on the windowsill. Erin took the desk chair; Lewis remained standing, his back to the door, as if guarding against anyone from coming in and disturbing this moment.

She said, 'I woke up because there was water dripping on my face. I was lying in the mud underneath a bramble bush, and everything hurt.'

She wasn't looking at them. She was staring at the curls of smoke emitting from the incense sticks.

'When something like that happens to you, you don't know what to expect from the emergency services. You're still in shock. That's the excuse I have for not realising sooner that the police's treatment of me was complete dogshit.'

Erin's mouth felt dry. She said, 'What did they do?'

'They told me I needed to take my clothes off. Just like that, like it was routine. All of them were blokes by the way. And when

185

I hesitated, one of them said, "Don't worry, he won't sniff your panties" and a couple of them started laughing.

'They gave me these overalls to wear when they interviewed me. It wasn't until later that I realised their questions were totally inappropriate. They asked if I had a boyfriend. They asked if I'd been drinking. If anything like this had ever happened before.' She grimaced. 'They just seemed... bored. The guy interviewing me – sorry, I don't remember his name – he said, "chances are there's enough evidence to say you two had sex, but not enough evidence to say you were raped. So I suggest you don't press charges."'

'The detective said that to you?'

She nodded.

Erin gritted her teeth.

'I didn't tell anyone this stuff for ages, by the way. It wasn't until about a year later that I told my mum. She complained. We were told there'd be an internal investigation. We never heard anything else. Then, when I started studying here, I needed a reference for a therapist, so I went to the police to ask for a record of the incident and the internal investigation. And you know what. They had no record I'd made a complaint.'

'You know what I'm going to ask you, Megan,' said Erin. 'Do you have any idea who he was? Your attacker?'

Megan shook her head. 'I'm sorry. He spiked me. I don't remember anything.'

Erin found it hard to keep the disappointment out of her face.

'There was one thing. I don't know if this helps. But the medical report showed it was Xanax he used. A couple of people at school were using it at the time, and I went with a friend once to pick some up. I don't know who the dealer was, but I remember the place. It was this warehouse on the waterfront. That was where everyone would go.'

'Do you think it's our guy?'

Lewis nursed his coffee cup anxiously. The two-hour drive from Bristol had wiped them out, so they'd decided to stop off for a coffee in a busy café in Wakestead's old town before they headed to their next interview.

'Got to be,' said Erin. 'I bet she started to feel the effects of the drug as soon as she was in that taxi queue. And he was there waiting for her. He approaches, tells her he'll look after her.'

'I'm a police officer, I'll get you home.'

'Exactly.'

'Now that one victim has come forward,' said Lewis, 'it might convince Maia to speak, you know.'

'I hope so. If Megan can't remember anything about her attacker, Maia's still our best bet.'

Lewis nodded, biting his lip. It looked like there was something else he wanted to say.

'I looked at everyone's calendars online,' he said, 'to see what they had on at around midday when Sophie went missing. I put it all in a spreadsheet. Obviously Tom was at the press conference. And Peters and Shergill were in a meeting together with the chief constable and the deputy chief constable. But Walker. He didn't actually have anything on, as far as I can see. There's no one who could vouch for where he was.'

Erin stared into her drink. She didn't want to go over this again.

'We can't keep doing this, Lewis.'

Unlike him, she'd resigned herself to it, finally. There you are, see; Tom did do it. You got him wrong. That was what Kapil had been about. Purging herself of any hope she'd been clinging on to. There was something cathartic to accepting it at last; Tom was a killer.

Lewis shuffled in his seat, agitated. 'The thing is,' he said, 'drugging a woman into unconsciousness…' He rolled his shoulders uncomfortably. 'Do we really believe Tom would do something like that?'

'Do you believe Walker would?'

'Well, I don't know. Between him and Tom, I'd sooner say Walker, I guess.'

Erin said nothing. She winced as a sharp pain shot up her temple. She was running on barely any sleep and her brain felt like it was trying to squeeze through the seams in her skull.

The memory of yesterday evening didn't bring her any pleasure. She thought of Kapil pulling his shirt over his bird-like shoulders and felt sick. But she'd ended it. Once and for all. She'd severed the tie, it was over, and she didn't want to go backwards.

Still, what Lewis was saying was right. Seeing how someone else behaved during sex had reminded her of everything she'd liked about Tom. His focus on the other person, his desire to please – that was tangible, something she could feel even now, as intimately as the china cup under her fingers. If what Tom really wanted was someone incapable of responding – of consenting – wouldn't she have seen that for herself?

Just then, a tall woman in a red coat appeared at their table. She pointed at them.

'You're the detectives on the Madson case, aren't you?'

Her voice had the cheerful note of someone who'd just recognised an old friend.

Lewis smiled uneasily. 'Anything we can help with?'

Immediately, she took the spare seat at their table. Erin's skin prickled. She didn't like this.

'I can't imagine what it must be like for you both right now. It's hard enough discovering a colleague might be involved in something like this. But it seems like you were genuinely close.'

Looking a little taken aback, Lewis nodded. 'Appreciate it.'

'Does it surprise you, everything that's come out since?'

Lewis gave a helpless shrug. 'We really couldn't say.'

'What about some of his previous cases? Like Alan Vogel's conviction? Could you tell me about that?'

Her eyes darted between them. The pain in Erin's temple sharpened.

'See, I'm writing a piece on DCI Radley for the *Examiner*. I'm aware that Vogel's appealing to have his conviction overturned.

Supposedly Radley framed him with false evidence. Do you think he could have done?'

Erin and Lewis looked at each other.

'We'll be off now.'

Erin pulled on her coat while Lewis downed the last dregs of his coffee.

The reporter was already backing up so she could walk with them as they headed out.

'I just want to give you the chance to clear things up on your side. Especially you, DI Crane. You were on the case. What do you think? Could Radley have planted that ribbon and framed Alan Vogel?'

The question shot through her. She threw the journalist a vicious look over her shoulder on the way out, and was disturbed by the way the woman's eyes lit up with satisfaction, as if that had been her end goal all along – provoking a reaction.

In the car, they were quiet. Erin wanted to say something to reassure Lewis, but her mind was blank. The woman's sudden appearance had shaken her and now she felt pain building in her chest as her heart beat faster.

Vogel again, always Vogel. What was it going to take to make this go away?

29

THEY FOUND HER IN THE garden. The receptionist let them out through the back door onto the patio, where Maia was smoking at a blue-green table near an apple tree. When Erin said her name, she turned around.

'How are you, Maia?'

Maia was far more apprehensive to see them than Megan had been. Her eyes went wide, darting between Erin and Lewis.

'This is Lewis. My partner.' Out of the corner of her vision, Erin saw him raise his hand jovially.

The chair legs made a horrible scraping sound against the patio as Maia, extinguishing her cigarette in the ashtray, started getting up.

'I know you want to help, Maia. And we know what's stopping you,' said Erin.

But Maia was crossing the patio, heading back to the house.

Last chance. Urgently, Erin said, 'Another woman's come forward. He did it to her too, Maia. She's willing to give us a statement. You wouldn't be alone.'

Maia opened the back door.

'But this other woman, she can't remember her attacker. She doesn't know who did it. You're the only one.'

Just as Maia was about to step inside, she went still. Her head was bowed.

'No one on our team knows about this,' said Lewis. 'No one's going to know about it until you say so. It'll just be us, talking.'

After a long pause, Maia lifted her head. She peered around the garden, as though someone might be lurking there amongst the hedges. Then she looked at them.

'Not here,' she said.

They went to the local church, where there was less chance of being overheard by someone at the housing association. Maia looked out over the graveyard, wrapped up tightly in her coat like she was ill. It was nearly October and the wind was pushing rust-coloured leaves over the graves. She and Erin sat together on a wrought-iron bench that was nestled underneath a deep bramble bush, protected from the wind, while Lewis crouched in front of them on the balls of his feet.

'Take your time,' said Erin.

A crow dropped down in front of them, fluttered its wings, and hopped over the graves, looking for worms. Maia stared straight ahead, deep in thought.

'He dressed well. Professionally. He looked like he took care of himself. And he was new to this. You can always tell when they're new. They're more polite.'

The wind swept through the trees with a sound like the crashing of waves. Erin didn't dare move.

'At first I thought, this one's not going to be so bad. We were just drinking and talking. And then the room started to spin. I don't remember what happened after that. I woke up in hospital.

'The police took me to the station for an interview. And he was there. And then I worked out what he was.

'He found a moment to talk to me when no one was around. I couldn't move. Couldn't speak. He said he'd taken photos of me while I was drugged. Naked. He said, if I tried to identify him, he would send them to my family and tell them I did sex work. And if that wasn't enough to convince me, then he would kill me.'

Erin couldn't breathe.

'So I said nothing. I kept quiet. But even then... I don't know if it was him or the other officers. But even though I kept quiet, a group of officers came by a few weeks later and told me I was under arrest. There was no one that could help me. Suddenly I was in court, and then I was in prison. My whole life had changed.'

'Would you be willing to identify him now?'

Maia said nothing. Erin felt like she was holding thin glass in her hand that could break and cut her at any moment.

'You can't protect me.'

'We can—'

'No. You can't. I'm not an idiot.'

'We're not working with anyone else on this, Maia. No one else on the force knows we're here.'

Maia breathed in shakily through her nose. Her hand clenched and unclenched in her lap.

'You don't have to make a decision right now.' Lewis's eyebrows were knitted together with sympathy. Erin felt a surge of warmth for him; he was good at this. 'Just as long as you know we're here and ready to listen. Either of us. Anytime, seriously. We're on call.'

Maia nodded, not looking at either of them. Erin realised how vulnerable this must have made her feel. They shouldn't push her too far.

But they were close now. Very close. She felt grateful that Maia walked ahead of them on the way back so she couldn't see how much her legs were shaking.

She went in search of Walker the next day. He was right; she needed to be completely open with him from now on. She had no intention of leaving him in the dark about what Maia had told them.

Walker was in a meeting room with someone, talking urgently. Instead of knocking, she found herself listening in just outside the door.

'I understand where you're coming from. Completely understand.'

Walker always sounded gentler and more reasonable when he spoke to someone senior. He continued: 'If we need more evidence, then I'm more than happy to keep building the case even after we've charged him.'

Who was he talking to? Peters?

'The report you've filed does not contain enough evidence to justify us contacting the CPS,' said a weary voice.

Erin recognised that voice. It was the investigator from the IOPC. Walker was trying to get them to charge Tom.

'We're still looking. We'll get it. Crane's doing a good job. We're coming at this from all angles.' Erin imagined Walker widening his gait and holding his hands up. 'Look, with the Maia Andrei case as well—'

'The link isn't strong enough, Walker.'

'That's not the only one. There's also Annie Dodds' case.'

Erin could hear her own shallow breathing.

'You're not seriously saying you believe Alan Vogel's claim that Radley could have framed him?'

'That's absolutely what I believe.'

Erin pressed her side against the wall. Since when had Walker thought that? Was it since she'd agreed to work with him? Had he decided it couldn't have been her?

There was a moment of silence.

'I worry that this has become personal for you,' said the investigator from the IOPC.

'Personal? There are a thousand things I would rather be doing than this. Quite frankly, I'd rather be wading through some lousy domestic case than this.'

'Until you find any forensic evidence that links Tom Radley to Sophie Madson's murder, I cannot recommend the CPS charges him.'

She heard the scrape of chair legs on the floor. They were coming out. Erin retreated down the corridor and stood around the corner.

She almost jumped out of her skin when Walker appeared round the corner a moment later. He looked her up and down.

'Crane. Didn't expect to see you there.'

Before she could say anything, he said, 'Any progress on Maia?'

Suddenly she didn't want to say.

'No.'

'That's a shame.'

They walked into the main office together. In that moment, she knew what she needed to do.

She said, 'There is something else we're looking into.'

'Oh yeah?'

'We think we know where the killer's buying Xanax from. We're going there tomorrow. If he's been there recently, there might be evidence. Shoe prints, that kind of thing.'

Walker stared at her. Erin searched his eyes for any sign of panic. But she found nothing.

'By yourselves?' said Walker. 'Do you feel comfortable doing that alone?'

'It's just to check the area. We don't need to bring SOCOs in unless we find something.'

'And what time is this?'

'First thing tomorrow.'

Walker studied her for a moment, then said, 'Alright. Give me a run-down afterwards,' and left.

She walked over to where Lewis was sat. Once Walker was out of earshot, Lewis leant in urgently. 'Are you talking about that warehouse Megan mentioned? Do we really need to go? And why tell Walker?'

'After work, you and I need to get in the car. I want to test something.'

She watched Walker stride across the office. She couldn't help wondering if he was silently panicking, working out the quickest route to the warehouse from here.

30

THE DARKNESS WAS CLOSING IN as they drove through the outskirts of Wakestead, in the direction of the warehouse. It was quiet here. There was no lighting down these streets apart from that which spilled out from people's houses. Pockets of light revealed a family having dinner together; a man exercising; a flat-screen TV bouncing muted colours around someone's living room. Gradually, the snapshots into people's lives disappeared. The houses became cold and empty; some of the windows were smashed or boarded up.

They parked down a small road beside the warehouse, with a view out onto the main road in front.

'This feels like a long shot,' said Lewis. 'What if he comes in the morning?'

'I said we'd be here first thing. If he wants to check the area, he'll come tonight.'

They turned the engine off so Walker wouldn't notice Erin's car lying in wait down the street. As the night drew in and the conversation died, it started to feel like they were huddled inside a freezing metal cage. Next to her, Lewis breathed warm air into his hands and rubbed them together.

Then a beam of ghostly light stretched across the road in front of them. A car's headlights. Erin's heart raced as the vehicle slid into view before promptly disappearing behind the wall of the warehouse. She stared at Lewis. They listened in total silence as the growl of its engine came to a halt. Whoever it was had parked just round the corner.

Lewis zipped up his coat and pulled up the hood. The two coats he wore didn't just provide protection against the cold – they also obscured his silhouette to anyone who might recognise him.

'Try and get as close as you can without being seen.'

'Got it,' he said, opening the car door. Erin watched him slink off down the road.

The next fifteen minutes were excruciating. She imagined Lewis reappearing with shaky legs and his hands clutching his chest, something dark dripping onto the pavement.

Finally Lewis shot round the corner. Erin stretched herself across the passenger seat and opened the car door. He bundled inside, out of breath.

'Did you see him?' she asked.

He got out his phone.

'Someone was in there alright.'

He scrolled through the photos he'd taken. Apart from the faint outline of some floorboards, caught in the fuzzy silver beam of someone's torch, all Erin could see was a sea of blacks and greys.

'Can't see a thing.'

'I don't know why I bothered, I thought just in case. Anyway I could hear him walking around. Sounded like he was wearing good shoes, smart shoes, you know. And it sounded like he was looking for something. I waited until he came out. But I'm sorry, I had to back up down a street, or he'd have seen me.'

'Did you catch the registration number?'

'No. But get this. I heard a police radio.'

Erin almost dropped Lewis's phone returning it to him; her hands had gone numb.

'You didn't tell Walker exactly where we were going, did you?'

She shook her head.

'It must have been him,' said Lewis, out of breath. 'We didn't tell anyone else that plan.'

Erin's heart pounded.

'Which means—' she began.

She couldn't bring herself to say it. Lewis finished her sentence for her:

'Which means it couldn't have been Tom.'

She paced around her living room. The journey home from the warehouse had frozen her toes to lumps of ice, but she didn't want to cuddle up under the covers. She wanted to keep moving.

There was condensation on the windows and her temple was throbbing. Itching to keep her hands busy, she retrieved the bottle of vodka from her bookshelf and poured herself a shot, which left a burning trail all the way down her throat. Then she sat next to the window, letting the alcohol's warmth spread through her.

The sheer certainty in Lewis's voice had sounded heavenly. Erin could have sat there listening to him repeat that phrase all night. It couldn't have been Tom. Tension lifted from her shoulders as she remembered the image of Lewis looking blissfully relieved, gripping the roots of his hair.

'We knew it, didn't we? We knew it wasn't him.'

Erin had felt weightless, like she might float off the car seat and through the ceiling at any moment. She had to really focus to pull herself back down to earth. 'Hang on a minute, just hang on. Whoever was here tonight was probably the one who attacked Megan.'

'So it's him.'

'But that doesn't mean it's Sophie's killer. We still don't know they're the same person.'

'Erin, come on. A young girl. Xanax. Someone in a position of control the victim couldn't name. It's him. It's the same guy.'

She sucked in air through her teeth. 'I bet it was Walker. Bet you anything. We need to just hope Maia does come forward and name him.'

'Walker still thinks we're going after Tom now, right?'

'Yeah.'

'Is there any chance he's going to go after Maia? Try and keep her quiet.'

'I reckon there is. Just in case, we can't tell him we're waiting for a call for her. We'll tell him she said she's not speaking to us.'

After that, they'd sat in silence for a few moments. Lewis reached out and gave her a brotherly shake of her shoulder. She put her hand over his.

Now, as she sat by the window, she thought how badly wanted to call Tom. She felt the need like a physical ache. She studied the ceiling, turned red by the refracting light of her bedside lamp. A memory hit her. Of the first time they'd had sex at her place. They'd ended up at the end of the bed, so the slanting sky light was above them and they could see themselves reflected in the black night, all bare skin and bitten lips. The wiry outline of golden ghosts. 'You look so good,' Tom had said into her neck. A needle of pleasure slid into Erin's spine, pinching her shoulders in. What she wanted. It was close now. She could almost reach out and grab it.

Someone had the washing on. She could hear the washing machine's gentle spin vibrating through the walls. An arc of light stretched around the walls as a car drove past outside.

She slid open the window and stretched her body to smoke out into the night. The nicotine gave her an intoxicating rush to the head.

She needed sleep. She might actually get some tonight. After she'd finished her cigarette, she took her plate through to the kitchen and started washing up in the sink.

The light in the room shifted. Erin looked up. The motion-sensor lights outside the front door had switched on. She could see the fluorescent glow across the mottled glass. She left the kitchen and went to the front door.

Nothing. No neighbour fumbling with the keys to their house. It must have been a cat, Erin told herself. But her heart was racing. She thought of Walker in that warehouse, searching through the darkness.

She stayed there, every muscle in her body straining as she listened out. She could hear the sounds of the town. The late-night shouting of errant teenagers. The low drone of cars moving around corners. She was about to go back inside when she heard the distant echo of a door opening and closing somewhere down the street.

She walked forward and leant over the fence. There was no one there.

31

Tom

TOM WATCHED ONE OF THE forensic team lift a woman's tights off the floor, dangling it in the air like an eel by his gloved hand, before cautiously lowering it into an evidence bag.

When he thought of prostitution, Tom pictured two extremes of the spectrum: high-end escorts – chandeliers and cocktail parties and private jets – or hollow-eyed women in dingy stairwells, with men who belonged to a dark criminal underworld circling nearby like guard-dogs. This very ordinary-looking house on Church Road, families next door, a pot plant clinging to life on the windowsill of the bedroom, Hello Kitty pillows on the bed, was not what he had imagined. It wasn't much, but it was someone's home. And last night someone had turned this home into a living nightmare.

Studying Maia Andrei's bed, Kapil put his hands in his pockets. 'His DNA should be all over this, right?' he said to the CSI in the doorway.

The CSI said, 'Sure. But so will the DNA of about ten other clients. You'll have a lot of suspects to eliminate. If we can work out exactly what he touched that will make this much easier.'

'OK. We'll ask the victim if there's anything she can identify.'

The CSI left. Tom stared at the back of Kapil's head as he surveyed the busybodies dusting surfaces for prints. No matter how much he tried to relax and focus on the case at hand, there was one thought that kept rising to the forefront of his mind, unignorable: it should have been him leading this.

*

Walker sighed loudly and coughed into the back of his hand. Maia flinched at the sound.

Reading the incident report, Walker scratched behind his ear. 'So what can you tell us about him?'

Maia's face paled. She said nothing.

'We don't have all day. Do you know the kinds of cases we have to put on hold when something like this comes up?'

Maia said, 'It's hard to remember.'

'Right. So what do you remember?'

Maia didn't say anything.

Walker blinked slowly, as if he was speaking to someone very stupid. 'I mean, you must have got a good look at him.'

Maia swallowed. Still she said nothing.

'It's just obviously, without a statement from you, it's going to be very hard for us to find him,' said Walker.

'I'm sorry. I don't know what to tell you.'

'Right. OK.' Walker looked around the room and shrugged. 'Well, this has been a waste of time, hasn't it? You're free to go.'

For a moment, Maia looked stunned. Then she shakily got to her feet and left the room.

Tom couldn't believe what had just happened. Walker was already gathering up his papers.

'Just like that? Shouldn't we have pressed her for more information? We didn't even ask what he touched in the room.'

'You heard her. She doesn't remember.'

'What about the Xanax? They must have got it from somewhere. We could ask the dealers if they know anything.'

Walker blew a raspberry. 'You want to kill yourself investigating something like this, be my guest, Radley. We don't even know for sure this guy spiked her. Maybe she took the Xanax herself, who knows.'

Walker's chair legs scraped against the hard floor as he stood up, getting ready to leave.

'Some women, honestly. If you don't want to end up in these situations, maybe don't do sex work?'

THE BLAME

*

Tom yawned into the back of his hand and looked at his watch. 6:42 p.m. By now, most of the force had gone home to their wives and families. There was no one around apart from a few seniors at the other end of the office as he turned on the kettle, made himself a tea and settled in at his desk, ready for at least another hour's work.

He wasn't usually in this late and it was especially depressing. The lights kept going out, so you had to stand up and wave your hands about like an idiot to restart them, and without the throng of bodies, the almost-empty office was like a giant refrigerator. But this was the only way. If he was going to investigate the case by himself, without proper backing from the super, he needed to do it out-of-hours, when no one was looking.

Taking a sip of tea and pulling his coat over his shoulders – it really was completely freezing in here – he looked up Maia's entry in the database and re-read her incident report. Walker and Manek were wrong to give up on her so easily. Even if she didn't press charges, didn't they have a duty to find out who did this? To dig a bit deeper than a five-minute interview with her? There had to be something they could find.

It had been a week since they had searched Maia's house, and there was very little to go on. There were no CCTV cameras down Church Road, so they had no hope of catching this guy on camera. And the forensic report that had arrived today showed that no traces of DNA were found on her body. As well as using a condom – and maybe gloves as well – they must have cleaned up afterwards, with Maia lying there. Whoever had attacked her had thought ahead.

Then he noticed something that caught his eye. Someone had looked up Maia's entry in the database. The detective's ID was logged above his in the bottom-right hand corner of the screen, marking their visit to this page just a few hours earlier.

Tom squinted at the name.

That was weird.

Why had this person wanted to look up Maia Andrei's details? They hadn't seemed interested before.

32

IN THE WAREHOUSE, THE FLOORBOARDS beneath their feet were green with moss. Above their heads, the slanting, rain-streaked windows opened up onto an expanse of overcast sky.

Together, Erin and Lewis circled the derelict space, taking photographs on their phones. The warehouse was almost completely empty apart from a pile of ash and a few beer bottles in one corner, where a group of teenagers must have drank the night away huddled in here like stowaways.

Later, when they showed Shergill the photos, he looked thoroughly underwhelmed. 'And why do you want a camera in this place?'

'It's hard to explain. But it's possible Sophie's killer might be meeting a dealer there.'

Shergill raised his eyebrows. 'I'll get someone down there as soon as possible.' Just as they were about to leave, he asked, 'Has Walker been alright with you lately?'

Erin's body tensed. 'Why?'

He shook his head. 'Nothing huge. It's just he asked if he could have a look through Sophie's laptop, as well as the burner phone.' In a resentful tone, he added, 'The implication seemed to be that you or I might have missed something.'

'What was he looking for?'

Shergill shrugged. 'He wouldn't say.'

As soon as they left Shergill's office and were walking down the corridor together, Lewis leant in. 'Missed something?' he whispered urgently. 'What's he up to?'

'I don't know. But he's trying to find out what we have on him. Do you know what that tells me?'

'What?'

She bit her lip. 'He knows we suspect him.'

'How would we have worked that out?'

'I don't know. But we need to take another look at what we've got. See if we can work out what he's looking for.

Inside the evidence room there were three cardboard boxes, each one filled to the brim with Sophie's belongings. Digging through the half-filled diaries, the schoolbooks, the clothes she was wearing the day she went missing, Erin was horribly reminded of how little progress they'd made since the hope-filled days at the start of the case. Weeks had passed and, instead of being returned to her parents, this stuff was still here, left to accumulate dust in the dimly lit evidence room of the Wakestead police force.

Next to her, Lewis pulled one box towards him, removed the burner phone from its plastic bag and started glumly clicking through it. She held in a sigh of exasperation. This was starting to feel like a massive waste of time.

'Maybe there was something in here we missed,' she said. 'Maybe Walker's already taken it.'

But then Lewis's hand froze.

'Wait a second.'

He peered closely at the phone before thrusting it in her face. The photo of Sophie naked was up on the screen. Erin looked between the photo and Lewis's gleeful expression and felt confused.

'I don't understand.'

'Look at it.'

'What?'

'The reflection.'

Erin was getting impatient now. 'What are you on about?' She didn't want to look at that violating image for a second longer. 'Lewis, that's grim—'

Then she saw it. The photograph showed Sophie on a white bed. Visible in the lower corner was a section of dark wooden flooring. If you looked closer, you could see the ghostly outline of someone's hand, curled around a phone.

Lewis said: 'She didn't get sent this. She took a photo of it.'

Erin's head spun. 'I don't get it.'

Lewis bit his lip. 'We know he blackmailed Maia with a photograph. But maybe he didn't mean for Sophie to see this. Maybe she found this in his house.'

'So what?' She felt irritated that she wasn't experiencing whatever epiphany had made Lewis's face light up.

'So she's taken a photo because she knows it's evidence. So maybe there's something in this she thought would help us.'

Erin looked closer at the faint shape of Sophie reflected in the photo. 'There isn't though. Nothing to help us identify the room she was in. If she had the opportunity to take other photos, maybe we would have more to—'

Then it hit her.

The tussle with Fraser. The yellow handbag splitting open.

'Wait. Those papers. The ones Fraser saw her picking up.'

Lewis's eyes went wide. 'She did have evidence. She was taking it to Tom. Why else would she have brought them with her that day?'

'Why not show it to him though? As proof she was telling the truth.'

'Maybe she still wasn't sure if she could trust him?' Lewis frowned. 'I'm more confused by why she wouldn't just have the evidence on her phone.'

'That I don't get. Maybe she felt more secure having physical copies of whatever these papers were. But I think there's something here. If he knew she had evidence, that would have given him a motive to kill her.'

Lewis reached up, running his hands through his hair in frustration. 'But none of this even matters, Erin. We don't have the copies.'

Erin's mind raced. They were so close. There had to be a way to get those papers, or at least find some trace of them—

Then she realised.

'Printers must keep a memory of documents, right? Her family's printer. Maybe they're still stored there.'

'Shit. In her house. This whole time.'

Her heart was pounding. 'Let's not get too excited. Maybe printers delete their memory after a certain point, I have no idea. But let's get SOCOs over either way.'

A shadow moved across the room. Her blood went cold as she realised that it must have been a figure through the square window in the door. She spun around and wrenched the door open. One of the probationers poked their head around the corner, looking cowed. 'It's Peters. He wants to speak to you both.'

Peters pushed an open newspaper across his desk. The headline leapt out at Erin in angry black lettering:

Has DCI Radley killed before?

Erin heard Lewis breathe in sharply beside her.

'Go on, have a read,' said Peters.

Tom Radley, the detective arrested in connection with Sophie Madson's murder, has been accused of planting evidence to incriminate Alan Vogel, who was sentenced earlier this year for the killing of school girl Annie Dodds eight years ago. Mr Vogel has always claimed to be innocent.

Peters said, 'Vogel's appeal isn't going away. Now the press have cottoned on. I hope I don't need to explain to you how bad this looks. Not one but two abuses of power. Under our watch.'

'He didn't frame him,' said Erin. 'He didn't.'

'Is that just a gut feeling? Or do you actually have evidence?'

Heat rose in Erin's face. 'I was there. He didn't do it.'

'I need something more concrete than that, Crane.' He jabbed at the page with a thick finger. 'Because this. I want this gone. Whether he did it or not, I want the truth to come out.'

Erin opened her mouth to say something but he was already turning away and picking up the phone to make a call; he was done with them. A wave of nausea swept over her as they emerged from Peters' office and headed down the corridor.

After a long silence, Lewis said, 'You never linked Vogel to the scene of the crime, did you?'

'The ribbon was missing from the scene of the crime. So yes we did.'

'Look, I know you found Annie's DNA in his house, along with the ribbon. But you never found any of his on her, right? I guess I just wondered… How do you know he's not telling the truth?'

Erin looked out of the window, at the silent storm of yellow leaves tearing from their branches.

'I just know.'

The prison officer let Erin inside the cell, gave one warning look to the inmate, and then closed the door behind him, leaving the two of them alone.

'Detective. Nice of you to visit.'

Vogel sat on the thin mattress of his bunk, weighty, toadlike. So she wouldn't have to look at him, Erin crossed the narrow cell and stood beside the tiny, barred window. A draft crept in through a gap between the wall and the window frame. The smell of damp was so overpowering Erin worried it would seep through her clothes.

'They tell me you're appealing the conviction, Vogel.'

He scratched his left arm through the sleeve of his grey tracksuit. 'I am.'

'DCI Radley had nothing to do with that ribbon turning up in your house. You and I both know that.'

'I don't know how that ribbon got there, detective. Someone put it there. And now I find out that one of the detectives who investigated my case has abused his position? What am I supposed to think?'

She looked out of the barred window, onto the grey quadrangle where some of the prisoners were playing football.

'DCI Radley hasn't been charged yet.'

'Well, I'm not waiting about until he is. I'm not spending the rest of my life here. The conditions in here are unacceptable.'

She remembered his house. The smell of dog food. The overgrown rose bush blocking out the daylight. Her jaw clenched. He still felt sorry for himself. After what he'd done.

She pulled up the metal chair out from under the desk and sat facing him. Only now did she get a proper look at him. The long eyebrow hairs curving down over the stupid eyes, still not getting it, even now.

'You're going to withdraw this appeal,' she said.

'I am not.'

'You're going to withdraw it because even if you're cleared of Annie Dodds' murder, you'll be convicted of historic child abuse. For which you're likely to receive a life sentence. The same as what you're serving now, Vogel. So it makes no difference.'

'Historic child abuse? What are you talking about?'

And here it was. The moment she'd been waiting for all this time. The sense of claustrophobia dissipated. Instead, every breath seemed to send a charge through her blood, heady and intoxicating.

'I've always wondered,' she said, 'is it that there were so many of them that you don't remember what they looked like… or has my face really changed that much?'

At first, his expression twitched with confusion. Then she saw him get it. His mouth opened.

She couldn't stop now. The moment was here and the rage was exhilarating.

'I suppose it would help if I looked more like my mum, wouldn't it? Dad's genes won out there, unfortunately. But Mum's face I bet you'd recognise. After the months you spent sat next to her on that sofa. Worming your way in.'

His mouth was moving soundlessly like a goldfish's. She could see how badly he wanted to buzz in the prison officer. Call for help. But there was nothing he could do.

Erin leant forward. Her face felt tight with anger.

'You're here because I put you here. You're staying because I want you to stay here. Try to leave, and a whole new nightmare will start for you.'

Never in her life had she felt more grateful to escape from somewhere. She wished the officer accompanying her would hurry up as he led her down the hallways of the prison, pausing to unlock each gate that blocked their way. Every step closer to the exit was a step away from Vogel and all the misery and pain he represented. She'd done it; it was over.

By the time she'd parked up at the bottom of her street, it was pitch black. She walked home, taking deep lungfuls of night air, trying to shake off the memory of Vogel's cold, damp room.

She only realised something was wrong when she noticed her shadow – a long, alien figure revealed by the harsh white of someone's headlights. She glanced over her shoulder. There was a car some way down the street. It was impossible to make out the driver. She turned back, trying to ignore her creeping sense of fear. But in the back of her mind, it occurred to her that the car was way below the speed limit, crawling along, almost like its driver was deliberately keeping their distance. Like they didn't want to be seen.

The growl of the car grew momentarily louder and then shrank away. She looked back again. It was out of view.

This was stupid. She tried to concentrate on her breathing.

Then she heard the sound again. Wheels rolling over the gravel. Should she look around? No. They'd know then that she'd clocked them.

There was a traffic mirror at the end of the road. From there, she might be able to see the car behind her. Perhaps even a registration number.

There it was, reflected in the dark mirror. A car sharking down one street and out of frame. She saw the bonnet bounce as the car rolled over a speed bump. Then it was gone. For just a moment she'd seen the silhouette of a man inside.

It was hard to tell in the darkness. But she was convinced she'd seen the metallic glint of Walker's car in the gloom.

33

THE NEXT MORNING, ERIN FOUND an empty meeting room and booted up her laptop. In the car park she had taken down Walker's vehicle registration number in her phone. Now she plugged the number into the NADC. She tapped her fingers anxiously against the surface of the laptop as the results loaded up.

Nothing. The database showed he had been captured on various CCTV cameras last night driving to and from work. But none of them were en route to the prison. And another search showed there were few cameras in her neighbourhood. So if he had been following her, she had no way of knowing. The same was true of the area around the warehouse. No cameras.

She stared at the white wall opposite her as the blood rushed around her head.

Lewis was pacing the interview room in agitation.

'She'll be here,' she said. 'It's only been fifteen minutes.'

Lewis checked his watch pointedly. 'Twenty now. What if she's having second thoughts?'

'She'll be here any moment.'

Erin hoped she sounded more confident that she felt. Every minute they spent in this nether zone seemed to stretch on for an age.

Suddenly her phone started ringing. Lewis whipped around like he'd heard a gunshot.

'I'm sorry,' came Maia's voice. 'I can't do it.'

Shit. Shit shit shit. The emotions crashing over her must have been all over her face, because Lewis shook his head in disbelief and put his head in his hands.

'If you need more time, Maia, that's absolutely fine. We can give you that.'

'I'm really sorry.'

Instinctively, she got up out of her chair. 'Maia, please tell me,' she said, 'did someone speak to you? Did he threaten you?'

The line cut out.

The receptionist who'd first shown Erin around the housing association stood wedged in the doorway, blocking their way in. Erin had to fight the urge to push past them and run down the corridor to Maia's room. Maia was so close. Just right there.

'She's already spoken with one of your colleagues. An officer stopped by yesterday.'

Erin and Lewis looked at each other.

'What was their name? The officer she spoke to?'

'I noted it down somewhere.' The staff member reached into her pocket for her phone and read something off the screen. 'There you go. Walker. DSU Walker.'

34

Lewis and Erin walked at pace down the corridor, towards the main office.

'Surely we can use this against him,' Lewis said. 'He's interfering with our case.'

Erin nodded. 'Let's get this all together in a report. The phone call Maia made to me. The staff member at the housing association who saw him. With this maybe we can get him knocked off Tom's case—'

The sound of a door clicking open made her jump. Turning around, she saw Adlington stood in the doorway to his office, grim-faced.

'Erin. A word.'

She exchanged a helpless look with Lewis.

'Can it wait?'

But he was always disappearing back into the room.

In his office, Adlington pulled out a chair for her. The sound of its legs scraping against the floor made her flinch. Reluctantly, she took the seat.

Not this. Not now. What she needed was to knuckle down with Lewis and plan their next move. They couldn't afford distractions like this.

Adlington looked tired. He wiped a hand over his face, then squinted at her through his glasses as though it was a struggle to keep his eyes open.

'Peters is getting jumpy,' he said. 'I need you to tell me where we are.'

'We're close,' she said.

He gave a huff of bitter laughter. 'Right. Well, that's good to hear. Who's your main suspect?'

She was surprised to realise that, for the first time, she wasn't sure she could trust Adlington. There was a probing tone to his voice that made her feel uncomfortable. The room felt claustrophobic; the walls too close and the overhead lights too bright.

'They're still nameless,' she said. 'But we think they may be responsible for a pattern of abuse over the years.'

'That doesn't sound like you're close.'

She squeezed the bones in her hands. 'It just needs time.'

'I know that,' he said. 'But you need to give us more. You're keeping us out of the loop. People are starting to notice.'

She was suddenly aware of the bowed heads in the main office, through the window. Under her collar, her skin burned. *People are starting to notice.* Adlington didn't know the half of it.

'A car followed me last night,' she said.

'Probably the press.'

'Maybe,' she said. 'Except they were just following. They didn't try to speak to me and they didn't get close enough to get a shot.'

He didn't say anything.

After a moment, she said, 'Looked like Walker's. If you ask me.'

She couldn't believe she'd said it out loud. She waited for Adlington to respond, holding her breath.

Adlington narrowed his eyes at her. 'Be careful, Erin.'

'He's following us. Everywhere I look, he's over my shoulder.'

'He micromanages—'

'This isn't fucking micromanaging. He's following us. He spoke privately with one of my interviewees. And then they cancelled my interview.'

Adlington grimaced. 'You think he was deliberately obstructive.'

'Yes.'

215

'And why would he be?'

'Because he's scared about what I'm going to find out.'

Adlington's face darkened.

'Walker has been voicing his concerns about you.'

'Of course he has.'

'Concerns that you're too emotionally involved—'

'No, no, listen,' said Erin. 'All this bullshit that he's pulling. He killed Sophie. He discredited Tom. And now he's trying to do the same to me.' She had to stop for a second to catch her breath. The words were spilling out of her as the paranoia she'd felt over the last few days came rushing in. 'Because he wants me to snap. Because that's what he needs. He needs you to think I'm fucking insane so they'll kick me off.'

'I know who Walker is. I've worked with him for years. You don't know him.'

'Yes, I do—'

'No, Erin. You don't.' He looked her up and down; the feeling of being scanned, analysed, made Erin grit her teeth. 'Are you eating OK? Sleeping OK?'

'It's not relevant,' she hissed.

'Of course it's relevant.' He was rubbing his eyes under his glasses, speaking quietly. 'It's all relevant. It's all so depressingly relevant.'

Looking defeated, he got to his feet. Before he left the room, he looked at her. 'If you go down this road,' he said. 'I will not vouch for you again. You are on thin ice.'

The lighter trembled in her hands as she held it up to her lips. She couldn't let Lewis see her like this. She needed to calm down. She looked round at the concrete pillars of the car park, relishing the emptiness of the space. Just as she drew in that first, relieving breath of cigarette smoke, the stairwell door opened.

Walker approached, hands in his pockets.

'Nasty habit, that, Crane. You ought to quit.'

She'd inhaled the wrong way when she saw him. The smoke burned in her nose. 'What do you want?'

'I've realised something.' He fixed her with a blue stare. 'I worked out a theory the other day. About why women don't commit as many murders as men.'

Her pulse drummed in her ears. 'Oh yeah?'

'When men go off their rocker, they're quiet about it. They keep to themselves. They hide away from the world. Until the day comes when they snap, and they smash a hammer into the back of someone's head. Their problem is they've stopped caring. They've dropped out of society. But you don't see that with women.'

'I guess not.'

'Women, they don't stop caring. My guess is they're more socialised. Even when they've lost it, they still want attention. So when they lose their marbles, they meddle.'

There was a little glint in his eye. Erin's pulse raced. Had he seen her look up his registration number? Was that possible?

She took a drag on her cigarette and exhaled, trying to look bored. 'What's this about?'

He leant in, lowering his voice. 'I found that bullshit spreadsheet you and Jennings made. Clocking who was where on the day Sophie Madson disappeared.' He smiled. 'What's your problem, Crane? Do you really hate us all that much?'

She brought her cigarette down. She didn't want him to see that her hand was shaking.

'I expect you both thought you were being very subtle.'

This was it. She'd been waiting for this moment and here it was.

'I've got something I'd like you to explain, as it happens.'

His eyelid twitched for a second. 'Go ahead.'

She reached into her jacket pocket and pulled out her phone. At the housing association, she'd asked to see the footage from the security camera just outside the building. The screenshot showed Walker heading up to the front door.

He was concentrating on keeping his face blank, but she saw it – a shadow in the eyes, a movement of muscle in his cheek, as he recognised himself in the photo. He looked at her and grinned through it.

'You can confirm that this is a photo of you heading into the housing association, where you spoke to Maia Andrei right before she cancelled my interview?'

'Don't you take that tone with me, sweetheart,' he sneered. 'You've got eyes. You don't need me to confirm it for you.'

'And what did you say to her?'

He straightened up, rolling his shoulders under his jacket. 'You weren't taking control of the situation, Crane. I urged her to come forward. Admittedly, I may have come down a little strong. I didn't know you had an interview with Maia, you see. Otherwise, I might not have taken the step I did. That's what happens when you sneak around. When you don't share information with your co-workers.'

'Is that why you asked Shergill if you could go through Sophie's laptop?'

Walker's eyes were locked onto hers. 'You think very carefully about what you're about to say to me,' he said.

The air around them was acrid with cigarette smoke.

The drooping rim of his eye gleamed red. 'You going to say it?'

She kept staring at him for a moment. Then she turned her head away, taking another drag on her cigarette.

'No,' he said. 'Thought not.'

She couldn't take any more of this. She turned away. Then she felt Walker grab her by the shoulder.

'You're loving this, aren't you?'

His eyes were narrowed to vicious slits.

'All your pride. All your arrogance, your reclusiveness. This is what you've always wanted, isn't it? An excuse to turn against your own team.'

He was still holding onto her shoulder. She tried to push him off but he only gripped tighter.

'Still struggling to see what he really is, aren't you?' He smiled nastily. 'You think I don't know what's been going on? You're a smart woman, Crane. But you've completely lost it. Radley's got you wound around his little finger like a loved-up schoolgirl.'

She couldn't believe he'd actually grabbed her. She tried to jerk herself free but he didn't let go. 'Get off me—'

'I'll tell you why I looked through Sophie's laptop. Because I don't believe for a second you'd tell me if you'd found anything about Radley there. So I had to look myself.' His fingers dug through her clothes. 'And do you know what? I found fuck all to do with Radley. But I did find something else that was very interesting... Annie Dodds. Sophie had Googled her. I'm not surprised the tech team overlooked it. Annie Dodds is a horror story and every teenager loves a horror story.'

She tugged her arm again, but Walker squeezed harder.

His face was pink and inches away from her. 'Except you know what was weird? The day she Googled Annie Dodds was the day before she died. So here's what I think. I think Radley must have discussed the case with her. Why, I don't know. But what I do know is it's too much of a coincidence to ignore. Maybe Radley told her Vogel was innocent. Bragged about putting him in prison. Then realised she knew too much.'

Erin had stopped struggling. Walker's blue eyes burned into her.

'He killed her to save his own skin, Crane. That's the awful fucking truth of it.'

She pushed him hard. Walker was grinning now. Without looking back, she tore through the fire exit and up the stairs with the blood roaring in her ears.

35

S HE CLOSED ALL THE BLINDS and sat on the edge of the bed with the lights down low, pressing her fingers over her eyes, sinking into the dark red. Somewhere in the distance, a dog started barking. The sound ripped through her.

She'd told Adlington she'd stay away, and, at the time, she'd meant it. They might check his phone record later down the line. They might even be watching his house right now. But she didn't care anymore. With the dog's barks echoing down the street and the heat from the radiators pressing in around her, she scrolled through her list of contacts, found Tom's name and hit call.

The dial tone seemed to ring out forever. The bookcase swam before her eyes as she waited, gripping the edge of the bed.

Just when she expected the dial tone to cut out, he picked up. She held her breath, waiting for him to say something. He didn't.

'I know we probably shouldn't be speaking,' she said.

Still nothing. Erin had a paranoid thought that it wasn't Tom who'd answered the phone, but Walker.

'Tom?'

'I'm here,' came his voice. 'What's happened?'

It was pathetic how quickly the heat climbed up her neck. His voice was low and clear and soft all at once. She wished she could fall into it.

'Can I see you?'

He did exactly what she'd been afraid he'd do – he hesitated. 'Erin—'

She couldn't even bear to let him continue and reject her out loud. 'Something's happened. I have to see you. Please, Tom, I have to see you tonight.'

Normally, the sound of her pleading voice would've filled her with self-hatred. But she was past that point.

'Alright,' he said. 'Do you remember where we spoke last month? By the river.'

'Yes.'

'Meet me there. Be careful no one follows you.'

Birdsong reached her from the riverbank as she emerged from the woods. There he was, walking down the path towards her. The undergrowth around them was completely dark. There was barely any light apart from the ghostlike blue of the river passing behind him. His face was in shadow.

'Has anyone followed you?'

'No.'

His eyes searched the trees behind her.

'They haven't, Tom.'

'Alright. This way.'

She followed Tom along the path until the riverbank flattened out. 'Watch your feet,' he said over his shoulder, just as Erin felt her boots sink slightly into the mud.

They were heading in the direction of a small boathouse. As Tom climbed up the steps, she peered underneath it. On the other side, the water lapped at the wooden stilts that raised the building out of the water.

'This is yours?'

'My family's. We used to come here when I was a kid. We had a boat that my dad would take out. The police don't know about it. We should be OK to talk here.'

There was a bed in the middle of the room, half-lit in a bedside lamp's fiery glow. She could see the cool silver river through the glass doors, which led onto a small balcony. A skylight in the ceiling cast a square of blue light onto the wall. On one side was a small kitchen unit where Tom shouldered off his satchel.

He didn't offer her a seat. Instead he pressed his back up against the wall by the kitchen units while she hovered in front of the closed door. His eyes studied her face.

'Someone's said something to you,' he said. 'Walker, I'm guessing.'

'He has a new theory.'

'About me?'

She nodded.

He glanced down angrily, jaw clenching. It made her grit her teeth.

'You can't keep reacting like that,' she said. 'You can't keep expecting me to be unaffected by these things.'

'Alright. What is it?'

She was suddenly finding it difficult to breathe. Her voice came out thin.

'Sophie Googled Annie Dodds' name the day before she died. Walker thinks she must have known something about the case. And that's why…'

Tom said nothing. His expression was grim.

'Did – did you already know what I'd done? Did you tell her? And did you worry she would—?'

The look of confusion on his face brought her a glimmer of hope.

'What? No. How does that link back to me at all? She was being abused, Erin. Maybe she wanted to see who in the force had actually put abusers in prison.' His eyes widened. 'Maybe that was how she found me. Maybe it was why she trusted me.' He shook his head in disbelief. 'I don't get it. Why's this got you worked up? Why did Walker—'

Then he worked it out. She saw the realisation in his eyes.

'You think I killed her to protect you,' he said.

Her skin burned underneath her clothes.

Tom looked out the window, at the water.

'I can see why you might believe that one. That's a nicer one. I prefer it too.'

She swallowed.

'Except I didn't know you'd planted that evidence until you told me, Erin. I didn't. Surely you could see that in how I reacted?'

He had a point. When she said nothing, he kept going.

'Even then... let's imagine I did know and that Walker's right and I did have a relationship with Sophie. Why would I be stupid enough to tell her my partner framed someone? And why would I then kill Sophie for knowing something I'd told her?'

He was right. The more she thought about it, the harder it became to picture the struggling. Lunging to throttle Sophie just because she knew something compromising about his partner. It didn't make sense.

Tom lowered himself into an armchair next to the kitchen and ran a hand through his hair. In a gentle voice, he said, 'It's not true, Erin. I didn't kill her.'

She breathed out for what felt like the first time in hours. 'Sorry, it's just – that one got to me.'

His hand was still in his hair and his legs were spread. He stared at the blue square of light on the wall, thinking. As she watched him, she thought how lonely he looked here. This small place must have been like a ghost house to him. *We had a boat that my dad would take out.* The image of a gangly sixteen-year-old Tom hanging out in this small retreat from the outside world made her feel warm inside. She wanted to fill in the gaps. She wanted to hear about the books read on the balcony while the river went past and the swims in the sweltering summer heat with pond weed tickling your feet and the nights spent laughing inside with your friends until two in the morning.

But the time when she'd have been able to ask him about the past felt far away now. He was damaged in a way he hadn't been before – or in a way he hadn't shown, at least. Maybe too much had happened for them to fall into the same rhythm as before.

'I've missed you,' she said finally.

The wrong thing to say. An understatement and overly sentimental; too much and too little at the same time.

He lifted his head and studied her. His eyes were tired.

'I don't want to hear it, Erin.'

He said it bluntly, with no satisfaction, just stating a fact. Erin looked back at him. She had utterly no idea what to say. Then he stared at the blue square on the wall again.

All she could manage was, 'I wish I could take it all back. I do.'

He glanced at her face and then at the floor. A moment of childlike vulnerability. It looked like he'd softened.

She pushed away from the wall and, as she closed the space between them, started taking off her shirt. A muscle in his jaw moved, but he didn't look up from the floor.

'I don't want you to – I don't want you to do that.'

She stopped. He still didn't look up. Her fingers trembled. She did the buttons back up. The rejection had knocked the air out of her lungs, like a blunt trauma to the chest.

'I'm sorry.'

She didn't know what to do. But she couldn't stay standing. She slowly sat on the floor in front of him.

His eyes kept slipping down her shirt. She knew he was imagining what she'd been doing before he'd stopped her.

'Do what you did before,' he said.

She started unbuttoning her shirt again. She heard him breathe in. He watched her fingers, eyes going hazy.

She knelt up to unbutton her jeans, then leant back to carefully pull them off. Her cheeks felt flushed with heat like she'd been drinking. When she was down to her underwear, she felt hyper-aware of the power of her own body. Its ability to transform them both. She leant back on her hands, and moved her feet apart across the bare floorboards.

Tom moved down, crawling. Erin felt a falling sensation. And everything else melted into nothing.

He fell asleep almost instantly afterwards. She could tell he was going to from the way he rolled on his back and pulled her towards him, like he was pulling up the sheets, and the way the arm holding her went as heavy as a dead weight. He must've been having bad nights. She moved closer and tried to fall asleep as well, but couldn't. The adrenaline was still singing through her body. Moving gently so as not to wake him, she looked around the room, at the shadows of the lamp casting shapes over the walls, at the unfamiliar ceiling, listening to the gentle sounds of the river outside.

Tom drew in a long intake of breath and moved his head on the pillow; not fully waking up, just stirring in his sleep. She touched his temple for a moment, feeling the soft skin there. Then she leant back against the headrest and imagined the dark water moving outside.

36

THE MOMENT SHE SAT DOWN at her desk the next morning, an email appeared in her inbox. It was Adlington, requesting a meeting in ten minutes' time. Any trace of calm she'd felt after spending the night with Tom vanished in an instant. *Walker*, she thought. He must have said something. But what? Burying her fear, she followed Adlington into an empty meeting room.

As soon as the door was shut, he placed one hand on the back of a chair, another in his pocket. He didn't look tired anymore. He looked furious. This was bad.

'I'm going to ask you something, and I need you to be honest with me,' he said. 'Have you or have you not been meeting privately with Tom?'

It felt like the seat had suddenly given way beneath her.

'Erin,' he said. 'Have you?'

'Where has this come from?'

'Someone gave us a tip-off. They claimed to have seen you and Tom meeting at a property by the river yesterday evening.'

'Who was it?'

'They chose to remain anonymous.'

'And who received the tip-off? Was it Walker?'

'That's not relevant.'

Harsh laughter escaped her. 'Jesus Christ. It was him. He followed me.'

'Meeting privately with Tom is exactly what I warned you about. I want a good explanation right now or I'm taking this to Peters.'

'I needed to know how he was.'

'That's not an excuse.'

'Adlington, think about it. Who would tip us off? If a reporter was following me, why wouldn't they publish this?'

'I don't know. Maybe someone actually has some integrity in this world? Or because you have a guardian angel looking out for you?' He stood up. 'This is your absolute last warning. Do not meet privately with Tom.'

Before leaving the room, he turned and said, 'This property. It belongs to Tom?'

She nodded reluctantly.

'Walker's going to search it.'

Erin felt a rush of panic. Search it? What did he expect to find there?

She was driving to the boathouse when her phone started ringing. Walker. Just seeing the name sent a shot of adrenaline through her. This couldn't be good.

She pulled over in a self-service station and called back. A man was filling up his Peugeot. The cars on the motorway flashed past against the backdrop of brambles and the silver sky.

'Crane. How are you doing?'

His voice was filled with self-satisfaction. This definitely wasn't good.

'What is it?'

'I thought you should be the first to know. We found a phone about twenty feet from Tom's boathouse. Smashed up. It's the same model as Sophie Madson's. Her actual phone, not another burner. The one we never found. Until now.'

The muffled roar of the motorway droned in her ears.

'I'm going back to the station now. When I get there, Tom's going to be waiting for me in that interview room. And I am going to personally charge him with the murder of Sophie Madson.'

The man had finished filling up his car. Its front door slammed shut. She watched the vehicle crawl away into the dark hedges.

'It's over, Crane.'

White-hot anger raced through her as she drove back to the station. This was why Walker had told her his theory about Vogel. Because he'd known she wouldn't be able to resist the urge to speak to Tom about it. He'd intended on following her. And she'd led him straight to the boathouse.

She ran all the way from her car into the office, ignoring the pain in her ribs, and, when she was there, opened the NADC on her laptop. If he'd followed her, this would prove it. Her head spun as she clicked on images of Walker's car captured on different CCTV cameras, trying to make sense of the routes he'd taken. She saw he'd driven to the boathouse an hour ago. She scrolled back further.

Her heart sank. He hadn't been picked up by any cameras in the window of time when she went to the boathouse with Tom. But that didn't make any sense. The leak couldn't have come from someone else. Could he have followed her on foot? Or perhaps – and the thought sent a shiver of electric fear over her back – he'd got someone else to do it for him.

She kept searching through the records. Finally she found something. A journey he'd made earlier that morning.

She grabbed her phone.

'Lewis,' she said when he picked up. 'I need you to get in your car right now.'

'What's going on?'

'I've texted you a postcode. I need you to go there and ask if they have CCTV. Check the footage from this morning between 8:15 and 8:30 a.m.'

There was the sound of breathing and rummaging around as Lewis typed it into Google. 'Huh? Why here?'

'8:15 and 8:30 a.m. If anything happens, call me.'

*

Erin was surprised to find herself alone in the observation room. She had expected Walker to summon the entire force to bear witness to this. But watching Walker pace back and forth in front of Tom, barely able to contain his excitement, she realised why he'd chosen to keep their interview discreet. He'd have all the time in the world to gloat in front of the team. There were things he wanted to say to Tom that could only be said in private.

Tom looked exhausted.

'Don't worry, Radley,' said Walker. 'Very nearly there now. Last time.'

He pointed a remote control at the screen on the wall, and up came a series of photographs taken on that morning's raid.

'The phone's so damaged we won't be able to see what was on it. But it's the same model Sophie Madson had.'

He strode around the table until he stood in front of Tom with his hands on each seat. 'Lying all smashed up just round the corner from your little boathouse.'

'I've never seen that before,' said Tom.

Walker smiled. 'Do you remember what I said to you, Radley, when all this started? Keep lying to me, because this is all going to come crashing down on your head. Well, now we're here, Radley. It's all crashing down. And you didn't disappoint me. Even now, you're still lying. Tom Radley, I am charging you for the murder of Sophie—'

Just then, the light in the room shifted. Unconsciously, Walker's eye flickered to the screen. And then his whole head turned towards it.

The picture on the screen had changed. They were no longer looking at the broken phone lying in the mud. They were looking at a CCTV image. Across the table, Tom stayed totally still, fixated on the screen.

The image showed the checkout counter of an electronics store. The camera was mounted above the cashier's balding head. There was no one else in the shot. Then another image replaced the first. It was almost identical, except now the cashier was serving someone: a man in his fifties with a black jacket zipped up to his chin and a lovingly maintained coif of silver hair.

Then, just in case they'd missed it, the screen zoomed in on what Walker was buying. A mobile phone.

Tom turned to look at Walker. But Walker never returned the gaze. After a few moments, he very slowly turned to stare through the one-way mirror. Erin, sat with the CCTV footage on laptop, felt her giddy satisfaction turn to dread.

She was ready for him when he opened the door. Walker was red in the face and his hands were shaking. Erin realised he was going to hit her. The chair crashed into her leg as she backed away, snarling, 'Don't you dare—'

He advanced across the room until his face was just inches from hers. 'I wouldn't hit a woman,' he said. 'So I'm going to have to hit him twice as hard.'

Then he stormed out, slamming the door shut behind him. A moment later, the door in the other room flew open. Tom leapt out of his seat. Walker crossed the floor at frightening speed, knocking over Tom's abandoned chair, which clattered to the floor.

'Come on, Radley. How did it happen?' He was shouting in his face, backing him up against the wall. 'I know it was you. I know you killed her. Stop fucking with me and come out with it. How? How did you do it? Tell me right now.'

Walker punched him. A sickening thud echoed around the observation room as the back of Tom's head collided with the wall. The blows kept coming, one after the other, while Tom sank further and further down to the floor.

Shock kept Erin rooted to the spot. Then she came to her senses and pelted out into the corridor. Walker had locked the interview room door. 'Walker!' she screamed. She smacked her palms against the wood until it hurt. No response. She ran down the corridor.

By the time the office manager had found the keys and let her in, the two men were horribly entangled on the floor. Walker had the front of Tom's shirt balled up in his fist. The space between his shoulder blades was dark with sweat and his sleeve was splattered with blood. Tom's head lolled back, red streaming from his nose.

Two officers launched themselves at Walker. He immediately released Tom, who crawled away, bearing his teeth at his assailant. The officers hauled Walker to his feet, pulling him back, but there was no need. All the fury seemed to have drained out of him in an instant. Erin looked at his fists, curled up by his sides. They were trembling.

She wanted to stay. She needed to help Tom. But the officers pushed her back out of the room. The air felt cool on her hot face as she emerged, disorientated, into the main office. Detectives and PCs had gotten up from their seats to see what was happening. She registered Peters brushing past her to stand in the doorway of the interview room, where he took in the scene before him with a look of abject disgust. Without looking at her, he barked, 'Crane. With me, now.' Heads peered over desktop screens as she followed him into his office.

There were cameras in the interview rooms. They watched the footage on Peters' computer in grim silence. Then he made her recount her version of events. Only once did he interrupt her, asking, 'How did you know where he was getting the phone from?' One eye scrutinising her from under a droop of skin. She explained that she'd taken a shot in the dark in assuming he'd bought the phone locally, and that she'd narrowed it down based on the electronics stores that were along Walker's route home. Peters was inscrutable. 'Lucky,' he said. It was impossible to tell whether he believed her or not.

By the time he dismissed her, the main office was totally silent. There was almost no sign of the commotion that had just occurred. She wondered where Tom was.

Then, through the narrow window in the door, she saw a silver head disappearing down the stairwell, towards the car park.

Walker had always kept at least three different suit jackets inside the wardrobe in the main office. He had collected them all up in their carriers and had them swung over his shoulder as he walked towards his car. He must have seen her approach, but he didn't acknowledge her until she was right beside him. 'Crane,' he said in an emotionless voice, not looking up while he laid out his suits in the boot. He was unrecognisable from the red-faced man she'd seen in the interview room, as though it was already years behind him. And yet there was something unnerving about how calm he looked. Erin realised she felt frightened of him.

'How did you know where the boathouse was?'

He closed the car boot. 'A contact.'

'Why were they following us?'

'I don't know. And I don't care.'

He shook his head. She knew what he was thinking. Twenty-four years of his life in this place, gone just like that.

'You've got this wrong, Crane,' he said. 'All wrong.'

'We'll see about that.'

He looked at her. Only then did Erin see how exhausted he really looked. There was no anger in his face this time. Just cold contempt. 'Listen. You are playing dirty.' His voice was low, rasping with fatigue. 'And one day soon, everyone's going to find out. And when they do, he won't be there for you like you were for him. He will let you take the fall.' Before she could say anything, he turned his back on her.

She watched the silver car pull away, absorbed into the pale sunlight that poured through the exit.

37

SHE OPENED ANOTHER BEER AND handed it to Lewis, who reclined on her sofa, resting the bottle on his chest and staring contemplatively at the ceiling. 'Do you think now's the time to involve the rest of the team? Tell them what Walker really is?'

She shook her head. 'Not yet. We still need more.'

Lewis lifted his head up so he could take a swig of beer. 'At least it will be easier now with him out of the picture.'

'No way.'

'Really?'

She looked at the closed curtains behind her sofa and imagined the silver car from the other night edging up her street.

'He went after Tom. Next he'll go after us.'

She felt a wave of tiredness. Her vision blurred. She had to lower herself down and crouch on the balls of her feet to stop from tipping over.

Lewis was next to her in an instant. She felt his hand on her arm. 'Erin? You OK?'

She breathed in and nodded. 'Just dizzy.'

'Sure you're OK?' He started getting up. 'You need a water or something?'

She pulled him back down. 'It's fine, it's fine.' It must have looked bad because Lewis was staring into her face as though she was on the verge of death.

She sat down. 'A water would be good, actually.'

He whisked off into the kitchen. She heard the sound of the tap running.

She knew it was mad, but her immediate thought was that Walker could have slipped her something. She tried to remember what she'd had that day. Could he have put something in her drink when she wasn't looking? Before he left?

Lewis came back with one of her mugs. She sipped greedily from it as he crouched down beside her.

'Thanks,' she said. She took a few more breaths in. Lewis's hand was on her shoulder. She might as well tell him, she realised. 'You don't think Walker gave me something? As in, Xanax?'

He raised his eyebrows. 'Xanax? Shit. What did you have at the office?'

'Not much. Coffee. Water.'

'You didn't eat anything?'

She shook her head.

'I mean, not to discredit what you're saying, but that's probably why then.'

She felt embarrassed she'd said anything. 'Yeah. You're probably right.'

'You need something? Like a sandwich?'

Erin rubbed her eyes. 'It's fine. It'll pass.' Already it was starting to. She could see clearly again.

'I really think maybe I should make you a—'

Then Lewis's phone buzzed. He checked it. Just like that, his attention left her.

'Some bedside companion you are,' she said irritably, pulling herself up.

'Sophie's papers,' he said, still staring at his phone. 'Forensics did find them on the printer. Sending them through now.'

Erin practically leapt up then, ignoring how heavy her head felt. Lewis threw himself down on the sofa and yanked open her laptop.

'Password?'

'I've got it.'

She leant over and typed it in, then clicked on her emails. There it was in her inbox – an email from one of the forensic investigators with four attachments. She opened it and clicked on the first one.

It was the naked photo of Sophie. She scrolled down to the next photo. Another girl. Around the same age. Eyes closed, skin pale and clammy, her sleeping body awkwardly draped over a cream sofa. Also unclothed.

'That's Megan,' said Lewis. 'Megan Sadler.'

Another photo. This one of Maia, lying on a bed.

She scrolled down again.

White noise roared in her ears.

It was Annie Dodds. And that was when everything came crashing down around her.

38

L EWIS STARED AT THE SCREEN, struggling to process what he was looking at. Erin was already stepping away from the sofa as the blood drained out of her.

'That's – that's Annie Dodds, isn't it? The girl from your case. The girl Vogel...'

Erin said nothing. The floor seemed to swim beneath her feet.

'So Walker was abusing her too? What the hell?'

He clasped a hand over his mouth.

'Maybe it's the same as it was with Fraser, Erin. Maybe Walker said he could help her get rid of him. But then... what if Vogel didn't kill her? What if Walker did?'

'I don't think—'

'There's got to be a connection, hasn't there?' Lewis stood up sharply. He was making big gestures, moving around. 'It can't be a coincidence, Erin. That's nuts.' He looked at her, hands frozen in his hair, eyes wide like a mad man's, almost grinning. 'We've got to talk to Vogel.'

Ice-cold fear rose in her stomach. 'No, we don't.'

'Erin, he's been telling the truth. He's innocent.' Lewis had gone back to her computer and was typing away. 'What prison's he in?'

'Lewis—'

'I'll get them on the phone now, ask to see him as soon as possible.'

'We're not calling anyone.'

She hissed the words through clenched teeth. Lewis looked up, wide-eyed, hands now frozen to the keyboard. Feeling a wave of guilt, Erin cleared her throat and said, in a quiet voice, 'It's – it's too soon, alright? We – we need to get the killer first. Before speaking to Vogel.'

Lewis stared at her. He gave a small nod.

'Sorry,' she said. 'I'm just – just tired.'

There was a long, horrible silence. Lewis's gaze had fallen to the floor. 'I'll let you get some sleep. We can talk about it tomorrow.'

Erin said nothing. He crossed the room and tugged on his jacket. Their beers sat half-finished on the table. 'See you,' she heard him say. Then she heard the sound of the door closing.

She barely made it out of the sitting room in time. She had to run down the corridor to get to the toilet before she vomited.

Afterwards she sat on the bathroom floor with her back against the wall. She clasped her hands together in front of her, pressing her face into her knuckles, and closed her eyes. There was no way out of this now. This was it.

She made it to Tom's as soon as she could. Seeing his face was almost too much to bear. Stepping into his arms, she pressed her nose against his collarbone and breathed in the smell of his soft t-shirt. He'd made two teas that were steaming on the kitchen table. She sat down on the chair that was closest to the wall, safe and tucked away, with a view of the door. It was warm in here. Tom had turned down the main lights but left on the lamp on a coffee table in the corner. It smelt of fresh laundry. Now that she was here, she never wanted to leave.

'Have you eaten?' he said.

She hadn't, but it was the last thing she could imagine doing now. 'I'm fine.'

He sat down next to her and leant forward with his arms resting on his knees. He didn't usually wear short-sleeved t-shirts like this. She looked at the smooth skin and the prominent blue veins on the inside of his arms.

'There's something I need to tell you,' she said.

He nodded.

'I'm scared you won't see me the same way once I say it.'

'It won't matter,' he said. The certainty in his voice only intensified her guilt.

'How can you say that after what I've thought about you?'

He didn't know. Once he did, she was certain he wouldn't feel the same. She looked away so he couldn't see the tears that were already filling her eyes. She spoke to her hands, squeezed together on the table top.

'There were four of them. Sophie found photos of them in his house and took copies. She must have wiped them from her computer. But they were still saved on the printer.'

He said nothing, just taking in what she was saying.

'All of them had the same ribbon in their hair. Annie's ribbon. And she was there as well. Annie. In the photos.'

'Annie?'

'It was our guy. Sophie's killer. He killed Annie too.'

The room felt airless. She stared at the floor, her breathing shallow.

After a painful silence, he said, 'So Vogel was innocent.'

Erin took a deep breath in but still felt suffocated.

'If I use this,' she said, 'I have to admit I put a man in prison when he didn't do it.'

He gripped her hands in her lap with both of his. Erin felt the smoothness of his fingers, the firmness of his grip.

'Erin. Listen to me. We can get around this. We never have to explain why the ribbon was in the room. It doesn't matter.'

'I put him in prison, and he didn't do it.'

'You didn't know that then. You were just doing what you thought was right. You didn't know he was innocent.'

The pity and understanding in his eyes was excruciating. It was twisting the knife into her.

'What if I did?' she said.

Unconsciously, Tom pulled back. It was such a subtle movement she almost missed it.

'What if I didn't know if he'd done it? And I framed him anyway?'

Tom said nothing.

'A long time ago, you asked me why I took it so far,' she said. 'I didn't tell you the truth. I took it as far as I did because… because it was the only—' She stopped, choking on her words, putting her hand to her mouth. She couldn't say it. She couldn't look at him and tell him.

She took a deep breath.

'Because it was the only way I could make him pay for what he'd done to me,' she said.

And it was out of her, and it was like a puncture or a wound, air rushing in and pain.

'I thought I could live with it,' she said. 'But I couldn't. I couldn't stand it.' She said it through clenched teeth. She could feel the hot tears rolling down her cheeks.

'I stopped us finding him. If I hadn't framed Vogel, we'd have kept investigating. We might have found him. Sophie's dead because of me.'

'No. No, don't say that.'

'She is. She is, Tom. Annie's family… I let their daughter's killer just keep walking the streets.'

'They can't know this, Erin,' he said.

She held her head in her hands. 'What do I do?'

'We can't use these photos,' he said. 'Tell Lewis we can't.'

'How? What do I say?'

'I don't know. But we'll think of something. We have to find another way.'

'Fuck. Fuck.'

Her tears dropped onto his hands.

'It's alright. It's alright.'

She leant forward until her face was in his lap.

'I'm so sorry, Tom. I'm so sorry for everything.'

39

S HE HAD THE DEEPEST SLEEP she'd had in weeks and still woke up exhausted. She wanted nothing more than to spend all day here, curled up in the sheets with Tom. But she had to get moving.

As she climbed up the river bank, she looked at the morning dew on the grass and the mist drifting up towards the trees. This was it. The case that was going to end her career. Something Walker had said came back to her out of nowhere. This is as high as you climb, Tom. She'd never imagined that, by the end of this case, those words would be true of her.

Tom was wrong. She couldn't ignore the photo. This was the most vital piece of evidence they had found so far, after weeks of trying and failing to draw a solid connection between the girls. There was no way she was throwing that away, just to save herself. She was going to follow this through to the end, no matter the outcome, and if that meant revealing what she'd done, then so be it.

She could have had thirty more years in this job. And it was gone. Breathe out, she thought, when she felt her stomach tightening and the shame coming in. What was done was done. She needed to accept the consequences.

Tom would be alright. That was what mattered. If she did this, he'd get out. He'd be back on the force and he'd have the career he'd always deserved to have. And she would do her time and start again. And that had to be enough.

*

It was late in the afternoon by the time she arrived at the station. Lewis looked up sheepishly as Erin approached their shared desk. He said nothing. The ghost of their last encounter was still written on his face.

'You were right last night,' she said. 'We need to look into Annie.'

He glowed. 'You worked on her case,' he said. 'Had she come into contact with the police before?'

'She was a witness in her mum's domestic abuse case. DI Danielle Cooper interviewed her.'

'Cooper… didn't she leave ages ago?'

'I know. To start with, I'd check Annie's files for signs that anyone else on the force came into contact with her. If there's nothing there, we might need to give Cooper a ring and ask.'

'I can do that. No problem.'

'OK. While you check Annie's files, I'm going to speak to Shergill. I think we need to tell him about Walker.'

Lewis bit his lip. 'Are you sure about that?'

'Neither of us were here when Annie's case started. We need to hear from someone who was. Besides, no one has any need to be loyal to Walker now. I think it's time.'

'OK. Let's do it.'

She sat in silence while Shergill played the tape, earphones in. His eyebrows creased as the second voice cut in.

'It's a police radio,' she said.

Carefully removing his earbuds, he asked, 'How long have you known this for?'

She considered lying. But decided there was no point, if she was really going to tell him everything – and she needed to. 'A couple of weeks now.'

His eyes narrowed. 'Why didn't you say when I first showed this to you?'

'We didn't know yet who we could trust,' she said.

Shergill nodded. He stared at the waves of audio, understanding their true meaning for the first time.

Grim-faced, he pushed himself away from the desk. He looked at her. 'Tell me everything.'

40

Lewis

LEWIS STIFLED A YAWN INTO the back of his hand. He'd spent the last hour reading through Annie's case file. So far, what he'd learnt was disappointing. After her body was found, the first on the scene were two officers he hadn't heard of before. He checked the force database and immediately saw why. One had transferred north; the other had retired the following year. Which meant neither of them had been here when the force had found out about Sophie's argument with Fraser. So it couldn't have been them.

Then he checked the file for the domestic abuse case. Just as Erin had said, it was Danielle Cooper who'd led the investigation and personally interviewed Annie. Lewis had a quick read of the interview transcript. There was no sign in there that Annie had spoken to any other officers.

Then something occurred to him. Maybe the killer hadn't been personally involved in the case. Maybe they'd seen Annie in the station – then got her details by looking at the case file. He clicked 'History' to see who had interacted with it.

As he stared at the entries, Lewis suddenly felt like he was drifting away from his own body; like the fingers on the keyboard were no longer his own. His heart had stopped.

Because, in the lead-up to Annie's death, someone had looked at the file three times. Once on the same day of her murder.

It was Shergill.

41

THE BEAM OF SHERGILL'S HEADLIGHTS transformed the road in front of them into tumbling silver waves.

'I think my house is the safest place to discuss this, just to be sure no one hears,' he said, eyes on the road. 'I'd suggest a pub, but you never know who might be there.'

'That's fine.'

They drove deeper into the countryside and through the woods, the tangled shapes of the trees turned into ugly caricatures in the darkness. Suddenly she felt a vibration in her pocket. She checked her phone. Lewis was calling. She hit cancel and turned it off. She'd ring him back later. For now she needed to give Shergill her complete attention.

In the quiet, he asked, 'I assume you've talked to others about this?'

'Lewis and Tom.'

'Who else?'

'That's it. We didn't tell anyone else. Just in case.'

Shergill nodded. He seemed to be taking a long time to process everything she told him. It was just shock, she guessed. The grim reality of it slowly dawning on him.

Eventually the headlights revealed the entrance to a cul-de-sac. The gravel crunched under the wheels as they glided in. He led her into the house, through the open-plan kitchen and into the living room, where he knelt to turn on the electric fireplace. It glowed amber in the cream-coloured room.

'I think I need a drink. Do you fancy one?' He was already opening the fridge. As if anticipating her, he added, 'I can order you a taxi later.'

She didn't really want a drink. But this wasn't Lewis or Tom. This was someone senior she needed to have on side. 'Sure.'

Shergill joined her by the sofa, handing her a glass of white wine. 'Please, sit down.' She took the edge of the sofa while Shergill settled into a green chair.

She started to explain everything. Maia Andrei. Megan Sadler. The warehouse. It must have been the feeling of letting it all out, like a balloon deflating, but she was exhausted by the time she'd finished. There was a hot pulse in her temple, steady and relentless like a drum beat.

'Four girls,' she said. 'Sophie Madson, Megan Sadler, Maia Andrei and Annie Dodds.'

'And you have digital copies of these photos? But not the physical ones?'

'That's right.'

She'd been thirsty and she realised that she'd gulped down her drink in no time at all. Her lips felt sticky. The air felt sticky.

Shergill's eyes moved from her face to the empty glass in her hand. He reached out. 'Top up?'

Judging by this sudden headache, that was probably a terrible idea. She shook her head. 'That'll do me.'

But he was already crossing the room and taking it from her hand. 'No, go ahead. One for the road.' She watched the narrow shoulder blades sticking through his shirt as he returned to the fridge.

Something was definitely up. Her face felt hot and her vision dragged slightly. Great – of all the times to get sick. She needed to seem resilient, not some withering flower who got knocked out by one drink.

Suddenly something occurred to her.

'Hey, Shergill,' she said, 'you'd not seen any photos like that before, had you?'

There was a pause, and then he said cautiously, 'No. I'd have said.'

'Obviously, it's just… can't you normally see when someone's deleted a file on a laptop? Or a phone?'

Another pause.

'Either they weren't on her devices to begin with,' he said, 'or someone helped her get rid of them.'

Had Walker managed to wipe the evidence? Was he technologically savvy enough to do that without Shergill noticing?

She still felt weird. She let her eyes rove the room, testing her senses, and moved her head slowly from side to side, surprised at how heavy it felt, like it was sloshing full of water. She let her eyes rest on the TV fixed to the wall opposite her. She could see a slither of herself reflected in the dark screen. Something about the image captured there was familiar.

Slowly it dawned on her. The walls. The sofa. She'd seen them before. She'd seen them in a photograph that must have been taken right here. Exactly where she was sat.

Sophie's photo. The one of Megan Sadler.

Shergill returned, wine in hand. The glass was ice-cold against her fingertips.

'You were saying,' he said, sinking back into his chair. The ice clinked in his glass as he took a sip, watching her.

Her heart was beating so fast she was scared he could see it causing gentle vibrations in her shirt. She blinked. He kept blurring to a smudge in front of her, like there was something in her eye.

A drop of cold moisture slid down onto the cuticle of her thumb. She looked down at the perspiration forming on the side of her glass.

She sat up, trying to look normal. 'Where's your toilet?'

She thought she saw his head jerk to one side in a swift, barely noticeable movement, as if he was considering saying no. But he gestured politely down the corridor. 'It's up the stairs. The first door on your right.'

'Thanks.' She got up and left slowly, aware all the time of Shergill's eyes boring into her back.

Once she was out of sight, she moved quickly but quietly. She shut herself in the bathroom, turning on both taps. It must have already hit her bloodstream. But she could still get some of it out. She knelt down in front of the toilet, curled two fingers down her throat and vomited up acid and wine into the toilet bowl.

When she opened the door, she half-expected to find Shergill stood there. But he was still waiting for her in the living room.

He felt too far away and too close all at once.

'You know,' she said, 'I looked up Walker's car in the NADC.'

One of Shergill's eyebrows twitched up.

'That's how I knew he bought that phone. Because I saw the journey on the database. And you know what else I saw? He didn't follow me to Tom's that night. Someone else must have done.'

Shergill still had the glass balanced in one hand. The wine inside was totally still.

'The same person who's been following me around a lot lately. I only saw the car in the darkness. I thought it was silver. But now that I think about it, metallic would be a better word. It could have been bronze. Or gold. Like yours.'

His dark eyes were shiny. 'I know this case has been hard on you, Crane.'

She said nothing. The fear was ebbing away. In its place came hot, pulsing anger.

'You saw Sophie had Googled Annie Dodds' name. You didn't say. You told me Walker was looking at her laptop so I'd suspect him. It was you. You abused those girls.'

Shergill held her gaze for a moment. Then he reached around and carefully placed his glass down on the table.

Turning back to face her, he said, 'There have always been things I wanted to do that women didn't want to do.' He looked at the carpet. His perspiring skin gleamed in the artificial flames from the electric fire. 'You don't know what it's like, living like that.'

'They trusted you. Because of what you represented.'

'They weren't aware of what was going on. I made sure of that. That's why I used the Xanax.'

'Sophie thought you were going to help her.'

'I had every intention of helping her. I gave her the burner phone so we could meet more easily to discuss options for how we would punish Fraser. Eventually I invited her to mine, and she accepted. I only used the Xanax on her once. One time. You see, I didn't want to have to use drugs. I'd always wanted to find someone who would let me do what I wanted, without them. And I felt we had developed a friendship of sorts. So I invited her over again and threatened Fraser over the phone in front of her. She was delighted.' He looked at the floor. 'Unfortunately, she didn't understand that I expected something in return. So I-I became angry. I felt I had no choice but to suggest I had something compromising on her. To make her understand that she couldn't just use me and expect to give nothing back.'

'The photo. You'd drugged her the last time she was round and taken pictures of her.'

'I was foolish. She reacted very calmly, so I thought she'd come round to my way of thinking. But then she asked to go to the toilet. And she must have gone into my bedroom then and found the photos. I had no idea until one of the team discovered the image she'd taken on the burner phone.'

'Only it wasn't just a photo of herself she'd found. It was photos of the other girls too. She recognised Annie. She took those photos as evidence and then she printed out physical copies, because she knew if anything happened to her, you'd delete them from her devices. Then the next day you followed her into town. After you saw her meet with Tom, you killed her. Then you destroyed her smartphone. You covered your tracks. It wasn't Walker we saw in that warehouse. It was you. Searching for evidence.'

'Sophie should've spoken to me. If she had, perhaps I could have prevented her death.' He said it in such a soft tone, as if it were a sad, distant event that didn't touch him.

248

'What are you talking about? You killed her.'

'This is what you need to understand, Erin. Annie's death was my fault. An accident, but my fault – I won't deny it. But I never killed Sophie. Tom Radley killed her.'

'Shut the fuck up.'

'Radley killed her, Crane.'

'Stop saying that. That's not going to work. That makes no fucking sense.'

'You need to listen to me, Crane—'

'No, you listen to me. This whole fucking nightmare's going to end. Everyone's going to know what you are.'

He clenched his jaw.

'That won't have made any difference,' he said quietly, nodding to the door she'd just come through. 'It hits the bloodstream very quickly. And you've had quite a high dosage. No matter how hard you try not to, you are going to fall asleep.'

She stood up, so quickly that stars exploded through her vision, and lurched into the kitchen, towards the door.

'Don't do that,' he said.

Phone in her hand and thumb over the on button – why the fuck had she turned it off—

A shattering noise exploded right by her ear. The air was still ringing with the sound as Erin felt her body tip forwards. Her open palms seared as they smacked against the tiled flooring. Hot liquid ran down the side of her face. The smell of alcohol burned around her head.

Shergill kicked her in the spine. The pain was blinding. She heard his voice, thick and mumbling and incoherent. 'I didn't want this. I didn't want this. Look what you've done.'

42

THE COLD TILES PRESSED INTO her cheek. Ignoring the pain, she lifted up her head. The door was just feet away. It might as well have been on the other side of the house.

Shergill had stopped kicking her. Where was he? Then she heard him – rattling around on the surface of the kitchen counters, searching for something. Fear shot through her. She tried to heave her body off the floor.

She had barely raised herself into a planking position when something hard and heavy landed on her back, pushing her back down. Shergill's knee, squeezing the air out of her lungs. Erin felty him yank her arms back. He was tying something around her wrists – an electrical cable. No no no. This was it. As soon as they had you tied up, that was it. She writhed underneath him. Over her shoulder, she caught a glimpse of his face and saw that it was trembling with concentration as he determinedly wrapped the cord tighter and tighter. She tried to scream but no sound came out.

He was gone again. Everything hurt but she tried hauling her body forward, crawling without arms, just shifting her weight inch by inch, barely moving. The totally clear sound of a kitchen knife being pulled out of its sheath sung out into the room.

Then it sounded like a wormhole had opened up in the middle of the kitchen. There was a yelp, a hard slap like a door being slammed and a hot scatter of something over her back like a rash. For a few moments, everything went black.

When she finally rolled onto her side and looked back into the kitchen, Shergill was on the floor, slumped back against the cupboards, neck folded back, with a dark stain spreading out across his white shirt. The knife he'd grabbed was on the floor in front of him, surrounded by a flurry of bloody footprints.

She felt the cable around her wrists start to loosen. Someone was untying her. Still she couldn't take her eyes off Shergill, staring back at her without seeing. His mouth had fallen wide open.

'Erin. Erin, Jesus Christ.'

A familiar voice. She looked round to find Tom crouching over her. The fear in his eyes made her suddenly scared that she was dying; an unreal idea, almost funny.

Then she heard the sirens coming.

43

Erin lay in his lap on the tiled flooring. She experienced the next stretch of time as a series of snapshots. She saw the cable discarded on the tiled floor. The bright kitchen lights reflected in a pool of Shergill's blood. Tom's hand holding hers against her stomach, his knuckles glowing white. It was as if she was travelling down a long dark tunnel, emerging into the world in intermittent bursts.

Then cool air was rushing over her face. Yellow lights flashed across the gravel of the cul de sac as the paramedics wheeled her towards the ambulance. She looked up at the ceiling of the vehicle while a paramedic wearing latex gloves thumbed through her hair. Fear kicked in as she realised that Tom was no longer with her.

The next thing she knew, she was lying in an unfamiliar bed, fighting her way out of a deep sleep. There was a blue curtain to her right. Somewhere in the room, a man snored loudly. She looked up and found Lewis leaning forward in a chair beside her bed, staring anxiously at her.

'Erin. How are you feeling?'

She felt like she was about to fall straight back asleep again. 'Alright.'

Her head was throbbing. She tried to sit up straight and immediately gave up. The snoring sound was coming from a man lying prostate in the bed opposite her with a thick padding of gauze over one eye. Out in the corridor, a nurse was telling someone which ward to visit.

'How long have I been here for?'

'Just the one night. The doctors are pretty optimistic you shouldn't have brain damage or anything.'

'That's good to know.'

'So you should be out soon.' After a pause, he added, timidly, 'I got you some stuff, by the way.'

Ignoring the pain in the back of her neck, she tilted her head to look at her bedside table, where there was an expensive-looking scented candle still in its box. Next to it was a card with a drawing of a weepy beagle and a caption reading, *Sorry you've been unwell.*

'WH Smith doesn't have many get-well-soon cards for people who've been beaten up, it turns out. And I got you this scented candle because I thought it might, be, you know...' he searched for the word '... calming. But apparently that's a fire hazard. So that can be for when you get out.'

'Thanks.' Erin stared at the offerings on the table. They looked excessive for a one-night visit. 'Are you... OK?'

He wrung out his hands, eyes filled with guilt. 'I should have been with you.'

'Don't be ridiculous. We didn't know.'

'What happened? Did he admit to it?'

She nodded. Even that sent a twinge of pain up her neck.

'Don't worry. We don't have to talk about it just now. Your mum's been in a lot. She's nice.'

'Is she alright?'

'She took quite a lot of convincing you weren't going to die. She cried on me a bit at one point.'

'Oh God.'

'Do you want to speak to her?'

She winced. 'Maybe not right now.'

'I'll call her.' He stood up. 'Say you're awake but too knackered to speak.'

'Thanks. That's really nice of you.'

Her attention drifted. She scanned the room and the corridor outside.

He was gone. Maybe she'd imagined it all. Maybe she'd got herself out of there.

Lewis said, 'Just so you know. Once you're well enough, they'll want to get your account of the incident. They haven't decided if it was manslaughter or murder.'

One of the investigators reminded her of a Shakespearean actor. He had a face like a horse and a slow, laborious way of speaking.

She hadn't been allowed to confer with Tom before giving her statement. That was the only thing that made her palms slippery with sweat during the post-incident procedure. Not because she had any intention of deceiving the two investigators. But because she didn't trust her memory to get everything right. The events of that evening came to her in fragments. She remembered her head lolling against Tom's stomach while the lights split across her vision. Everything has happened so quickly. What if she said something that contradicted his account in some small but crucial way?

It took two gruelling hours all in all. Next Erin and Tom would write up their statements – something they were allowed to do together, to agree on timings and locations. Another chance to catch them out. After that, there'd be god-knew how many more interviews before the IOPC reached their conclusion, deciding whether Tom should be let off or charged for Shergill's murder.

She'd found sleeping in the hospital hard. There was always noise coming from somewhere. A machine quietly whirring in the darkness, loud breathing, the rattle of trolley wheels down the corridor. She'd wanted to get out so much that she'd lied through her medical assessment, ignoring the signals her body sent her. Now they weren't so much signals as alarm bells. On the drive to Lewis's house, there was a dull, throbbing pain where her right kneecap had crashed into Shergill's kitchen floor and whenever she turned her head too far, it sent a shooting pain up the back of her neck.

Once he'd let her in – offering her a helping hand down the

corridor, which Erin rejected – Lewis boiled the kettle. He looked more relaxed than he had in weeks.

'The news is crazy. DI Crane survives cop-death-battle. It's amazing.'

Erin rubbed the back of her neck. She didn't want to imagine the press hysteria right now. 'God, I never want to hold a press conference ever again.'

He turned around and handed her a tea, raising an eyebrow at her. 'Got someone here to see you,' he said.

It was funny. Because she'd always thought that Lewis had never got it. But she realised then that he did, at least on some level. It was the secret smile over his cup, the way he gestured with his thumb into the corridor and retreated further into the kitchen to give her some space. She abandoned her tea on the side and left the room, pulled along as if by an invisible thread.

He must have slept over. Pushing open the door to the guest bedroom and finding him there, sat on the bed, made the room around him shudder and pull out of focus. He was wearing grey tracksuits and a black t-shirt and his hair was messy and un-styled. He'd been looking at his phone but when she came in he looked up and put his phone in his pocket and rolled his head back, smiling.

She couldn't pull him in close enough. His warm body up against hers, collarbone against her chin, breathing him in.

'Lewis rang me and told me what he'd found. When he said you and Shergill were gone, I thought the only place I could try was his house. When I saw you both, I thought…' She felt his hot breath against her ear as he moved his head closer. 'Christ.'

'It was him,' she said. 'He was Sophie's abuser. He killed her.'

'I know. Lewis worked it out just in time. Did he confess?'

She nodded. 'You should've heard him, Tom. He still didn't admit to Sophie's murder. He tried to palm that off on you.'

'He didn't want to make it any worse for himself.'

Her teeth clenched. 'Fucking coward. Still couldn't admit it, even then.'

'Do you remember anything after that?'

She frowned. The stretch of lost time had a physicality to it. Like silver shapes moving in a dark room. 'I remember him dying. After that, I don't know.'

'We were on the kitchen floor for a while. You said he'd given you something but you couldn't get the word out. The paramedics on the line told me I needed to make you throw up. I had to put my fingers down your throat. And I had to keep waking you up.'

Erin felt her face go red with embarrassment. 'Great. That's great to hear.'

'They put me in handcuffs immediately. They wouldn't even let me go to the hospital with you.'

She buried her nose in his chest. Then something flickered in the back of her mind, like a street lamp stuttering briefly to life. She lifted her head.

'Did we speak about something?'

Tom looked at her. 'What?'

'I don't know... I felt like you said something to me. Something important.'

He looked puzzled. 'You weren't very chatty, Erin. You could barely form words. I talked you through what I was doing and that an ambulance was coming. That was it.'

She rested her head on his chest again. She could have sworn there was something, but she couldn't think what.

44

IT WAS STRANGE, RETURNING TO her old life. There were things that she hadn't noticed she'd let slip until now. For one thing, her place was a state. It must have been months since she'd properly cleaned it and as a result everything was coated with a fine layer of dust, while the coffee table was piled up with unopened envelopes and adverts for takeaways that had been posted through the letterbox. She'd lost weight too, which made sense, although she hadn't noticed until she tugged on a jumper that had always been one size too big and realised it now doubled as a small tent.

She felt nervous about her first day back, as though she was starting work all over again. She looked like she'd crawled out of a grave; green bruises around her hairline and staples in her head. When she'd first bumped into Adlington on the way in, he'd stared at her and said, 'God, look at the state of you.' She was just replying, 'I was about to say the same,' when he'd cut her off with an abrupt hug, the first he'd ever given her and probably the only one he ever would.

With Peters, she went through everything they had against Shergill, including his confession. Once she was finished, he looked out the window. 'Things will be different from now on,' he said. 'The new Super, Warren… he's solid; he'll do a good job.'

Erin stared at him, not understanding. 'Guv?'

He said, 'This is my last week.'

Which, like an idiot, she hadn't seen coming.

'I've had a long run-up. I knew if Radley was ever charged, that this would be on the cards. But I hadn't expected this.' He sighed.

'For years, right under my nose. On my patch.' He shook his head. 'Nothing else for it. It's the right thing.'

She looked at the overflowing spider plant and Peters' coat up on the rack and his weathered hands clasped together on the table. A part of her had really thought that, once the killer was caught, things would go back to normal. How naïve she'd been.

As the days passed, Erin soon found herself wishing Shergill had lived. After everything they'd been through, Megan and Maia deserved the chance to testify against their attacker in court. But dead, Shergill could not be prosecuted for the crimes he'd committed. So the police issued a statement a few days later to conclude that the head of digital forensics was responsible for the murder of Sophie Madson and two counts of sexual assault. The evidence linking him to Annie Dodds' death, however, was deemed insufficient, meaning the CPS would have to review her case. Erin had to bury her anxiety. There was still a chance Vogel would be released. Still a chance they would find out what she'd done.

The day they closed Sophie Madson's case was quiet, almost peaceful. After Erin had made her statement, she avoided taking further questions from the reporters and left through the fire escape with Tom and Lewis in tow. They didn't turn on the radio. They didn't go home and watch the coverage of the press conference on TV. Instead, the three of them walked into a pub on the far outskirts of Wakestead, where the rugby was playing on telly, ordered a drink, and none of them said a word.

45

I T WAS A BRIGHT DAY in May – sour smell of apples, sun drying the roads, rain still glittering in the leaves of the trees – when the IOPC released their report saying that Tom's actions had been justified. Erin almost ran two red lights driving to his after work.

The White Hart was a cramped pub; they usually gave it a miss. But around the back there was a sloping garden with picnic tables and a low-hanging cherry tree. It was just warm enough to have your arms bare and only feel a slight breeze prickling over the hairs on your skin. Midges were dancing in a shaft of early evening sunlight.

She watched Tom take a sip of his pint. He absentmindedly stroked her knee under the table. It had been ages since she'd sat like this, just watching life go by. On another table, a woman in a summer dress drank strawberry ciders with her partner, at their feet a ridiculous-looking dog that could have doubled as a huge wig, panting happily. Shrieks of laughter filled the air as their two kids ran circles around the garden.

'They dissected it to death,' he said. 'Trying to work out if there was any way I could have restrained him without killing him. But it's easy to say that, isn't it? When you're sat there pen-pushing and analysing the situation from a distance. In the moment, you just don't think like that.'

She pulled back a strand of hair that had caught in her mouth. 'Personally, I'm pretty glad you didn't stand there umming and ahhing about how to peacefully restrain him.'

'I didn't see another option.'

'When all this started, if you'd told me the guy we were looking for would be dead, I'd have been glad,' she said. 'But now, I'm not so sure.'

'Why?'

'It just doesn't feel that real sometimes.'

'People believe you. They know Shergill did it. That's all that matters.'

'I'd have wanted everyone else to hear what I heard. For him to say it in court.'

Tom face hardened. 'I'm glad he's dead. Based on what you'd said, if he'd lived, he'd have just kept trying to pin it on me.'

'Sorry. I didn't mean that…' She reached across the table to touch his hand. 'I wouldn't have wanted it to drag on any longer for you.'

She got the impression she was happier about the IOPC's report than he was. There was a tiredness behind his eyes that had been there since the start of all of this, and even months later it still hadn't left yet.

He squeezed her hand and took another sip.

'I'm sorry,' she said. 'I think for some reason it just doesn't feel over to me. There's still so much we don't have. We don't have him right there, at the scene.'

'We have statements from victims. We have photos of them in his house. We have a confession.'

'I'm not doubting that he did it,' she said quickly. 'It's just… I want more.'

She bit her lip. Seeing he hadn't convinced her, he put his elbows on the pub table and leant forward.

'I understand. Not that I feel the same way you do, if I'm honest. I want to see the back of it.' He squeezed her hand. 'But we've lived with this case. You more than anyone. It's been the reason you get up in the morning. The last thing you think about at night. I know you can't just switch something like that off. I know it takes time. But I'm just trying to reassure you that what you're feeling is this idea that you're not allowed to move on. But you are. Because we did it. He might be dead, but he's been done for it. You can put it to rest now. You owe it to yourself.'

'Yeah. You're right.'

He looked at her empty glass and necked the last of his pint. 'Do you want another one?'

'Go on. I don't want to be sober again til Monday.'

Before he left, he kissed her on the forehead. It left her with an afterglow of pleasure as she watched the two kids chase each other up and down the garden path, but once it faded, something else crept in to replace it: a dark, gnawing feeling of doubt.

That wasn't how she'd expected him to react.

46

Tom

AFTER HOURS, TOM MUCH PREFERRED the evidence room to the main office. Here, without any windows, it was easier to convince yourself it was a reasonable time of day and not – he checked his watch – past 7 p.m. There was something almost tranquil in the silence of this dusty room as he pulled open the drawer containing the evidence bags from Maia Andrei's case.

The first thing he found were price lists and shift rotas, which Maia had organised. For a second, he got hopeful he might find some client details noted down there. But no, of course not – these documents weren't useful to him. He placed them back inside the drawer and pulled out the other evidence bags. Most of them contained Maia's clothing, which forensics had already found didn't have any DNA traces on them. The other noteworthy item was a receipt they'd found in Maia's waste paper basket.

Tom studied the crumpled note. No way would this be of any help finding the killer.

Then he spotted it.

His heart leapt. Actually. Maybe it would.

The CCTV from outside the wine shop came through the next day. Kapil had all but lost interest in the case, so Tom didn't even bother telling him it had arrived before he sat down at his desk to watch it.

The receipt had just one item on it: a bottle of wine, bought from West Green Wines, a wine shop in Wakestead, on the night of the attack, at precisely 10:16 p.m. Opening the clip, Tom tried to lower his expectations. The researcher had already warned him the footage outside the shop was of extremely poor quality. They were right. You could hardly even make out the faces of those who parked up and went to the wine shop before re-emerging and driving off.

At precisely the time noted on the receipt, he saw a man get out of one car and disappear off-screen briefly before returning to get back inside.

He froze the clip. His heart sank with disappointment. Sure enough, it was too dark and the footage was too grainy; their face was blurred and their body swamped in a large, knee-length coat.

Then Tom's blood turned cold inside his veins. But not because of the shadowy figure. It was the car he'd climbed inside.

He didn't look up the registration number. He didn't need to. That exact same number plate was visible through the window to his left, under the shade of a willow tree outside the station, where a car was parked belonging to someone he saw every day. The same person whose ID details had been registered in the history of Maia's case file.

The buzzing in his head reached a fever-pitch.

You, he thought. It was you.

Shergill barely even looked up from his computer when Tom approached his desk the next morning.

'Alright, Radley?'

'I wondered if I could have a word with you?'

Everything about Shergill's posture said he didn't think this was worth his time. He rubbed between his eyes and said in a dismissive tone, 'I'm pretty busy this morning.'

'It's urgent.'

Shergill let out a sigh of frustration as he got up. The air around them felt heavy; Tom could have been wading through cement as they crossed the office together, and his hand seemed to turn the doorknob in slow motion when he let them into one of the empty meeting rooms.

Once the door was closed, Tom said: 'I wanted to ask you about a case.'

Shergill scratched behind his ear. 'Sure. Which one?'

'Maia Andrei's case. The sex worker who was attacked.'

He watched Shergill carefully for his reaction.

The hand behind his ear had frozen. A sudden grey layer of fear masked his face. 'Right. Well, if you need anything, I'd be more than happy to help.' But his voice was clipped, his tone flat.

'Why was your car in the area that night?'

There were some silences you could feel in the air. This was one of them. It seemed to draw in closer, cracking around them.

Shergill said very slowly, like he was struggling to form words, 'What are you talking about?'

'Your car. It stopped outside West Green Wines that night.'

'Oh yeah. I forgot I was there. Picking up a bottle of something. I was seeing a friend that night.'

'The bottle. Was it a chardonnay by any chance? The same chardonnay you used to spike Maia Andrei?'

He couldn't believe he'd said it out loud. He thought his heart was going to burst out of his chest.

Shergill swayed on the spot.

Tom heard his own voice say, 'I have to report this to Peters, Shergill.'

Shergill was biting down so his jaw stuck out horribly. After a few moments he swallowed, straightened up. 'It wasn't what you think it was. It got out of hand.'

Tom shook his head, speechless.

Shergill said, 'The way I want to have sex is my business. Nobody else's. She knew what she signed up for. The overdose – it was an accident. A total accident.'

Tom couldn't believe how controlled Shergill sounded, how calm.

Was that true? Could it have been an accident? Tom felt doubt creeping in. He tried to push it down.

264

'Even if it was, I have to report it. You can't – you can't seriously ask me to ignore this.'

He wished he sounded more confident – he noticed a slight tremor had entered his voice.

'Tom. This is not as bad as you think. The other detectives will see that, trust me. Ratting out a fellow officer over something like this. It doesn't look good, Tom. You haven't been here long. You don't know how it works. No one will trust you ever again.'

Tom turned to leave. Then he felt Shergill's hand fasten around his arm.

'Tom, please. If you help me out, I'll help you out. In any way I can. I know it's been hard for you here. I can change that. I can put in a good word with Peters. I can see to it that you get the top cases.'

Tom snorted.

'I'll give you anything. Anything, Tom.'

How quickly and shamelessly he changed tracks. It was stunning. Tom realised then – this man would say anything.

'Tom,' Shergill said, 'just give me a chance to explain. Please—'

Tom pushed through the door, tugging his arm free from Shergill's grip.

Escaping that room felt like pulling himself out of a sinkhole.

Tom stared up at the ceiling in the darkness.

All day, Shergill's words had echoed around his head. *The way I want to have sex is my business. Nobody else's. She knew what she signed up for. The overdose – it was an accident. A total accident.*

They'd never actually heard Maia's side of it. Could Shergill have been telling the truth? Physically, she had been almost unscathed – the medical report had showed she only had very slight internal bruising, the kind you could get from normal rough sex. Maybe she really had consented to everything.

He couldn't help thinking that the rest of the force would side with Shergill, and not her, if all this came out. Walker's reaction to Maia Andrei showed just how little respect detectives had for sex workers. In which case, there was a very real risk that dredging up something like this would do him no favours. And he was isolated enough as it was.

Tom turned over in his bed, wrapping the sheet tighter around him. He needed to stop thinking like this. Even if it wasn't the attack he'd first imagined, Shergill had still been involved in a case that could have ended in a woman's death. One way or another, he had to tell someone.

This was too big to take straight to Peters, so the next morning when he reached the office, Tom went in search of Kapil. He needed to share this with a peer first – someone who could confirm he wasn't going insane, that this was really happening, and they needed to do something about it, fast.

Finally, he heard a voice that sounded like Kapil's coming out of one of the meeting rooms, where the door had been left slightly ajar. He almost barged straight in. But then he heard another voice that made him stop – a low muffled voice, so quiet he almost missed it.

Peters.

'It's a big one, Manek. A double homicide in Grange Park. Looks like it could be gang-related. Sure you're ready for something like this?'

'Absolutely.'

'Good to hear. I want you and Radley to take the lead on it.'

Tom couldn't help it. Despite everything, his heart soared. A double homicide. Their first.

There was a moment of silence, then Peters said, 'What's that face for?'

'I think it might be better if I lead this one by myself.' Kapil's voice.

Tom felt a tight pressure building between his ears. He leant carefully into the door.

'And what makes you say that, Manek?'

Peters sounded almost impressed that he was offering to take it alone. This was bad.

'I'm not sure Tom's ready.'

'Why?'

'I'm guessing you haven't seen the video?'

More silence; he imagined Peters shaking his head.

'He puked during a post-mortem. Must have some fear of blood or something. He seems like a smart guy, don't get me wrong. But something like this, a double homicide... you know, it's intense.'

Stomach churning, Tom waited for Peters to question Kapil, retort, defend him, anything.

Instead, through his nose, Peters let out a faint huff of laughter. 'He chucked up.'

Silence. Kapil nodding, maybe. Tom pictured that smirk glinting in his eyes.

The sound of shuffling papers. 'Fair enough. You take the reins then, Kapil. I'll let Radley off the hook on this one.'

The conversation moved on, and Tom stopped listening after that. Dazed, and not knowing what to do with himself, he stumbled over to his desk. When he got there, he realised he'd been clenching his hands into fists the whole time. Opening them, he saw his palms were marred with red half-moons where his nails had dug in, hard enough, almost, to split the skin.

After about ten minutes of staring into his computer, stunned, unable to even read the words on the screen, he realised Kapil had arrived at his side.

'Alright, Radley?'

He was stashing something away inside a folder. Clearly he hoped Tom wouldn't see what it was. But Tom already knew. An incident report. The beginnings of a brand-new case.

'What were you speaking to Peters about?'

'Huh?' Kapil's eyes went wide. Then he said, 'Oh. Nothing. He just wanted an update on the sex worker case. Anything to report there, by the way? Any movement?'

Tom looked at him. 'No,' he said, 'No movement.'

*

Once Kapil was gone, he returned to Shergill's desk and asked if he could have a word. Leaving the office with Shergill in tow, Tom thought how surreal this was – a senior detective, whose respect he'd have given anything for just weeks ago, now following him like a puppy, watching his every move with wide, anxious eyes as Tom led him to the car park and closed the fire escape door behind them.

'I haven't told anyone yet,' he said.

He hated the way Shergill's face lit up with hope.

'But that doesn't mean I won't,' Tom added quickly. 'I just… need to think about things.'

'Of course. Of course.'

What was he doing? This was awful. If someone could see him now… He stuffed his hands in the pockets of his coat as a chill gust of wind hit him in the chest, suppressing the thought. He needed to just come out with it. Get this over with.

'How much influence do you actually have over things here?' he said in a low voice, ashamed to hear the words come out of his mouth.

Shergill said, 'Peters listens to me.'

'But you don't make the decisions.'

'No. But you'd be surprised how much difference a senior detective's opinion can make to someone's career.'

Tom paused, watching the wind sweep through the trees outside the car park.

'Could you get rid of someone?'

'Who?'

Was he going to do this? Really?

'Kapil Manek.'

He said it so quietly it was almost a murmur.

Shergill raised his eyebrows in surprise. But he said nothing; he knew not to push it.

'If there was a serious enough complaint raised against him. Or if there was evidence that he'd stepped out of line, or missed something crucial,' he said, 'then he might be dismissed. Especially as he's so new to the force.'

'What if there isn't something like that?'

Shergill stared hard at the wall. Then his eyes darkened.

'I think there's a way we can make this work for both of us.'

Tom listened to the gentle patter of raindrops on the roof of his car.

He should have left ten minutes ago. Much longer sat here parked outside his flat and he'd be late for work. But he physically couldn't move. He was paralysed with fear, his mind racing.

Was he really going to do this?

He forced himself to turn the engine on. The windscreen-wipers rocked gently back and forth, squeaking rhythmically. He took a deep breath and began the short drive to Wakestead police station.

He could hardly believe it when he found himself stood in the doorway to Peters' office. The chief superintendent arched an eyebrow at him in surprise.

'I have something to report,' Tom said.

After he'd arrived home later that evening, when he was hanging up his suit jacket in the wardrobe, Tom's phone rang.

'Radley,' said the voice. 'This is Peters.'

Tom had never received a call from the chief superintendent before.

'I wanted to make you aware that we've decided to let Kapil Manek go,' he said, 'after what you told us.'

'I understand that.'

Tom made an effort to sound like this was the first he'd heard of it. But the truth was he already knew. Just an hour earlier, as he was about to leave the office, someone had come barrelling into him round the corner. It was Kapil, coat on, a bag slung over his shoulder. He looked mortified. Tom felt like he'd lifted a stone to find a spider recoiling underneath.

'Have a good one, Radley,' he said quickly. There was a flash of nervous hazel as they briefly made eye contact, and then Kapil made a rush towards the exit.

At the far end of the room, Tom had seen Peters and the other senior managers packing up. Clearly they'd just ended some kind of meeting. One Kapil had been present for that they'd felt the need to do after hours.

On the phone, Peters said, 'He was leading that case. To miss something so glaringly obvious… it's not good enough.'

Tom drew in a deep breath of satisfaction.

'So I wanted to thank you,' Peters continued. 'If you hadn't persevered with that case, we'd have missed a criminal operation that has no place in Wakestead.'

Tom pictured the arrest. Officers rapping on the door. Shouting through the letter box. Boots thundering up the stairs. Maia Andrei and her housemates emerging from their room in their dressing gowns, slow-footed and bleary-eyed in the morning. If Tom hadn't found those documents in the evidence room, showing they worked together, he'd have had no proof they were using the house as a brothel. But the existence of those price lists meant Kapil had failed to notice a criminal operation being carried out right next door to young families' homes.

After Peters hung up, Tom sat on his bed and pulled from his satchel an assortment of papers, held together by a paper clip. Before he'd left, he'd photocopied the single receipt from West Green Wines, and then printed out a still of the CCTV footage showing Shergill's car parked outside the shop, at the exact time the wine was bought. With digital evidence there was always a risk Shergill would find and delete it. Now he would always have the physical evidence to threaten Shergill with, if necessary.

He looked up from the papers, facing the full-length mirror on his bedroom wall. Nowadays he hardly recognised himself. It must have been this new routine. He'd made a concerted effort in recent weeks to exercise more and eat better. Now the sorry sight he usually saw in the mornings, of a pallid, skinny thing in his boxers, was a distant, shameful memory. His shoulders were broader, his body leanly muscled, his cheekbones more prominent.

Looking at his dark eyes in the mirror, Tom decided he never wanted to see that other person staring back at him ever again.

47

Erin and Tom had brought a bottle of red wine round to Lewis's flat, along with a pack of bread rolls that they piled into a large bowl and placed in the centre of his dinner table. Lewis crashed his own equally large serving bowl against it while slopping spaghetti bolognese onto their plates.

It had been an unusually boozy week. The night before, the force had crammed into the Bull and Butcher to welcome Tom back and give Peters a proper send-off. 'Shame he didn't give a speech,' Lewis remarked, twirling an impressive forkful of spaghetti.

'As if we'd have heard any of it in that pub,' said Tom.

Lewis imitated Peters' hoarse whisper, which made Erin sneeze up her wine.

As they ate and drank, she felt a glow of contentment. It was as if nothing had changed since they first came round for dinner all those months ago, when the case had barely begun. Lewis had done the lights the same way – the overheads turned off, lamps glowing from various corners of the room – and his hair was sticking up in all directions from where he kept running his fingers through it, and talking at a hundred miles an hour just like he had that night when he'd first starting coming out of his shell. Tom, reclining on the faded green sofa, was his old self again – relaxed, confident, miraculously untouched by his ordeal. She suddenly felt deeply grateful for both of them. After everything, they were still here.

It was somewhere near the end of the second bottle where things started to feel strange. They'd been knocking them back pretty hard.

Erin was aware that she was laughing like an idiot at everything. Thank God things were further along with Tom now or she'd have been mortified by the ugly snorts she was making.

But she could tell from the fiery glow in his cheeks and from the size of his gestures as he spoke – unusually theatrical for him – that the drink was getting to Tom most of all. Erin went to fetch another bottle from the kitchen and when she was rooting around for a corkscrew, Tom came up behind her and started kissing her neck. She elbowed him playfully. 'Fuck off.' Reflected in the window, she could see Lewis picking mince out of his teeth while he scrolled through his phone, and the sight wasn't exactly setting her loins on fire.

He kept going. It was getting annoying now. She looked at their reflection, Tom's face buried in her neck, her own expression strangled, and felt weirdly uncomfortable. She pressed her hand on his chest and disentangled herself.

'How drunk are you?' she said, elbowing him again. His eyes didn't focus on hers.

Afterwards, when they were back in the sitting room, she felt annoyed with herself for being so boring. This was stupid. Tom was the last person she should ever feel uncomfortable around.

If he was thinking about it too, there was no way of knowing. He topped up their glasses with the new bottle.

They'd started bitching about the IOPC. The room felt hot and Lewis and Tom's faces gleamed pink in the lamp light.

'They're useless,' said Lewis, crashing his glass down on the table. 'I heard about one copper from Banbury. He was accused of getting rough with some kids. It was pretty bad. They'd gotten gobby with him so he'd grabbed one of them by the throat and bent him backwards over a railing at the park. The kid had bruises on his neck and everything. But obviously the copper said the bruising was already there, he'd had a fight with a friend, blah blah blah. The inquest dragged on for six months and nothing even came of it.'

Tom scoffed. 'And that's it. You're immediately under arrest, you're immediately suspended, all your colleagues know. That's it.'

Lewis looked startled. 'Oh, I meant – you know I think he did do it; it was three accounts against his.'

'I know. But even if he had done it, he didn't deserve that,' said Tom. There was an awkward silence.

'You mean, the inquest should have been shorter?' said Lewis. 'Because I agree that—'

'No. I mean that kid should have kept his mouth shut.'

The room tilted. The red wine in Erin's mouth felt thick like tar as she swallowed it.

'It's the arrogance, that's what it is,' Tom said, playing with the stem of his glass. 'It's the arrogance of them. To think that what was just ten minutes… maybe less, maybe two minutes of pain and discomfort for them warrants inflicting years' worth of damage on someone else.'

There was a pain deep in Erin's chest.

'Well, he assaulted them,' she said in a quiet voice.

Tom shifted in his seat. 'That man's career would have taken him years to build. How is it fair that all of that was for nothing? Just because of one mistake. One incident that a person can't get over just because they don't have what he has. They don't have the nerve. He's giving back to society in more ways than most people do in their lives. And what are they? They're nothing.'

After that, they were silent. Tom drank from his glass. Lewis was nodding politely but his eyes had gone wide.

'I don't know, I guess it's hard to say what happened,' he said even-handedly.

In the taxi home, Tom was self-satisfied and glazed over. Something about having a driver seemed to calm him down, at least. He asked how the driver's night was going in a voice that almost seemed sincere. He had one hand on her knee, and the touch was comforting this time instead of pinching.

'Did you mean what you said?' she asked.

His expression was lethargic when he looked at her, eyes drifting. It was hard to tell if he knew exactly what she meant. 'I got carried away,' he said.

The warm glow of dimly lit lamps greeted her on the way into his house. An enticing trail into each room. It was just like the time she'd come here that night, when she'd told him the truth about Vogel. She liked it that he did things like that. Small, thoughtful things to make the place more pleasant for her. Calm down, she thought. He'd just gotten stupid and drunk and emotional. So had she.

He stepped closer. Erin felt a wave in her stomach, as though she'd driven over a hill. 'God, I missed you,' he said abruptly. He tilted his head forward, placed a hand on her cheek and started kissing her. For a moment she felt like she was watching what was happening from outside her own body. Then Tom's hands moved under her clothes, moving from her stomach to her back. Her heightened emotions melted away, physical sensations gradually winning over. She was being an idiot. Everything was fine.

But the feeling didn't last long. Because that was when it came back to her, as they were crawling over the bed in the darkness. Crystal clear, like the memory had been perfectly preserved in her brain, just buried out of sight, and something had dislodged it from its hiding place.

'Did we speak about something?'

'What?'

'I don't know… I felt like you said something to me. Something important.'

Tom started kissing her neck and running his fingers over her scalp. She stared at the ceiling.

She didn't know what made her remember it. Maybe it was the darkness and the sensation of his fingers in her hair. But suddenly they were back on that kitchen floor again, tangled together. Because he'd been gripping her hair like that too when he'd leant in and whispered, 'What did he say, Erin? What did he say to you?' And her answer had been so mumbling and incoherent she couldn't quite remember it. But it must have been something like he said he abused girls… killed Annie.

'What?'

And then something like *said you killed Sophie.*

She'd been slipping in and out of consciousness, speaking without thinking, barely registering what was going on. But she remembered the next questions. Because she'd had to really think to understand what he was saying.

'Did he mention papers? Receipts?'

What? No.

'Did you record the conversation? Erin? Did you?'

No… No. Didn't record it. And he'd stopped asking questions then. As if that was all he needed to know.

Tom's bathroom mirror was fitted with LED strips on the inside frame, casting his chest in a golden glow as he angled his face towards the glass and dragged the razor through a mask of shaving foam. The window was open an inch to let the steam out and bring the birdsong in. Refreshed after her shower, Erin sat on the floor, propped up against the wall of the bath, her bare legs cool on the tiled flooring.

Just a week ago, she would have given anything for this moment. A Saturday morning with no time for anything but each other. Him stood there, golden and unreal. Why would she want to do anything to ruin this?

But she was going to. It was out of her control.

'How did you know where Shergill lived?'

Tom bashed the razorhead against the edge of the sink. He frowned into the frothy water with his head bowed. 'What?'

'How did you know his address?'

Looking up, his eyes found hers in the mirror. Then, bringing the razor up and returning attention to his face, he said, 'We had drinks at his house once. Years ago. Before you joined.'

'Right,' she said.

She waited to see if he'd add something else. But he stayed silent.

The razor glided under his jawline.

'It must have been hard to remember,' she said. 'It felt pretty out of the way.'

Eyes flashing to hers in the mirror again. 'It was difficult finding the lane. But I got there.'

There was a gentle but nudging reminder in that last phrase. *I got there. For you.* Soon he was finishing up and running a white towel over his face. She found herself looking to see if he'd nicked himself. But his skin shone unbroken in the mirror.

48

WHITE NOISE TUMBLED AROUND THE stairwell as the rain fell outside. Erin looked at the soft line of Tom's profile against the grey wall. He stared at the window, eyes filled with hostility.

How had they ended up here? She tried to remember. They'd hardly said a word to each other on the drive to work. In fact, ever since yesterday, long, uncomfortable silences had repeatedly come between them – until, as they approved the office in his car, something had sent Tom over the edge.

Shergill. Tom had brought him up of his own accord and Erin, trying to defuse the tension, had said: 'I hope I don't seem ungrateful for what you did.' She wished she hadn't said it. That particular sentence had provoked an immediate reaction from Tom, who tightened his grip on the steering wheel. He'd marched up the stairwell in silence until she'd said that she wasn't going into the office with him like this, couldn't work with this hanging over them, and now he was leaning moodily against the wall.

'You do seem ungrateful,' he said. 'You think it was easy doing something like that? You don't think it's bothering me just a little bit? Shergill left people behind, you know.'

'I know that. You can't change what happened.'

It took a huge effort to keep her voice quiet and controlled. She couldn't handle an argument like this. Because she couldn't bear to think what it meant.

'But you think I shouldn't have,' he said. 'Because you think it would help you answer these questions that keep spinning around your head. Because you can't drop it.'

'You said you wanted to investigate this with me.'

'I am. I'm perfectly happy to do that with you. It's just I can feel what you're thinking – I can feel that you're angry with me for killing him. But I didn't have a choice, I didn't see another option, to get you out of there. Can't you see that?'

All this time she'd been clinging to a tiny vestige of hope. Now, with every word that left Tom's mouth, that hope was dwindling away. She felt empty.

The rivulets of water streaming down the window created a constantly moving, hallucinogenic mask over his face. Looking at him made her throat tighten painfully.

She said, 'I feel like you're going away. I don't know. Like you're planning an escape or something.'

He looked at her. After a few moments, he said, 'I'm not going anywhere.'

If she'd had her eyes closed, just the gentle tone of his voice might have been enough to reassure her. But the words felt wrong coming from the person in front of her. There was reproach in his eyes and he made no move to touch her like he normally would have, just stood against the wall with his hands behind his back.

'Look, never mind. I have a meeting in ten. I'll catch you after,' he said.

She watched him climb up the last stretch of stairs. When he was halfway, she heard herself say: 'Tom.'

He stopped but didn't turn around.

'If you'd made a mistake… I would listen.'

He stayed very still for a while. Then looked back over his shoulder. The expression on his face startled her. He looked lost; in a way he never had over the last few months, in a way he never had in all the time she'd known him.

He breathed out deeply and turned on the spot. 'Erin—' he began.

THE BLAME

The door in front of him swung open. Three officers piled down the stairs, talking loudly. Whatever Tom had been about to say – and Erin was certain he was going to say something – she saw him decide against it in that moment. He headed back up the stairs. As the door closed behind him, Erin was suddenly struck by the painful memory of him pushing her through that door all those months ago, when he'd kissed her in this stairwell. Back then the world had felt full of possibility. It seemed so far away now. She waited until she heard the voices of the officers fade and the door downstairs bang shut. Then she rested her body against the bannister. There was a dull ache in the pit of her stomach. Because she knew that kiss was the safest she had ever felt with him – and would ever feel. It was over.

She gave herself a few moments to reset, and then she began advancing up the stairs. It was time.

She had to tell someone.

49

ADLINGTON FOLLOWED HER INTO THE meeting room in obedient silence. She closed the door behind her. Her stomach churned as she considered what she was about to do.

'I've been looking at Shergill's case,' she explained once he'd sat down. She remained standing. 'I know it's a bit of a leap. But I don't think we can rule out the possibility that someone here might have been helping him...'

She stopped talking when she noticed the look on Adlington's face. And then it sunk in. Where they were. The white walls all around them. Except for one side, where a double-sided mirror glinted ominously. Adlington had placed a recording device on the table in front of them where one light glowed an accusatory red.

'There's something we need to talk about, Erin,' he said. 'Isn't there?'

At first she stayed where she was, open-mouthed, too shocked to move. Then, slowly, she sank into the seat in front of him.

Adlington's hand was laid flat on the table. He stared at it for a few moments, tongue making a tent in his cheek, like the words he was going to say were something solid he could spit out. Then he pulled off his spectacles and rubbed the space between his eyes.

'I didn't believe it at first. I thought, of course not. Of course not Erin. And then I thought about it for longer. And I realised that, in fact, it made sense. Perfect sense. And I realised I'd been a fool.'

His voice had gone horribly quiet. Erin had heard him speak

like this in the early days when they'd interviewed together. This was how he sounded when he had a suspect across the table in front of him; someone he had no respect for whatsoever. Her heart fell.

No. It couldn't be this. It couldn't.

He took a deep, shaky breath in.

'Tampering with evidence, that's a sackable offence in itself. A gross miscarriage of justice.' He looked at her. 'But framing a man for your own personal gain. For your own vendetta. Without regard for the victim or their family.' He shook his head. 'Unbelievable.'

The walls were shrinking in. The recycled, air-conditioned air pressed closer. Adlington's face, filled with contempt, was unbearable to look at.

She swallowed, even though her mouth was totally dry. 'Adlington, please listen to me—'

'No, that's enough,' he said. 'We're done here. You're out. You're off the force.'

She needed to say something now. Defend herself. Like any suspect in this room would. But she couldn't. Her thoughts were scattering, dispersing, like fragments of ash from a fire spreading into the air.

'I watched you back yourself into a corner time and time again throughout this case –' his voice was low '– so convinced that you were on your own. Did you ever stop to notice who was standing there behind you? Vouching for you, every time? When Walker was trying to get you off the team, do you know who was there making sure Peters kept you on it? All because I didn't believe a word he said about you. When I should have done.'

Slowly, reality was creeping back in, materialising around her. Vital signs returning; she could feel her heart thudding painfully in her chest. A reminder. This wasn't over yet.

She stretched her arm across the table. 'Adlington, listen. Walker's saying this because of what I did. As revenge. He's saying this to discredit me.'

To her surprise, that sent a shadow of confusion over Adlington's face. He stared at her.

'It wasn't Walker who told me this, Erin.'

At first, she didn't get it. She looked at him like he was mad.

And then it hit her.

Of course it wasn't Walker. There was only one other person this could have been.

She watched her hand slowly curl up on the table. The chair had disappeared beneath her.

'Let me tell you what happens now,' said Adlington. 'You'll be arrested for abusing your authority to pervert the course of justice. I've already referred this to the IOPC. They'll be here soon to question you.'

But she barely even heard him. Adlington's voice was just a muffled background noise, like the sound of rainfall. She was back in the stairwell. Tom opposite her, warping shapes over his face. Something behind his eyes, like a decision he'd made a long time ago. His presence next to her in the car. Calmly shaving in front of the golden mirror. All that time, all those small silences. Planning. Mentally preparing himself for this moment.

Where was he now? Out in the main office, pretending to work? Getting on with it; interviewing someone in another room? Or drinking a coffee across the street, putting as much distance between himself and her as possible?

Because this was something he'd felt he had to do. And there could only be one reason why.

'I really thought...' she heard herself say.

She looked at Adlington. She realised that tears were falling down her face.

'He did it. He did kill her. Tom.'

Adlington was shaking his head. 'Don't do this, Erin.'

'He wouldn't have done this if it wasn't true. It's been him all along. Can't you see that?'

'We'll wait for the IOPC in the custody suite,' said Adlington.

'You know you have a choice about how it works now. I don't want them to grab you. I don't want them to cuff you. I want you to walk out with me.'

All the defiance had drained out of her. She nodded and rose unsteadily to her feet.

The eyes of every officer in the building burned into her as she followed Adlington across the main office. Passing the glass box that was Peters' old office, she noticed a tall figure stood inside, talking to the new chief superintendent with their back turned to her. She knew instantly that it was Tom. She waited for him to see her. She wasn't leaving until he did. Until he looked her in the eyes and she could confirm for herself that this was real. But as Adlington gently placed a hand on her shoulder, steering her in the direction of the custody suites, as she shook, unable to feel her legs, Tom, still deep in conversation with the chief superintendent, never once turned around.

50

Tom

'Tom, can I have a word?'

'Of course.'

As Lewis closed the door to his office and sat down, Tom saw he was wearing a dark-green fleece over his suit. 'Going somewhere?'

Lewis hunched forward in his chair, fists balled up inside the pockets of his fleece. 'It's my interview today. With the IOPC. About Erin.'

It had been two weeks since her dismissal and Tom still hated hearing Erin's name spoken out loud. He realised Lewis was waiting for him to say something. He shifted in his seat, sitting up straight.

'OK. Well, I can tell you what they asked me in my interview, if that would help you prepare—'

'No, it's—'

Lewis chewed his bottom lip.

'If I say how affected Erin was by Vogel. How traumatised... will that help her?'

The expression in his eyes was painfully earnest.

'Surely it will,' he continued. 'I mean, she can't have been alright in the head to do what she did. They must be able to see she wasn't thinking straight. Surely they'll see that and...'

Tom should have seen this coming. He'd thought Lewis would be quick to move on from Erin, once he knew the truth. But that had been naïve. They'd spent too long investigating together for that.

Tom made himself take in a deep, slow breath.

'We shouldn't be trying to help her, Lewis.'

'Why?'

Because I can't afford to. Because I need her to be totally discredited. Or else they'll listen to what she has to say.

Tom pushed away from the table and rubbed a hand over his face. His skin felt hot and clammy.

'It's our job to find the truth and tell it, Lewis. That's what we do.'

'I know she made a mistake. A big fucking mistake. But I get it, Tom. I get why she did what she did. You do too, right? I mean, what Vogel did to her… How can you just… write her off like this?'

Tom's throat tightened. He had a sudden memory, it must have been a month ago – that recent? – of Erin in bed beneath him, Sunday morning, her hair tangled between his fingers, breathless and curling up with laughter because of something he'd said to tease her. Not anymore. Gone. Gone for ever. If Lewis had any idea. The things he'd had to give up. The dreams he'd had to say goodbye to. And here he was, acting like Tom had thrown her away in an instant, like it was nothing.

'She knowingly framed a man for a crime he didn't commit. If anyone else had done that, would you be able to look past it?'

Lewis's mouth had been open. Now he closed it.

Tom breathed in deeply.

'I know it's hard. But we need to put this behind us now. If we have an ounce of respect for this place and the work we do here, we need to move on. So don't exaggerate. Don't lie. Just give the IOPC the straight facts.'

Had that worked? It looked like it had. To his relief, Lewis was nodding in agreement. But then his gaze flashed down to Tom's hands. Tom realised he'd been gripping the edge of the desk this whole time and his knuckles were bone-white. Immediately, he let go – but too quickly, and Lewis saw. Uncertainty flickered across his face as he got up to leave.

Tom needed to make sure he didn't make a beeline for someone else next. So instead of returning to his desk, he stayed in the doorway, watching Lewis go. Relief spread through him when he saw him reach the doors to the lift and step inside with his head bowed, not having said a word to anyone.

Just as Lewis disappeared into the lift, Tom's phone started ringing. A cold sweat broke over him as he read the name on the screen. Walker. He picked up.

'How are you, Radley?'

He hadn't heard Walker's voice since the day he'd attacked him. The nonchalant tone with which he spoke made Tom feel nauseous with anger.

'What is this about?' he asked.

'Did I really hurt you that badly?'

Tom clenched his teeth. Few things had brought him more pleasure than seeing Walker dismissed. He'd hoped he'd never have to hear from the deranged DSU again.

Walker's voice turned serious. 'Listen, there's something you should know,' he said. 'Erin. She called me. Just now.'

Tom's heartbeat accelerated. 'What did she say?'

'She thinks you did it, Radley. Thinks you killed Sophie Madson. She's claiming she's found evidence.'

His blood was pumping hot around his head. He held his breath, waiting for Walker to continue.

'I don't believe you did it. Not anymore. I lived and breathed this case and couldn't find any evidence against you. Crane also couldn't tell me what she'd found, so I call bullshit.'

Tom let out the breath he'd been holding in.

'So here's what I think. I think she's planted something to try and stitch you up. Just like she stitched up Vogel. I think she called me to try and get someone on side, seeing as she's got no one right now.'

He could sense Walker was about to hang up. But Tom couldn't shake the feeling that something was wrong here. 'Why are you doing this?' he asked.

'Look, I did what I had to do. In my position, you'd have done the same.' His voice hardened. 'Besides, it's Erin. She can't handle anything or anyone that doesn't fit into her little moral universe. And she'll stick you if you don't any way she can. I don't necessarily like you, Radley, but I'm not going to let her get away with this again. So I'm telling you, flag it with the Super.'

The resentment in Walker's voice relieved him. He had started to worry that Erin could have gotten to him. But no, Erin was the reason his career had come to such an abrupt, humiliating end. He wanted to make her pay for it.

'Walker,' he said. 'Thank you. I know you didn't have to tell me.'

For a moment the former detective paused. Then he said, 'No. I didn't. You should remember that.'

It took all Tom's self-restraint not to run every red light he saw. He felt completely awake, like he'd been thrown into an ice-cold bath.

As soon as the call ended, he'd taken the lift downstairs, walking calmly so as to not draw attention from any of the officers, then bolted across the car park and got in the car.

He had to reach the boathouse. If it was still there, then Erin was bullshitting, and he was in the clear. If not, he needed to act – fast.

He tried to calm down by telling himself he would talk her round. He'd never had trouble making her believe him before. He wouldn't now.

But then the guilt yawned open inside him, threatening to swallow him up. If only none of it had happened. If only he hadn't—

Not worth thinking about. Everything was going to be fine. He was going to go in and get out of there in five minutes. Then he was going to throw what he found to the bottom of the river.

The boathouse creaked like an old ship as he crossed the floor. He crouched down next to the loose floorboard, prising it up from its place. A wave of relief washed over him. They were still there. The receipts and the still from the CCTV camera, which he'd kept as collateral against Shergill, just in case.

So Erin hadn't taken them. Did that mean she was planning to plant evidence after all? Walker had told him…

'Thought I might find you here,' said a voice.

He felt a jolt go through him. In front of him, the windows seemed to warp and bend. He tried to steady his breathing. Couldn't. He looked over his shoulder.

A small woman had stepped through the front door and was watching him calmly with her hands in the pockets of her coat.

51

Slowly, he rose to his feet. But Erin had seen enough already. She'd seen the look of open-mouthed fear on his face.

'Good hiding spot, that. Even Walker didn't find it when he searched this place.'

She watched him look silently down at the space he'd uncovered. Then, feet fixed to the ground, shoulders rigid, his eyes met hers. 'You – you planted this.'

'We both know I didn't.'

He stared at her, his face blank but eyes alert, searching hers for an answer.

'Yes, you did,' he said. 'Walker told me you were going to.'

'Walker told you I'd found evidence. And you immediately ran home and made straight for that floorboard.'

She saw it drop through him, heavy as a stone. She saw that he got it. He looked out of the window at the gently rippling water. When he looked back, he was smiling bitterly. 'You told Walker to call me. You did.'

She took a step forward. 'When Shergill attacked me, you asked me if he had mentioned papers. Receipts. This was what you were talking about, wasn't it?'

Tom nodded to himself, eyes to the ground. She could see that thoughts were racing through his head. When he finally looked up, something had changed. The suspicion had left his face. His eyes were pleading with her.

'Whatever you're imagining,' he said. 'You're wrong. That's not what happened.'

This was it. The interview she'd been waiting for all this time. She couldn't risk saying anything that might stop him talking. But she couldn't stop herself from saying, gently, in a quiet voice, 'No more lies.'

He nodded. Then he bit his lip, looking around the studio. 'Can we – can we go somewhere else?'

'No. We'll stay here.'

Tom flexed his hands. She'd always liked his hands. His long fingers and the prominent knuckles and veins. He was staring wide-eyed at the ceiling. Trying to work out where to start.

When he looked back at her, the air around them went totally still.

'I knew about Maia,' he said.

Erin felt a thin line of pain sliver up her chest and into her throat.

'I saw CCTV of Shergill buying a bottle of wine on the night Maia was attacked. I'd found the receipt at her house. I confronted him about it. He denied it. Obviously. But I knew what had happened.'

She waited as he drew in a deep breath. She was too afraid to even move.

'I wanted to turn him in. I did.' He breathed out deeply. 'I'm so ashamed that I didn't. But Shergill… he threatened me. Said he would ruin my career. Get me taken off the force. That was why he got Kapil Manek struck off. To prove he could do it.'

She swallowed. She hated the confused way her body reacted when it was pinned under his gaze; the wave of heat that crept up her neck.

'So you let Shergill get away with it. And because of that, he was able to hurt others. Megan. Sophie.'

Tom looked at the floor. 'I was young. I made a mistake. Knowing now that it might have saved Sophie, I'd give anything to go back and change what I did.'

'As soon as you met Sophie, you must have known that Shergill was involved. But you led us on this wild goose chase anyway. You tried to convince me it was Walker.'

'I was afraid you'd find out what I'd done. What I'd hidden. But I swear, I had nothing to do with Sophie's death.'

She shook her head. 'That's unforgivable. Doing that to me. Screwing up the investigation. Unforgivable.'

He edged forwards, tentatively closing the distance between them. 'I know how you must feel about me. I'm so sorry for what I did. You're right. I was trying to save my own skin. But we got him. Shergill. In the end. That's what matters.'

'If all this is true, and you didn't kill Sophie,' she said, 'then why did you say what you did to Adlington? Why did you want me out of the picture?'

'Because you wouldn't stop,' he said desperately. 'Everyone was going to work out that I'd known about Shergill. And you were still thinking that I'd killed her. I could see that. I couldn't – I couldn't take it anymore.'

Now he reached out to hold her hand. 'I shouldn't have done it, Erin. I'm so sorry. I'll do anything to make you trust me again. I'm not a killer.'

She felt the warmth radiating from his skin. A moment of dizziness hit her, like all the blood had left her head.

'It's good to hear you say that,' she said. 'But it's not true, is it?'

Tom's eyelid quivered. His hand on hers loosened.

'When I spoke to Shergill the night he died, one thing was clear to me: he was telling the truth. And when we spoke about Sophie, there was no memory in his eyes. No guilt. Because he genuinely saw himself as innocent.'

Tom's hand left hers. 'That's just what he wanted you to think, Erin—'

'You asked me, when we were lying in Shergill's kitchen, what he'd told me. Whether I recorded the conversation. Why would you ask that? What possible reason could you have?'

292

He opened his mouth to speak, but she kept going.

'When you came in and found Shergill on top of me, you killed him without hesitation. You killed him because you couldn't have him talking.'

'Erin, that's not—'

'On the day Sophie Madson was killed, Shergill was at a meeting an hour before she called the police. You were nowhere to be seen. That gap of time that's always been there. It's still there.'

For the first time, she didn't feel anything as she looked at him. She didn't know who she was looking at.

'It's you, Tom. It could only be you.'

His eyes went dark and a muscle in his upper lip twitched. 'No one's going to believe you.'

Out of the darkness: 'Alright. Let's stop this now, Tom.'

Lewis was standing in the doorway to the boathouse. Tom stared at him as if he'd just appeared out of thin air. Unconsciously, he pulled away from Erin. He looked between each of them, shaking his head.

'You can't be doing this to me,' he said. 'After everything—'

'Tom,' said Lewis. 'Give up. It's over.'

'I know what this has been like for both of you. I know what you had to go through for me. But after all that, after everything, you're going to let Shergill win?'

'How are we letting him win?' Lewis's voice was cold.

'We know it was him. He'd confessed to almost everything. He just didn't want blood on his hands when it came to the trial. So he pinned it on me – the one everyone's been trying to pin it on since all this started. Why would I kill Sophie Madson?' His eyes were wild as he turned desperately from Lewis to Erin. 'Give me one reason why I did it.'

'I don't know why,' said Erin. 'But I know it was you.'

Tom flinched. He rounded on Lewis. 'Lewis, I don't know what she said to you. But don't you see what's happening? I'm responsible for her getting kicked out so now she's trying to get me out. Don't you see what she is?'

Lewis said, 'I know what she is, Tom. None of us worked you out though, did we?'

Tom's lip curled. 'This doesn't prove anything,' he said. Then his eyes lit up. 'It was Walker. It must have been.' Erin scoffed but he kept going, speaking loudly and urgently. 'He must have been helping Shergill. Behind the scenes, this whole time.'

To her surprise, when Lewis next spoke, his voice was soft. 'Mate, please,' he said. 'Please just stop. It's over.'

Then the reality of it dawned on him. Tom's whole body seemed to sway on the spot and he took a shaky step back as if to regain his balance. His face had drained of colour. Wild-eyed, he stared out through the window at the lapping water. 'You bastards,' he said under his breath. 'You fucking bastards.'

Lewis continued, calm and professional as anything: 'You kept these papers so you could threaten Shergill with them if you needed to. Because you knew what he'd done. But you chose to say nothing.' Every word sank into Tom; his eyelids fluttered and his jaw clenched. 'Maybe you even met him here so there'd be no phone calls between you and no other evidence of a relationship. To discuss Sophie's murder. And perhaps a broader cover up and payment—'

'Payment.' A horrible snarl. 'You think I-I murdered someone for *payment?* What the fuck is wrong with you, Lewis—'

'We don't know why you did it, Tom,' Erin cut in. 'We want to know. This is your chance to tell us how it really happened. Or people will create an uglier story. You know they will.'

He hadn't looked at her once while she spoke. Most likely he couldn't bear to. The muscles in his neck clenched as he swallowed.

'It's not fair,' he said. 'It was an accident.'

He said it so quietly, in such an unfamiliar voice, almost like a child's, that for a few moments they just stood there, wondering if they'd heard him right.

Lewis was the first to break the silence. 'Tell us how it happened,' he said quietly.

Even though he was looking the other way, she could see there were spiteful, bitter tears in Tom's eyes. He shook his head, grimacing. '*No*,' he said, again so quietly she could barely hear.

'It will feel better, Tom,' said Lewis, stepping forward and reaching out to place a hand on his shoulder. 'I promise it will.' His hand had barely made contact before Tom recoiled as though he'd been burned. His head snapped around and he backed into the corner of the room, shaking his head.

'Don't you fucking work me!' he was yelling. 'Don't you fucking use that routine on me, Lewis!'

Erin didn't dare breathe. They watched as Tom took in quiet, shuddering breaths with his back against the wall, his hands clenched in his hair, forearms hiding his face. She could see just from the corner of his mouth that he was crying silently. Then slowly, he let his body slide down the wall. He curled up.

Erin didn't want to touch him. She didn't have it in her to anywhere near him. But Lewis slowly crossed the room and crouched down beside him. Sensing him near, Tom's foot flinched away and the hands in his hair tightened. His face was hidden but they could see his shoulders were shaking.

Neither of them said anything. There was no point now. She felt that instinctively and she knew that Lewis did too, without either of them having to so much as look at one another.

After a few long moments, Tom took his hands away from his face and hugged his shoulders. His face was wet with tears.

'When it – when it happened,' he said in a rasping voice. 'When she died… it broke my heart.'

And just like that, all of the air left the room.

52

Tom

5th September, the previous year

IT WAS ONLY AS THE crowd of local reporters were leaving that Tom realised he was being watched. The side of his face prickled. He looked around to find the Old Cross's car park almost empty of people apart from one young woman. She was outrageously pretty – brown eyes and a full mouth in a small face, like a doll. He smiled at her and she blinked nervously. Then she drifted over towards him.

Was anyone else here? Tom did another quick scan of the car park. If she was interested, he was hardly going to turn her down. But only if no one caught him in the act.

'Detective?' She was holding a number of sheets close to her chest as though worried he'd steal them from her.

He straightened up. 'Anything I can help you with?'

'I wondered if I could talk to you,' she said. 'It's to do with Alan Vogel's conviction.'

Her eyes were large and determined. Not interested, then. Maybe she was a relative.

'Do you know Vogel?'

But she was already shaking her head. 'No, no, it's just... I have some information.' The way she said it was tight-lipped, covert. What was with this girl?

'OK,' he said. 'It was good of you to come forward. Any parent or friend with you today?'

She shook her head.

'Alright then. And what exactly is this information related to?'

She looked between each of his eyes, and then said, 'I don't think he did it.'

And then the whole atmosphere changed. Tom looked her up and down, taking in the papers clasped to her chest. What was in there?

'What's your name?'

'Sophie Madson.'

'Sophie,' he said. 'We might need to go somewhere a little more private, is that OK?'

It was what she'd come here for. She nodded.

Tom led her to the car. As they strapped themselves in, he considered taking her to a café, but decided against it. Hopefully this wouldn't take too long. Besides, he was slightly self-conscious of how it would look to passers-by; him having coffee with a pretty teenager.

'Maybe we'll park up somewhere quiet,' he said. 'Then I can drive you home. Where do you live?'

'Beech Tree Lane.'

A cracking sound almost cut her off; the police radio cutting in, an officer putting out a call.

'Sorry about that,' he said, as they set off. 'I'll need to keep it on just in case.'

'That's fine.'

'We'll stop off on the way to yours. So, tell me. What's this about?'

She looked out the window, her soft profile blurred against the bright sunlight. 'Is there a way I can tell you but… no one will know I said it?'

'What you're asking about is witness protection,' he said. 'For now, we can say this is between us. Off the record.'

After a pause, she said, 'You definitely wouldn't?'

He turned off the roundabout at Wakestead town centre.

'I promise. It's off the record.'

Maybe this was something big. He'd been cautious before. But now he was certain he needed to hear whatever this was about.

Wakestead town centre had dissolved into the distance. Now they were driving past hedgerows and fields turned pea-green in the sunlight.

'Yesterday...' she began.

Tom glanced at her; she was still looking out the window and he could see she was chewing the inside of her mouth.

'What?'

'Yesterday, I saw a photo of her. Annie Dodds.'

'What do you mean, you saw a photo of her? Where?'

'It was with photos of other girls. Four altogether,' she said.

'Where did you see this? Whose photos?'

'It's complicated,' she said. 'A friend. But not really a friend. I needed their help with something. Last week, I was at his house. We had a couple of drinks. And—'

'What?'

'I don't know if I can trust you.'

'Anything you say is confidential until you tell me otherwise.'

The papers were lying flat in her lap. She held her hands protectively over them. 'I fell asleep. I woke up in the morning, not being able to remember what had happened. He drove me home. I thought maybe I was just ill. But then yesterday he invited me over again—'

A high-pitched noise had started sounding in Tom's ear. Slowly building.

'I'm such an idiot,' she said, her voice thick with tears.

'It's ok. Go ahead.'

'He was saying he expected something in return for...helping me. I told him no. He started to threaten me. He said "I could make your life very difficult, you know. You don't know what I've got on you." He made it sound like he'd taken photos of me or something.'

Tom noticed her hands were trembling over the papers.

'So I said I was going to the toilet, and I went looking for whatever it was. That's how I found the photographs, in a drawer in his room. Of girls unconscious. Without any clothes on. I was one of them. He must have drugged me the last time I was there. I'm worried he… did something.'

Oh fuck.

'And there was a photo of Annie Dodds. I recognised her from TV.'

Tom's mind was racing. They'd never come across anything like this with Vogel. No camera; no evidence of other girls being involved. Who was this person?

'I photographed the images as quickly as I could. I had two phones and I started taking photos on the second as well, just in case. But I only managed to photograph one – the picture of me – before I heard him calling my name up the stairs. I went down and said whatever I needed to say to get out of there. Eventually he got comfortable enough to let me go. I ran home. I googled Annie's name, to check I was right. And it was her. And that's how I found your name. I thought maybe you could help me.'

Tom's heart was beating faster. 'This person. Do you know how he met these girls?'

'I have a theory. I might be wrong.'

'Go ahead.'

'In some of the reports I found online about Annie Dodds, they said something like "local authorities were aware of her". Police and social workers. I think maybe that's what they had in common, the girls. I say that because that's the only thing I had in common with Annie.'

Tom didn't like where this was going. The distress quivering off her felt suddenly deadly, radioactive.

'I thought I was in control of the situation,' she said. 'But I did exactly what he wanted me to do. I was part of a pattern. He killed Annie… and if I don't say something, I'll be next.'

It couldn't be this. It couldn't be.

And then she said it, loud and clear, unmistakable. 'His name is Ben Shergill.'

The world was falling around him. He could no longer feel the steering wheel.

'Do you know him?' she asked.

All the blood had drained out of his head. He needed to park. He needed to park right now or he was going to crash the car. He made himself breathe deeply, praying she'd interpret his long silence as thoughtful and collected.

'Who've you spoken to about this?'

'You're the first person.'

Thank God. That was good. That was good.

'Not even your parents?'

She shook her head. 'I was…' She choked a little. 'I don't know – ashamed of what they'd think of me. The reason I knew him, Shergill… it wasn't a good reason.'

'I'm going to park somewhere,' he said. 'Is that OK?'

'Yes.'

He had to concentrate hard to keep the car moving in a straight line and find the beginning of a footpath into the woods. He pulled up on the grass.

'How did this start?'

'He came up to me once on the way home from school. He wanted to know if my coach was causing me trouble, because a couple of officers had seen us arguing. The truth was he was. My coach, Fraser, he'd hit on me. Someone half his age. And he suspended me because I said no. I was angry. I wanted to get back at him. I know how bad this sounds. But I thought maybe Shergill could help me get him arrested. Scare him, I don't know. Shergill said he would help me. Even called him up to threaten him. I see now what he was doing.'

'These photos,' he said. 'You said you took pictures of them?'

'Yes. And I printed copies too. This morning.'

She turned the papers over in her lap. Tom's vision went hazy as he processed the photographs printed on them.

There she was. Maia. His stomach lurched.

So Shergill hadn't stopped. Worse than that. He'd killed. And the photo of Maia, that dark-haired girl, cemented Tom's place in this domino chain. A point where it could've stopped but hadn't. He thought he was going to be sick.

'Are these the only copies you have?'

'The only physical ones. I have digital ones as well. But I thought I had to have the physical thing. He's in Digital Forensics, right? I was worried, if I talked to you, my phone might be confiscated, and he might…'

He made a point of nodding, as if taking in what she was saying, but really he was using this moment to scan the woods. No one was around. He couldn't risk being seen with her like this. He needed to act fast.

'I'm going to make a call. And then I'll be right back.'

He realised he hadn't looked at her in a while and flashed a nervous smile in her direction. He immediately wished he hadn't. It must have looked artificial because she smiled back cautiously, eyelids fluttering. He slammed the door shut behind him. He couldn't even look back at her as he turned and headed towards the shelter of the trees.

The shadows on the forest floor were bright green and seemed to ripple as the leaves above him moved in the breeze. The birds were singing. He stumbled into the woods, barely able to feel his feet or the ground beneath him. His only instinct was to get as far away as possible.

He needed to calm down. There was a force crushing against his windpipe. He started breathing out through his mouth; in one two three and out one two three. This didn't have to lead back to him. It was Shergill she was accusing; Shergill who would be charged if this went any further. She had no way of knowing or ever proving that Tom had known what he was. There was nothing connecting him to any other girl Shergill had touched.

Nothing, except Maia's case. Just thinking about it made him want to curl in on himself. If anyone ever drew the dots between him and that case… He couldn't bear to think about it.

And then there was Shergill himself. If he was going down, there was no way he wouldn't also take the opportunity to bring Tom down with him. And then everyone would know. Everyone. Peters. Walker. His parents. Erin. Everyone would know he'd found out about a girl's abuse and done nothing.

He didn't know where he was going. He wanted more than anything to buy himself just an hour of time. To find some quiet, sheltered area and just think and come to a reasoned conclusion about what to do next. But he didn't have an hour. It was too risky. These woods were quiet but anyone could walk through at any moment.

That thought sent cold fear sinking through his guts. He looked around wildly. No one. But for how long? What if some dog walker came out from the trees?

He stopped walking. He reached out blindly for the mossy bark of a tree trunk and steadied himself there. He couldn't afford to lose sight of the car. He had to stay here, in this gut-wrenching limbo, and figure out as quickly as possible what to do next.

Call Shergill. Call Shergill and work out how to nip this in the bud right now. But if he did that, then he was admitting to some kind of involvement with him. Moreover, he was drawing a traceable connection between them. If Shergill was ever investigated, they would pull his phone records and see the call in there, an admittance of a relationship, a confession.

No, he had to sort this out on his own. He had to find a way of reasoning with her.

She was only a teenager. She'd be scared about what this meant for her reputation, her safety, her family. He could appeal to her fears: did she really want to put her family through this? Did she know how infrequently girls like her were believed or how often the media tore them apart?

Another option was to offer her protection. He could say he'd make sure Shergill would never touch her again, as long as this stayed between them. But then again, he thought, she'd been brave enough to confront him over this. Knowing she was capable of speaking out, how could he ever be confident she wouldn't one day decide to come forward?

He was sick with adrenaline. He could feel his heart beating with painful, relentless force. He had a strange image of pulling apart his chest, slipping a hand into his ribcage and massaging the thing like an animal until it slowed down.

No, he couldn't reason with her. The only thing he could do was accept what was going to happen. She was going to report Shergill. There would be an investigation into whether he really had killed Annie and abused Maia and that other girl, which – given the photo evidence – a jury would almost certainly say he had. And then Shergill would reveal that Tom had known all along. He might even have the evidence to back it up. The police systems would have records of Tom asking for and looking into the CCTV footage that had ultimately proven Shergill's guilt. Maia's prison sentence alone was enough to incriminate him.

If the court believed Shergill, then it could mean prison for Tom too. Blank walls and sneering faces and empty years. He'd be a disgrace to everyone he knew. His parents, his friends, his colleagues. Everything he was, everything he'd thought he'd ever be – gone.

No. It wasn't fair. It was Shergill who'd abused those girls – not him. He had to talk her out of this. And he needed to start now, while he had the time.

As walked slowly back to the car, he felt nothing except a cool, calm determination.

She looked up when he climbed back inside.

'What did they say?'

'What?' It all came back to him when he saw the expectancy in her face. 'Oh. Yes. I was just ringing my partner to clarify the details of the Vogel case. I didn't mention what you told me. We need to handle this carefully.'

She nodded. He was the one who had the authority here, he reminded himself. She didn't know what the process was. He had to take advantage of that to convince her to do what he wanted.

'It was really brave of you to tell me this,' he said. 'I know how hard it must have been for you.'

'I was worried you wouldn't understand. Because he's one of you.'

'It's not really like that. Shergill's on the tech side. It's different,' he said. 'I'm sorry. I know it must be hard to speak about. But do you know for certain whether Shergill sexually assaulted you?' He needed to know what had happened. That was the only way he could strike the right note with her.

She grimaced. 'What do you mean? I was naked in the photo. So he must have done.'

'But you don't know for certain that he did? You didn't go to a doctor afterwards? You don't have any other evidence, apart from these photos?'

She shook her head, looking, for the first time, a little doubtful.

'I always make sure girls who've been through something like this know what they're getting into. I'm sorry if this is hard to hear. But I think you need to hear it.'

She blinked at him in surprise.

'Statistically speaking, girls and women in your position often lose cases. If that happens, it will be painful. It could cost your parents a lot of money in defamation. It could come up in search engines when employers google your name. It might make it hard to compete. Or even get a job.'

She had gone very still.

'And you need to consider his status as well,' he said. 'The fact that you're coming against an authority figure in the community makes it less likely people will believe what you say.'

'But the photos I just showed you. They prove he assaulted me, and those other girls.' There was a question mark in her voice.

'Can you prove they came from Shergill's camera?'

She shook her head.

'See, that's a problem. As soon as he finds out you have those photos, you're right, he'll wipe them from all of his devices. He'll deny having a connection with you. There'll be no evidence that he knew Annie or those other girls.'

'What are you saying? That I just… drop it?'

He clasped his hands together in his lap and took a breath in, as if this was really difficult for him to say. 'If I was in your position,' he said, 'I would never meet Shergill ever again. I would stay well clear of him. But to protect myself, and my family, I would not take this any further. I wouldn't press charges.'

She looked shocked. 'But Annie… and what he did to me… Surely you have to investigate that?'

'You're right. And I will. Discreetly, in my own time, so Shergill isn't suspicious. But this –' he pointed at the photos '– this is not enough to take this forward right now. It's insufficient evidence. The best thing for you to do right now is leave this with me and not press charges. Don't even tell anyone. You don't want to burden your family with this.'

His heart was crashing against his ribcage. She sank back into the passenger seat, looking with confusion at the papers in her hands, clearly shocked that their contents hadn't achieved more.

Then something made her sit up straight.

'No,' she said. 'I need to do it. I need to speak with my parents. I've kept them out of it for too long.'

Alarm spiked through him. 'You don't need to do that. I think, for now, it's best that it stays between us.'

'Why?' she said.

Fuck. Fuck, fuck, fuck. 'I don't think they would understand. They don't know the criminal justice system like I do, Sophie. They'd push you to take it too far and you'd regret it. Trust me.'

'If that's what they'd think, then I should do it.'

Aren't you listening? 'I just don't want you to throw away your life like that. I don't want you to ruin your future.'

There was a look of dark determination in her face as she looked into the wood. 'He already did that to Annie,' she said.

He couldn't think of anything to say.

She turned to look at him, and now her eyes were bright with conviction. 'I'm going to do it. Not just for me. I have to do it for them.'

He felt sick. He looked into the green wood, teeming with sunlight, and watched a leaf gently flutter to the ground.

'Do you mind driving me home?' Her voice sounded far away.

'I think we should stay out here for a little bit longer.'

'Why?'

'Because you wouldn't want to rush into anything.'

'It's OK, don't worry. I can walk from here.'

Then he heard the car door open.

The muscles in his arm jolted. A hand that looked like someone else's had reached out and grabbed her arm. He stared at it in disbelief, unable to comprehend what his body had just done.

Sophie didn't move. She stared at him with fierce eyes and cheeks ablaze. His stomach churned.

He tried to steady his voice. 'I really think we should stay here and talk for a bit longer.'

Her chest rose and fell shakily. 'Can you let go of my arm?'

'I'm just trying to help you, Sophie. Everything's fine. Please.' He hadn't meant to say that. It came out automatically, but he hadn't been able to keep the desperation out of his voice. He sounded untrustworthy.

'Let go.' And now she pulled, first in a single jerking motion, and then much harder as she scrambled backwards over the seat, towards the open door. She was stronger than he'd expected. For a moment her hand slithered out of his grasp but he caught her by the wrist before he lost his grip entirely. And then she started screaming. Whole body turned away from him, head out of the car and into the wood.

It was horrible. Her wailing jumped and skidded through him.

'Sophie, please, please, be quiet, it's OK—'

He didn't know what he was saying. Suddenly her head ducked down. She wriggled her free hand inside the pocket of her jeans. She was going for her phone.

'Don't, don't—'

It flashed white and menacing in her hand. Cold fear tumbled through him. Now he didn't care anymore. He threw himself forward, knee colliding with the gear stick. But it was too late. She'd started the call. He saw the number: 999.

She yelled into the phone: 'I'm Sophie Madson, I'm—'

He jammed his forearm against her windpipe, crushing her body into the car seat. The phone slipped through her fingers and fell down the side of the seat. She didn't stop screaming so he covered her mouth, trying to muffle the sound. Her free hands were pummelling his ribs. He twisted his body across hers and flailed desperately for where the phone was trapped down in the gutter beside the seat. There was a blast of noise as the police radio cut in briefly, and then out – please, please could they not hear that. Her feet kicked the glove compartment again and again. His hands were sweating so much the phone slipped through his fingers twice. Finally, he managed to end the call. He threw the phone out of the car and into the grass.

It was real now. It was happening. This was a runaway train and there was nothing he could do to stop it.

He felt so angry at her for the call that the first blow was easy. He didn't even see it hit. He wrestled her down, flat across the two front seats. Blood on her white teeth and the overpowering smell of perfume. Her nails clawing at his face.

The second blow was the hardest of them all.

When Tom had finished speaking, none of them moved. If Erin had even tried, it felt like she would have shattered into pieces. Still crouched down beside Tom, Lewis was motionless apart from the tears silently climbing down his cheeks.

Outside, the light was turning yellow as the sun went down and for a moment she could focus on nothing but the dust circling in a shaft of light and the sound of birdsong coming in through the window. It was the kind of beautiful summer's evening teenagers would spend drinking and smoking by the river. Sophie should have been walking home down Beech Tree Lane in the long shadows, her gym bag over a sunlit shoulder.

'I didn't mean to do it. It was all so fast. I didn't know what I was doing.'

Hearing his voice again brought her back into the room. This was the part where the killer tried to forgive themselves. They allowed themselves to imagine that, by finally saying it out loud, they had been purged of what they'd done.

She wasn't going to let it happen.

'They called you in,' she said. She had to lower her voice to make sure it remained steady. 'After the call was reported, you were one of the first they called in. And you put her body in the boot of your car.'

Tom's face scrunched up with pain and he shook his head. 'Erin, please, I can't. I know what I've done. I can't bear it.'

She ignored him. 'Shergill didn't destroy Sophie's phone. You did. You drove through the town with her body in your car. When we had that meeting, Sophie wasn't in the woods or on the roads or in someone's house. She was downstairs. In your car. All her family out looking for her, thinking she might still be alive. All of us out searching. And you knew.' Her fingernails were digging into her palms so hard she might have drawn blood. 'We saw photographs of the post-mortem,' she said. 'You were right next to me. I saw what happened to her face. That was you. You did that to her.'

She had to keep blinking to stop the tears from blurring her vision. They were staring straight at each other now, tears pouring down his face, and it was gone now, all of it, and there was nothing inside her but disgust.

'I would do anything to take it back,' he gasped. 'I wish she'd never spoken to me.'

'Stop talking like you didn't have a choice. You did it to save your own skin. After you decided Maia wasn't worth it. And Sophie wasn't worth it. That none of them were worth it.'

He wiped his nose on his sleeve and started backing up against the wall, sitting upright. 'You'd have handed yourself over, would you, Erin?' he snarled through his teeth. 'If you had the choice, you'd choose someone you didn't know? Over yourself? Because that was the choice I had. And I decided I wanted my life. I worked hard for it. I worked so fucking hard for it.' Helpless and self-pitying.

Lewis was shaking his head, eyes to the ground. 'Listen to yourself, mate.'

Tom scrambled up off the floorboards. 'As if you'd have had the fucking nerve, Lewis, to rat out a senior detective like that. As if either of you wouldn't have done the exact same fucking thing I did.' Moving erratically, he darted towards them and then back again, jabbing an accusatory finger at them. 'Do you have any idea what I did for you two? I took you both with me, this whole time. I was here. I killed him. For you. For you, Erin.'

All the pent-up emotion was exploding out of him. It meant they only had a few moments left.

'There's no point, Tom. Lewis has been wired up this whole time. Everything you've said, the others have heard. Officers are on their way.'

Tom's mouth opened and his body swayed in a slow, underwater motion.

Slowly, Lewis lifted himself to his feet and unclipped the handcuffs that had been attached to his belt, out of sight.

Tom reacted like he'd been electrocuted. *'Don't you fucking dare.'* His hands suctioned to the wall behind him and he pulled himself along the length of it, away from them. His chest rose and fell with rapid breaths. 'It's not happening. It's not happening.' And then, when Lewis started to walk calmly towards him, he launched himself away from the wall, making straight for the door.

Lewis whipped around to face her. 'Erin.'

But Tom hadn't even made it to the door before it was pulled open, flooding the room with light. There was no hesitation. No emotion. As the officers swarmed around him, one of them gave orders in cold, militaristic barks: 'Hands up. Against the wall.'

She'd expected him to give himself up with dignity. She really had. But as she looked away from the crowd of uniformed bodies, not wanting to see any more, all she could hear was snivelling – 'No.

No, no, no. Listen to me' – and, in every word, the rasping outrage of someone who still thought they could talk their way out of it.

Adlington had followed in after the officers but, instead of joining them, he crossed the room towards her. She knew from the contempt in his eyes that he'd been listening to Lewis's recording of the confession all the way here. He held out a pair of handcuffs.

'This one's yours,' he said.

She looked at them for a moment and took in a long, deep breath. A few days ago, the mere thought of this moment would have sent a mad tidal rush of blood to her head. Tom's arrest on a plate in front of her. But now, with the handcuffs right in front of her, she felt nothing.

She shook her head. 'No, it's not. You do it. Or Lewis. I'm done.'

She looked from him to Lewis, who was hovering beside the officers with his hands folded. His eyes went bright with pain when they met hers. She hoped he understood from the way she looked at him. Without saying a word, she slowly made her way towards the door.

Just as she reached it a desperate voice cried out, muffled with tears: 'Erin, don't leave. Please, please. Erin help me—'

She left the boathouse without looking back. The soft earth sank beneath her feet. She felt a cool sensation on the back of her hand and looked up. Summer rain was falling.

EPILOGUE

IT WAS ONE OF THOSE Decembers that arrived with the full force of winter. Santas glowed in shop windows as Erin battled against the cold winds that whipped down the high street. She pushed into the busy pub, grateful for the wave of warmth that hit her, and found a booth at the back of the room, tucked away, out of sight.

She almost didn't recognise Lewis when he came in. It had only been seven months since that day at the boathouse, and she'd expected the same gawky DS to come strolling into the pub. So when a confident-looking man in a suit with a neat haircut walked in, she thought for a horrified moment that Tom was back. Her discomfort must have shown on her face because there was a veil of tension between them when they ordered their drinks. It was only once they were sat in their sticky booth and halfway through their pints that they started to ease back into their old selves.

'How's Chris?'

Lewis's new partner; he'd mentioned him over text. He made a so-so motion with his head. 'He's got a lot to learn. But he'll learn.'

She felt a smile tug at her lips. 'Get you.'

Lewis smiled, embarrassed. 'Have you seen Adlington recently?'

'I don't think he wants to see me, Lewis.'

'He does.'

She shook her head, not looking at him. She had never admitted to planting the ribbon. In court, the judge concluded that Tom had framed Vogel as part of his efforts to conceal Shergill's crimes from the world. His ruling had led to Vogel's release, and spared her a prison sentence. But it hadn't been enough to save her career in the force or repair her relationship with Adlington, who assumed she'd either helped Tom, or at the very least known about the ribbon and chosen to say nothing.

There was something else Lewis wanted to ask her, she could tell. Eyes nervously searching her face, he said, 'What about him?'

He didn't need to say who he meant.

Erin stiffened. 'No,' she said. 'Have you?'

He nodded. Maybe she should have seen it coming, but she was shocked.

'He's lost weight. He doesn't leave the cell much, I think. Just stays there. Reading a lot, apparently.' After a moment, he said, 'He asked after you.'

She looked at the cracks in the wooden table. She didn't want to imagine Tom thinking about her.

Lewis was fiddling with the coaster, turning it round in circles by its corners. 'There's something I've been thinking about a lot lately. I don't know why, but I can't get over it.'

She waited patiently for him to continue.

'He picked me because I was inexperienced. Naïve.'

She clenched her jaw and said nothing. She'd suspected the same thing too.

'When I realised that –' he shook his head and scoffed '– it's pathetic, isn't it? That shouldn't hurt. But it does.'

'He underestimated you. More fool him.'

'He underestimated you too.'

Erin really didn't want to talk about Tom. She took a sip of her drink and said nothing.

There was something else Lewis wanted to say. He leant forward conspiratorially. 'You know, someone joined the other day who'd been sacked from the force before for roughing someone up in an interview. They appealed a year down the line and blamed it on PTSD they got on the job. The tribunal let them off. It got me thinking. You could go to a tribunal. You know, make your case to re-join.' His eyes had lit up. 'I'll help. I'll say whatever. I'll say police work turned you into a complete basket case if you need me to. I'll say you had to dive under your desk whenever the coffee machine went off.'

She smiled and shook her head. 'I'm barred for gross misconduct, Lewis. My name's on lists. It's like having a criminal record.'

It was sweet, but he'd clearly been genuinely hopeful that this was going to solve it for her. His chest deflated and he clenched his jaw. 'That's so shit.'

'It's fair.'

She was telling herself that, and they both knew it. Accepting that she could never again go into police work, let alone be a detective, had hurt more than she could have imagined, like cleaving off a limb in one devastating blow. When she'd decided to join the police, it had lit a path into an otherwise dark and unclear future. It was the way she'd made sense of herself for years. Now all the lights had gone out one by one.

The temptation had been to drop out entirely. Limp off and hide out somewhere remote and out of sight. Maybe she could herd sheep in deepest rural Wales or work on a salmon farm in Norway. But it turned out that plane tickets and remote huts were surprisingly expensive and most Norwegian salmon-farmers actually had quite extensive experience in aquaculture. So she'd gone to stay at her mum's for a bit instead.

That hadn't felt good. Raising the white flag and making it official that everything had gone to shit. But after a few days, she'd started to settle in pretty comfortably to her early retirement. In fact, she and her mum were getting on better than they ever had, laughing at daytime TV on the weekend, going out for cigarette breaks together. Part of the reason for that, Erin suspected, was she hadn't gone into too much detail about any of it – neither the sacking nor Tom's imprisonment. She'd left it all at the door when she'd first wheeled her suitcase in.

The truth was she did think about visiting Tom. She already saw him everywhere she went. Queuing up for coffee outside the station, passing her in the street, propping up the bar of the Bull and Butcher, wearing the same black coat with the collar turned up. Part of her wondered if seeing him in person would make these visions stop. But she knew it wouldn't. So she never did.

He'd been put away for twenty-two years. He'd be approaching sixty by the time he was let out. Assuming he ever was. Far from bringing her any satisfaction, thinking about that relentless stretch of time stirred a dull ache in her stomach. After everything that had happened, she still found it hard to separate the man who'd crumbled into misery and self-pity in front of her that day from the man who'd been beside her for over a hundred interviews. Who would rifle through his wardrobe to find her a blanket when she lay in bed insisting she was warm enough or, while talking to her on his sofa, pull her foot into his lap and gently squeeze it up and down in an act of absentminded tenderness. Sometimes one of these moments returned to her with startling clarity. She'd learnt to let them pass.

Maybe you never fully closed the door on the things that happened to you. Maybe it wasn't so much a case of building a barricade, but – if the ghost opened it and had a wander round – learning to leave it to be.

'Ready?'

Erin nodded. Maia zipped up her coat and locked the door behind her, while the Labrador panted happily, already straining against the lead, nose pointed towards the end of the garden.

They followed a footpath across some farmers' fields. Erin looked around at the rugged landscape – at the sheep and the black earth. Their boots sank into the mud.

Maia had been doing well ever since the case was closed. She had left the housing association several months ago after getting a job waitressing at a local café.

She said, 'All those times I trusted Shergill and Tom, never suspecting a thing… Walker was right. I was blind.'

Maia watched as the dog pulled on the lead, alerted by a squirrel in the hedgerow. She shrugged. 'There's no point thinking about it.'

'But I got it so wrong. If I hadn't, Shergill could have been charged years ago.'

She watched carefully for Maia's reaction. Erin suddenly thought how beautiful she was, with her green scarf pulled up to her chin and the wind gently blowing her dark hair.

But Maia shook her head. With a confidence that surprised Erin, she said, 'It doesn't matter, does it?'

Erin had no idea what she meant. Of course it mattered. She stayed silent, feeling uncomfortable.

Maia said, 'Because the girl that happened to isn't here anymore. She's gone. The only thing that matters is the next person. Every girl that comes after me.'

Erin and her mum were smoking in the overgrown garden one night, sat at the rickety green table, when her mum said, 'There's something we need to talk about, isn't there?'

Erin looked up in surprise. She didn't think she'd ever heard her mum say something like that before.

Her mum's eyes were fixed on hers. 'I... I suspected it.'

Erin felt her stomach twist. She had wanted to get away from it here, in this familiar place, with the wind blowing through the trees, but she couldn't. Here, after all, was where it had all started.

Her mum bent forward and tried shakily to light her cigarette. The spark stop-started in and out of life. It was painful to watch. Just as Erin tentatively reached out to help her, the flame caught. Her mum turned her face away. Erin watched the smoke drift up as she spoke.

'I recognised his face in the news, when he was charged. Of course I did. I know I was out of it back then, when I was with him, but I could never forget what he looked like.'

She tapped the ash off the end of her cigarette, shivering in the cold. Her dyed-blonde hair was ghostly white in the beam from the light on the outside wall.

'And then I saw you were the one who'd investigated him. You and

Tom. But you never mentioned it. Never said anything. After that, whenever you came round, you were… different. You were carrying something. Hiding something from me. And I… I worked out why. At least partly why.'

The cigarette trembled between her fingers.

'I understand why you couldn't tell me, love. I know I fucked up. I know I did.' Her voice caught in her throat. 'All these things you were doing to protect me. After I brought someone into our lives who did that.'

'It's not your fault—'

'Don't tell me that. I put you in a place where you couldn't talk to me. And I have to live with that. I can't take back what I did. And maybe things will never be completely alright between us. But I'm going to be there. From now on, I'm going to be there. And the first thing I'm going to do is get you out of here. It's nice for me, having you here. But you can't stay. There's nothing for you here.'

One morning, when she was having coffee by the steamed-up window in the kitchen, Walker rang.

'So this bloke called me up the other day. He told me about a case that went cold seventeen years ago. His mum went missing when he was little. Not the sort of woman who'd walk out, by the sounds of things. Solicitor. Good job, good family. On the day of her disappearance, she was seen arguing with a man who turned up at her office. No one's seen her since.'

'And why are you telling me this?'

'Because after your work on the Vogel case and the Madson case, it sounds like something right up your street.'

Erin lowered her coffee cup. Was he mocking her? She gritted her teeth. 'I'm barred, Walker.'

'You don't have to be in the police to work as a detective, Crane. Use your imagination. With your experience, I reckon you'd do alright for yourself, running your own practice.'

'Really? I don't know if gross misconduct looks great to clients.'

'Depends what paper they read. Some people have gone so in for the Radley stuff they don't seem to give a shit what you've done.'

She felt a flicker of hope.

'Listen, you're not doing anything else, are you? So why not?'

Her heart was beating faster. 'Would you want to join?'

'Would I want to work with zero job security and no consistent income when I have three mouths to feed? And you driving me up the wall every day? Let me think about that. No. No, I wouldn't.'

She bit her lip, feeling pissed off, until he continued: 'But would I if I were you? If I was your age and had nothing to lose? Yeah. Then I might do.'

'I'll think about it.'

When she hung up, she looked through the window at the wall of trees at the bottom of the garden, blurred by the condensation. All her childhood, she'd imagined them as giants advancing on the house. Stretching their limbs over the wooden fence, breaking it down to come and swallow them up. Now, for what seemed like the first time, the trees were still.

ACKNOWLEDGEMENTS

I am hugely grateful to everyone who played a role in bringing *The Blame* to life.

Thank you to my brilliant agent Kate Nash, whose guidance, intuition and unfailing enthusiasm have made this book better in so many ways; to Jamie Hodder-Williams, Laura Fletcher and the whole team at Bedford Square for their faith in the story and all their hard work to get it out into the world; to Donna Hillyer for her eagle-eyed copy-editing; and to everyone who lent me their thoughts during my research, especially Graeme Johnson, for his invaluable insight into the world of policing and for always taking the time to answer my one million questions. Any factual inaccuracies in police procedure are either my error or there to serve the plot.

Last but not least, a huge thank you to my wonderful friends and family and to Sam, for all your loving support.

ABOUT THE AUTHOR

Charlotte Langley works as a newspaper journalist and is a fresh, breakout voice in gripping psychological police dramas.

Bedford Square Publishers

Bedford Square Publishers is an independent publisher of fiction and non-fiction, founded in 2022 in the historic streets of Bedford Square London and the sea mist shrouded green of Bedford Square Brighton.

Our goal is to discover irresistible stories and voices that illuminate our world.

We are passionate about connecting our authors to readers across the globe and our independence allows us to do this in original and nimble ways.

The team at Bedford Square Publishers has years of experience and we aim to use that knowledge and creative insight, alongside evolving technology, to reach the right readers for our books. From the ones who read a lot, to the ones who don't consider themselves readers, we aim to find those who will love our books and talk about them as much as we do.

We are hunting for vital new voices from all backgrounds – with books that take the reader to new places and transform perceptions of the world we live in.

Follow us on social media for the latest Bedford Square Publishers news.

@bedsqpublishers

facebook.com/bedfordsq.publishers/

@bedfordsq.publishers

https://bedfordsquarepublishers.co.uk/